PLEASANTVILLE

Also by Attica Locke

The Cutting Season
Black Water Rising

PLEASANTVILLE

Attica Locke

HARPER

An Imprint of HarperCollins*Publishers*

PLEASANTVILLE. Copyright © 2015 by Attica Locke. All rights reserved. Printed in the United States of America. No part of this book may be used or reproduced in any manner whatsoever without written permission except in the case of brief quotations embodied in critical articles and reviews. For information, address HarperCollins Publishers, 195 Broadway, New York, NY 10007.

HarperCollins books may be purchased for educational, business, or sales promotional use. For information, please e-mail the Special Markets Department at SPsales@harpercollins.com.

FIRST EDITION

Library of Congress Cataloging-in-Publication Data has been applied for.

ISBN: 978-0-06-225940-0

15 16 17 18 19   OV/RRD   10 9 8 7 6 5 4 3 2 1

per te, Saro
ci vediamo li

AUTHOR'S NOTE

This is a work of fiction. Any resemblance to persons living or dead is coincidental and not the author's intent. Pleasantville is a real place, but portions of its history and geography are fictionalized here for the sake of a good story.

Any politician worth his salt knows the road to elected office passes through Pleasantville.

—JAMES CAMPBELL, *Houston Chronicle*

Election Night

TEXAS, 1996

They partied in Pleasantville that night, from Laurentide to Demaree Lane. They unscrewed bottle tops, set the needle on a few records, left dinner dishes soaking in the sink. They sat on leather sofas in front of color TVs; hovered over kitchen radios; kept the phone lines hot, passing gossip on percentages and precinct returns, on the verge, they knew, of realizing the dream of their lifetime, the ripe fruit of decades of labor and struggle. They were retired army men, some, grown men who wept openly in front of their TV sets as the numbers started to roll in. They were doctors and lawyers, nurses, schoolteachers and engineers, men and women who had settled here in the years after the Second World War, in Pleasantville, a neighborhood that, when it was built in 1949, had been advertised over the city's airwaves and in the pages of the *Defender* and the *Sun* as the first of its kind in the nation—"a planned community of new homes, spacious and modern in design, and built specifically for Negro families of means and class," a description that belied the rebellious spirit of its first inhabitants, the tenacity of that postwar generation. For, yes, they endured the worst of Jim Crow, backs of buses and separate toilets; and, yes, they paid their poll taxes, driving or walking for miles each Election Day, waiting in lines two and three hours long. Yes, they waited. But they also *marched*. In wing tips and patent leather pumps, crisp fedoras and pin-striped suits, belted dresses and silk stockings, they marched on city hall, the school board, even the Department of Public Works, holding out the collective votes of a brand-new bloc as a bargaining chip to politicians previously reluctant to consider the needs of the new Negro middle class, and sealing, in the process, the neighborhood's unexpected political power, which would become legend over the next four decades. And it was hard not to believe it had all been leading to this.

Channels 13 and 11 were already calling the local race, putting Sandy Wolcott and Axel Hathorne, a Pleasantville native, in next month's runoff for the mayor's seat, and Houston, Texas, that much closer to getting its first black mayor in its 160-year history. Channel 2 was running a concession speech by Councilman Lewis Acton, who looked to finish a distant third—and word was now spreading down the wide oak- and elm-lined streets of Pleasantville that the man himself, their onetime neighbor, Axel Hathorne; his father, Sam "Sunny" Hathorne, patriarch of one of Pleasantville's founding families; and key members of the Hathorne campaign staff were all coming home to celebrate. From Gellhorn Drive to Silverdale, folks freshened up coffeepots, pulled the good gin from under the sink. They set out ice, punch, and cookies and waited for the doorbell to ring, as they'd been told Axel wanted to knock on doors personally, shake a few hands, just as Fred Hofheinz did the night Pleasantville helped put him in the mayor's office, and Oscar Holcombe before him—celebrations that wouldn't come close to tonight's.

The girl, she wasn't invited.

But she didn't expect to be.

She had played her small part, put in hours on the ground, knocked on some doors, and now what she wanted, more than anything, was to go home. At the appointed place, the corner of Guinevere and Ledwicke, she waited for her ride, her blue cotton T-shirt a thin shell against the damp night air. It was well above seventy degrees when she'd left home this afternoon, and she'd never meant to be gone this long, but she was due a bonus, a little extra cash in her pocket, if she unloaded all the leaflets she'd been given to distribute. She was too smart, or proud, to toss the lot of them into a trash can at the neighborhood community center as others before her had tried, only to be fired the second the ploy was discovered by the campaign staff. This job meant more to her than to the others, she knew that. She was six months out of high school with no brighter prospect on her horizon than moving up to the cash register at the Wendy's on OST where she worked part-time, so she'd pushed herself a little harder, made a show of her unmatched fortitude and productivity, pointedly staying past nightfall, a plan she hadn't thought all the way through, as evidenced by her lack of a decent coat or even a cotton sweater, and the fact that she was flat broke after spending what little money she had at a pay phone at the truck stop on Market Street. Once more, she checked to make sure the last leaflet, the one she'd saved and carefully folded into a neat square, was still inside the front pocket of her leather purse. Rooting around inside, she checked the time on her pager, the one Kenny had bought her when he left for college, promising they'd make it work somehow. Had he called? She scrolled through the phone numbers stored in the tiny machine. How long would she have to wait out here? It was already coming on nine o'clock, and she knew her mother would worry. She could picture her right now, smoking a Newport out the kitchen window, still in her pink nurse's scrubs, and listening to KTSU, *All the Blues You Can Use*, glancing every few minutes at the yellow sunflower clock above the stove, wondering why her daughter wasn't home yet. The girl crossed her skinny arms across her chest, a defense against the night air, which seemed cooler here at the southernmost edge of the neighborhood, where the base of Ledwicke ended abruptly, running smack into the lip of a wide, untamed plot of scrub oak and weeds and tall, clawlike trees. This far to the south the streetlamps in Pleasantville gave out, and she was all too aware that she was standing alone on a dim street corner miles from home, with nothing but the low, insistent hum of an idling engine as unwelcome company.

He'd been watching her for a few minutes now, the nose of his vehicle pointed east on Guinevere, the body tucked under the low-hanging branches of a willow tree, so that she could make out no more than a man's rough silhouette behind the windshield, sharp angles outlined by a faint yellow light coming from a window on the side of a house across Ledwicke from where she was standing. His headlights were dark, which is why she hadn't seen him at first. But he was facing in her direction, his engine running, his features wearing an expression she couldn't read in the dark. She couldn't tell the make or model of the vehicle, but it was the height and width of a van, or a truck of some sort.

Run. Just run.

It was a whisper inside her own skull, her mother's voice actually, calling her home. But she should wait for her ride, shouldn't she? She felt a stab of uncertainty, a panic so sharp it made her eyes water. Everything hinged on this one choice. *I should wait for my way out*, she thought, still wanting to believe a way out was possible, but already knowing, with a creeping certainty, that this night had turned on her, that her disappearing had already begun. She knew she'd made a mistake, knew even before she heard the van's door open. *Just run.*

Jay Porter stood on his own lonely street corner clear across town.

It was late that same night, a little after eleven, when he got the call that someone had broken into his office on Brazos Street, just south of downtown, about half a mile from the Hyatt Regency. He could see the twinkling white lights of the high-rise luxury hotel from the corner of Brazos and Anita, where he was waiting on the squad car that ADT had assured him was on its way. The hotel sat on the other side of the 45 Freeway, the dividing line between the city's corporate heart and Jay's neighborhood, a clunky mix of old Victorians turned over for business, glass-and-brick storefronts, record shops, barbecue stands, liquidation centers, and the shell of an old Montgomery Ward. He'd hung out a shingle here last year, finally moving out of the cramped office in the strip mall on W. Gray, paying cash for this place, which was falling apart when he found it, a foreclosure that had been sitting empty for years. The house was a modest Victorian with good bones and an open floor plan and a room upstairs for his law library, a place where he could write his briefs away from the phones and the noise on the street. It was the kind of house Bernie would have liked to call her own, even more than the rambling suburban three-bedroom ranch they'd settled in a few years after their youngest, Ben, was born—a fine house, sure, but one he could hardly distinguish from half a dozen others on their block. Rows and rows of beige brick and lacquered wood, their subdivision was the real estate equivalent of a box of drugstore chocolates, pretty, but dull.

Jay had refurbished the eighty-seven-year-old Victorian himself, as if his wife might *yet* have the chance to spend slow afternoons on its wraparound porch, as if they might still have a shot at starting over. He half-expected to walk through the front yard's wrought-iron gate one day and find her sitting there, on the white two-seater swing he'd built himself. The house, with its bottomless demands and clamors for his attention—missing doorknobs and broken light fixtures, the floors he'd stripped by hand—had saved his life during the worst of this past year. He thanked it daily for putting tools in his hands, all those long, idle afternoons when he let his practice go to shit.

There'd been three break-ins in the area since June.

Even the Hathorne for Mayor headquarters on Travis got hit, and much political hay was made in the *Chronicle* over the former police chief's seeming inability to secure his own campaign office. Jay's place had been raided in July, when thieves had taken the back door completely off its hinges. They'd made off with a drill set from Sears and a color TV, a little pocket Sony on which Eddie Mae had watched gavel-to-gavel coverage of the O.J. trial, plus some petty cash and a gold bracelet of hers. A week later he'd had the alarm system installed.

They must have come in through a window this time.

When he'd pulled up to the house, the headlights of his Land Cruiser had swept the front porch, lighting up pieces of broken glass. There were shards of it still scattered across the porch's wide slats, a rough pile in a semicircle just under the first-floor window, the glass lying where it had fallen, the scene strangely preserved, as still as a snapshot. Whoever had broken in tonight had exited the house a different way, or was, at this very moment, still inside. Jay, who didn't keep guns in his home anymore, not since the kids, had a single registered firearm, and it was right now sitting useless inside a locked box in the bottom drawer of his office desk. Hence his patient vigil across the street, waiting for the cops. There was nothing in that office that he couldn't live without, not a thing in the world he would put before the need to get back home to his family in one piece. He wasn't trying to be a hero.

The Crown Victoria came riding low, with its light bar off, its tires crunching loose gravel in the street. The officers pulled to a stop at an angle that brought the front end of their cruiser to rest nearly at Jay's feet at the curb, its headlights hitting him square in the chest. He instinctively raised his hands.

"Porter," he said, loud and clear. "This is my place."

The woman was youngish and short. Her hair was slicked back into a tiny nub of a bun, and her lips were full and pink, a dime-store rose that most women abandon in their twenties. She came out of the car first, one hand on the handle of her service weapon, already en route to the front door. She nodded at the sound of his name, but otherwise said nothing as Jay unlocked the front gate.

"You been inside?"

Jay shook his head, stepping aside to let her pass.

He handed her the key to the front door.

The woman's partner was taking his time. He was slow getting out of the car, slow coming up the front steps, not the least bit of tension in his stride. For all Jay knew, this might have been the fiftieth break-in they'd handled tonight. He was older than the woman, but not by much. Jay didn't believe he'd set foot into his fourth decade. He wore a mustache and a hard part on the left side of his head, and he smelled heavily of cologne as Jay let him pass. Crossing the threshold, he too put a hand on the handle of his pistol. Jay followed them into the house, the soft creak of the pine floors beneath their feet the only sound in the dark. He felt along the wall for the light switch, the one between the front door and Eddie Mae's desk. It cut a shaft of light through the center of the waiting room, shadows scattering like startled mice. The younger cop was in motion, down the main hall toward the back of the house, the storage closet, and the kitchen. Her partner was walking up the stairs. There was the law library up there, plus the conference room. Downstairs, Jay inspected Eddie Mae's desk, opening and closing drawers. Then he walked down the hall to his own office in the rear-left corner of the house, the room closest to the back door, which was standing wide open. "Must have been the way they got out," he heard behind him. It was the cop with the mustache. "I didn't see anything upstairs." His partner likewise had nothing to report from the kitchen. She had already holstered her weapon and was reaching for an ink pen. Within ten minutes they filled out a full incident report. Jay could see nothing that was missing: not his checkbook, or the sterling letter opener he hardly ever used, not his collection of LPs and 45s, obscure R & B pressings from Arhoolie and Peacock Records, including a mint-condition copy of A. G. Hats's *Belle Blue*. It was the Texas blues of his childhood, music that can't be replaced on CD. He had a turntable in here too, an old Magnavox he kept behind the door, also untouched. He checked both the petty cash and the metal lockbox with his .38 revolver, which was right where he'd last left it, stowed away since the very morning he'd moved into this office. It took the officers more time to inspect his gun license than it did to fill out their paperwork. Whoever it was, they guessed, maybe the alarm had scared him off. It looked as if someone had simply opened the back door and walked out. The cops did a cursory search of the backyard. It was a tiny, blank square of grass, and a single glance was more than sufficient to wrap up their entire investigation. "Okay," Jay said, shoving his hands into the pockets of his slacks. He walked the cops to the front steps, zipping his windbreaker. Another dispatch call was coming in, something about a 22-11 over on Crawford Street, just off Wheeler. The one with the mustache lifted his radio first, and then the two of them were off. Jay locked the gate behind them, watching through the wrought-iron bars as the squad car peeled down Brazos Street, this time flashing its red and blue lights. Back inside, Jay walked to the hall closet to get a broom. He would need plywood too, or at least a thick piece of cardboard, something he could put over the broken window for the night, or however long it would take to get a guy out to fix it. He'd painted the house oyster gray, but had otherwise left the exterior, including the original windows, intact. Replacing this one would cost him at least two hundred dollars.

The broken window sat just to the side of Eddie Mae's desk, and if tomorrow's temperature was within even ten degrees of what it was now, Jay's entire day would consist of listening to a long recitation of the ingredients she would need to buy for a home remedy to fight the bug that was inevitably setting up shop in her throat and lungs. He could picture her shivering, clearing her throat every fifteen minutes, and eventually asking for a long lunch so she could hunt down some chicken soup. The thought, at this hour, as he stood broom in hand, actually made him smile. It had been nearly twenty years now, the two of them working together. He'd put her through school, set up a trust fund for her grandkids, from the portion of the civil settlements that was Eddie Mae's cut. Back when the money was still rolling in, of course, when Jay still had more than one client. She was now a certified paralegal, shopped exclusively at Casual Corner, and had narrowed her choices of coiffure down to two wigs, both of a color that occurs in nature. But Eddie Mae was still Eddie Mae, and there wasn't

a day she didn't think could be better passed over a few beers
and an early dominoes game. She was nearing seventy now,
stuck in a house full of kids, and, aside from one grandson at
TSU who worked part-time at a Radio Shack, the only one with
steady employment. She weekly cursed Jay for setting up that
"dang trust," giving her progeny an excuse to perfect the art of
waiting—and forcing her to work out of the house thirty hours
a week just to get some peace and quiet. She was one of the few
constants in Jay's life, and he'd come to love her for it, the parts
of their daily life that he could set his watch by.

Jay held the metal dustpan in his left hand. He felt his forty-
six-year-old knees creak as he squatted beside Eddie Mae's
desk, aiming the bristles of the wooden broom at the spot
where dozens of pieces of broken glass *should* have been.

And that's, of course, when he saw the thief's mistake.

There wasn't a single shard of glass inside the house.

The floor beside Eddie Mae's desk was bare, covered only by
the corner of a hand-woven Indian rug he'd bought at Foley's.
The glass is on the wrong side, he thought. It was so obvious to
him now that he couldn't believe he hadn't realized it before.
He couldn't believe the two officers hadn't noticed it either.
But, hell, they'd given the incident no more than ten minutes of
their time, and Jay knew if he weren't paying a monthly service
fee to the alarm company, HPD wouldn't have sent anyone at
all, not with the pressures on the department being what they
were. Houston's crime problem was as much a part of its cultural
identity as its love of football and line dancing, barbecue and
big hair, a permanent fixture no matter the state of the local
economy or the face in the mayor's office. Two law-and-order
candidates—Axel Hathorne, former chief of police, and Sandy
Wolcott, the current district attorney of Harris County—were
running to change that. There was probably no greater evidence
of the electorate's singular focus—the widespread fear that

Houston would never pull out of the shadow of the oil bust that had devastated its economy in the '80s, wounding its diamond-crusted pride, until it got its crime situation under control.

Jay pulled himself upright. He rested one hand on the tip of the broom's handle, taking in the staged scene. If someone had broken in through this window, as Jay had originally thought, the intruder would have kicked the window *in*, raining glass exactly where Jay was standing now, still holding the empty dustpan. But someone had actually kicked this window from inside the house, pushing the glass *out*, and onto the front porch, where Jay had first seen it. Someone wanted Jay to think he had come through the front window, when all the while the back door had been opened with as much ease as if Jay had unlocked it himself. Someone either picked the lock, he thought, or had a key. The window and broken glass were just for show. It was a pointed, if unsophisticated, sleight of hand, and more effort than he imagined the average two-bit crook, looking for tools or jewelry or cash for drugs, would bother with. It suggested that Jay had walked in on something he didn't as yet understand.

The phone on Eddie Mae's desk rang.

The sound so startled Jay that the dustpan dropped from his hand.

It fell straight to the floor, the metal edge cutting into the soft pine, leaving a small dent in the wooden board beneath Jay's tennis shoes. As he reached across her desk for the telephone, he knocked over a picture frame and Eddie Mae's dish of butterscotch candy. On the other end of the line, he heard a light cough, and then a familiar voice. "Everything all right down there, Counselor?"

It was Rolly Snow.

He was calling from the alley behind the Hyatt Regency, where Town Cars two, four, and six of his fleet of Lincolns were parked, waiting to pick up any stragglers from Sandy Wolcott's victory party, which was still raging, her supporters reveling in the night's surprising turn of events. Axel Hathorne had been favored to win by a wide margin, with more than 50 percent of the vote, to become the Bayou City's first black mayor. But the race had quickly tightened when Wolcott entered, late and hot on the fuel of her newfound fame. She'd beaten Charlie Luckman, arguably the best defense attorney in the state, in a high-profile murder trial last year, one that brought her national attention and a spot on Court TV offering hours of analysis during the O.J. trial. She got a six-figure book deal. She went on *Oprah*. And it didn't take long for somebody to see in her rising star a shot at city hall. Wolcott quickly got her name on the ballot, stealing Axel Hathorne's law-and-order platform right out from under him, and now the two of them were heading into a runoff in thirty days. The party at the Hyatt showed no signs of slowing. If Rolly was lucky, some drunk potentate or campaign official would forget which car he'd arrived in and slide into the back of one of Rolly's Rolling Elegance Town Cars instead. In a black suit and his Stacy Adams, a black braid tucked beneath the starched collar of his shirt, he had been catching a smoke with two of his drivers, sharing a plate of shrimp they'd paid a busboy twenty bucks to hand-deliver, when ADT called. Rolly's was the second name on the alarm company's contact sheet. He called Jay's house first. It was Ellie who'd told him her dad wasn't home.

"She's still up?"

"Was when I called."

Jay sighed. He'd told that girl to get off the phone.

It was the last thing he'd said before he walked out the door. She had a trigonometry test in the morning, and he'd told her in no uncertain terms to hang up the phone and go to bed. This was almost becoming a nightly thing with them, this tug-of-war over the telephone. It wasn't boys yet, that he knew of. Just a couple of girlfriends, Lori King being the closest, who had a near cannibalistic attraction to each other, gobbling up every word, every breath swirling between them, as they talked and talked for hours on end—the same girls who looked at Jay blankly if he asked them so much as what they had for lunch that day, the classes they were taking this fall, or even the names of their siblings. They were a species of which he had no field knowledge, sly and chameleonlike. In the presence of an adult, and especially one who was asking too many questions, they went as stiff and dull as tree bark. Tonight was the first time he'd let Ellie stay alone with Ben. There was no way to get a sitter this late, and Rolly, he knew, was working, and uninterested, frankly, in meeting two cops at Jay's office. He'd had no choice but to leave, to lock the front door and promise he'd be back in an hour.

"I can swing by the office if you need me, after this wraps up."

"Yeah, why don't you, man," Jay said.

For whatever reason, he didn't mention the odd details of the break-in, the degree to which the staged scene made him uncomfortable. Instead, he asked Rolly to drive by the place a few times through the night, to make sure nothing funny was going on. "I can give you a couple hundred bucks for it," he said, offering something close to Rolly's old hourly rate, back when he still did pickup work for Jay as a private investigator. They'd worked together off and on for years, Rolly running a one-man operation out of his bar, Lula's, and when that closed down, meeting clients at the garage where he kept his fleet of Town Cars. "Looking into stuff," as Rolly liked to call it, had never been more than a sideline gig, a source of income, sure, but also his own personal gift to the world, like perfect pitch or a throwing arm like Joe Montana's, a talent that would shame God to waste. He made bank on the car service company and had plans to buy his first limousine next year. These days, he only ever "looked into stuff" for old friends.

"On the house, Counselor," he said.

Jay hung up the line and bent down to pick up the dustpan.

He started for the hall closet, but then stopped himself a moment later, pausing long enough to right the picture frame on Eddie Mae's desk. It was a snapshot of her first great-grandchild, a pigtailed girl named Angel. The butterscotch candies had scattered across the desktop. Jay was picking up the pieces one by one when he heard a faint thump overhead, the sound of a heavy footfall, like the heel of a boot landing on a wood floor. He looked up at the tin ceiling tiles, rows of beveled bronze, and swore he heard it again. The gas lamp in the ceiling was swaying slightly from the weight of whatever was going on upstairs, the light pushing shadows this way and that. Jay felt his breath stop.

Someone, he thought, is still in this house.

He started for the phone first, but his mind went blank. He couldn't for the life of him remember even two of the numbers for Rolly's mobile phone, his pager either. An emergency call to 911 would waste time he didn't have. It had taken the beat cops nearly fifteen minutes to get here, and it would take a hell of a lot less time than that for Jay to end up on the losing side of a confrontation with whoever was locked inside this dark house with him.

He went for the .38 next.

It was in the lockbox still sitting on top of his desk.

He couldn't remember the last time he'd held a pistol like this, but this one seemed to remember him, the metal warming to his touch. He gripped the gun at his side as he stepped from his office into the center hallway, glancing at the ceiling, wondering what it was that awaited him on the other side. The back of his neck was wet with sweat, the windbreaker sticking to his skin. He unzipped the jacket, peeling it off, arm by arm, as he moved toward the stairs, pressing himself against the side of the wall as he climbed the steps. Upstairs, the overhead lights were all off. He felt his way through the dark, keeping his cover, confident he knew the lay of this property better than anyone else. There was the law library up here, plus the conference room, which he used for makeshift storage, filled with stacks of boxes he hadn't bothered to unpack after the move last year, files going all the way back to the Ainsley case, his first big civil verdict, against Cole Oil Industries. He heard a crash, glass breaking, coming from that direction. He ran to the conference room, which sat right above Eddie Mae's desk downstairs, stepping inside just in time to see a silhouette standing by a newly broken window. He smelled hair grease and alcohol, plus something else coming off human skin, the sour punch of marijuana, curling the hairs in his nostrils. He reached for the light switch and raised the .38 at the same time.

The kid froze.

And so did Jay. He had a clean shot, but he couldn't move, pierced through the heart by the kid's eyes, red rimmed and black. He was nineteen or twenty, baby faced but tall and lanky like a ballplayer. He wore a flattop fade that had seen better days, and his pants came up short of his ankles, details Jay was storing without even realizing he was doing it. The kid didn't raise his hands, but neither did he run, and Jay wondered if he had a knife or, worse, a gun. They were in a standoff of sorts, he and Jay, which, as the seconds ticked away, began to feel almost like a dare. Jay had his shot, which the state of Texas said he was well within his rights to take. *Shoot. Just shoot.* It was a whisper inside his skull, a reckless impulse he didn't know was still there. Slowly, the kid raised his hands. "Come on, Mr. Cosby," he said, eyeing the middle-aged black man standing in front of him. "Let's keep it light, old man."

Jay felt his grip on the gun slip. He glanced toward the telephone on the conference room table, judging its distance versus
his speed. He took his eyes off the scene for only a second, but
it was long enough for the kid to make his move. He kicked at
the remaining glass along the bottom of the window frame and
pushed his lean frame through, moving as fast as a rat through
a tunnel. Jay had a line on him, had the .38 still in his hand. But
he couldn't do it. He couldn't shoot this kid in the back. The kid
looked over his shoulder once and, inexplicably, flashed Jay a
smile. And then he jumped. Jay ran to the open window, careful not to cut himself on the glass. Down below, the kid landed
in the grass with a grunt, scrambling to his feet in one ceaseless
motion. He scaled the low-lying gate and took off on foot to the
south, running toward Wheeler Avenue, the border between
Jay's neighborhood and Third Ward.

Jay stood in front of the window, his chest heaving.

He knew he'd made a mistake, knew it before the kid even
hit the ground.

It was that smile, for one, the openmouthed taunt. But also
the peculiar circumstances of the break-in, the staged scene
downstairs and the feeling he'd had that someone was playing games with him. And now that someone was gone, had
slipped off into a night already dampening at this hour into a
wide, white fog that would cover the city by dawn. There was a
dagger of glass still hanging from the top of the window frame,
and in the harsh white light of the conference room, Jay caught
a glimpse of his own reflection. He hadn't shaved in days, and
the curls on his chin were coming in a steel gray. His eyes had
gone flat and dull with age, like two coals forgotten in a fire.
Jay hardly flinched at the sight. He was four years shy of fifty,
he had two kids who deserved a hell of a lot better than they'd
been handed in this life, and his wife had been dead a year.

He was going home.

Part One

CHAPTER 1

The first time Jay hears the name Alicia Nowell he's sitting in his car, at a stoplight, Thursday morning on his way to take Ellie to school. Ten-year-old Ben gets dropped off first. He's had a hard time with school, almost since his first days of kindergarten, and by the third grade Bernie had pulled some strings at the school district, where she was working at the time, and got him enrolled in a special program at Poe Elementary, which starts a half hour before Ellie's classes at Lamar High School, another placement Bernie orchestrated. It's just the two of them in the car, Jay and his daughter, the station set to KCOH. Ellie has control of the dial Mondays and Wednesdays. Tuesdays and Thursdays are Jay's turn. Fridays are theoretically Ben's to program the radio, but he's claimed, more than once, not to care what they listen to, and Jay usually cedes those mornings to his daughter as well. She's quiet today, face pointed to the passenger window, her arms folded across the puffy expanse of her black Starter jacket, her chin and the bottom half of her face tucked below the zipped collar. She's hardly spoken since they left the house, just a few mumbled words as Ben climbed out of the Land Cruiser, reminding him not to forget his lunch. To Jay, there hasn't been so much as a "Good morning." They got into it yesterday after school, over this business with the telephone. Jay was short with her, he knows. He has only two settings when it comes to his daughter: either calm and solicitous, gentle in any inquiry about her thoughts and concerns, or else he becomes stony and impassive: the more words come out of her mouth that he finds misguided or unreasonable in some way, the more he thinks she's pointedly dismissing the wisdom of his judgment, the way *he* would do things. It is an ugly trait of his that Bernie often called out, managing with just a few words to bring him back to his better self. But his wife knew him better than his daughter does, and he knew his wife better than he knows his teenage daughter. There are things she knew about her family, not secrets so much as hard-earned intimacies, that she inadvertently took with her, leaving the rest of them to fend for themselves in this new, foreign land, meeting daily at the kitchen table, or passing in the hallway, without their shared interpreter. She, more than anyone else, knew Jay's tendency to mask fear with brooding, knew his panic too often takes the form of withholding, a silence that can suck the air out of any room. With his daughter, it's something he's still working on.

It didn't help that he was exhausted last night, having slept not a wink on Tuesday. He lay in bed for hours that night, before finally getting up and padding across the toffee-colored carpet to the armchair by Bernie's side of the bed. He fished through the pockets of his pants until he came across his copy of the cops' report. He called the precinct and asked to make an amendment to his earlier statement, the one made in haste without, he now realized, a proper inspection of the property by HPD officers. He mentioned the funny business with the downstairs window, the details that pointed to some kind of scheme, and the kid, of course. Jay was clear in his description: "nineteen or twenty, black male, with a flattop hairdo, and he was tall, six two maybe, and skinny, real skinny." Not a bit of which the desk cop was willing to deal with over the phone. He would leave a message for Officers Young and McFee, he said. Soon after ending the call, Jay flipped over the cops' report and jotted down every bit of it he could remember. He checked on his kids, covering Ben's feet with his Ninja Turtles comforter and turning off the radio in Ellie's room. In the kitchen, he made himself a drink. Three fingers of Jack and a handful of ice cubes.

Sipping in the dark, he tried to make sense of the break-in. Why the staged scene, and why, of all places, did he find the intruder, a nineteen-year-old kid, in the very room where Jay's files are kept? The whole thing left a bad taste in his mouth, one that kept him drinking. Time was, he would have sat hunched over his kitchen table all night, trying to piece together a conspiracy out of the broken bits and pieces of a night like this. He'd passed whole decades that way, in the dark, guided only by the sound of his panicked heartbeat. But that felt like a lifetime ago. Jay had, for the most part, made peace with himself and the facts of his early life: the Movement, his arrest and criminal trial in 1970, when he'd been indicted on conspiracy charges and had come within a juror's breath of going to prison for the rest of his life. They were less a plague on his psyche now than a distant source of pride. Kwame Mackalvy, his old comrade turned foil turned friend again, was right. They *had* been about something once. The marches and the protests, the demonstrations for a democracy that wasn't hollow inside. It *had* mattered. They'd made a difference in people's lives, including the lives of the two kids sleeping down the hall. And Jay had tried to do the same with his law practice, first with Cole Oil, winning $56 million for Erman Ainsley and the remaining residents by the salt mines, where the petrochemical giant was illegally storing and hoarding crude oil, black, greasy globs of which were coming up through the grass in his clients' backyards. More than the money, for Jay the real win had been a trip to D.C. the following year, helping Ainsley pick out a suit for his testimony before a congressional hearing on the Coles' business practices, charges of price gouging and wreaking environmental havoc. It was here that Jay thought the oil company would *really* be made to pay. But the investigation never made it out of committee; the fever for justice was lost somewhere in the turnover of congressional seats in '84, when nearly every candidate out of Texas and Louisiana got donations from Cole Oil or its executive officers. The judgment itself has gone unpaid, held up on countless appeals for well over ten years now. Neither Jay nor his clients has seen a penny.

Ainsley is dead now.

It's Dot, his elderly wife, to whom Jay speaks about the case, and one of her grandkids, a dentist in Clear Lake who demands updates on a monthly basis.

Still, the Cole case was a turning point for Jay.

It was only a month after the verdict that Jay took a call from a local official in Trinity County, not even ten miles from the town where Jay was born. The woman spoke so softly it seemed she was whispering into the telephone. A lumber company out of Diboll, she said, was driving across the county line and dumping wood waste in a makeshift and wholly illegal landfill just outside the town of Groveton. The arsenic the company used to pressure-wash and treat the wood was leaching into the soil, seeping into the groundwater. There were calls coming in from local residents. One woman had twelve dead chickens on her hands. Another swore she could smell death in her ice water. Jay had driven up Highway 59 that afternoon, stopping in Diboll first, and then tracing the back route he imagined the lumber mill was using. Sure enough, just off Farm Road 355, within plain view of a neighborhood of chain-link fences and chicken coops, home to a majority of Groveton's black population, Jay was able to take pictures of a massive pile of rust-colored, rotting wood chips and pulp, steaming poison after a cold winter rain. Two days later, he met with Groveton's beleaguered mayor and walked out as the city's official counsel in the matter of *City of Groveton v. Sullivan Lumber Co.* A week after that, he filed the papers at the courthouse in Lufkin, stopping on his way to have a tense lunch of chicken salad and boiled peanuts with his mother at his childhood home in Nigton, the two avoiding so many topics that they'd hardly said anything at all.

There were many others after that—DDT residue found in a neighborhood of trailers and mobile homes near a plant in Nacogdoches; a hazardous waste site contaminating the well water in the town of Douglass; a chemical plant illegally dumping its runoff in a Latino neighborhood in Corpus Christi—the out-of-court settlements growing in proportion to his reputation.

The Cole deal is still his biggest payout to date, money he has yet to see.

He sends Thomas Cole a Christmas card every year, and he waits.

He's a more patient man now, more measured and wise, he hopes, and less paranoid than his younger self, less quick to see the whole world as a personal attack on him, liars and spies at his back. There are no more pistols under his pillow, an argument his wife won years ago. Most days, he holds his head up for *her*, keeping a promise he made long ago: to get right in his mind, for her and for their kids, the two of them more beautiful than he feels he deserves.

The radio station is still running a postgame analysis of the general election when Jay turns onto Westheimer, about a block from Lamar High School, pulling into the parking lot of the dry cleaner across the street. He lets his daughter walk the rest of the way on her own. KCOH is heated up this morning, taking calls in the run-up to *Person to Person*, its daytime talk show, Phil Donahue for black folks. There's no shock about Clinton heading back to the White House, so today's topic on 1430 AM is closer to home: the runoff next month between Axel Hathorne and Sandy Wolcott. The question: *How the hell did Dallas get a black mayor before Houston?* "It's 1996, people," the host, Mike Harris, says, before the station cuts to a wrap-up of the morning's big news.

The story of the missing girl has already played twice.

By the seven-thirty segment, she has a name: Alicia Ann Nowell. Jay reaches for the volume. Ellie has her books in her lap. She reaches for the door handle but doesn't move right away, pulled in by the story as well. According to the radio, the girl, a Houston native, did not come home Tuesday night. Early reports indicate she was last seen in the neighborhood of Pleasantville, at the corner of Ledwicke and Guinevere, a few miles from her home in Sunnyside. At the mention of Pleasantville, Ellie turns and looks at her dad. Jay is tapping his fingers on the steering wheel, his brow creasing deeply. The story ends with an emotional plea from the family for information. Jay can hardly make out the mother's words, so choked and garbled are they with panic and tears. It's already been two days. "My name is Maxine Robicheaux. Alicia Nowell is my daughter. Please, please, if you have seen my child, please call your local police station, tell somebody something, please." The news reporter goes on to describe Alicia as eighteen and black. She was last seen in a long-sleeved T-shirt, blue. Her ears are triple pierced on both sides. "I have to go," Ellie says, opening the car door.

Jay turns off the radio, watching as she starts toward the school.

She stops suddenly and runs back to the car, her hair springing loose from the collar of her jacket. She favors Evelyn, Bernie's sister, more than her mother, but more than anyone else she looks like Jay's sister, Penny, who lives in Dallas. Ellie is fairer than either of her parents, redbone they used to call it in the country. She has freckles across her nose and forehead, and her eyes are the very color of her aunt's nickname, copper and full of fire when she laughs or sings, which she does when she thinks no one is listening. It's Ben who is the spitting image of his mother, down to the dimple in his left cheek. Jay rolls down the passenger-side window so Ellie can lean in and tell him, "Ms. Hilliard wants to see you."

"Which one is that?"

"The principal."

"What's that about?"

She shrugs and then waves, saying she'll get a ride home with Lori's mom, adding that Mrs. King said she could pick up Ben too. "Bye, Daddy."

"Elena," he calls after her. But she's already gone, swallowed up by the crowd of teenagers moving across the street. It's mild outside, but bright and sunny. Across Westheimer Road, Jay can hear the snap of the halyard against the school's metal flagpole. He traces his daughter's movements as long as he can, but eventually loses sight of her in the crush of students, at least a dozen of them wearing nearly identical puffy Starter jackets, girls tucked inside their private cocoons, trapped somewhere between childhood and the coming chrysalis. Jay can still remember the day Ellie was born, can still remember holding Bernie's father, Reverend Boykins, who wept openly in the hospital parking lot, Jay saving his own tears for the moment he brought his daughter home, a fall day like this one.

Officers Young and McFee keep their three-thirty appointment, stopping by Jay's office at the tail end of their shift. They're day cops usually, seven to four. Tuesday night they'd been picking up overtime. By sunlight, McFee looks a little older than Jay originally thought, and she's Latina, no matter the last name. She has her hair slicked back into the same tight little bun. In the entryway to Jay's office, she hovers, barely filling half the door frame. She's letting her partner take the lead. Young, to Jay's dismay, hasn't written down a single word. He's holding a notepad and is clicking the top of his ink pen.

"He was in the room where my files are kept," Jay says. "Wouldn't figure a kid like that to be interested in anything he couldn't trade or pawn before the sun came up."

Young nods, a gesture more of appeasement than agreement. "But you said yourself that nothing was actually stolen from the property."

"The case files up there go back more than *ten* years," Jay says. "It would take nearly that long to go through every photograph and sheet of paper to know if any of it is missing." The phone on Jay's desk rings. From down the hall, Eddie Mae hollers his name. Since her eldest grandson installed their phone system, she's learned to forward calls to his office, but she won't fool with the intercom, not when it's just the two of them in the office half the time.

"Mrs. Delyvan is on the phone for you."

Jay sighs.

He has to take this call.

"Did you see him take anything?"

"Well, no."

"He have anything in his hands?"

Looking back, Jay can see only one thing: the smile on the kid's face, a split second before he leaped out the second-floor window. Of course he didn't see if the kid had any stolen goods in his hands; he was looking for a gun. "If you hadn't walked out of here without doing a proper search, you might have actually found the kid upstairs, had a chance to pat him down yourself."

"One more time, Mr. Porter," Young says, his thick jaw brick-like and unyielding. "There *was* no one upstairs. I checked the place myself."

"I didn't see any sign of a suspect downstairs either," McFee says.

A suspect, Jay thinks, not *the*.

Suddenly, the very existence of a perpetrator is under suspicion, as if Jay imagined the whole thing, or made it up, or maybe broke into the office himself, which for all he knows is what the cops are *really* thinking, the two of them on the verge of opening a separate investigation into a potential insurance scam. He resents the two cops for making him feel crazy, for making him feel that he can't trust his own eyes.

The phone on Jay's desk rings again.

"That's the Delyvan woman, Jay!"

"Look," the cop says. "Officer McFee and I have no problem amending the initial report, Mr. Porter, adding in your description of the intruder and the bit about the misplaced glass." He delivers that last part as if he were describing the plot of an Agatha Christie novel. This isn't a murder mystery, he wants it known, just a simple case of breaking and entering, one of thirty or forty on a given night in the city of Houston, depending on the weather. "But I will also add words to support my opinion, based on ten years on the force, that I did not see ev-

idence of an intruder in your place of business at the time my
partner and I were present."

Jay holds up a finger, not the one he wants to, mind you, but
a single index finger to indicate he needs to answer this ringing
telephone.

"Mrs. Delyvan," he says, picking up the line.

"Jay, this is Arlee calling."

"Yes, ma'am."

Jay's office is one of the smaller rooms in the house. It sits opposite the kitchen on the other side of the house, where, at least
once a week, Eddie Mae has a pot of red beans on the stove. He
can smell the pork fat and brown sugar from here, the smoky
scent passing through two walls and filling every inch of the
room. The window behind his desk he's propped open with
an ancient text on Texas civil statutes, borrowed from his library upstairs. It's strikingly uncluttered for a lawyer's office.
But he hasn't carried a full caseload since his wife died; he's
been turning away all new business and clearing out the old.
His entire practice has come down to a single class action suit,
Pleasantville v. ProFerma Labs, a case he kept because it was
local, close to home, and close to his kids; he wouldn't have
to travel, and there would be no trial, that much he was sure
of. Last year, when two explosions from ProFerma's chemical
plant threatened to burn one of Houston's most storied neighborhoods to the ground, it was Jay Porter whom the residents of
Pleasantville called, what should have been a slam dunk. Half
the city had watched the smoky scene on their television sets,
orange embers flying into folks' backyards, lighting up roofs
and wood-frame houses, and Jay was sure the case would never
see the inside of a courtroom. ProFerma had every incentive to
settle the matter quickly. But a year and a half later, they're no
closer to a deal. The company has yet to make a serious offer.
Arlee Delyvan was the first to sign on as a plaintiff.

She was one of "the original thirty-seven," one of the three dozen or so families who'd settled into the first homes in Pleasantville when the neighborhood was built in '49. Dr. Delyvan, who'd been a pediatrician, bought a four-bedroom, ranch-style home on Tilgham. It came with a his-and-hers two-car garage, with room enough for his Ford and his wife's blue Lincoln Continental. Mrs. Delyvan, a widow, is in her late seventies and volunteers part-time at the Samuel P. Hathorne Community Center, where she's calling from now. As Jay is ever in the business of maintaining his clients' trust, he takes their calls, day or night, no matter the topic.

"You heard about the girl, I guess," she says. "Alicia Nowell?"

It takes a moment for the name to land. When it does, Jay swallows a clump of dread that's suddenly lodged itself in the back of his throat. "I heard something on the radio this morning, yes, ma'am," he says.

"They're saying somebody might have grabbed her out here."

"That's what I heard."

"Well?"

She waits for him to say more, to put two and two together, or in this case, two plus *one*. Alicia Nowell makes three girls now who have gone missing in and around Pleasantville. The first one in '94, the second last year. Two girls, more than a year apart, is a mean coincidence. Three girls is officially a problem.

Jay puts his client on hold and tells Officers Young and McFee that he wants a look at the amended incident report whenever it's ready. He has Eddie Mae see them to the door. Then, sitting down in the rolling slat-back chair behind his desk, he again picks up the line. Mrs. Delyvan sounds heated, her voice hushed, but stern. Nobody, not anyone on the radio, not the newspaper, no one has mentioned a word about the other girls, both of them local, raised in Pleasantville, their families about to pass another Christmas with no answers.

"This one was from south of here, Sunnyside," Arlee says, spitting out the word like an unwanted seed. "But a child is a child, and here's another one who seems to have just disappeared off our streets." She sighs heavily into the phone. "Her parents have been calling here nonstop. I'm afraid I don't know much more than they do, what little I've heard on my street. It was Elma Johnson who saw the girl, standing at the corner of Ledwicke and Guinevere. Elma was at her kitchen sink, rinsing a head of cabbage, when she looked out her window and saw this Nowell girl, same description her parents gave the police, standing alone at the corner. She had a purse in her hands but nothing else and looked to Elma like she was waiting for someone." She kept looking up the north side of the street, watching cars coming from that direction. Arlee added that Clarence Watson and another woman over on Pleasantville Drive both believed they'd seen the Nowell girl before, or at least a girl who looked a lot like her, passing out Hathorne campaign leaflets. "But that's impossible, Jay. The Voters League, we made our endorsement on *Sunday*," she says, speaking of Pleasantville's voting organization, the most important and influential community institution of its kind in the city, a group almost as old as the neighborhood itself.

Pleasantville's home precinct, number 259 in Harris County, Texas, is known as one of the most vote rich in the state, and the Voters League, therefore, holds a lot of sway. It's a level of political power the people of Pleasantville cherish because they built it out of thin air back in the early 1950s, when they fought the city and the all-white school board to get an elementary school for their new neighborhood, a school that wasn't overcrowded and underfunded, like those in Denver Harbor and Fifth Ward. It took nearly a year of pressing the mayor, but finally the residents, their numbers growing each time they marched on city hall, got their state-of-the-art school. And got something even more valuable in the process: a place to vote. It eliminated the need to split Pleasantville into arbitrary sections, with some residents voting in existing precincts to the north and some to the east and west, by creating a single precinct of consolidated black voting power, nicknamed "the mighty 259" by more than a few mayors, city council members, state senators, governors, and congressmen, who know the neighborhood's power to swing an election. There is and always has been a culture of civic engagement that defines the neighborhood as much as its wide, clean streets with pink and white crepe myrtles lining each side, its legendary Christmas banquets and Sunday barbecues, the gin and whist parties on Saturday nights.

Bottom line: folks in Pleasantville *vote*, always have.

And in numbers unmatched almost anywhere else in the state of Texas.

"It's no secret we're pushing for Hathorne, the hometown boy," Mrs. Delyvan says. "But we made it official on Sunday. Pleasantville is going for Hathorne all the way. By Sunday night, his campaign pulled out of here, instead putting their folks on the ground out near Memorial, places like Tanglewood and South Post Oak, parts of the city that were still up for grabs. Sunday till the polls closed on Tuesday night, there wasn't a soul from the Hathorne campaign working these streets. We were expecting Axel, sure, some high-level staffers and family members. But I don't know what that girl was doing out here."

"You talk to Axel?"

"I left a message with his nephew, Neal, the one running his campaign."

"What about Sam?" Jay says, meaning Axel's father.

"I'm told he's aware of the situation," she says. "But it's been two days."

"Right," Jay says, hearing the hint of desperation in her voice, the drumbeat at the edge of this entire conversation. The first girls, Deanne Duchon and Tina Wells, were found exactly six days after they went missing, their broken bodies discovered a year apart, but no more than a hundred yards from the same creek, and rumors ran rampant across northeast Houston that each of the girls had been alive up until a few hours before she was found in the field of brush. Around Pleasantville, there has always been a sense that if the police department had acted sooner, if the girls had been from River Oaks or Southampton Place, one or both lives might have been saved.

"There's still time, Jay. She might be out there somewhere," Arlee says, making clear her belief that the cases are most certainly connected.

Jay believes it too.

The thought crossed his mind the second he heard the news.

"You know the Duchons still got that girl's room closed off? Every last thing in it just the way she left it, her car still sitting right there in the garage, a little yellow Mustang Betty bought her when she turned sixteen, a month before she went missing."

Jay slides his hands into his pockets, looking out his office window. He still has Bernie's car. With Evelyn's help he was able to pack up most of her clothes, on a day when the kids were at school, but her Camry is, like Deanne Duchon's yellow Mustang, still parked in his garage. He still sits inside it some nights, after the kids have gone to bed.

"Elma, Ruby, Joe Wainwright, and me," Arlee says, "we called a meeting on the issue, to see if we can't put pressure on law enforcement, let them know that Pleasantville takes the lives of these girls seriously." Jay would have expected no less from them. They are a group of people who believe there isn't a single problem that can't be solved with a meeting, a neighborhood that believes deeply in the power of its number, and Jay respects them for it. Their activism preceded his by more than a decade, and he is, at forty-six, ever aware that he walks daily in their debt. "We think you ought to come tonight, Jay." He reaches across his desk for his Rolodex, looking for the number for Alice King, Lori's mother, knowing he will not be picking his kids up before dinner. "What time?" he says.

"Ruby will set out the coffee around six."

"Yes, ma'am."

He changes into a fresh shirt. In the back bathroom, he gives himself a good shave, his first in a week. Next, he calls Mrs. King to make sure it's all right if the kids stay a little late. Ellie's upstairs with Lori, she says. Ben is right there with her in the kitchen. "I want to go home," he says as soon as he comes on the line. Of all the after-school help Jay regularly relies on, the King household is Ben's least favorite. Lori's two older sisters are in college, and there isn't anyone in the house anywhere near his age. He spends most of his time in the Kings' kitchen, teaching Mrs. King to use her computer, while she asks him at least five times an hour if he's hungry. Ben's version, of course. "You guys okay?"

"Yes, sir."

"You minding Mrs. King?"

"Yes, sir."

"Okay, I'll be there as soon as I can."

"Yes, sir."

"Love you, son."

"I love you too, Dad."

Ben makes it easy. Their affection for each other is pure and unguarded, nearly elegant in its simplicity. Ben always says exactly what he means, or else he hardly speaks at all. It's a trait that Jay respects, mainly because he recognizes it in himself. It's not fair, really, the ease with which he and Ben get along, or that Ellie got stuck with the parent least equipped to raise her. Jay reaches for his suit jacket and tie and heads down the main hall, telling Eddie Mae he'll be out for a while. She's on the computer, fiddling with her AOL account. "Rolly called," she says, motioning toward the broken window, still covered in cardboard. "He mentioned something about Tuesday night."

Jay sighs. "You know I have to ask."

"I ain't give nobody a key, and you know it."

"I know you wouldn't *give* it, Eddie Mae, but I'm thinking more about the number of people in and out of your house and whether one of them might have made a copy, might have got some idea in his mind that this was an easy target."

"You wondering if my family tried to *steal* from you?"

"I said I had to ask."

"Them boys ain't half right, but they ain't all wrong neither."

Jay fishes for his keys, in his pocket. "Don't hold it against me, huh?"

Eddie Mae waves off the thought. "You want to take some beans? It's some rice in there too, and beer," she says, which Jay guesses she might have already cracked into, judging by her plump, flushed cheeks and the nearness of five o'clock. "Do me a favor," he says on his way out. "Take another look around and make sure no one took anything, would you? Tomorrow, I'll poke through the files upstairs, just to make sure we didn't overlook something that may be missing." He turns and walks through the front door, down the steps, and through the wrought-iron gate, heading toward his car.

On impulse, he drives past the Hathorne campaign headquarters, a block over on Travis. The windows of the brick storefront are papered with red-white-and-blue posters, featuring both the campaign slogan (HATHORNE FOR HOUSTON!) and photos of the man himself, Axel Hathorne, in his late fifties now, tall and hook nosed, like a hawk, nicknamed "the Axe" when Jay first met him, nearly thirty years ago, back when Jay was a student and activist at the University of Houston. Despite the name and his reputation as a ballbuster, especially when he was a beat cop patrolling the streets of Fifth Ward and Kashmere Gardens, baton in hand, Jay always found Axe to be one of the better men to wear the uniform. To his comrades in COBRA and AABL, his few buddies in SNCC, he frequently spread the word: if an arrest was coming, better to turn yourself in to a man like Mr. Hathorne than risk an arrest at the hands of a beat cop with no interest in, or understanding of, the racial justice movement. Axel had said publicly that he'd rather see black men marching in the streets than climbing through back windows—words that had pissed off both sides of the racial divide—when he was first appointed to run the police department, by none other than Cynthia Maddox, the city's first woman mayor, and the first woman to break Jay's heart.

It's odd, he thinks, that Hathorne hasn't gotten out ahead of the story of the missing girl. Axel grew up in Pleasantville after all. Jay would have thought a former police chief with an eye on the mayor's office would have lined the streets of Pleasantville with men in blue, had cops knocking on doors and checking every field and creek within a five-mile radius. The door to his campaign headquarters is propped open by a cardboard box, out of which a young staffer is distributing campaign T-shirts to a line of volunteers that stretches all the way to the kosher bakery next door. They're eager teenagers, some, and others as old as or older than Jay, men and women in tattered jeans, getting paid a few bucks to pass out campaign leaflets, papering neighborhoods across the city; every election season, Jay clears their junk mail from his doorstep. For the marginally employed, it isn't a bad gig. From the front seat of his car, Jay watches the line of volunteers as each is handed a clipboard, a stack of pamphlets, and a campaign T-shirt, blue with long sleeves. Just like the one Alicia Nowell was last seen wearing.

CHAPTER 2

Rolly spent Tuesday night in the backseat of his car, a '92 Lincoln with gold detailing on the hood, the only one in his fleet of ten that his regular crew is not allowed to drive. Around one in the morning, he'd dropped off his last fare, a Wolcott campaign straggler who spent most of the drive to West U. on his two-way pager, and then he swung by his garage on Telephone Road, to change his clothes and pay the staff, two hundred cash to each of his drivers. He put a cooler of beer in the backseat, and a bag of peanuts and some Fritos from the vending machine in his front pockets, and then he drove south to Jay's office on Brazos, parking, for the purposes of surveillance, a half block from the nearest streetlamp. He killed the engine and cut the Lincoln's headlights, settling in for his night watch. He munched on salted peanuts and juiced the battery on his mobile phone, plugging it into the cigarette lighter. He has a gal he's seeing out to Hitch-cock, halfway to Galveston; she doesn't sleep but a few hours a night and is always up for a call from Rolly. He can't predict where the romance is headed. Hitchcock is forty minutes away, an hour in traffic, and his little miss is without a car or a bus pass. She stays in a two-bedroom house with her daughter and two of her grandkids. He swore he would never mess with an older woman, but this one is six feet in heels with a tight little ass, and she has his nose so wide open he can smell a raindrop from two miles away. He knows he's in deep trouble.

He was dialing her number when a suspicious car came up Brazos, cruising to the north. It was a Nissan Z, black, and Rolly got three digits off the license plate as the car, unexpectedly, slowed in front of the gate to Jay's office. Before he could catch the other three numbers, the driver cut the Z's front and rear lights. The door swung open, and someone got out, a man cut-ting a tall, lanky figure. He paced in front of the gate, as if scop-ing the place, as if he expected something was about to jump off. Rolly felt for the grip of the Colt .45 in the waistband of his black Levi's. But stopped himself when he realized Jay had given him no clear instruction as to what to do in the event he ran into trouble. Calling the cops was not Rolly's style. But neither did he want to start something out here without knowing what he was getting into. He cleared the Motorola's screen. But before he could call Jay, he heard the car door slam. The driver of the Nissan Z revved the engine and quickly sped off, heading in the general direction of downtown. Rolly managed to eye an-other piece of the license plate's puzzle. This morning, he ran the four digits by a friend at the Department of Public Safety; 5KL 6 matches the first four digits of only one black Nissan model Z in the entire state of Texas, registered to a Jon K. Lee in Houston. "Might be nothing," Rolly says on the phone now.

Jay, who doesn't like to talk while driving, has pulled off the 610 Freeway, the first exit past the bridge over the Ship Channel, less than a mile from the village of Pleasantville. He's idling in the parking lot of a Circle K. On the back of a receipt, he writes the name and address of Jon K. Lee. "Funny thing is," Rolly says, "he filed a notice with the Department of Public Safety that his '96 Nissan Z was stolen last month."

He must be calling from the tiny office in his garage. In the background, Jay hears the thump of a car's stereo. When not on a call, his drivers play cards mostly, smoke and drink. The garage has the feel of a barbershop or a fraternity house, a place where men and boys go to willfully lose track of time. Jay makes a note about the stolen car. "'Preciate it, man," he says.

"Not a problem, Counselor."

Jay turns off his car phone, stowing it and its long cord in the compartment beneath the Land Cruiser's armrest. He goes into the convenience store and buys himself a Coke. The place has already put up Christmas decorations, cheap tinsel and paper wreaths hanging from the ceiling. It's still three weeks from Thanksgiving, on its own a rough current to cross for two kids who lost their mother, but nothing like the emotional shit storm that's waiting for all of them come December. Last year they rented a house in Corpus. Unplugged the TV and went fishing every day. Evelyn stopped speaking to Jay for a week. She'd had a tree out, everything ready at her place. But he never showed.

From the parking lot, he turns onto Clinton Drive. At the Gethsemane Baptist Church, he turns left on Flagship, coming into Pleasantville at one of its southern borders, arriving, within a few turns, at the corner of Guinevere and Ledwicke, the spot where, as far as anyone knows, Alicia Nowell was last seen.

Jay slows at the intersection.

The streets are empty tonight, and the scene in his rearview mirror is dim. Behind him, Ledwicke, the neighborhood's major north-south connecter that leads to the Samuel P. Hathorne Community Center, the pool, and the football field, ends at the edge of a wide area of wild woods. It's a rare block of undeveloped land in a city that wears its disdain for proper zoning as a badge, its belief in industrial growth as a democracy's birthright, penciled in just behind the pursuit of happiness. Pleasantville, in particular, has become surrounded by industry over the last twenty years, ever since the 610 Freeway was built against the residents' strident opposition. Besides the chemical plants that moved in, there's now a Budweiser brewery nearby and a six-acre factory that produces plastic packing materials, all on what used to be open prairie.

Elma Johnson's house stands on Guinevere, facing south. It's a cream-colored four-bedroom with Tudor accents and a Carolina cherry tree in the front yard. Jay's been inside once before. In her living room, he sat over her kidney-shaped coffee table as she'd signed the voluminous plaintiffs' forms, joining, at that point, sixty-seven of her neighbors and friends. From her kitchen window, she was the last to see the girl. Alicia was standing on the corner where Jay is parked now, maybe fifty feet from the tangle of trees in the open field, a dark maze of thorns and brambly vines. There's a soggy creek that cuts through the woods there. If Jay hadn't spent nearly ten grand earlier this year having it tested for the chemical SBS, or polystyrene-butadiene-styrene, the accelerant in last year's fires, he'd never have known it was there. It's completely hidden from the street, the reason someone chose it as a final resting place for the first two girls.

Jay still remembers the second girl.

She slipped away, must have been, the day Bernie checked in for her last stint at St. Luke's, on the cardiac floor that time because oncology had no more beds. Tina Wells had gotten off the school bus one afternoon and never made it the thirty or forty yards from the bus stop to her front door. Her mother, on the evening news, couldn't speak. It was Pastor Morehead, from the Pleasantville Methodist Church, who spoke for the family.

"This is a little girl," he said. "Someone's child."

Bernie watched it all from her hospital bed, and she woke the next day asking if there'd been any news. She worried over that missing girl for days, wouldn't let anybody change the channel on the TV if the news was on, hoping for an update. Jay sat through it, fidgety and uncomfortable, staring into the hall, waiting on the next doctor or nurse to come in, listening for the soles of shoes squeaking on the linoleum outside. And when nearly a week went by with no answers, no happy ending, on TV or in that tiny hospital room, or in the pages and pages of her medical chart, Bernie finally said she thought it would be best if she were the one to talk to Ellie, their fourteen-year-old daughter, about what was happening to her mother, that she wasn't coming home the way anyone wanted, and there were things she thought her girl needed to know to go on without her. Jay felt relieved and grateful at first, Bernie taking this off his shoulders, and then ashamed of himself, his bald cowardice. He excused himself and went out to the hall, where he leaned his face against the cold wall tiles to keep from puking.

Tina Wells was found the next day. She'd been fifteen, Ellie's age now.

A car rolls up behind Jay and honks.

He's been idling for a couple of minutes, blocking the intersection.

He waves an apology to the driver, then scoots his car along, heading toward the community center, where Arlee was when she called, and where Jay assumes tonight's meeting is being held. The car behind him, a black Cadillac, honks again, just as the driver pulls alongside Jay. The rear window slides down. Sam Hathorne is sitting in the back passenger seat, alone.

"Follow me," he says, before rolling up the tinted window.

The Cadillac picks up speed, zooming ahead of Jay. At the turnoff to the community center, Hathorne's driver keeps going, and Jay follows, unsure where they're heading until the Cadillac turns onto Norvic, pulling up in front of the Hathorne family homestead, a sprawling ranch-style house painted russet brown and set back from the street by thirty yards and twin magnolia trees shading damp grass. The driver steps out of the car first. Sam Hathorne opens the rear passenger door on his own. He comes out smoothing his suit jacket and holding out a hand for Jay. "Arlee told me you were coming."

The two men meet at the start of the house's brick walk.

"Sam," Jay says, shaking his hand.

"I thought it'd be more comfortable if we met here."

Samuel P. Hathorne, "Sunny" to a number of the old guard, men and women who've known him since '49, who raised their children alongside his, is no more than five feet six in boots, a pearl gray ostrich pair on his feet now. He is barrel chested, with a torso that narrows to the tip of a V at his small, nearly birdlike waist. He wears wire-rimmed glasses, black across the tops of the lenses, and he keeps his silver hair close to the sides with a lift at the front, giving him an extra inch in stature. Sam moved his family into the first single-family home at Pleasantville's founding, had, in fact, been the unofficial liaison between the Negro community and Mel Silverman and Bernard Paul, the developers who dreamed up the town. Sam, even way back then, decided who would benefit from his connections, who would get a home loan from his bank, Southern National—which he'd built over the years from a few thousand dollars to the premier black bank in the state—and who wouldn't, who got to buy into the most coveted new community for black folks in the city and who didn't. He was the unofficial "mayor" of Pleasantville, the man to see if you had a beef with a neighbor, or needed a reference for a job or a loan, of course. And if Sam Hathorne wouldn't give you the money, he would tell you who would. He was one of the first to organize the new residents in their many fights with city hall over city services, spearheading that campaign for the elementary school, and he's had the ear of folks in city government ever since. He is the funnel through which power flows, from city hall to the north side. A walking conduit for Pleasantville's needs, he's simply beloved in these parts. He still owns the house on Norvic, though most people know he doesn't really live in it anymore, and most folks forgive him for it. A lot has changed in Pleasantville since 1949.

His driver, a fair-skinned black man in a navy suit, gray shirt, and tie, lights a cigarette as Sam leads Jay toward the front door of the house. Eighty now, he walks with a slight limp, favoring his right leg. He pats Jay warmly on the back and asks him what he's drinking tonight.

Inside, there's a fire going. But the mood is somber.

Arlee Delyvan nods to Jay when he walks in. She's wearing black slacks and a gray sweater. Next to her on the Hathornes' leather sofa are Ruby Wainwright, tall and lean like her husband, and Elma Johnson, a dark-skinned woman with a head full of finger curls. She sits stone faced, a gold-rimmed china cup resting on her lap. Trays of tea cakes and honeyed ham sit on the coffee table, untouched. The men in the room hover over a standing ashtray, curls of white cigarette smoke reaching up toward the ceiling.

Sam Hathorne pours himself two fingers of Crown Royal.

"Turn that off," he says, nodding toward a wooden stereo cabinet and record player, on which a lick of blues guitar is playing.

When no one heeds his instruction, he crosses to the stereo and lifts the needle off the record himself. "Axel called the family," he says, taking a hearty swallow of his whiskey. "This morning, Axel spoke with the girl's mother and stepfather."

The handful of neighborhood folks who've gathered, Jay's clients each of them, have congregated in the sitting area of the living room. But around a long, elegant dining room table are faces from the campaign Jay doesn't recognize: a heavyset white woman with stick-straight gray hair running down the back of her blue Hathorne T-shirt; a white man in his late forties, in brown slacks the exact color of his neat, close-trimmed hair; and a young black guy in shirtsleeves and slacks, who'd been on the phone when Jay walked in. He flips his cell phone closed, pushing down the antennae with his teeth. He's the youngest in the room by a decade.

"This is my grandson, Mr. Porter," Sam says. "Neal Hathorne." Neal shakes Jay's hand.

"Heard a lot about you, sir," he says.

Up close, Jay can see the family resemblance. He's on the short side, like his grandfather, but he has the same caramel-colored skin as every Hathorne Jay has ever laid eyes on, the same diamond-sharp features that tell the legend of distant Cherokee blood running through the entire brood. Their bright, honey-colored eyes stare out at him from portraits and photographs across the plush living room. Axel in his dress greens from the army; Ola, Camille, Delia, and Gwen, the four beauties, in graduation uniforms, cotillion whites, and wedding gowns. There are two doctors among them, a banker, and a professor of engineering, the Hathornes having produced a line of incredibly accomplished children. Grandchildren too, if Neal is any indication. This one graduated law school at the University of Texas, Sam says, smiling, full of elder pride.

"He's running his uncle's campaign."

"And we're on top of this, trust me."

He can't be more than thirty, slim as a department-store model, and handsome too. "You Ola's son?" Jay asks, thinking he sees a resemblance there.

At the question of his lineage, Neal turns, caught off guard. "No."

He offers nothing further, neither as a courtesy nor as a clarification.

Jay glances again at the family portraits on the walls, trying to place the young man, to divine from which Hathorne he sprang.

"We're in touch with the police department," Neal tells the others.

Behind him, the front door opens and in walks Johnetta Paul. "What the hell, Sam?" she says, trailing a smoky scent of Shalimar. She's wearing a custom pantsuit in fuchsia, her signature color, her braids woven into a rather large, boxlike structure on her head. She is the incumbent councilwoman for District B, which includes parts of Fifth Ward and all of Pleasantville. Like Axel Hathorne, she is heading into a runoff on December tenth, having been ill-prepared for a challenge from a political upstart out of Clinton Park. "I'm getting calls, Sam, one month before the goddamned runoff I'm getting calls from people wanting to know how scared they should be," she says. She's a woman in her fifties, but carries herself like an impatient, overly made-up teenager, flitting restlessly.

"Where is Axel?" she demands.

"At the *Chronicle*'s offices downtown."

"Well, tell him to get his bony ass down here."

"He's meeting with the editorial board at the paper, making another pitch," Neal says. "We barely secured their endorsement in the general."

"And that's only because the *Chronicle* couldn't figure out a way to sell papers in this city if the editors didn't endorse the first viable black mayoral candidate in memory, especially against a Pop-Tart like Wolcott," the white woman says. "But we can't necessarily count on their support again. Behind the scenes, everything I'm hearing on the ground is that the paper is pushing for Wolcott." Then, remembering herself, she turns to the room, as if meeting new members of the campaign's team. "Marcie Hall, communications director."

Arlee and Ruby Wainwright exchange a glance, but say nothing. Jim, Ruby's husband, frowns.

"We did well on Tuesday," Sam says. "But some of the numbers were *troubling*. Bob Stein at Rice is polling the new landscape, tracking where Acton's votes are going. We've got twenty-nine days to push this thing our way."

"*Our* way, exactly," Johnetta says. "*I* was the first one on the council to come out for Axel, the 'Pleasantville ticket,' you called it, and *I* don't intend to be dragged down 'cause Axe is too slow to get on top of this thing."

"Sit down, 'Netta," Sam says, the pet name only fueling the long-standing rumor about the real nature of their relationship. "Unless you've already forgotten who put you in that council seat in the first place," he says, not bothering to look her in the eye, not needing so much as a glance to shut her up.

"What are the police saying?" Jay asks, getting back to the girl.

"They've opened a case," Neal says.

"That's it?" Johnetta says.

"That's a start," Neal says. "And not as easy as you might imagine. The girl was eighteen. She was living at home, but as far as HPD is concerned, Alicia Nowell is an adult female. For all they know, she doesn't want to be found."

"What about the others, Sam?" Arlee says.

Mr. Wainwright clears his throat. He's a retired engineer, and he speaks in a deep baritone, hands clasped behind his back. "Did the police detectives indicate a belief that the cases are connected? This girl and the others?"

"We didn't really get that far."

"Well, what *did* they say?" Johnetta says.

Neal sighs. "We've left several messages at the precinct. Axel left word with the chief downtown. We'll let you know as soon as we hear back."

Arlee is stunned. "You haven't even *talked* to them?"

"Good lord," Johnetta says.

"Sam, what is going on here?" Arlee says.

Keith Morehead, youth pastor at the Pleasantville Methodist Church, one of the youngest clergymen in the community, is in jeans and sneakers. "Why aren't we meeting at the community center? There're a number of families who've expressed their concern to me personally. I'm sure they'd like to be heard on the issue."

"Why aren't the Wellses here? Or Deanne's parents?"

"I wanted us to be able to speak freely." Sam pours himself another bump of whiskey. "Grief and guilt cloud things," he says, leaving Jay to wonder to whose guilt he's referring, why that word would enter this room. "We have a young woman missing, in my neighborhood, Axel's old stomping ground, a story that will get out of our hands if we let it, and at the worst possible time." Neal opens his mouth to speak, but Sam shakes his head, hushing him. "I thought a gathering here, among friends, people we trust, was the more prudent approach," Sam says. "Arlee, Ruby, you know as well as anyone how meetings at the center can easily get off track, veering into arguments over deed restrictions and what kind of punch to serve at the next PTA meeting. Especially in the last few years, with the newer folks coming in."

There are nods of recognition around the room.

These are some of the oldest families in Pleasantville.

What was once a segregated oasis, a black Levittown where flowers grew and families thrived, now seems hardly worth the gas money for young black professionals, not for a daily commute ten miles past downtown, not when they can buy property *anywhere* these days. No matter the best efforts of the old-timers to keep the neighborhood as it's always been, to secure its borders, keep the money in and the newcomers out, there are, every year, new families who are buying their way in, working-class blacks from places like Fifth Ward and South Park, and Latino families from the north side, who see in its quaint, tree-lined streets their chance at the American dream. You can't put up fences on change.

"It's been two days," Arlee says. "Three, when the sun comes up. We're losing time every hour that passes, every hour there's a killer still out there."

"We don't know that's what this is, Arlee," Sam says.

"We'd be fools to think otherwise," Mr. Wainwright says ruefully.

"It's been *two* days," Arlee says again. "Deanne, Tina, whether HPD wants to say so publicly or not, those girls were still alive at this point. You all saw the reports. If HPD had made a bigger push to find them, who knows how things might have turned out for them, for their families. I imagine the Duchons and the Wellses might have cause for a civil suit against the department, if they wanted to go that route." She glances across the room at Jay, who feels put on the spot, aware too late that Arlee had something like this in mind the second she called his office this afternoon. He had come tonight to offer what support he could. His heart aches for the girls' families. But he is in no position to consider a lawsuit against the police department. Sam follows the look between them, Jay and Arlee, wrongly assuming that this was planned.

"You can't be serious," Marcie says.

"I'm in the middle of the biggest fund-raising push of the campaign," the man in the dark brown slacks says. "We're waiting on a dozen five-figure checks right now. Any word about this would be a disaster."

"We're on top of it, Stan," Neal says. Stan, the moneyman, Jay thinks.

"I love you, Sam, I do," Arlee says, looking at him, one of her oldest friends. "But I am not putting your campaign ahead of these girls."

"Suing the police department won't do a thing for Alicia Nowell right now," Sam says, and Jay is inclined to agree.

"Elma," he says. "You saw her Tuesday?"

"Tuesday night, 'bout a quarter to nine. She was just standing by herself."

Vivian Hathorne, Sam's wife, emerges from the kitchen. She leans against the door frame, cupping a tumbler filled with a clear liquid she's sipping too slowly for it to be anything other than vodka. She's wearing a navy skirt, a lace apron tied around her waist. She was a schoolteacher once, back before Sam's bank set them up in comfort and style. Viv is taller than her husband, and round in every place he is stick straight, her hips opening like a rose beneath her narrow gold-plated belt. She wears her hair in a thick braid, streaked with pewter; it rests dramatically across the front of her left shoulder. She is, even in her late seventies, utterly striking. Johnetta, at the sight of her, rolls her eyes. "What's her name?" Viv asks, her voice soft and bell-like. "The girl?"

"Nowell," Arlee says. "She wasn't from around here."

"What was she doing in Pleasantville?"

"She work for your uncle's campaign?" Jay asks.

He remembers the description of the blue, long-sleeved

T-shirt she'd been wearing. And the reports from at least two residents in the area that Alicia was leaving leaflets on doorsteps in the hours before she went missing.

"She wasn't on the payroll, no," Neal says.

"Which means what exactly?"

"She wasn't *employed* by the campaign, that much we know."

"Which is exactly what everyone in this room needs to say if asked," Marcie says, looking up from her legal pad. Her upper lip is sweating.

"Was she a volunteer?" Jay asks.

"Was she?" Vivian says, alarmed. "Sam? Was she working for Axel?"

Sam, staring into the bottom of his glass, doesn't answer right away.

"Sunny?" It's Mr. Wainwright, pushing for an answer.

Neal sighs. "The truth is, we don't really know."

"She was off the books?" Jay says. He makes a gesture with his right hand, rubbing his fingers together to suggest the untraceable cash that might have landed in Alicia Nowell's hands, street money to get out the vote.

"Every campaign does it," Neal says.

True, Jay thinks. But if the missing girl was indeed volunteering for Axel's campaign, it will mean nothing but trouble for the former police chief.

Johnetta, sensing the political danger of being in this room for even another second, tucks her purse under her arm. "I wasn't here," she tells Sam. "Until you fix this, I wasn't here." She makes a quick survey of the room, eyes lingering on Jay Porter, probably wondering if she's already hit him up for a contribution to her reelection campaign, before deciding now probably isn't the time. She turns to Mr. Wainwright. "Lend me a smoke, would you, Jim?" She waits for him to light it, then turns on her black heels and walks out.

At her exit, Vivian says, "Don't let that woman in my house again."

"We don't keep records of all our volunteers," Sam says.

Not the ones paid under the table, Jay thinks.

Now, more than ever, he understands why the meeting was moved from the community center at the last minute. The building may have Sam's name over the door, but it's city property, open to any resident, or any member of the press for that matter. This room, with its curtains drawn, is Sam's domain. "You have to disclose the possibility," Jay says, looking at Sam first, then Neal. "You can't play coy with the cops, not about this."

"We're working in-house to look into it," Neal says. He pulls his phone from his pocket, checks a missed call on the screen, then flips it closed again. "As of right now, none of our staffers remember her, nor does Tonya Hardaway, our field director, remember assigning her to Pleasantville. But if she was working for us, we have every intention of cooperating fully with the investigation."

"Last reports had Alicia in a blue shirt, long sleeves," Jay says.

Sam nods, but is unmoved. "Her mother said she never heard anything about her daughter working for a campaign. She didn't follow politics."

"The color might have confused some people," Neal says.

"Clarence and them," Jim says, looking at Arlee, in particular, "they may have seen a blue shirt and just assumed she was walking for the campaign."

"So you didn't have anybody in the field Tuesday?" Jay asks.

"In Pleasantville?" Neal says, glancing at his grandfather. "No."

"She wasn't one of ours," Sam says, as if willing it so.

"You guys were out here celebrating though, weren't you? Axel and the campaign going door-to-door?" Jay says, repeating the rumors he heard.

"Ruby set out a pound cake," Jim says, looking at his wife.

"It's still sitting on my kitchen counter," she says, crossing her arms in irritation.

"We weren't able to make it to every house that night," Sam says, glancing from his grandson to Marcie, the communications director. "But the bottom line is, the campaign has no knowledge of the girl or what happened to her."

"We've put together a search, first light tomorrow," Arlee says. From a leather tote at her feet, she pulls out a roll of paper, weathered at the edges. She unfurls the map across the coffee table. It's Pleasantville, each block broken into tiny squares, pencil marks scribbled on each plot of land, notes about the residents in every house in the entire neighborhood. It's the Voters League map. "We'll attack this like any other canvass, like every outreach we've ever done, on any and every issue that affects this community. House by house, we'll find out who saw what on Tuesday. We'll start to piece together her last hours."

"Pastor Jennings at Gethsemane, and Pastor Williams at Hope Well Baptist," Morehead says, "we're all planning to make statements during this Sunday's services, warning our congregations about the threat. I'm advising folks to meet their schoolchildren at the bus stops if they're able. Students, the girls especially, should walk in groups of two or three, everybody in before nightfall. The Blue Hawks," he says, speaking of the boys' basketball team he coaches at the rec center, "we're thinking of starting a patrol group for the neighborhood. We're asking folks to be on the lookout for any strange faces hanging around."

"You still having problems with the trucks?" Jay asks.

Arlee nods, and Jay makes a note to call Sterling & Company Trucks first thing in the morning. It isn't a part of his official duty as Pleasantville's civil attorney on record, has nothing, in fact, to do with the chemical fire. But for years Sterling has been allowing its commercial drivers to cut through the neighborhood on their way to the Port of Houston, and a while back Jay agreed to intervene. He sent a few strongly worded missives on his letterhead, but apparently these aren't doing the trick, because two, three times a week, Sterling's drivers still tear through in 18-wheelers and oversize box trucks, men who have no business in Pleasantville. "I'll get on it tomorrow," he says. It would give him something to do.

CHAPTER 3

By Friday morning, her picture's in the paper.

The *Houston Chronicle* runs a small piece in the City Section, page 2.

When she first sees the girl's face, Lonette Kay Phillips is sitting in the front room of her duplex on Marshall Street in Montrose, in a run-down, redbrick colonial that rests directly behind the West Alabama Ice House, where Lonnie passed a good amount of time the previous night, drinking her way through the world's weirdest blind date. It's a high school graduation picture, black gown and fingers cupping her chin, the whole deal, surrounded by three inches of copy, more than Lonnie would have thought the *Chronicle* would spare for the occasion. Back when its rival, the *Houston Post*, was still alive, the *Chronicle* had ignored the stories of the two girls who had disappeared off the streets of Pleasantville, their bodies found less than a city block from where Alicia Nowell was last seen. Lonnie, who had a Shiner Bock and two arsenic-white Hostess Donettes for breakfast, wipes the powdered sugar from her fingers onto the thighs of her jeans and lights a Parliament, staring at the Nowell girl's face.

She's pretty.

But they all are at that age.

Seventeen, eighteen, god don't make much ugly, not for girls like these, with mothers and fathers who check their beds at night, make sure the front and back doors are locked. In Lonnie's experience, it's time and circumstance that sully a complexion. She must have aged ten years the first time her daddy let her walk out of the house and into the car of some boy who couldn't be bothered with more than a honk from the driveway, the dented tail end of his Le Mans already pulling out into the street. "She looks like the others," she says, exhaling smoke. On his desk, Jay has the newspaper open to the same page. He called Lonnie first thing this morning, hoping she could help, remembering that she'd written about the other girls when she was still at the *Post*. "You know her?"

Jay shakes his head. "She wasn't from the neighborhood."

"Yeah, I read that."

The article was written by Gregg Bartolomo, a beat reporter she used to see here and there around the offices on Texas Avenue, back before she unceremoniously jumped over to the *Post* in '92, at the promise of, among other things, a promotion and an expense account, both of which she'd happily trade now for the chance to be gainfully employed again. She hasn't landed anything solid in the year since the warm day in April when the venerable *Post* folded, catching the city of Houston and the paper's staff by surprise. The *Chronicle* piece says that the girl was raised in Sunnyside, and that she lives with her mother and stepfather, Maxine and Mitchell Robicheaux, both of whom were questioned by law enforcement. It's more information than came out at the neighborhood meeting last night, Jay tells her. Either there are aspects of the investigation that the Hathornes were purposefully keeping from the folks in Pleasantville, or there's information the cops are purposefully keeping from them.

A graduate of Jesse H. Jones High School, Alicia Nowell has a part-time job at a Wendy's on OST, just east of 288. She was not scheduled to work on Tuesday, November fifth, but she'd left her apartment that afternoon. The information about her clothing is repeated here, that she was last seen in a long-sleeved blue T-shirt and jeans. There is no mention of the Hathorne campaign or whether the missing girl has any connection to its staff. The cops are treating this as a missing person case, but because the girl is eighteen, it's suggested that she could have simply walked off somewhere of her own volition. A boyfriend is mentioned, a young man who is a student at Lamar University in Beaumont, some ninety miles away.

"Sad," Lonnie says.

"Folks in Pleasantville think it's starting up again."

"You talk to Arlee Delyvan?"

"Last night."

"She took it hard, Arlee."

"They're scared."

"Ought to be."

Through the phone line, Jay hears her exhale, working up to something.

"Look, I was going to call you," she says.

"One of these days."

"How are the kids?"

"Fine," he says. He never knows how to answer that question.

"Maybe I'll come by sometime."

"You should."

There is a pocket of silence between them, deep enough to hold regrets for both of them, their relationship having thinned over the past year or so. Jay is unable to remember who stopped calling whom first. She came to the funeral, of course, but they'd barely spoken, Jay sitting with Ben and Ellie all the way up front by the cherrywood casket, a few feet from where Jay had recited his wedding vows. It was the first eulogy Bernie's father, Reverend Boykins, had declined to deliver in his own church; he'd woken that morning barely able to stand. Jay wouldn't wish this life on anyone, the nights he sits in his backyard, staring up at the sky, wanting, stars and all, to pull the whole thing back like the lid of a tin can, anything to see his wife again. It's the reason he drove to Pleasantville last night, the reason he called Lonnie this morning.

"How much do you remember about the story?"

"Deanne Duchon," Lon says, starting with the first girl. Jay scribbles the name on a legal pad, taking notes. "She was walking home from a friend's house. Four blocks, after sunset. But she never made it. Her dad had told her not to drive. She had a brand-new Mustang, but he told her it was a waste of gas to drive it just four blocks. He must have told me that story ten times."

"They have a suspect?"

"There was a name. I'd have to look through my notes."

She glances across the hardwood floors of her apartment, past the ratty futon, where there's a narrow, built-in bookshelf near the front door, and, below it, a sagging cardboard box, which she carried out of the *Post*'s offices eighteen months ago, loading it into her VW Golf before heading home, lugging it into her apartment and dropping it by the door, where it's sat every day since, a dusty reminder that she was once a writer, a real one. She has often prided herself on being less openly sentimental than her colleagues. That April morning last year, when news came that the paper's owner was pulling the plug, Lonnie had not hung around for the postmortem. While her co-workers stood dumbfounded, so blindsided that they had still been working on stories when their desk phones started ringing, Lonnie grabbed every piece of paper she'd ever scribbled on, combing the corners of her cubicle for anything she might have missed. Short of swiping the desktop Mac she wrote on, she got everything. By the time security started ushering folks out of the building, Lonnie was already a mile up the Southwest Freeway. She would cry later, she told herself. Only, the thing is, she never did. No tears, just beer and cigarettes for breakfast, whole days watching Sally Jessy and Montel. The box was meant as a kind of insurance policy, a way to start over when the time was right. There are at least a hundred stories inside, pieces she'd researched, bits of knowledge trying to find their way to the light of day. She's pitched a few, tried to sell herself to the *Statesman* in Austin, the *Morning News* in Dallas, the *Star-Telegram*, *Texas Monthly*, even *Texas Highways*. But no one local is hiring, and the *Chronicle* won't have her back—a feeling that's mutual. "I can take a look," she says. "I had started a bit on the second girl last year. The same name came up, I remember. Almost from the beginning, HPD was looking at similarities between the two cases."

"Maybe you and this Bartolomo guy could compare notes."

"Ha."

In the old days it would have been unthinkable, reporters from rival papers sharing information. The whole system was set up for one to keep a competitive distance from the other; however they duked it out on the front pages, chasing scoops and stories, there was an understanding that they made each other better. But Houston is a one-paper town now, the first major city in the country to try to run a democracy with a

single journalistic checkpoint, a single voice guiding four million people through a maze of complex issues.

"They organized a search, Arlee and the Wainwrights," Jay
says. "They're block-walking to gather any other information
on who might have seen what. If this is what they think it is,
then there's not a lot of time."

"No, there isn't. I'll give Bartolomo a call, see where they're at
with this. Mike Resner, the detective on the first cases, I think
he's still over in the Northeast Division. Might be worth a call
there too."

"It might put folks at ease out there, if they had a better sense
of what's going on with the investigation," Jay says. "I think
there's a hope that finding this girl might lead to answers about
the other two, offer some peace for the families. Between the
fires and this, Pleasantville could use some good news."

"Hey," Lon says softly. "I'm glad you called."

"Me too," he says, hanging up.

When he looks up, Eddie Mae is standing over his desk. She
must have come in sometime while he was on the phone. She's
still wearing her overcoat, and she's holding a stack of pink
message slips in one hand and a Jack in the Box cup in the
other. The bank called, she says right off, some problem with
the line of credit for the Pleasantville case, and the Arkansas
folks are at it again. The Pritchetts, plaintiffs ten through seventeen in the class action suit Jay filed against Chemlyne Industries in Little Rock, Jay's last time in a courtroom, have been
at each other's throats since they took a deal—two days before
Jay's closing arguments, and against his strident counsel. The
ones with any money left are constantly fighting with the ones
who have long since gone back to being broke, albeit with shiny
cars in their driveways and pounds of tenderloin in the deep
freeze. "B. J. Pritchett wants to sue his brother Carl for defama-
tion," Eddie Mae says. "Something about a collection of Nancy

Wilson records B. J. said he would buy off Carl and never did, and Carl going around town calling his brother a cheap son of a bitch. B.J. wants *you* to handle the matter in court. He's got a five-hundred-dollar check already made out to you as a retainer." She rolls her eyes.

Jay sighs. He curses the day he ever set foot in Arkansas.

Looking down at the desktop, where the newspaper is still open to the story of the missing girl, Eddie Mae cocks her head, staring, slantways, at the black-and-white photo of Alicia Nowell. "What's it been now?" she says.

"Three days."

"I'll pray for her."

"Was there something else?" Jay says, folding the newspaper in half.

"That lady from the trailer park called again, the one out to Baytown. She and her neighbors, they're still having problems with their water. She's convinced something's leaking out of the oil refinery down there, some runoff that's tainting every-thing. It's got so she won't even cook with it no more."

"Give her the list of referrals."

"You won't even meet with her?"

"Not taking clients, Eddie Mae, you know that."

She presses her lips together, quietly weighing whether this is the time to get into it with him. The one time she brought up losing a girlfriend to cancer, he'd quickly shut her down, not wanting to hear other people's ideas of what they thought he was living through, or to turn grief into a contest, one he would always win. He could never bring himself to shame someone's good intentions.

"That it?"

"No," she says. Reaching into the pocket of her peacoat, she pulls out a small rectangle of paper, frayed at the edges. "I did like you said, looked this place up and down, everywhere except the conference room upstairs, which you said *you'd* go through." Jay nods. "I didn't notice anything missing," Eddie Mae says. "But I did find this." She holds out a business card.

Jay takes it into his hands.

On the blank side, he sees his own name, scribbled in pencil, followed by the address of his law office, 3106 Brazos. "You think he dropped it?" Eddie Mae says, meaning the young man who broke into the office on Tuesday night.

"Where did you find it?"

"Under the couch in the waiting room, just a few feet from my desk," she says. "Wind must have blown it there. It was just a piece of it sticking out."

Jay flips the card over.

He leans back in his chair, staring at it.

"Weird, ain't it?" Eddie Mae says.

"Yes, ma'am, it is," Jay says. If whoever broke into his office inadvertently left this behind, it seems the intruder purposefully sought him out. And that doesn't make up even half the weird part. The name on the front of the professionally printed business card, in clean block letters, is JON K. LEE. The man with the stolen Z, Jay remembers. A car that matches the exact description of the one idling outside this very building late Tuesday night. According to his business card, Mr. Lee is an executive in the legal department of Cole Oil Industries. "Son of a bitch," Jay mutters. He feels a lick of heat across his forehead as he reaches across his desk for the telephone. Anticipating a show, Eddie Mae takes a front-row seat, setting herself down in one of the chairs across from Jay's desk, sipping her watery Pepsi as Jay dials the number on Mr. Lee's business card. It rings three times before a secretary picks up. "Mr. Lee's office."

"Jay Porter calling for him."

"Oh." There's a note of surprise in the woman's voice. He imagines his name is familiar enough in the halls of the Cole

Oil Industries legal department, considering the nearly fifteen years he's been after Cole and its money. He's never heard of Jon K. Lee. There was a Darryl Whitaker in legal, he remembers. He was first chair in '83 when Ainsley's case first went to trial. But Whitaker left years ago to work for a lobbying firm in D.C. Since then, there's been a revolving door of young attorneys working the endless appeals, offering every six months or so to settle with Ainsley's family and the other plaintiffs, always for a small fraction of what Jay had won for them in court. "One moment, Mr. Porter."

Jay hears the line click, then a man's voice. "This is Jon Lee. What can I help you with?" He sounds young, young enough to drive a Z, Jay thinks. Either it's all he can afford, or he's still chasing the kinds of women who are impressed by that sort of thing. Another ten years at the Cole trough, and he'll be in a Mercedes for sure. Jay wonders how long he's been paying bar dues.

"I'm trying to understand why I found your business card in my office."

"I'm sorry, who is this?"

"You working the Ainsley case now?"

He wouldn't have figured Thomas Cole to pull a dirty stunt like this, breaking into his office, but how else to explain the coincidence?

"I think you've got the wrong number."

"You had a car stolen a few weeks back, right? A Nissan?"

"How do you—"

Lee stops suddenly. "Lisa, can you get off the line for a sec," he says, waiting for the departure of his secretary. A second later there's another click, and then the line goes dead completely. Jay pulls the phone from his ear, staring at the receiver. He dials Lee's number again, but the call goes straight to voice mail, two, three more times. Jay hangs up, feeling the rush of

heat again, downright panic about what this means. "Get upstairs," he says to Eddie Mae. "There's an inventory sheet inside
the front of every box, every file we ever started for the Cole
case, from Ainsley on down." Eddie Mae nods. She filed most
of that paperwork herself. "Go back to the beginning, the first
briefs, Ainsley's deposition, all the way back to 1981, and make
sure every piece of paper, every videotape, everything is accounted for." He reaches for his car keys.

"Where are *you* going?"

"Can you also pull our billing records for '81, '82? Accounts
payable."

"Why?"

"Just do it, please."

Eddie Mae looks up, cocking her head to the side, noting the
tension through his neck and jaw. Jay carefully avoids her eye.
There's no way she could know what he's thinking. There's only
one person who knows what he did, years ago, which didn't win
him the biggest case of his life so much as ensure he wouldn't
lose it—and his wife is gone. "Pull the records," he says.

CHAPTER 4

Cole Oil Industries moved its headquarters in the fall of '91, from a towering high-rise in downtown Houston to a sprawling glass-and-stone industrial park outside the Loop, parking itself off the Southwest Freeway on Beechnut, right across the street from Brown & Root, its biggest competitor in the great rebirth of the military-industrial complex. Both had made a fortune in government contracts during George H. W. Bush's Gulf War, Brown & Root providing logistical support to U.S. troops in Kuwait, and Cole Oil managing oil-field production in Iraq. The construction of the brand-new, state-of-the-art complex was an act of optimism ahead of the '92 elections, a Bush win promising a wide, patriotic path into untapped markets in oil-rich nations previ-

ously closed to American money and interests. Texas didn't
see Bill Clinton coming.

It's a twenty-minute drive west from here.

When the freeway is clear, Jay's done it in less than fifteen.

Tucking Jon K. Lee's business card into his front pocket,
he starts down the steps of his office, stopping short when he
sees Jim Wainwright coming up the paved walk, the front gate
swinging closed behind him. Jim is a tall man. He played forward for the Prairie View Panthers before his time in the army,
most of it spent in segregated housing at Fort Polk in Louisiana,
and afterward finished his graduate studies at Texas Southern,
then called Texas State University for Negroes. Even ten years
into his retirement, it's rare to see Mr. Wainwright, a former
engineer, out of slacks and a tie. His look this morning, blue
jeans and a paint-splattered PV sweatshirt, reminds Jay of the
grim search out in Pleasantville. It stops him in his tracks. *Tell
me we weren't too late.* Jim shoves his hands into the pockets
and shakes his head. "Nothing so far," he says, words that fill
Jay with relief. Jim stands quiet a moment, his brow tensed into
a deep wrinkle.

"I need to talk to you, Jay."

"You want to come inside?"

Jim hangs back. "Let's take a walk, son," he says.

They make it up the block, past the print shop and a nude
furniture outlet, before Jim says a word, stopping in front of
the Diamond Lounge, a small blues bar. He pulls on the door's
brass handle, and a warm rush of air pours out into the street,
carrying the scent of tobacco and peanuts, which are roasted
daily on a stove top in the back. The lights are up inside, showing the cracks in the leather booths, the untended sticky spills
on the polished concrete floor. There's half a drum set on the

corner stage, and a few empty and crumpled paper cups from last night's show. Mr. Wainwright, who looks like he's had one hell of a week, plants his feet in front of the leather bar and orders a scotch and water. By Jay's watch, it's only 9:40 in the morning. The guy behind the bar slides a beer in front of Jay, unsolicited. He would ask for a glass of water, but he doesn't want to leave Jim with the feeling that he's drinking alone, not when Jay can feel a brick-size confession about to fall off the man's chest. Mr. Wainwright takes a sip of his scotch, sucking air through his teeth as it goes down. "You're in trouble, son," he says.

"Excuse me?"

"I like you, Jay, I do. And when the tragedy hit last year, when the fires were still burning, I was one of the main ones said you were the man to call."

"Thank you," Jay says cautiously.

Jim finishes the rest of the scotch in one gulp. His hand shakes as he sets his glass on the bar top. "But it's a lot of us involved in this thing. What, three hundred plaintiffs or something like that?"

"Four hundred and eighty-seven," Jay says.

He finds himself reaching for the beer, taking a swallow without thinking, anything to wet the back of his suddenly dry throat. It's a Michelob, ice cold.

"Well, there's some out there, Jay, who ain't happy with the way things are going. I think a lot of folks, myself included, thought we'd be further along in the process by now. Ruby and I, we've been lucky, least as it goes with the doctors and stuff. There's some up to the north side of the neighborhood got their kids on inhalers now, in and out of clinics. And I know you know this stuff too. But my house, others on my street, the money we paid to fix things, my roof, resodding the lawn, the repaint on my wife's car and mine, that's money we're not

seeing back." Mr. Wainwright picks up his glass, as if he forgot
it was empty, and then sets it down again. Under the bare bulbs
of the Diamond Lounge's main room, the white hair against
his deep brown skin makes a halo effect. "I put my faith in you,
and that's good enough for me, but there's some out there that
are feeling strung along."

They're not the only ones, Jay thinks.

He's put out his own money too. Nearly thirty thousand to
test the soil and the water out there, another fifty grand to two
researchers at Baylor to study the long-term medical effects of
the chemical burn on adults and children, and over a thousand
hours at forty-five bucks a pop for an investigator to take plaintiff and witness statements, the same woman he used in Arkansas for the Chemlyne trial. Not to mention money he's loaned
to more than a dozen families in Pleasantville, newcomers,
ones who bought in late to the neighborhood, who still have
young kids, college to pay for, braces, school trips and summer
camps, piano lessons and new shoes every six months, the ones
who can't easily afford to cover what insurance won't. While
they wait for settlement checks to start rolling in, Jay has paid
out of his own pocket to patch their roofs, redo drywall dam-
aged by the fire hoses, or pad out the rent money needed for a
temporary apartment while repairs are done on their homes.
Pleasantville is his entire practice now, and he'll go broke if he
can't settle it soon.

The truth is . . . he's planning to retire after this. Ellie's college
and Ben's, pay off the house, the whole bit, and then he's going
to sit down somewhere for a few years, take as long as he wants
to figure out what the point of any of this has been, what grace
he's meant to make of his flesh and bone, the breath that won't
stop, even if his wife has none. He's going to lie down somewhere and *wait*. Jay is forty-six now, which might as well be
sixty in black man years. Kwame Mackalvy had a heart attack

last year, was in the hospital for a week afterward, scared out of his mind. Jay took him peanut brittle and copies of *The Nation* and *Jet*, shook the man's hand when he left and said they'd get together real soon. Kwame, still Lloyd to Jay, his old running buddy, he'd hung on long enough to get released from the hospital, only to drop dead in his front yard two days later. Bernie's dad had a prostate scare this summer. Penny, Jay's baby sister, is on three different medications to lower her blood pressure. It's hard some days not to view life as little more than the space between diagnoses, the rest between twin notes of tragedy and catastrophe. And Jay doesn't want to spend his knee-deep in other people's problems.

He hasn't told Eddie Mae yet, hasn't said the words out loud to himself.

But he's through practicing law.

He reminds Jim, "We got ProFerma up to seven-point-five in just the last few months." It's another bullshit number, he knows, and one that had taken at least ten meetings to get to. He is actually trying to reach fifty million, to come close to what he did with the Cole case, what he still, for personal reasons, considers his proudest moment as an attorney. Fifty million would mean over seventy thousand dollars for each family. It isn't enough, but nothing ever would be, and seventy grand could patch a house, pay off medical bills, even get a kid to college. The trick is to arrive at that number without a trial.

A trial he can't do.

He just doesn't have it in him anymore.

He never really got over Arkansas, his last big case, those months and months he spent in court while his wife, unbeknownst to him, was dying at home. And for what exactly? It's hard not to look back and see the whole thing as a waste. How do you bill a client for the hours you should have been by your wife's side, for time you can't get back?

This infighting among plaintiffs, different views on how to proceed and impatience at the glacial pace of the legal system, that's to be expected, and he tells Wainwright so. "No, this is bigger than that," Jim says. "There's a group of them, Jelly Lopez and Bill Rodriguez, they're talking about going with another lawyer. I wanted to say something last night, but it wasn't the right time."

"No, of course not."

"They've already met with someone."

"Who?"

Jim reaches into the back pocket of his jeans and pulls out a folded Post-it note, on which he'd carefully printed the name. "Ricardo Aguilar."

"Never heard of him."

But it explains something strange ProFerma's lawyer said during their last meeting, a lunch at Irma's downtown. Drunk on Patrón, his slim, pinkish face sweating from the heat of raw chiles and the buzzing neon signs, he'd boasted that he happened to know the community's bottom line, and it was less money than Jay was proposing, even suggesting some folks might take as little as a few thousand dollars and a buyout of their property. At the time Jay took it for a bluff, but now he wonders if ProFerma has been illegally talking to someone behind his back.

Mr. Wainwright nods to the gentleman behind the bar, raising his glass for a refill. Jay takes a second pull on his Michelob. Jelly Lopez, Jules to his employers at ConocoPhillips, where he works as a drilling supervisor, was one of the last to sign on as Jay's client, filling out the plaintiff's forms in Jay's office, his wife clutching her purse in her lap while he asked five questions for every two on a page. Why did Jay need to know this about him? Why did Jay need to know that? What did his annual income, his medical history, or his wife's family's educational background have to do with the fires or getting Pro-Ferma to pay to replace the air ducts in his house, to clean the water his kids drink? He's high maintenance, to put it mildly, but certainly not the worst Jay's ever seen. He was in a hurry to see somebody pay for what was done, and Jay understood. Jelly and Bill Rodriguez are neighbors. They share a fence on Berndale, and their kids are in the same preschool class. Bill's son was diagnosed with asthma in April. "I wouldn't have put much stock in it, some of the new folks just wanting a say in how things are done," Jim says, "not wanting to feel hemmed in by all our voices, the old guard, folks who've been in Pleasantville for some forty years, since we were younger than them. You know we vote on any and everything out there, even what color to paint the trim on the community center. But majority rule don't feel much like a democracy if you're always sweating from underneath it." He gives a nod of thanks as the bartender pours another glass of Ezra Brooks. Overhead, the music coming through the speakers slows. They're playing a Texas favorite now, A. G. Hats, the first track off his album, *Belle Blue*, the only one he ever recorded. A run of black keys, followed by the familiar voice, thick and slow as honey. *See, dreams the only thing I got, the onliest way I know how to live . . .*

"But this thing is gaining a little steam," Jim says. "And not just with folks like Jelly and Bill." From his other back pocket he pulls a letter-size piece of paper folded in thirds. He holds it out for Jay. "This has been making the rounds since before the election. Might have come out of Acton's campaign, or more likely something Wolcott had her people send out."

It's a flyer, printed on a mimeograph machine, the kind that used to reside in every school and church office in the country, making loads of smudged copies. There is probably one collecting dust in a back room at the Pleasantville community center right now, and it occurs to Jay that the author of this flyer must

have known that too, as this leaflet was clearly designed to
appear as if it originated within the community, as if a group of
concerned citizens were reaching out to their own. The words
are in black and white, but fuzzy around the edges. There are
exclamation points going all the way down the page, starting
with the heading across the top.

WHO IS REALLY LOOKING OUT FOR THE CITIZEN
OF PLEASANTVILLE!
BEFORE YOU CAST YOUR VOTE!
DEMAND AN ANSWER FROM AXEL HATHORNE
ABOUT HIS SUPPORT FOR THE
BUFFALO BAYOU DEVELOPMENT PROJECT!
AND
WHAT IT MEANS FOR OUR FUTURE!
THIS COUDL BE THE MOST IMPORTANT VOTE IN
PLEASANTVILLE'S FUTRE!

"What's the Buffalo Bayou Development Project?" Jay asks.

"It's another stab at the River Walk thing, turning the banks
of Buffalo Bayou into a city showcase, with restaurants and
shops, boat rides up and down the bayou." Jay cringes at the
memory of his own boat ride on Buffalo Bayou fifteen years
ago, the late-night leap to save a drowning woman, an act of
chivalry that nearly got him killed. But he doesn't know how a
development deal miles up the bayou would affect the neighborhood of Pleasantville.

"Who knows?" Jim continues. "But folks are skittish. They
told us the freeway would modernize things." He's speaking of
610, the Loop that circles the city's center. "But that only boxed
us in on all sides, all these plants and factories moving to the
area, in our backyard. Who knows if ProFerma would have set
up shop here without the highway being built? Development in

this city is like a cancer, spread every which way, eating every-thing in its path. They start talking hotels, restaurants, tourist pulls, all up and down the bayou and out to the Ship Chan-nel, and who's to say they won't tear right through the back side of Pleasantville? The bayou's not even a mile from us." He stares into his glass. "We should never have let those factories in, should have laid down in the streets against it, like we did with the freeway. We should have fought it."

"And you asked Axel about it, the bayou thing?"

"Yes, we did, at the candidate forum last weekend."

"And?"

"And," Jim says, sighing, "I hate to say, but he sounded like the rest of them, like any other politician coming out to court our vote. The flyer's got folks jumpy, worried, like maybe Axe isn't telling everything, not until the runoff."

"You really think that of him?"

"Not before this," Jim says, tapping the flyer with his index finger. "We all want this lawsuit wrapped up before our prop-erty values go down any further, Jelly and them too. That's what I'm trying to tell you, Jay, why you're vulnerable in this thing. There's some out there want to settle and then sell and get out of Pleasantville for good. It ain't me, but Jelly and them are putting real pressure on the rest of us to reach a resolution sooner rather than later. Apparently, this Aguilar thinks he can walk us for ten million right now."

Jay does the math in his head, frowning to himself.

"What's Bill Rodriguez going to do with thirteen thousand dollars ten, twenty years from now when his kid's asthma turns into something worse?" For Jay, it's always about the kids, the main ones who suffer from our choices long after we're gone. Any deal that doesn't look two generations ahead is useless. It might put a Cadillac in the driveway, but it won't secure a future.

"More like sixteen thousand," Jim says. He's done his own math too.

"How's that?"

"Aguilar says he'll drop his commission to twenty percent."

"Who is this guy?"

"Jelly knows him. They went to UT together."

A 20 percent commission on a ten-million-dollar settlement, that's a cool two million. And Ricardo Aguilar is making a grab for it. It's against the rules of the Texas State Bar Association to proposition another lawyer's clients, but Aguilar could always say it was Jelly who reached out first, which as far as Jay knows is exactly how it went down. "We've been wanting to get Axel alone on this issue," Jim says. "Without Sam and the young fellow, Neal. But Axe is running for mayor of Houston, not Pleasantville, and he's all over the place these days. And then this thing with the girl happened, and, well, it just got lost."

Jay folds the flyer, tucking it into the inside pocket of his suit jacket.

"I appreciate you sharing this with me."

"Like I said, I like you, Jay." He picks up his drink, finishing it off. "But Jelly's already circulating a petition, getting signatures on the issue of seeking new counsel. There's only so much I can do to slow this down."

He looks at Jay under the harsh white lights of the club.

It's Jay, he suggests, who will have to save his own ass.

"My next scheduled sit-down with ProFerma's lead counsel isn't for another month," Jay says. "I can move that up, go at them more aggressively." Jim nods, liking the sound of that. "They've been dicking around with the numbers, excuse my language. But I have an evidentiary strategy in mind, some cards I was holding until we got closer on the numbers." Jay is bluffing a little, just to make clear he isn't sleeping on the job. What he doesn't need right now is a rumor about a development deal making his clients skittish and apt to take less than they deserve. "You let the word get back that I'm on this thing, and that no one should be too fooled by flashy promises. A lot of times these guys say they'll take a lower commission fee, and then jack it up to forty percent when there's a trial."

"At least he's willing to talk about a trial."

There it is, out in the open.

Jay's trepidation about, or downright fear of, standing in a courtroom again—it's not as well hidden as he thought. "There's not a one of us don't know what you been through this year," Jim says. "But the families out there, myself included, we've been through a lot too. We need a fighter, son." He reaches into the pocket of his jeans for his wallet. From inside, he pulls several bills, leaving the bartender an extra ten for his time. To Jay, he says, "You still have my vote."

"Thank you, sir."

Jay watches him go, the bar's padded door swinging closed behind him. The bartender offers him another beer, but Jay shakes his head. The first one left him feeling foggy and loose limbed, weak against the wind that just blew through him. He's never lost a client before. Lord knows he can't afford to start now.

CHAPTER 5

Jon K. Lee will have to wait, Jay thinks, as he walks to the Hathorne campaign headquarters, one block over on Travis. The volunteers are out this morning, a line of them wearing long-sleeved T-shirts, a deep, patriot blue, with the slogan HATHORNE FOR HOUSTON! in white. A staffer, a young black woman in braids, is handing out stacks of door knockers, glossy leaflets to be left on front doors across the city. The leaflets show Axel's picture, an image of the candidate surrounded by a handful of men in blue. The Houston Police Department endorsed him in the general, and there is every reason to assume it will back him again in the runoff against Sandy Wolcott, the D.A., who easily scored the endorsement of the Harris County sheriff. The battle of the law-and-order candidates has made for one of the oddest campaign seasons in Houston's history. Inside the storefront's glass doors, there are more volunteers at a phone bank in the front part of the office. At a square of four card tables pushed together, they sit on folding chairs, copies of the county voter rolls splayed out in front of them, each volunteer hunched over a script and a telephone. Jay can hear their one-sided conversations: *Hi, I'm_____, and I'm calling to ask for your vote for Axel Hathorne. Mr. Hathorne is a Houston native, and the first African-American police chief in the city. For nearly forty years, he's fought to keep our streets safe.*

"Can I help you?"

Jay turns to see the staffer with the long braids, pulled in a ponytail off her face. Coming in from outside, she's got a large, bricklike phone cradled against her ear as she bends down to dump a surplus of leaflets into an open cardboard box. Standing upright, she rolls up the sleeves of her fleece pullover, eyeing Jay with more than a little curiosity. In his suit and tie, he stands out among the jeans and khakis, sneakers and T-shirts in the office. Nor, in this getup, would he ever pass for a member of the press. "You Detective Moore?" she says. The mention of a police officer catches Jay off guard, and before he can correct her assumption, the woman, moving fast, eager to check one more thing off her list, walks to a dented metal desk a few feet from the makeshift call center. "The station said you'd be by," she says, holding up a finger to slow a staffer headed her way with a clipboard. "I'm the field director," she says to Jay. "Marcie normally handles Neal's schedule, along with Axel's. But Tuesday, Election Day, everything was get out the vote, and I actually put together the schedule for that day." She hands him a spreadsheet with detailed blocks of times and locations, and the names of the campaign's key players, including the candidate himself. "It's about what you'd expect, nothing out of the ordinary. There *was* one thing, though," she says, her brow wrinkling.

"Tonya!"

Down a roll of thin carpet comes Marcie in acid-washed jeans and a Hathorne T-shirt, walking from the back offices, which are really just a series of cubicles set apart by fabric dividers. She's breathless, damp with sweat. "Melanie Lawson at Channel Thirteen wants to tape a segment with Axel, history in the making, maybe some stuff with his dad, that sort of thing, to air after the debate tomorrow night, but they have to get a crew over here today to tape."

"They're at the Hyatt all day, doing debate prep."

"Neal on his mobile?"

"Yes."

Marcie turns, noticing Jay. "You were at Sam's last night."

"What?" Tonya says, looking confused at first and then panicked. She smiles tightly, eyeing the campaign schedule in Jay's hand, but too timid to ask for it back in front of Marcie, her superior, for all Jay knows. In fact, the more anxious she seems, the more curious Jay is to know what exactly is on that schedule. He folds it and tucks it into the inside pocket of his jacket. "Just came for a bumper sticker," he says, grabbing a blue HATHORNE FOR HOUSTON! decal from the corner of a call-center desk, before walking out and heading for the Hyatt.

Rolly has a connection at the hotel, a guy behind the front desk, who, for an ounce of hash every two weeks, provides any guest needing a ride the phone number for Rolly's car company. For the same deal, he's more than happy to get Jay a room number, sending him to a two-story suite on the seventh floor. The Hathorne campaign has had it for the past two nights, leading up to tomorrow's debate on Channel 13. It's one of the few on the floor that use a bolt lock instead of a key card. Through the door, Jay can hear the steel lock turn, just moments before

Vivian Hathorne answers the door. She's in a black sweater, something silky and wine colored peeking from underneath. Below, there are black slacks and slippers on her feet. She is, as he last saw her, holding a glass in one hand.

"They haven't found her, have they?"

"That my fish?" a voice behind her calls out.

Vivian opens the door wider, giving Sam Hathorne a view of their visitor.

Down the short hallway that leads to the suite's main room, Jay's and Sam's eyes meet. Sam smiles stiffly.

"Come in," Vivian says.

Jay follows her down the hallway into the suite, passing a guest bathroom and a kitchenette before entering the main room. The suite is bigger than his first apartment, the one-bedroom in Third Ward where he and Bernie started a family, Ellie sharing a room with them for the first two years of her life. There's a private bedroom on the suite's lower floor, and a short, curved staircase leading to another upstairs. In the living room, furniture has been pushed off to the sides. The TV has been turned to face a back corner of the room. There's a mess of wires coming out of the back of it, one of them leading to a video camera set up on a tripod in the middle of the room, facing a mock debate setup. Axel Hathorne, all six feet of him, stands behind the lectern on the left. He's in a Rice University sweatshirt, a bib of paper towels around the neck and two different shades of brown powder and foundation on each cheek. Behind the second lectern, Russell Weingate, a University of Texas political science professor and campaign consultant, is playing the part of Axel's rival. The wall of glass behind them offers a postcard picture of Houston's glittering skyline. Across the room, a young white guy wearing a Blues Traveler T-shirt sits in front of a television screen, a pair of headphones resting on his neck, next to a young woman wearing a nose ring and a tool belt filled with cosmetics. She's checking her work on-screen. Neal stands behind her, his arms crossed tightly.

"Let's go through that last bit again," he says.

Russell Weingate is wearing a sweater vest over his button-down shirt, jeans, and black sneakers. He takes off his glasses, wiping them with the untucked tail of his shirt. "The projections for tax revenue from Kingwood in the next year alone have changed even the hardest hard-liners on this issue," he says. "Wolcott has always supported pulling the town of Kingwood into Houston, which is on message for her. 'Smart, low-risk growth.' You're weak here, Axe."

"I still say it's spreading the city's infrastructure too thin."

"Can I get you a drink, Mr. Porter?" Vivian says.

"No, that's fine."

Sam takes a last pull on the cigarette in his hand. He grinds it out in a crystal ashtray resting on a nearby table. "Bring me a Coke, would you, Viv?"

"Axel?"

"No, I'm fine, Mama."

Neal turns from the TV screen and sees Jay for the first time. Axel is already walking from behind the lectern, yanking the paper towels from his collar.

"Jay Porter," he says. He pats Jay on the back, shaking his hand. He's got a good three inches on Jay but never seems to tower. His manner is affable and open, a practiced demeanor meant to mitigate the power of his height. He's relaxed in his later years, a long way from the stern and unforgiving cop with the cutting nickname. He seems happy to be away from the lectern.

"Nice to see you, Axe," Jay says. He, after all these years, remembers the man fondly, remembers when Hathorne was the only name he trusted on a police force filled with good ol' boys.

Axe went easy on Jay a few times, and on Bumpy Williams and Lloyd Mackalvy, even one time declining to arrest them during an anti-police brutality march through Fifth Ward, despite pressure from higher-ups to come down hard. "They're just walking," he'd said to his superiors.

"You too, man," Axel says to Jay. "How're your kids?"

Neal sighs. "Guess this means we're taking a break."

Vivian returns from the small kitchen. She hands a can of Coke to Sam, and presents Jay with a glass of water he never asked for. Resting a thin hand on his forearm, she again asks if they've found the girl. Sam shakes his head matter-of-factly. "Jim would have called." Frankie, Sam's driver, enters the hotel suite next, cradling two greasy take-out bags. Sam clears a space to set down the food, Styrofoam containers of catfish and slices of white bread, damp with steam.

"Viv, honey, check if they got some hot sauce in the kitchen."

"She didn't work for us, by the way," Neal says to Jay.

"It's true," Axel says. "Neal and Tonya did a top-to-bottom search, and there's no paper, no eyewitnesses that put her anywhere near our offices or our campaign. No one in the organization remembers her. The description of her clothing on the day in question, it's likely just a coincidence."

"Axe is on top of it," Neal says. "We've talked to the lead detective."

"Detective Moore," Jay says offhand.

"That's right," Axel says, a little surprised to hear the name coming out of Jay's mouth. "He's heading the case out of the Northeast Division."

"We're cooperating fully. We turned over records, answered all their questions," Neal says. And yet, Jay thinks, Detective Moore is this morning on his way back to campaign headquarters, hunting that schedule, a copy of which rests in Jay's pocket right now. "They know about the planned search. We made them aware of the residents' concerns, to say nothing of Alicia Nowell's family."

Axel sighs heavily. "I told her parents to call night or day."

"I still don't know why we can't put this on the current police chief somehow," Neal says. "The other girls went missing on his watch too."

Sam shakes his head. Russell too.

"It nullifies the department's endorsement if we tear them down publicly," he says. "It's a fine line to walk. But HPD is key for us."

"Plus, I don't want to go negative," Axel says.

"Well, the chief's not the one running," Neal says, glancing at his grandfather. He has the same nut-brown coloring as Neal, but the Hathorne similarity stops there. For the life of him, Jay still can't tell where the boy came from. "Don't think Wolcott's not storing up a reserve on *you*. I'm telling you, it's a mistake to not strike her first. We've got her affair, just say the word."

"Wolcott?" Viv says.

"With a married cop during her first trial, a *witness*, no less."

Sam shakes his head. "It's not the right time."

Vivian turns to Axel with a plea. "You'll find the girl, won't you, son?"

Sam tells her their son is doing everything he can, short of going out in the streets himself.

"That's not a bad idea," Axel says.

Sam shakes his head. "We need you here, son. We finished barely three points ahead of Wolcott. You need to go to sleep and wake up thinking about how to widen that gap before December tenth. The runoff is—"

"It's been four days," Jay says. "She's been missing *four* days."

Sam looks across the room at Neal, who nods once and then quickly turns to the makeup artist and the tech guy in the ratty T-shirt. "Can you excuse us a moment?" As the two shuffle out of the room, they all watch in silence—Jay, Axel, Sam and Vivian, Russell Weingate, and Neal, of course, who waits until the door catches before speaking again. "Look, the campaign is going to release a statement today, outlining our assistance on the case, Axel's ties to the area, his concern for the family of the missing girl. Marcie is drafting it now."

"But we'd like to keep Axel as far away from this as possible," Sam says.

"Campaign statements, interviews with the cops, we're handling it all."

"We don't ever want him to have to lie about Tuesday night."

"Lie?" Jay says, staring at Axel.

The candidate shrugs. "It's nothing, really."

"*Lie* is probably too strong a word," Neal says.

Sam sighs. "There were plans made for Tuesday night, big stroll down Pleasantville's streets, knocking on doors, folks wanting a handshake, the way things have always been done. But the night got past us, and in the end—"

"You never showed," Jay says, realizing. He remembers Ruby Wainwright's description of the celebratory pound cake that sat untouched on her kitchen counter. "So you were never in Pleasantville Tuesday night?" he asks Axel.

"No one from the campaign was."

"Which we'd rather not have advertised," Sam says.

"We've had the precinct in our column since Axel filed papers to run," Neal says. "We can't afford to lose our core support over a few hurt feelings."

"Where were you then?" Jay asks Axel.

"Dinner with a few donors downtown."

"Eyes on the prize," Sam says, dabbing at the grease on his chin.

Neal turns to Jay. "We appreciate you checking on the situation. It was good of you to come last night, but we've got this handled." He puts a hand on Jay's shoulder, the gesture a naked attempt to usher Jay out of the hotel suite.

"Actually there's something else."

From his coat pocket, Jay pulls out the folded-up copy of the flyer, the printed accusations against Axel and his campaign over the Buffalo Bayou Development Project. "You got some folks in your old precinct worried."

Axel takes the paper from Jay, unfolding it.

His lips move slightly as he reads the words.

"What is this?"

"We're tracking it down right now," Neal says. He and Sam exchange a look. It's clear they knew about the flyer already, and their candidate did not.

"What is the Buffalo Bayou Development Project?" Jay asks.

"Nothing that anybody in Pleasantville ought to worry about," Sam says.

Axel is still holding the flyer. "Where did this come from?"

"It's Acton or Wolcott," Neal says; "it came out a few days before the general."

"It's a dirty trick is what it is." Sam pushes away the leftover bits of food, reaching into his pockets to light a cigarette. He's on his good leg mostly, his left hip swung out to the side, boot dug into the carpet. "You see they made it look local, like someone in *my* neighborhood has a problem with Axel, as if anyone in Pleasantville would put out anything like this without coming to me first," he insists, coming dangerously close to saying, "without *asking* me first." Through a helix of smoke, Sam studies Jay, doing the math in his head, how a flyer distributed to the residents of Pleasantville made it into Jay Porter's hands. "Who gave it to you?" he asks, even though he knows Jay better than that. He trusts Jay, that's always been clear. Hell, Jay wouldn't have signed his first client in Pleasantville without Sam saying it was okay, that Jay was the best out there, especially for a case like theirs. But, early on, Sam discovered that being "mayor of Pleasantville" wouldn't grant him special access to Jay's process or progress, which he had on more than one occasion insinuated was his due. No, the case was Jay's, and his clients were entitled to his discretion, even now.

"Doesn't matter. The point is there are some folks out there worried about what this means, whether this is another threat to the neighborhood. There's a group out there talking about selling and getting out of Pleasantville before the next blow comes," Jay says, pointing to the bayou development flyer. "The same ones pushing for a cheap settlement in the civil lawsuit, just to wrap it up quickly. So you can see why this would present a problem for me." The mobile phone in his pocket rings. He checks the screen, but doesn't recognize the number. He lets it go to voice mail.

Axel shakes his head. "This isn't even a part of my platform. It's not in any of the campaign literature. How would anybody think to put this out there?"

"It's Wolcott," Neal says. "This has Reese Parker's name written all over it. Mailers, that's her thing. When she ran Blanchard's campaign in Dallas, she was sending out letters all over the city, letters from black preachers hinting that Blanchard's unmarried opponent, Dale Ackerman, was living outside the laws of the Bible, taking care to point out his close friendship with one of his male aides. It was a week after the election before anyone realized nobody'd ever heard of a single name signed to those letters. The preachers, the church names, she just made it up whole cloth. Rove in Austin was so impressed, he hired her to work George W.'s race for the governor's seat. I would have thought she'd have hopped onto a national race by now, especially with rumors about Bush making a run for the White House. I don't know what she's doing fucking around with a mayor's race in Houston." He plops down in a nearby chair, seemingly exhausted by the force he's up against. "We've been negotiating a price for Acton's endorsement. We're working on a number. He's a greedy bastard, and an asshole, frankly. But I don't think he'd stoop to this."

In Jay's pocket, the Motorola trills again.

"You planning something along the bayou?" he asks Axel directly.

"No, not at all."

"They're using this to paint him as a fool." Sam puffs on his cigarette. "The bayou project is a boondoggle, a money pit," he says. "And everyone knows it."

Russell Weingate nods. "The BBDP is just a commission, a few developers with deep pockets, that's all. Every election cycle, they court the candidates, write a few checks, make their pitch." For decades, folks have been dreaming up ideas to build something grand along Buffalo Bayou, like the River Walk in San Antonio: restaurants, shops, and luxury hotels with views of the water, anything but the weeds and concrete that surround it now. "And every cycle the candidates nod and act interested, and then they cash those checks and nothing ever comes of it. No one can seriously think that just 'cause Axel met with the commission *one* time that he's serious about this thing. That commission's a dinosaur. They've been around for at least fifteen years."

"Since Cynthia's reign," Jay says, his tongue nearly tripping on a name he hasn't uttered in years. Cynthia Maddox, the former mayor of Houston, Texas, current booster for Axel Hathorne's historic run for office, and the woman Jay has long suspected of turning him over to the feds in '69, of being an undercover informant, one, or a girl in over her head, two, a believer who sold her soul to save her ass. It was a betrayal that gutted Jay's life, stole from him love and faith when he needed them most. "Isn't that where *she* ran into trouble her last years in office?" he says. It was widely reported back then, in the pages of the *Post* and the *Houston Chronicle*, that she used taxpayer money to have the Army Corps of Engineers survey the land along the bayou for construction, and then nothing ever got built.

"That's not all Cynthia's fault," Axel says.

"You can't put the whole oil bust on her," Sam says. "Those early investors fled because the city's economy collapsed, *everything* dried up."

"Only no one remembers it that way," Russell says. "And now it looks like Wolcott and her attack dog Parker are trying to turn Cynthia's support of Axel into a liability for him, like he's pushing her old ideas."

"This is just to scare people," Neal says.

"Well, it's working," Jay says.

His phone rings again. Irritated now, he snatches it out of his pocket. He flips open the mouthpiece, barking a less than cordial "Hello."

It's a woman's voice. "I'm sorry to have to call you on your cell phone."

"Who is this?"

"This is Ms. Hilliard, Mr. Porter."

"Who?"

"From Lamar High School."

"Is Ellie okay?"

"Oh, yes," she says. "She's sitting right here in my office."

Hilliard, he remembers. The school's principal. "That serious, huh?"

"I'm afraid so, Mr. Porter."

He sighs. "I'll be right there."

He flips his Motorola closed. "Gentlemen," he says. He reaches for the flyer. "You need to clean this up before it gets any further out of your hands." He folds the paper, tucks it back into the inside pocket of his jacket. "If there's a message I can convey to my clients to put them at ease about the threat of any proposed development, I sure as hell wish you'd tell me."

"There is no threat," Sam says, openly bristling at the idea that anyone or anything would come between him and his beloved Pleasantville, his tiny fiefdom by the port. "I appreciate your concern for the community's feelings on this," he says. "But anything more that needs to be said will come from me."

A tiny worm of a frown inches across Axel's face. But he never says a word. Between the two of them, it's hard not to wonder whose political dream is being fulfilled, that of the son or the father. Had he been born in a different time, Samuel Hathorne might have made his own run for mayor of Houston, instead of settling for the office that was within his reach: "mayor" of Pleasantville, and city hall's ambassador to the colored community, delivering votes in exchange for working streetlights or a new middle school—what neighborhoods like River Oaks and Memorial took for granted as their due. Everything in Pleasantville had been fought for and protected by Sam Hathorne, who led with a strong, steady hand. In the parlance of his day, he was what black folks used to call the Head Nigger in Charge, a title that was high praise or a deep insult, depending on the speaker's tolerance for obsequiousness as a political tool. Sam knew the game better than anyone else, and he played his hand. "I'll take care of it," he says.

CHAPTER 6

The polished halls of Lamar High School are empty when Jay arrives, somewhere in the middle of third period. He's spent surprisingly little time inside the school. In two years, Ellie hasn't yet found her way into any clubs, sports teams, or school plays, spending most of her time with Lori King. Besides a couple of parent-teacher conferences, he's mostly viewed his daughter's high school years from a distance. Bernie worked a few fund-raising events early last year, even chaperoning the freshman fall dance, which Ellie didn't attend. Jay was always working. He's never met the principal, Ms. Hilliard, and feels somewhat embarrassed by his surprise at seeing a woman nearly a decade younger than he is. Somewhere in his mind he must have been carrying an image of his own principal, Mr.

Cleveland Simms, at the colored high school in Lufkin, a thirty-minute bus ride from his boyhood home in Nigton. Debra Hilliard is in her late thirties, soft-spoken and no taller than her students. From behind her desk, she smiles at Jay. Ellie is sitting in the chair to his right. She looked at him once when he walked in and gave a small shrug.

He's made himself a promise not to get upset until he hears her side of the story, whatever this is about. Innocent until proven guilty, and all that. He's been in a hot seat before and believes his daughter deserves no less than what he got. This isn't a courtroom, of course; Ellie is certainly not up against the kinds of serious charges he was in 1970, when he was, hard to believe, only four years older than she is now. Still, he feels a strict allegiance to his kid. He has very nearly tired of the pity thrown on his family, every tough conversation couched in professed understanding of the Porters' difficult situation, the pain they must be in, all of it just a run-up to whatever criticism they were going to lob anyway.

Ms. Hilliard, as far as Jay is concerned, can skip the big speech.

"What'd she do?"

"I like Ellie," she says.

"I do too."

"She's smart, incredibly conscientious with her peers, and dedicated, I would have said a week ago, to her schoolwork." She shoots a glance at Ellie. "And I know it's been a hell of a year for your family, excuse my language."

"What did she *do*?"

"Okay, Mr. Porter," she says drily. She's a black woman with shoulder-length hair, dangly silver earrings peeking from behind the strands. She's wearing a cotton button-down, rolled up at the sleeves, and blue slacks. She clasps her hands on the desktop. "I guess it's more what she *didn't* do." She looks at

Ellie again, giving her a chance to come clean. Ellie, her black
Starter jacket across her lap, fiddles with the zipper.

"I skipped class," she says softly.

"Classes. She's skipped *classes*."

"Elena?"

"I'm sorry, Dad."

She has her head down, but Jay thinks he sees tears, actual
tears, in her eyes. The skin on the back of her neck is flushed,
her cheeks plum with shame. "Once last week, and two times
this week," Ms. Hilliard says. "The girls left the campus without
permission. I'm afraid I'm going to have to put her on suspension. I'll be speaking with Lori King's mother as well."

"You're going to punish her for missing school by having
her miss more school?" Jay says, squirming a little in his chair,
angry, but not sure with which one of them. Debra Hilliard
smiles tightly. She opens a top drawer, pulling out a blue pad of
suspension slips. She scribbles a few words across the top, sliding the paper across the desk for Jay to sign. "I think the hope
is that this gives the two of you a chance to talk. And you, as
her parent, to find out what's going on with Ellie." Jay reaches
across the desk and signs the principal's order. "It should be
two days," she says, "but we'll count today as a full one and
leave it at that. She can come back on Tuesday." She looks over
at Ellie. "I'm rooting for you, Elena. It might not seem that way
now, but I'm on your side."

Jay stands. "You too, Mr. Porter," the principal says.

"Let's go, Ellie."

He grabs her backpack from the floor, nodding once to the
principal before escorting his daughter into the hall and down
the main stairs. Outside, in the parking lot, Jay, on an impulse,
holds out the car keys for Ellie. She stares at them, her eyes
still damp. "Really?" She looks at her dad, incredulous at first,
then breaking into something resembling a smile. She's had

a learner's permit since she turned fifteen in September, and they'd made a deal to get on the road together at least once a week, which is not that easy with just the three of them in the house; Jay is not comfortable having Ben in the backseat while his sister learns to drive. But it's a few hours before Ben's out of school, and they might as well take the opportunity at hand. "Why not?" he says, letting her know he still trusts her, hoping she shows him the same in kind. He walks around to the passenger door, climbing into the Land Cruiser, and waits for her to get behind the wheel.

"You hungry?"

Ellie is busy adjusting the side mirrors, and doesn't answer. She's focused on getting the car started, so nervous that Jay has to remind her to put her foot on the brake. When the engine finally turns over, he tells her to pull out of the parking lot and make a right on Westheimer. Neither of them has had any lunch, and he offers to buy her a late breakfast at the 59 Diner, pancakes and eggs.

Ellie nods, her hands gripped at "ten and two" on the steering wheel.

"You're doing fine," Jay says. He leans forward, checking the side-view mirror. A pickup truck pulls up close to them, almost kissing the Land Cruiser's bumper. Ellie hardly notices, stopping short at a yellow light. Jay braces himself against the dash. "What's going on, El?" he says. "Why'd you skip school?"

"It was just a few times."

"That's not really going to help you."

When the light changes to green, the car behind them honks twice.

Ellie jerks the car forward, laying hard on the gas. "I don't know what to say, Dad. It was wrong. I knew you'd think it was wrong. I messed up, and I'm sorry." She tries to turn to say this directly to him. But he tells her to keep her eyes on the road.

"Why were you crying back there?"

"It's embarrassing," she says. "All that talk about being on my side." She rolls her eyes, and for whatever reason, this makes Jay smile. "So where'd you go?" he says, pointing for her to make a right turn on Shepherd. "You guys taking off from school. Hope it was something good," he says. "This was Lori's idea?" He looks at his daughter behind the wheel. She's biting her lip, silent.

"Okay," he says, leaving it for now. "You're out for the rest of the day, and you're grounded until next weekend. We can talk about the rest when you're ready." He squirms in the passenger seat, unused to the view from this side of the car. He's screwing this up, he's sure of it, sending the wrong message, that he's weak and uncertain. But he just can't work up the outrage right now.

"She asked me to go with her," Ellie says finally.

Jay turns to his daughter, surprised to hear her speak. "Lori?"

Ellie nods.

"Go where?"

"To the clinic, the place on Main, by the Astrodome," she says, speaking of the old football stadium, which has sat empty since the Oilers left for Nashville. The neighborhood has dulled since then, which isn't saying much. The Astrodome had been the crown jewel of an area of town otherwise filled with pawnshops and *taquerías* and one aging, midrange hotel. Jay can't understand why Lori would go all the way the hell out there to see a doctor.

"She's sick?"

"Dad," she says, exasperated by his dimness. "She's pregnant."

"Lori?" She might as well have told him the girl had joined the circus.

Lori is only fifteen. *Fifteen.* Just a few months older than

Ellie. He turns to look at his daughter, seeing a body closer to its first bike ride than motherhood. He doesn't even know if she's kissed a boy. He feels a sudden panic at the thought of her behind the wheel, a child steering two steel tons.

"But you can't tell her mom."

"Elena, I can't promise something like that."

"You can't, Dad," she says, taking her eyes off the road, swerving a little into the next lane. He reaches for the wheel. "I swore I wouldn't tell. I wouldn't have told you at all except I promised Mom." Her voice catches on the last word.

"What?"

"I promised Mom I would never lie to you," she says. "She said it wouldn't be fair, that you were going to have a hard enough time as it is, but it's not fair to me either." This, Jay soon discovers, is where the tears are coming from. Ellie wipes at them with the back of her hand. They're still a few blocks from the diner, but Jay tells her to pull over. She yanks the wheel and turns the car into the parking lot of a Kwik Kopy. Jay pulls up the hand brake. He reaches for his daughter, who is shaking now. She collapses in an awkward heap across the armrest. Jay holds her up. He can feel the dampness of her tears on his neck.

"I got you," he says. *I got you.*

For one furious moment, he actually hates his wife for putting this on Ellie, hates her, in fact, for every day that's passed since she went out like a light one warm November afternoon, not even a word to him when he left the room for five minutes, just long enough to show Ben, again, how to switch the TV signal to VCR. Those last few days at home, Jay had sent Eddie Mae to Blockbuster with a hundred dollars, told her to bring back anything PG and under, just lots of it, something a nine-year-old boy could watch while his mother died in the next room, all those long hours in the house while they waited, times neither Ben nor Bernie could stand another good-bye.

"No more," she told Jay. Ben watched movies, and Evelyn, god bless her, kept the food coming. That last morning, Bernie asked for a cheese sandwich, of all things, and a cup of tea, and then she slept for hours. It must have been close to five when Jay stepped out of their bedroom. The sun was setting, he remembers. The nurse, the only one in the room, said Bernie spoke only once. "It's okay," she said, just before she went.

They have a quiet dinner at home, the three of them, spaghetti for Ben, chicken and dirty rice for Jay and Ellie. Ben, who likes to sit at the table with his legs crossed under him in the chair, talks football, making guesses about the playoffs, still two months away; much to his father's chagrin, Ben favors the Cowboys. But what can you do? Jay thinks. Nobody sticks around for nothing anymore, and a boy's got to have a team to pull for. Ellie jumps the second the phone rings, two seconds after taking her last bite. "Can I, Dad?" she says.

He nods, letting her go.

It's technically Ben's night with the dishes, but Jay offers him a hand, and the two of them knock it out in no time, and then Jay pretends to watch *Family Matters* with his son. Really, he's thinking of his daughter, and whatever is going on behind her closed bedroom door. He thinks of Mrs. King, likewise locked out of the details of her daughter's life. If it were him, he'd want to know. It ought to be criminal, actually, for one parent to keep something like this from another.

At about a quarter to nine, the doorbell rings.

It's Lonnie at the door, a surprise.

She comes into the house carrying a cardboard box. "I caught up with that reporter, Bartolomo," she says. "Wasn't much there, either because he doesn't have it or he still somehow thinks I'm playing for the other side. One paper, I reminded him. There are no more sides." She holds out the box, which is strangely damp on the bottom. Jay takes it from her hands. She's wearing a Mizzou sweatshirt and black jeans. She smells like nicotine and root beer, a bittersweet scent that suits her. "But I thought we might want to look at some of my old notes from the first two girls." And then, as if it's just now occurred to her that she hasn't laid eyes on him in nearly a year, hasn't been inside his house in as long, she goes in for an awkward pat on Jay's back. "Where are the kids?"

Jay nods toward the den, a wide room with exposed ceiling beams, just past the formal living room and the kitchen. He follows Lonnie, the sagging cardboard box pressed against his chest, setting it down beside the leather sectional, where Ben is lying, flat on his stomach. "Lonnie!" he says when he sees her. She opens her arms as he jumps toward them. There used to be a time—after the Cole story broke, Lonnie getting her byline on the front page of her old employer, the *Houston Chronicle*— when she spent a great deal of time with Jay's family, coming over to dinner at least a couple of times a month. Ben grew up around her, in fact. She left the *Chronicle* in '92, met a girl she liked and bought a little house in the Heights, and waited for her star to rise at the *Post*, careful to keep her private life private this time, convinced it had caused her problems at the *Chronicle*. And then from out of nowhere the shit all fell apart. First the *Post* went, then the girl, then the house. The losses hit Lonnie hard, and depression made her scarce. And then Bernie got sick, and they kind of lost the thread of their unlikely friendship. Jay and the kids, they haven't seen her in months. She gives the little one a hug, asks him how his gin rummy game is going. She taught him to play when he was six. Jay offers her a beer, leftovers from the fridge. She shakes her head, peeling off her sweatshirt and reaching into her back pocket for a pack of Parliaments. "Not in the house," he says. She nods, remembering, and slides the sweatshirt right back on. "Let's take this party outside then," she says. She hefts the cardboard box against her hip, heading for the patio. Jay opens the sliding glass door for her. "Where's El?" she says, as they settle on opposite sides of a wrought-iron table, the weight of the cardboard box listing it to one side. The house is a one-story ranch, more wide than deep. The rest of the lot is all yard, a cool, green expanse stretching a quarter of an acre to a wooden fence.

"'Preciate you doing this," he says, nodding toward the box.

"Please," she says. "Do you have any idea what I've been doing for the past two months?" She pulls the cigarettes from her pocket again, fishing out a book of matches too. "You ever heard of something called 'online dating'?"

"No."

"Good," she says, lighting a Parliament. "That's part of my pitch. Old shits like you who read magazines to keep up with what the young folks are doing, even if just to shake your heads at their foolishness. AOL, that Internet company, they've got these chat rooms. And there's something called Match.com. Apparently, it's a thing, meeting people on your computer," she says, shaking her head at the sheer absurdity of it. "You tell people what you like, what you're into, and see if they'll write you back. The same personals shit that paid half our salaries at the *Post*, only now you can lie about your height in the privacy of your own home." She blows a line of smoke into the dark, and Jay smiles. He's missed her, he realizes. "In the past six weeks, I've put on my best 'straight girl' jeans, and been on a dozen of these blind dates, each guy a bigger asshole than the last. Actually, the assholes I prefer. It's the ones that look like they're going to take my purse when I go to the bathroom that scare the shit out of me. The last one ate his fingernails at the table. He actually called me 'Ma' twice." The amber-colored deck lights are on a timer, and they went out a few moments ago. Jay waves a hand, and they snap back on. He wishes he'd grabbed a beer for himself. "Anyway, I'm thinking of writing a feature about it, hoping it's something a major monthly might be interested in."

"How's your money?"

"It ain't great."

"You need a little something, I can—"

She waves him off at first. But then, thinking it over, she says, "Yeah, maybe." She sucks the Parliament to the filter. "It might come to that."

She stubs out the cigarette with the heel of her leather boot.

"Where's El?" she asks again.

"On the phone," he sighs. "She's *always* on the phone."

"Fifteen," Lonnie says. "I remember."

She lifts the flap of the box, revealing a mound of loose paper. "This is it, by the way. Everything I walked out with last year. I pulled some of my notes on Deanne Duchon and Tina Wells this afternoon. No news on the search, huh?"

"I don't think so."

From the box, Lonnie pulls out a crinkled batch of note-book paper. "I'm thinking about going out there tomorrow, see what's what." Jay can see his inquiry this morning has stirred something in her, stoking a reporter's curiosity.

"What did Bartolomo say?"

"Well, the girl was definitely working on a campaign, the search is on for which one."

"Neal Hathorne was adamant. She wasn't working for them."

Lon shrugs. "The information is sketchy, all of it coming from her boyfriend, this kid out in Beaumont. I personally don't understand why they're taking his word on every god-damned thing. But that's all I got out of Bartolomo. I don't know if that's the *Chronicle*'s angle, or the cops'. But that's the current line of pursuit. It's a hot story, right in the middle of a runoff campaign. The boyfriend, they were in high school together, at

Jones. He says the school had a candidate forum in the spring, for their government classes. Acton was the only one who came in person. The others sent reps from their campaigns. But there was definitely some amount of recruiting going on, you know, 'Come work for us, see the process from the inside,' that sort of thing. The boyfriend, he says Alicia really was into it, taking a couple of business cards." She exhales slowly.

Jay can hear the TV inside, a Coca-Cola commercial.

"What about the other girls?"

"That's the thing that's weird," she says. "I mentioned the names Deanne Duchon and Tina Wells to Gregg Bartolomo, and I got nothing. Here he is reporting on a missing person case, in the same neighborhood where two other girls went missing, and he acts like he's never heard their names before. Either he's fucking with me, still playing keep-away, or he honestly is as shitty a reporter as I remember. It's like it's not even a thing for them. The *Chronicle* isn't putting it all together, not on paper, at least."

"Can I?" Jay says, reaching for her stack of notes.

"Yeah," she says, handing it over. She brushes back a lock of hair hanging loose from her ponytail. It's a fair, nutty color, and greasy at the roots. Across the table, she watches Jay flipping through the pages and pages of her cubelike print handwriting. He pauses over a couple of crude drawings, each showing the bare outline of a human form. "Resner, in the Northeast Division, he wouldn't give me a copy of the autopsy reports, but he was kind enough to leave me alone with them, long enough for me to make my own rough copy."

"It's a Detective Moore working this one."

"That's what I heard," she says. "Res and I, we spoke this morning. He was cagey about the whole thing, telling me to direct any questions to Moore."

Looking down, Jay cringes at the crudely drawn silhou-

ettes of Deanne Duchon and Tina Wells. Here on paper, they
are mirror images of each other. Each figure has an X marked
across the throat, and the following notation, in Lonnie's handwriting: *fractured hyoid bone (strangulation)*. Down the arms
and legs, there are more notes: *little to no bruising (no defensive
wounds)*, followed by a question mark. And the worst of it, the
words scribbled near the tight V between the legs: *semen on
the inner thighs (no sign of vaginal penetration)*. Jay feels a sour
heat at the back of his throat, his dinner threatening to come
back up.

"Jesus," he mumbles.

"He messed with them, using their little bodies to get off. But
they weren't raped, not according to any legal definition of the
word," Lonnie says, stubbing out her second cigarette. "Tina
Wells's hymen was still intact."

Fifteen, Jay thinks.

"But check out the time of death," Lon says. "Both girls."

According to the autopsy report, Deanne Duchon was alive
as little as eight hours before she was found in the creek. With
Tina Wells, it was estimated at as little as five hours before she
was discovered. "He didn't kill them right away. They were alive
somewhere for five days," Lon says. "And found on the sixth."

"You mentioned there was a suspect?"

"Yes, a guy by the name of Alonzo Hollis."

The patio lights go out.

Jay waves a hand overhead, and the lights come on again. He
should go inside and switch the setting, he thinks, and maybe
pour a whiskey. He could use a drink right now. "How'd the
cops come to Hollis?"

"Eyewitness statements," Lon says. "Mike Resner, when he
was working the cases, he walked the streets of Pleasantville.
HPD was slow to react to the abductions, I'll give you that, but
I'll never say Res didn't take the cases seriously. He talked to

everybody out there, trying to put together any last sightings. The girls' families, their friends, the whole heart of their lives was in Pleasantville. So he worked it out there. And one thing came up in both cases."

"What was that?"

"A trucker."

"A trucker?" Jay says. "Was it one of Sterling and Company's?"

Lonnie was just searching for the name in her notes. "You know it?"

Jay sighs.

The visit from Jim Wainwright, the talk with the Hathornes, picking up his daughter from the principal's office . . . amid all that he forgot to call the trucking company. "They've been a problem for a while—their drivers speed through Pleasantville as a shortcut to the port. They pick up goods coming off those ships and move 'em out onto the highways, the rail yards to the south."

"Well, back in '94, it wasn't a truck driving, but rather *idling* on Guinevere, on the back side of Gethsemane Baptist Church, the very day Deanne went missing. And it wasn't an eighteen-wheeler, but a van with a white guy, midthirties, sitting at the wheel. Same thing last year, a white van, idling on the edges of the neighborhood the day Tina Wells disappeared. At least six people reported seeing a van just like it before. One of the local pastors, he'd made note of the van's number, the one painted on the side, identifying it as one of Sterling's fleet. The guy was planning to call the company to complain. He never did, but when Res and his partner came knocking, he showed them the number, which he'd written on a napkin. It was still sitting on the front seat of his car. That van was assigned to a driver by the name of Alonzo Hollis. He had shit for an alibi, other than he was at home, sleeping one off between shifts. He gave the same story last year. He has at least one prior, for sexual battery back in the eighties. But the kicker, the thing that raised the hair on the back of my neck," she says, pausing. "There was another girl. A might-have-been, I should say. It was in the early part of last year. It never made any of my stories. Res and his partner asked us to hold it. But there was a guy matching Hollis's description hanging around that truck stop on Market, at the northeast entrance to the neighborhood. He was messing with a teenage girl in the parking lot. Don't ask me what she was doing at a truck stop at eleven o'clock at night. But the guy tried to jump her, an eyewitness said in a report that got filed away in the Northeast Division. Apparently, the guy tried to pull her into the van before the witness scared him off. The witness said Hollis got in his van and took off."

Jay glances again at the notes from the autopsy report. "So, what, he takes them somewhere and then dumps them back in Pleasantville when he's done?"

"That was the working theory. The van, that makes him mobile."

"So why didn't they arrest him back then?"

"There was a problem with their case, a big one."

"What?"

"It wasn't his semen." She reaches for the pack of Parliaments, lighting another. "From the D.A.'s point of view, there just wasn't enough there."

"Which was Wolcott?"

"Her office, at least," she says, exhaling smoke. "I can tell you what else. The police department, they're going to protect her on this. Tobin, the current chief, he hates Axel, but publicly the department has to support one of their own. But according to Resner, they're hoping for a Wolcott win. I guess they don't want ol' Axe looking over their shoulder for the next two years."

"What do *you* think of their suspect?"

"I think Alonzo Hollis was the best, and *only*, lead they ever had."

"And you trust this Resner?"

"As much as I would any cop," she says.

"He would have passed all this on to Detective Moore, right?"

"Can't see a reason why he wouldn't."

Jay taps the tabletop. "Tomorrow's Saturday."

"Day five," Lonnie says.

They both know Alicia Nowell is running out of time.

Lon stays for ice cream with the kids, Blue Bell peppermint, Ellie's favorite. She comes out of her room and seems genuinely happy to see an old family friend. She doesn't mention the headline story in her life, the pregnancy of her best friend, but she's surprisingly chatty about other things—a sewing class she and Lori are thinking about taking, and whether her dad will let her see *Set It Off* with her friends this weekend—and Jay is struck by the energy of having another person in the house, the veil it lifts. Maybe Lonnie can come for dinner sometime, he says, make a real evening of it. "I'd like that," she says.

Later, the kids asleep, Jay and Lon stay up talking over a few beers.

Gingerly, he asks about Amy.

"She says she's confused."

"There someone else?"

"Her ex-husband."

"Ouch."

She shrugs. "She comes around still," she says. "I don't know."

"She the reason you never left town after you lost the job?"

"I have yet to admit that to myself, Mr. Porter."

"Enough said, Ms. Phillips."

He backs off, and they finish the last of the beer in silence.

It's nearly eleven o'clock by the time he walks her to her car, the dusty white VW Golf. Without a word said, he slips her two hundred-dollar bills, money he pulled from his wallet when she wasn't looking. She tucks it into the pocket of her jeans, somehow knowing an elaborate or lavish thank-you would embarrass them both. "You look good, Jay," she says. "You and the kids."

"We'll be all right," he says.

"Yes, you will."

He's still a little undone over this Lori thing, not sure how or when to break it to her mother, still wondering if it's the right thing to do. He's about to ask Lonnie to throw some light his way, give him some idea of how to handle this, when he spots a black Nissan Z parked across Glenmeadow, idling at the curb. Heart thumping, he starts for the car, walking across the street at an angle. "Jay," he hears Lon call behind him. As he nears the driver's side of the Nissan, he can smell marijuana burning inside, a coil of smoke winding in a stream through a crack in the driver's-side window. Inside the car, the smoke is so thick that Jay can't see a soul. He raps on the driver's-side window as the engine revs. The driver, whoever it is, peels away from the curb, tearing down sleepy Glenmeadow, tires squealing. Jay watches it go, catching the same four characters on the Texas plates that Rolly reported earlier, 5KL 6, plus the last two, a 7 and a 2. It's Jon K. Lee's stolen car, the one that was outside Jay's office the night of the break-in. "What in the world was that?" Lonnie says.

"Trouble," he says.

CHAPTER 7

Market Street cuts across the northeast corner of the city, running from Fifth Ward all the way out to Pleasantville in the east, and beyond. Pockets of it are residential, to the west and out near Phyllis Wheatley High School. But the piece Jay is driving on now, past Wayside and the railroad tracks, is all warehouses and manufacturing outfits. Before the fire, ProFerma Labs had its plant on Market. Pete Washington, plaintiff number 223, used to watch the smoke from its stacks from his living room window. ProFerma was home-brewing polyvinyl chloride, or PVC, with the permission of the EPA, of course. It was the illegal storing of polystyrene-butadiene-styrene that made Jay's case. Whether it was human error that caused the explosion (a careless cigarette maybe) or a freak accident, a lone spark in the atmosphere looking to start something, it didn't matter. ProFerma was never supposed to be storing that shit in the first place. If people had known about it, they could have sued the company years ago, and maybe prevented millions of dollars in property damage, medical bills, and physical trauma, not to mention the tens of thousands of dollars the city's fire department spent on overtime, putting out a fire that burned for days.

The company is long gone. It left behind the burned shells of its manufacturing plant and warehouses and set up shop in Duncan, Oklahoma, men driving from as far as Little Rock when they heard the company was hiring.

Sterling & Company Trucks had been its neighbor.

Jay pulls into the parking lot, about a quarter after ten Saturday morning, the earliest he could get out of the house. Evelyn had agreed to watch the kids, but she does not stir before eight on weekends. He steps out of the Land Cruiser, dew still on the edges of the tinted windshield. He put on a suit for this, gave himself a fresh shave, all to walk, businesslike, through Sterling & Company's doors.

The general manager is a man by the name of Bob Christie. He's thick through the waist and neck, with naval tattoos ringing his right forearm. "Our sales team doesn't work Saturdays," he says as he leads Jay into his office. It's square and sterile, flat carpet under cheap bookshelves lined with plastic binders, and thin rows of fluorescent lights overhead. There are no windows, just pictures of trucks and vans, the entire Sterling fleet photographed as lovingly as a flotilla of spectacular ships. There are drivers in almost every framed photo, all of them in black STERLING & CO. TRUCKS T-shirts, standing in neat rows around the gleaming trucks. Jay wonders which one is Alonzo Hollis. White guy, midthirties, Lon had said. He scans the faces in the pictures, just as Christie sits, picking up a small pad on his desk. "If I can get some information from you about your trucking needs, then I can have someone call you first thing Monday with a proposal. What kind of company did you say you run?" He looks up, taking in Jay's suit, seemingly making a personal thread count and factoring that into his bottom line. Outside, Jay can hear the roar of engines rolling, 18-wheelers pulling out of the company's lot, making a slow crawl onto Market Street.

"I didn't," he says.

Confused, Christie leans back in his chair a little. It squeaks beneath his heavy weight. He taps the tip of his pen on top of the white pad on his desk.

"I'm actually here about one of your employees, Alonzo Hollis."

"What is this?" Christie says, eyes narrowing.

"My name is Jay Porter, Mr. Christie."

"You're that lawyer."

"Among other things."

"What in the world is this shit?" He rocks back and forth in his desk chair, which squeaks like he's suffocating a mouse. "You want to see the memo I sent out to my staff? At this point, even the secretaries know better than to cut through Pleasantville. I made it plain as day the hell that would rain down on anybody crossing Market Street to get to the port. I made it very clear."

"Alonzo Hollis," Jay says. "Was he working Tuesday night?"

"Look, we cooperated fully with the cops, so unless you got a badge inside that suit somewhere, I think we're done here," Christie says, standing.

"It's a simple question, and one you might save yourself a lot of trouble by answering now. Be something for the folks in Pleasantville to find out you knowingly sent a murder suspect back into the streets of their neighborhood."

"Hollis was never charged with anything."

"Yet."

"I told you, we are cooperating fully."

Jay notes his slip into the present tense. "Then answer the question."

"Good-bye, Mr. Porter."

So Hollis's name *has* come up again since the latest girl went missing, Jay thinks as he leaves Christie's office. He's on the phone with Rolly before he makes it to his car, asking for another favor. He has a name and not much else.

"I can work with it," Rolly says.

He's out to Hitchcock with his girl and a house full of grandkids, but he'll see what he can do from there. "This the one messed around with those girls?"

"According to Lonnie, he's number one on the cops' list."

"That don't always mean shit. You know better than anyone."

"The girl's still out there, man."

"Say no more," Rolly says. "I'm on it."

Jay calls Lonnie next. She's already at the search site.

He crosses Market Street into Pleasantville, passing the truck stop where she said yet a fourth girl narrowly escaped abduction, a man looking a hell of a lot like Hollis trying to snatch her into his van. The image lingers in his mind as he drives into the heart of the neighborhood, rolling up to an eye-catching scene.

They're everywhere on foot, men and women in white T-shirts, each with Alicia Nowell's name printed crudely in Magic Marker across the back. They're carrying clipboards, notepads, knocking on doors, chatting up their neighbors. If Jay didn't know the grim reason for this show of force from the community, he might think this was the most aggressive get-out-the-vote campaign in Pleasantville's history. The parking lot of the community center has been made over as headquarters. There are card tables and folding chairs set up on the graveled asphalt, and a large number of familiar faces drinking coffee out of Styrofoam cups. Jay recognizes Jelly Lopez standing with his wife and two other families from Berndale Street. He gives a friendly wave to his client. Either Jelly doesn't see him, or he's rolled up the welcome mat on his lawyer.

Jay continues on.

He parks a block over and then walks back to the community center on foot, the sun making every effort to push its way through the gauzy clouds overhead and making him squint. Against the white T-shirts, the hazy sunlight makes a strange halo effect, creating an army of angels for Alicia.

Sandy Wolcott is wearing one.

Axel Hathorne's competition has slipped a T-shirt over her button-down blouse just in time for her on-camera interview with a TV news crew. It's only Fox 26, but still, Jay thinks, look who got herself some free airtime. And a crowd. The missing girl's parents are standing within arm's reach of the candidate. Wolcott, in fact, puts her arm around Maxine Robicheaux as she offers words of support for the search effort. All of it caught on camera, pixels lining up in her favor ahead of tonight's debate. Maxine's husband, Mitchell, seems about fifteen years her senior. He's unshaven and awkward looking in a too-tight white T-shirt. He must be at least six feet four inches, with hands the size of small grapefruits. He towers over Wolcott and Maxine, gazing off toward Guinevere and the fateful corner, and the untamed brush beyond. There are pockets of white behind the bare branches of the trees, where volunteer searchers are combing the woods. Next to Maxine is Pastor Keith Morehead. The pastor has crossed political lines to offer the family his support. Behind him, the players on the youth basketball team he coaches are dressed in white T-shirts too.

"I'm not concerned about tonight's debate," Wolcott says to the reporter. "The second I heard about the search, I put down everything and got out here as fast as I could. I can't imagine being anywhere else actually, not when one of our own is in trouble," she says, claiming Alicia as family. She gives Maxine a gentle squeeze.

"Are you suggesting canceling tonight's debate?"

"Not at all," Wolcott says. "I think Houston needs to hear from its candidates for mayor. It's just that some of us are more prepared to answer the city's tough questions than others. I don't have any notecards to study. So I'm here to help." She offers a warm smile, pinched with an appropriate amount of concern. Jay's never met her and has no reason to believe she's being anything but sincere. But the moment feels strained, a tin note of opportunism ringing in Jay's ears, a flash of elation caught behind the tortoiseshell glasses she started wearing when she announced her intention to run, when talk of her pale green eyes and the height of her stiletto heels starting getting too much play in the press. With Reese Parker's coaching, she's crafted a more somber on-screen persona.

Johnetta Paul, who must have heard the whir of a video camera from a block over, comes speed-walking down the sidewalk in front of the rec center in heels, a white search T-shirt belted over black slacks, a pink blouse underneath. She presses in on Wolcott's left side, squeezing into the frame, practically reaching for the reporter's microphone to make her *own* statement of consolation to the family, to stress *her* commitment to finding the girl alive.

Wolcott has a number of staffers out here with her, including a middle-aged woman with acid-blond hair processed to within an inch of its life. Standing back a few feet, she's watching her candidate like a proud mom witnessing her kid's first time on-stage. She's drinking a Big Gulp and talking on a mobile phone and smoking all at the same time, her blue eyes disappearing into the peach folds of her fleshy skin. "That is Reese Parker."

Lonnie has sidled up beside Jay, her face pink and dewy from the sun.

"Wolcott's campaign manager?"

"Consultant. And professional shit stirrer."

She reaches into the pocket of her denim shirt, pulling out her Parliaments. "Fifty bucks says Parker called Fox herself."

"How long have you been out here?"

"Long enough," she says, lighting a smoke. "Come on, let's walk."

They move away from the crowd, walking alongside the fence that rings the basketball courts. There's a wide grass field behind it, where local kids play league sports, football in the fall and soccer in the spring. Jay can see the back of the elementary school from here. "Have you seen this?" Lonnie says. She pinches her cigarette between her lips and from the same shirt pocket pulls a folded-up sheet of paper. It's the flyer, the same one Jim Wainwright showed Jay yesterday morning, the anonymous complaints about the Buffalo Bayou Development Project screaming in capital letters across the top. Lonnie blows a stream of smoke into the air and taps the top corner of the flyer. "I've heard from three different people that she was passing these out."

"Alicia Nowell?"

Lonnie nods. "Tuesday wasn't her first time in Pleasantville."

Jay wrinkles his brow. "Are you sure?"

"Blue T-shirt, this girl," she says, pointing to a copy of the missing girl's graduation photo that's poking out of her shirt pocket. "Three different people, Jay, on three different streets, said she left one of these leaflets on their doorsteps. This was *last* week sometime." She pinches off the smoking tip of her cigarette, grinding out the red cherry in the damp grass, and pockets the butt.

"This isn't Hathorne's," Jay says.

"I know. A friend of mine works opp for their team, guy who

used to write for the *Post* too. He says the word internally is she wasn't theirs."

"What do you mean, 'opp'?"

"Opposition research," she says. "He wouldn't breathe a word of the dirt they've dug up on little Miss Sandra Dee over there, but I sure as shit wish he'd root around in Parker's closet. I happen to know she spends a lot of time in there."

Lon smiles wide, waiting for him to take the bait.

Jay would just as soon have no idea how she knows that.

He looks at the flyer. "This means Alicia was either working for Acton—"

"Or Wolcott," Lonnie says, finishing the thought.

"Easy enough to put Alicia in a blue T-shirt to make her look like a Hathorne worker, an insider with some concerns about the direction of the campaign."

They both turn to catch a glimpse of Wolcott and her crew, Reese Parker and the other staffers following as the cameraman and the news reporter shadow the candidate. Wolcott is across Ledwicke, talking to her potential constituents, half of whom Jay is fairly certain didn't vote for her in the general.

"You think it's theirs? Parker and Wolcott's?"

"If it is, then coming out here sure is damn good cover," Jay says, shoving his hands into his pockets. Maxine and Mitchell Robicheaux have been left standing in the parking lot of the Samuel P. Hathorne Community Center, aimlessly watching the activity all around them. Ruby Wainwright brings them coffee, offers Maxine a seat away from the crowd. "They're wasting that girl's time with a photo op," Jay says, shaking his head at Wolcott's performance for the camera, "when the real story of what she was doing in Pleasantville is right here," he says, pointing to the flyer. They're going about this all wrong. He remembers the white van, the fact that each girl was kept alive for days. "Wherever she is, she's not here."

"You want to roll to the Northeast?"

The cell phone in Jay's pocket rings.

He pulls out the black Motorola and answers.

Rolly got an address for Hollis, he says, page 223 in the phone book.

"Easy as pie," he says.

"Look like someone's home?"

"No car, no movement outside."

"Any sign of the girl?"

"No," Rolly says. "You want me to start something, knock on his door?"

"Be careful with it, though. If he smells trouble, thinks you're a cop sniffing around, he may spook, panic even, and we may never find the girl."

"The day I pass for a cop, take me to a field and shoot me."

Half Chickasaw, half Louisiana Creole, Rolly Snow is an ex-con who did time with one of Jay's friends from his Movement days. Part of his gift as an investigator has always been the fact that he doesn't look the part—with his long, braided hair, black as ink, and the initials of his name tattooed across his right hand. Jay can picture him behind the wheel of his El Camino Real, the pickup that comes out whenever a job requires it, when a Town Car would be as out of place as a hat on a horse's head. He's parked a few houses down, he says, with a clean view of Hollis's front windows. "I'll play it smooth," he assures Jay.

Jay closes the flip phone, sliding it back into his pants pocket.

He glances again at the Robicheauxs, Maxine's hips spilling off the sides of a cheap folding chair, a line of sweat running down her hairline, weaving through a mesh of pressed hair, the roots untended for the last five days. *Five days.* She keeps rubbing her hands along the front of her thighs and rocking back and forth in the chair, her body moving on memory, old muscles aching for the child she once rocked in her arms. She looks up, her gaze landing on Jay. From where he's standing, he can feel the weight of the bags under her eyes, her face as wrecked as that of Tina Wells's mother, the day she wept on the TV in Bernie's room at St. Luke's. He gives Maxine a polite nod. She gives him the same, rocking back and forth in the folding chair. Jay turns to Lonnie and says, "Let's go."

Detective Resner is Lonnie's contact, so she drives, she and Jay making up the rules of this partnership as they go along, slipping into an easy give-and-take that reminds him of those weeks and months when they met fifteen years ago while nosing around Cole Oil and its illegal business practices, finally coming together to compare notes. He couldn't have brought that case to court without Lonnie's help. She was an uncommonly good reporter, if a little preachy on the page, a ninety-five-pound engine fueled by nicotine and the heat of her own fanaticism when it comes to virtue, her unshakable dislike of liars and scoundrels of all stripes. It depresses him to think of her wasting her time and talent trying to sell a bunch of bullshit stories to second-rate magazines, or to think that she's having trouble with her rent.

The Northeast Police Station is a one-story brick building, as flat and wide as a prison block, its image a forewarning for those led in handcuffs through its doors. Lonnie parks her hatchback in the front parking lot, pulling up the emergency brake just as she sees Gregg Bartolomo pacing in front of the building, in one hand a slim notebook and in the other a bulky Model T cellular phone, an ancient-looking thing probably doled out by his employer. Lonnie had one just like it when she was at the *Post*. "He's calling something in," she says, reading it in his gait, the way he pitches forward on the balls of his feet. "He's got something," she adds, reaching for the door handle.

Bartolomo sees them coming and practically runs. He's Jay's height, maybe a little smaller, with an olive complexion that's settled into a deep butternut color with the onset of middle age. He presses a button on the phone, turning it off, and hops into the front seat of a red Ford Fiesta. He rolls up the window as Lon approaches, shouting through the glass, "Is it the girl?"

"I should never have given you anything," he says, locking the doors.

"They make a break in the case?"

He guns the engine, drowning out the sound of her voice, the equivalent of sticking his fingers in her ears. "Asshole," Lonnie mumbles.

Jay ignores them both and heads for the front doors of the station. Inside, there's a uniformed cop behind the front desk, an ancient white man with a case of rosacea and thinning hair and a phone receiver cradled against his ear. There are other phones ringing in the station, and Jay hears the clang of type-writers in the distance. He can see the tops of balding heads above the divider behind the front desk, where senior offi-cers are working, but the reception room is otherwise empty, save for a light-skinned black man sitting on a bench near the door. It's Frankie, Sam Hathorne's driver. He stands when he sees Jay, a look of recognition and also relief shooting across his face.

"Something's wrong," he says right away. "He's been in there too long. Sam is on his way. He's got Axel calling around now."

"*Who's* in there?"

"Neal."

Frankie tells him he was instructed to drop Neal at the station house. The cops had a few more questions, they'd said, about the girl working for Hathorne.

"Neal thought it could wait," he says. "They got the debate tonight and everything. But Sam said it might look bad, you know, not cooperating when the girl is still missing. I was supposed to run him out here and back to the hotel. But they took him back in one of them little rooms and he ain't been out since."

"An interrogation room?"

"They won't let me in there."

"I can get in there," Jay says. The words tumble out, like beads let loose from a string, a surprise to him as much as anyone.

Lonnie enters the station behind him.

She nods at the desk officer and gives her name, an old routine from her reporter days. "They still think she was working for Hathorne," Jay says.

"I'll talk to Mike," she says, as the desk cop waves her forward.

"She was working for Acton or Wolcott, *tell* him."

Lonnie nods as she steps through the opening of a low swinging gate that's the same faux-wood finish as the divider separating the desk from the rest of reception. The cop has allowed her past the threshold, opening a path to the desks and detectives behind the room divider. Jay waits for the cop to take another call, his head bent over some form, and then he turns and asks Frankie where they took Neal. Frankie points down a brightly lit tiled hall to the left of the station's front desk. Jay moves purposefully, portraying for all the world a man who knows where he's going and what he's getting himself into. INTERROGATION ROOM 1 and INTERROGATION ROOM 2 sit directly across the hall from each other. The door to room 2 is closed tight. But unlocked, Jay finds, when he walks in unannounced. The detective sitting across a table from Neal Hathorne doesn't turn at the sound, sure in the assumption that the only folks roaming free back here are other cops. It's Neal who looks up in surprise. In a light blue shirt rolled to his elbows and black slacks, he's seated at the table, facing the door. He has one foot propped on the knee of his other leg. It falls to the floor when he sees Jay. It's this thudding sound that gets the cop's attention. He glances over his shoulder, and then literally does a double take.

"Detective Moore?" Jay says, taking a guess.

The cop stands. "Who are you?"

"I'm his lawyer."

"What?" Neal says.

He looks back and forth between Jay, a man he's met only twice, and the cop who's had him in this little room for hours. A pinch of anxiety shows on his face, in the crinkle of his brow. The detective, a black man old enough to have served in the Northeast when Axel was still stationed here, holds out two hands, blocking Jay from coming any closer. He's wearing a woven sports coat that doesn't match his pants. "He didn't ask for a lawyer."

Jay looks at Neal. "You want a lawyer?"

"He's not under arrest."

The word sets off something in Neal. "Arrest?"

He stands, the muscles on his slim forearms twisting as he presses his hands onto the tabletop. He's wearing glasses today, a pair of wire rims that somehow make him look younger than he is. "They're just asking me a few questions," he says, presumably to Jay, but he's looking at the detective, wanting Moore to confirm this. The detective steps around Jay, leaning into the tiled hallway, searching for backup. But Jay knows the detective is flying solo. There's a pane of mirrored glass cut into the wall behind Neal's seat, on the other side of which, Jay guesses, sits an observation room. If there were officers monitoring this little chat with Neal Hathorne, they would have flown into the

room the second Jay stepped inside. The detective hollers down
the hall for an assist. He steps back inside, turning to Jay and
shaking his head. "You can't just come in here."

"I can if he asks for a lawyer."

"He's not being interrogated."

"Oh, is that right?" Jay says, making an exaggerated show of
looking around the room. Two uniformed officers appear in
the doorway, one with a hand on his holster. Jay shoots Neal
a look, silently encouraging the young campaign manager
to consider why he's in this small, boxlike room. Neal sighs,
shoves his hands into the pockets of his softly wrinkled slacks.

"He can stay," he says.

The detective turns to Neal. "What's that?"

"I want a lawyer," Neal says. "He can stay."

The detective turns from Neal to Jay, the surprise guest. He
seems momentarily unsure of how to play the situation. Finally,
he waves off the uniformed cops, shaking his head to himself,
before stepping aside to let Jay cross the room to his client. "I'll
need a chair," Jay says.

CHAPTER 8

They found her purse and wallet, separated by two hundred yards and a drain ditch, in the weeds along a deserted stretch of road by the Port of Houston, a good quarter mile from where the residents had been concentrating their search efforts. With Jay in the room now, there's no more need to tiptoe up to it. The facts are what they are. Detective Moore lays them out before Jay and Neal: a faux leather hobo bag, the stitching on the straps coming undone; and a pink nylon wallet, Velcro at the seams and open to the center, the slots for credit cards empty and one prom photo sticking out, Alicia and the boyfriend, Jay thinks. The wallet is too thin to have ever held more than a few dollars. Beside it are other details of the young girl's life: Bonnie Bell Dr Pepper lip gloss; a mechanical pencil with basketballs printed on it; a tin of face powder; Bayer aspirin; a tampon, its outer packaging torn at the corners; a dusty pack of Tic Tacs; a folded-up copy of the Buffalo Bayou Development Project flyer; and a small black pager. The items are set on a plastic sheet, and Detective Moore doesn't touch any of them, especially avoiding the pager, to which this conversation, half an hour after Jay sat down, has finally circled around. Until its discovery, Alicia's parents had no idea she owned a pager, let alone why Neal Hathorne's mobile number would be on its screen. His was the last number received, a little over an hour before Elma Johnson spotted the girl through the curtains of her kitchen window. *She was waiting on someone*, the woman said.

"Help me out here, Mr. Hathorne," Moore says. He's removed his jacket, letting it hang on the chair back behind him, and rolled up his shirtsleeves. "How is it that your cell phone number showed up in Alicia Nowell's pager?"

"I have no idea. I never met her."

Jay reaches out a hand to stop him, almost as he would if one of his kids was riding next to him in the front of the car and he put on the brakes. "Let's be clear," he says, "none of this means Mr. Hathorne was in contact with Alicia, only that someone in possession of the seven digits that make up his phone number happened to punch in those numbers when paging Alicia Nowell."

"What's her pager number?" Neal says, pulling out his phone.

He starts scrolling through his call list, ready to clear this up right now.

Again, Jay holds out his hand.

"Look, we're here to help. We all want the girl found safe and sound. Which is why we can't afford to waste any more time. It's been *five* days."

"No one is more aware of that than I am, Mr. Porter." Moore

turns his attention once again to Neal. "She wasn't working for your uncle's campaign?"

"No," Neal says. "I told you, I never met the girl."

"Then *again*, Mr. Hathorne, why was your phone number in her pager?"

"I think we've established that's not getting us anywhere," Jay says.

"Did you call her?" Moore asks.

Beside Jay, Neal's left leg is pumping up and down underneath the wooden table, as he sits hunched over his mobile phone, scrolling through what must be dozens of phone numbers he's dialed in the last few days. The restless, rat-tat-tat motion rattles the one chair leg that's shorter than the others, not to mention what it's beginning to do to Jay's nerves. He remembers the heat that soon gathers in these little rooms, breath souring by the hour without food or water. He's been on this side of the table before, both as a lawyer and as a suspect. From his pocket, he pulls a folded copy of the same bayou development flyer, comparing it with the one on the table. "This, right here, this is evidence the girl was working for Mr. Acton or Ms. Wolcott, right before the general election. She was leaving these on front steps, in mailboxes, all around Pleasantville."

Moore wears a thin mustache, blacker than the hair on his head, and Jay tries to understand the kind of vanity that would make a man dye his mustache and not bother with the rest of it. The detective pinches his mouth into a tight line, pondering something. The heat's on him too. Jay notices sweat rings under his arms. Neal leans back in his chair. He seems to newly consider the chain of events that led him to this interrogation room, and he whispers a single word under his breath, the name of Wolcott's highly paid campaign consultant. "Parker." It's the first moment since Jay walked in that Neal appears to grasp that he might actually be in some trouble here, that there might be forces working against him that he can't see, let alone control; the mere thought of Reese Parker's hand in this stirs more fear than the detective ever did. "I swear to god, if this is some kind of a stunt."

Then it worked, Jay thinks.

Wolcott is walking the streets, on camera, making a public show of looking for the missing girl, while Hathorne's right hand is holed up in here. Neal flips open his cell phone again and starts dialing.

"Not here," Jay says.

Moore doesn't touch the flyer. He seems wholly unimpressed. Jay tries to explain. "If Alicia was handing these out, she wasn't working for Hathorne."

"She *wasn't*. How many times do I have to say it?" Neal says.

"You spoke at her high school," Moore says. "You remember that?"

"What?"

"Alicia Nowell, she went to Jones High School."

"So?"

"So you visited the school in the spring, before she graduated."

"No, I didn't."

He shakes his head, marveling at how crazy this all sounds. Then he leans back in his chair again. A moment passes before he realizes his mistake.

"Jesus, I did," he says, looking at Jay and then Detective Moore, as if he wants to apologize for having said the wrong thing. "They held a candidate forum, for the students, a government class or something like that. Acton was the only one who came in person. I was there for Axe. Wolcott sent some low-level staffer."

"We have reports that you spent some time talking to Ms. Nowell."

Neal shakes his head. "I don't know what to say. I don't remember her."

"Neal." Jay holds out a hand, again to stop him from talking. He wants to steer the conversation back to Acton and Wolcott, the fact that members of one of their campaigns might have sent Alicia into Pleasantville, may have, for all they know, arranged to pick her up after her shift ended. Maybe *that's* who she was waiting for, standing alone at the corner of Ledwicke and Guinevere.

"There were reports that you slid her your business card."

"I pass out a lot of cards. We're always looking for volunteers."

"Right, and between that and your phone number in her pager—"

Neal sighs. "I *could* have called her—"

"Don't," Jay says.

"There are some numbers in here I don't recognize," he says, holding up his cell phone. He seems nervous now, aware of his previous mistake, and yet here he is again, changing his story on a dime. He tries to lay it all out now, talking too much. Neal graduated from law school, twenty years after Jay, so he's technically a lawyer, but one without a bar card or an animal instinct for avoiding traps. "It's possible one of them belonged to Alicia Nowell," he says. "But it doesn't mean I knew it was her pager. I've called a lot of people during the campaign. And I still carry a pager too. If someone pages me, I call back, leaving my cell number. To be honest, I might have thought it was Acton's people. Since the primary, I have a list of people a mile long, from Acton's communications director to his second cousin, all with their hands out, wanting money in exchange for his endorsement. It's possible I called her back, put my number in her pager, not even knowing who I was calling."

"Just as it's possible that someone *else* paged Alicia and

punched in Neal's number," Jay says to Detective Moore. To Neal, he says, "*Stop* talking."

"Can we take a look at that phone?"

"Not at this time," Jay says.

"Might point us in a right direction."

"You seem pointed in a direction already."

"Where were you Tuesday night, Mr. Hathorne?"

"You don't have to answer that," Jay says.

"You're not serious?" Neal says to the cop. He asks Jay, "Is he serious?"

"I got a girl out there in the streets somewhere. I'm damned serious."

"Alonzo Hollis," Jay says. "Any idea where *he* was Tuesday night?"

The cop stares at Jay, as he runs a finger along the edge of the table, exercising his own right to remain silent, mocking Jay's earnestness, his arrogance at thinking he knows more than a seasoned detective. But Jay doesn't give a shit what Moore thinks of him. "Be interesting," he says, "for Alicia Nowell's parents, let alone the *Chronicle* and the city as a whole, to find out that HPD had a suspect in two nearly identical abductions and didn't pursue him, all the while wasting time questioning Neal Hathorne, nephew of the former police chief, who, other than trying to get Axel elected, appears to have been minding his own business."

"We're working on Hollis's alibi," Moore concedes.

"So are we," Jay says. It comes out stronger than he intended, as if he's already building a defense, when one hasn't been required, when the breadth of his investigation is an ex-con skulking around Hollis's place in a rusty El Camino.

Moore leans back in his chair, resting his hands on a tiny roll of gut that's spilling over his belt. "You knew a girl named Tina Wells, didn't you, Neal?"

"What?"

"Tina Wells, you knew her."

Jay turns to look at Neal.

This time Neal holds up a hand, to let him know it's okay. He *wants* to talk. "I've spent my whole life around Pleasantville. Of course I knew her."

"Deanne Duchon too," Moore says. "You went on a date with her once, didn't you, before she died? You're twenty-seven, twenty-eight years old?"

"Twenty-nine," Neal says.

"She was a little young for you, don't you think?"

"Jesus Christ," Neal mutters in anger.

"Let's go," Jay says to Neal. He stands, unexpectedly light-headed on his feet. He feels a hot, blood-rushing regret about walking in here, unsure what came over him, why he thought any of this was worth the risk. "Acton or Wolcott," he says to the cop. "She was working for one of them. Follow the flyer if you want to get a picture of her last hours."

Neal is still seated, still talking. "I escorted Deanne to the Pleasantville Christmas party, like three years ago. It was something my grandfather and her dad cooked up when her date dropped out at the last minute. It was nothing."

Jay grabs him by the arm, pulling him toward the door.

"We're done here."

"Where's the girl, Neal?"

"This is crazy," Neal says to the cop.

Jay opens the interrogation room's door, shoving Neal out of the tiny box and into the short, tiled hallway. The air is cool out here, perfumed with the strangely reassuring scent of copier fluid and coffee. Jay starts for the front of the station house, Neal right behind him. "What the hell was all that?" he says, pointing back toward the interrogation room. "Keep your voice down," Jay says. He doesn't know who's listening. The number of folks in the reception area has grown, but Lonnie is nowhere to be found. Instead, there's a message from her on his cell phone. "Resner's hands are tied," she reports. "The cases aren't linked, not officially. The Nowell girl is Moore's and his partner's. Resner was told in no uncertain terms to let them run it. But I did get from Mike that all the reports about Neal meeting the girl, all the way back in the spring, they're coming from the boyfriend." He also graduated from Jones High School this year, she says.

The door to the station house opens.

Sam Hathorne walks in. Sam, in a black overcoat dotted with raindrops, removes a dove gray fedora from his head. He marches directly to his grandson, putting two protective arms on the young man's narrow shoulders and looking him over, head to toe, searching for any injury to his body or his pride. On the phone, Lon's smoker's voice continues in Jay's ear. "I'm going to check him out, the boyfriend," she says in her voice-mail message. "Beaumont's just out Highway 90. You think you can find a ride back to your car?"

Jay hangs up his phone, sliding it into his pants pocket.

To Frankie, he says, "Can you drop me somewhere?"

Sam hands his hat to his driver. He turns to Jay, wrapping one of those protective arms around him too, unexpectedly pulling him into the family circle. He smells of tobacco and English Leather aftershave. "Ride with us, Jay."

Outside, fat, doughy clouds have closed over. There are patches of wet cement across the surface of the police station's parking lot, but the sudden, unexpected rain, rolling in while Jay and Neal were holed up inside, has mostly faded now. He wonders if the search was called off, with Alicia Nowell still out there somewhere, her parents coming up on another sunset with no answer. Neal rides in the front of the Cadillac, next to Frankie. Sam and Jay are sunk into the leather seats in the back. Sam lights a cigarette, flipping the metal lid of the ashtray in the door's armrest. On cue, Frankie lowers Sam's window a crack, using the driver's-side console. "Turn that off," Sam says, and Frankie snaps off the blues playing on the car's radio. A. G. Hats, sounds like. "Sorry, sir," Frankie says.

Neal is already on his cell phone, presently in a heated conversation with Lewis Acton, played out on speakerphone for the benefit of his grandfather, who listens stoically. "We had a deal, damn it," Acton is saying. "Don't think I can't and *won't* walk my endorsement right over to Wolcott's headquarters. She and I could have a joint statement out before the cameras start to roll tonight."

"For half your price," Neal says. "I know for a fact, Wolcott's bottom line is twenty, cash. That works for you, go right ahead. We'll win without you."

"How do I even know that thing is real, and not some negotiation tactic?"

"Oh, it's real," Neal says, looking down at a copy of the BBDP flyer.

"Well, I didn't put it out."

Jay looks down at his Seiko. It's after three o'clock by now. He leans toward Frankie in the driver's seat. "Can you drop me in Pleasantville?"

"Can't, sir," Frankie says, catching Jay's eyes in the rearview mirror. "We have to get Neal to the debate site. Axe is already at the venue, waiting."

"We're just a few hours from start time," Sam says.

"I can bring you back after I drop them."

Jay, feeling trapped, sinks back into the rear passenger seat, the smell of Sam's cigarette smoke making him squirm a little, pushing old buttons, making him want things he can no longer have. Sam looks over at him, and gives him a fatherly pat on his leg. "You did a good thing for Neal back there."

"I didn't do it for Neal."

"Axe has been on the phone all day trying to get to the bottom of this," Sam says. "But they're freezing him out, saying it looks bad for the current chief, with the department endorsement and all that, like he's taking orders from Axel, like he's running things. But it's going to look real bad for Tobin when Axe is in the mayor's office, and that turncoat motherfucker has to answer for why he had Neal holed up in there like that, insinuating god knows what. We've got to move before this story gets way the hell out ahead of us." He takes another pull on his cigarette, short and black as a cigar, blowing smoke through the crack in the tinted window. It mixes with the steel-edged scent coming off the Ship Channel and the refineries that line it: Shell, Exxon, and Cole Oil, of course, the greedy bastards pumping money onto tankers at this very moment. Jay has a fevered thought that giving up smoking in this chemically soaked city was a fool's wishful thinking, that he might as well bum a smoke from Sam right now and put himself out of his misery, ride out his remaining years with a friend always in hand. What difference did it make, really? Bernie never touched the stuff, liquor either, never did a thing more dangerous than breathing the very same air that's burning through Jay's lungs right now. He can see a line of barges down below, the exhaust from their engines melding into the nickel black clouds in the sky. It's frighteningly easy in this city, moving as residents do from one air-conditioned box to another, to forget how many questionable materials are moving through Houston, Texas, on any given day.

"It's Wolcott, I'm sure of it," Neal says, hanging up the phone. "Reese Parker had her hand in this somehow. I wouldn't put it past her to drop my name in connection with the case, just to get a story or two, dominate the news cycle for a day and crush any momentum we get off the debate tonight."

Sam, in the backseat, nods vaguely. "Parker plays dirty, always has."

"What about Wolcott's affair?" Neal says. "The guy, the cop, he resigned this week. If now's not the time to bring that out in the open, then when is?"

"Axe doesn't want to go dirty."

"Axe isn't in the car right now," Neal says, turning to look at Sam. "I never would have figured you to be gun-shy. They're ahead of us by a mile in fund-raising, Pop. And if we start losing donors over this, we can forget catching up to them with TV. We might as well stop cutting the ads right now."

"We hit them, they hit us back," Sam says. "It's a long game, Neal."

And none of it, Jay thinks, explains Neal's phone number in the girl's pager. It didn't sound right at the station, and it doesn't make any more sense now. Jay stares at Neal across the interior of the car. "Where were you Tuesday night?" he says.

"Excuse me?"

"Tuesday night. Where *were* you?"

"You're kidding, right?"

Frankie looks from Neal in the front seat to Jay's reflection in the rearview mirror, before quickly turning his eyes back to the road, the white concrete of the 610 Freeway. The car falls silent for a moment, no sound except for the soft scratch of Sam carefully stubbing out the small black cigarette in the ashtray in the armrest. Neal wrenches 180 degrees in his seat, turning head-on to face Jay, his erstwhile savior and now a man who appears to have dearly pissed him off. "I was running a campaign," he says bluntly. "It was election night. I was *every-where.*" He sounds edgy with exhaustion, put out by the idea that he's had time for anything other than political victory, winning a ground war. "The Women's League, the west side, Alief, the teachers' union, the ILA on Navigation, the Teamsters, the fucking chemical workers, churches, every polling place from Highway 6 to damn near Pasadena. I was everywhere, okay? Everywhere."

CHAPTER 9

The first mayoral debate ahead of the December tenth runoff is scheduled as a standard Lincoln-Douglas type deal, two lecterns on a stage, this one being put on by the *Houston Chronicle* and Channel 13, the local ABC affiliate, and hosted by the political science department at the University of Houston. Jay can't bring himself to set foot on that campus tonight for any number of reasons, not the least of which is the prospect of running into one of Axel Hathorne's biggest supporters, Cynthia Maddox, a woman whose power to upend Jay's life and rattle the contents of his rib cage he doesn't feel like testing tonight. "Drop me off up here," he says to Frankie, when they're a block from the university's main entrance on Calhoun, practically jumping out of the car before it rolls to a complete stop. He nods a quick good-bye to Sam, and then watches the Cadillac continue on without him, turning right into the college. Standing on the curb, sun going down, Jay calls for a rescue, asking Rolly to come give him a ride back to his car. Rolly says he can do him one better. "I got something," he says.

Alonzo Hollis, come to find out, is a six-foot, 180-pound former marine and ranch hand—born to and raised by a Pentecostal preacher, and strict father of six, in the tiny town of Needville, south of Sugar Land—who, late into his twenties, liked to hang around high school football games in his hometown, eventually running off with a sophomore who worked the concession stand, marrying her as quick as he could in a courthouse in downtown Houston, a forged parental consent form in his hand.

His now *ex*-wife, who at the ripe old age of twenty-three is as bitter as a baby persimmon, was more than willing to spit out a long list of the man's shortcomings at the slightest provocation, like the appearance of Rolly Snow on her doorstep, the heels of his silver-tipped boots chipping away at her crumbling concrete steps, his smile tobacco stained and wide. He had talked his way into the house using one of the oldest cons in the book. Lucifer himself probably showed up to Jesus's house at least once or twice, claiming to have the twenty dollars he owed him. Rolly told the young woman in the T-shirt and cutoff shorts that he owed his old buddy Alonzo a little piece, money he'd put on a ball game, tempting fate by backing the Aggies against Alabama. The screen door had opened wider at the mention of money. "How much is it?"

Rolly shook his head, appearing sheepish.

Naw, he said.

He'd rather give it to 'Lonzo himself, apologize for being a dick about it.

"You expecting him anytime soon?" he said. "I could wait a minute."

Like every mark before her, Kyla Hollis had every intention of getting a hold of that money for herself, even if it meant hosting Rolly in her sitting room for half an hour and giving him the last two beers in the house. Once inside, he excused himself twice, claiming a trip to the bathroom, but instead searching every inch of Kyla's home. There was no sign of the girl. Alonzo either.

Still, he thought he might be able to get something out of the former Mrs. Hollis. There is a certain kind of gal who goes in for a guy like Rolly—his long black hair, the tats across his hands and forearms—and little miss cutoff shorts could have been his for the taking. Time was, he would have tipped himself for his trouble, made a pass or a squeeze, laid a guiding hand on a lady's back as he led her to the bedroom, letting her talk and talk when the deed was done, getting all the information he was looking for. But he was in deep with his girl, the grandmother in Hitchcock, and ultimately passed on twenty-three-year-old tail, he tells Jay. He seems proud, actually, wanting someone else to bear witness to his self-restraint. They are riding in the cab of the El Camino, traveling north on Calhoun toward the 45 Freeway, windows down on a rare starry sky, the late-morning rain having cleared out the smoky breath of industry, laying bare the city skyline. Somehow, in the last half hour or so, the night had turned pretty. Jay hasn't heard from Evelyn or his kids after trying to reach her at her place and his. He keeps his cell phone on his lap. Across the front seat of his pickup truck, Rolly keeps tapping at the pack of cigarettes in the front pocket of his shirt, stopping himself each time he realizes he's doing it, trying his best to show his utter respect for a man who won't smoke in front of his kids. He doesn't light up around Jay anymore, except for marijuana, which he claims doesn't count.

"The whole thing cost me fifty bucks, what I said I lost on the football game. But it was worth it to get her talking. And talk she did," Rolly says, his hair whipping in the wind. "She can't stand the man. Thinks he's a roach and a rat and every other low-down living thing, calls him the 'bleacher creature' 'cause he still hangs out at high school games, ogling cheerleaders and girls half his age. It took her a while to see she was just look-ing for a way out of small-town Texas, that Hollis ain't shit. She kicked him out of the house when he got fired."

"Fired?"

"The trucking company let him go three months ago."

"What?"

"That's what I said to her, like that was the first I'd heard it."

"Where's he working now?"

"Some low-rent tire shop, one of the chains," Rolly says. "But the ex-wife says he wouldn't have been at work Tuesday night anyway because he was supposed to be at her place. Whatever do-it-yourself divorce settlement they worked out, it included having him watch their kid a couple of times a month."

"Kid?"

"I know," Rolly says, as surprised as Jay by the plot turn. "Not a baby picture in the whole fucking house." He pulls onto the on-ramp for the 45 Freeway. "The point is, Alonzo Hollis was due at Kyla's house Tuesday night, and he never showed. And she hasn't heard a word from him since." He glances at Jay again, the freeway lights pulling shadows like warm taffy from every corner of the truck's cab. "Tell the truth of it, I walked out of there thinking she knew I wasn't no friend of Hollis, that I was sniffing around about something else, and Tuesday night set off alarm bells. I get the distinct feeling she *wanted* me to know Hollis wasn't where he was supposed to be."

"So he's not living there anymore then."

"No, but I know where he is. I swiped this when she went into the kitchen," Rolly says, tapping an envelope that's on the dash. It's a piece of Hollis's mail, on which Kyla had scribbled a forwarding address.

It's a street Jay recognizes, somewhere out near Aldine.

"If he isn't working for Sterling," Jay says, "you really think he'd drive all the way back to Pleasantville, hoping to find some girl walking alone at night?"

"Depends."

"On?"

"On whether he'd gotten away with it twice before."

"You want to roll on him?"

"What choice we got?"

Jay glances at his watch. Wherever his kids are, it's dinner-time. This may be the longest he's been away from them in a year.

"Hey," Rolly says, tapping his fist against Jay's knee. It's been nearly twenty years since the day they met—when Rolly walked into Jay's law office, those five hundred cheaply carpeted square feet in the strip mall on W. Gray, asking for help with some girl troubles that had unexpectedly turned legal—and he can practically read Jay's mind. "Nothing jumps off in a half hour, we cut out."

"Deal," Jay says.

The place in Aldine is a two-hundred-unit apartment complex, one of those sprawling rental communities the size of a small college campus that pop up along big city freeways across the South, promising a pool and a weight room and an easy twenty-minute ride into downtown, or wherever your twelve-dollar-an-hour job is. This one has the nerve to call itself Beechwood Estates.

"Shit," Rolly mumbles when he sees it.

And Jay, on his own, can immediately see the problem.

For whatever cover a place like this offers, its very uniformity promising anonymity for snoops like Rolly, it also gives off no hint of the character of the man they are seeking. There are no shoes lying about, size ten or twelve, no toys or hollowed-out barbecue pits or shopping bags at the curb, and no trash they could poke through looking for a pay stub, no way of knowing which bag of garbage inside the metal bins in the complex's parking lot belongs to Hollis.

They've got his apartment number, and that's about it.

The door to the unit marked 27-A is on the first floor of the complex, across an alley from the main parking lot, the one closest to the entrance to Beechwood Estates. It's a distance of about twenty yards from Hollis's front door to the truck, which Rolly parks in a dark spot underneath the carport. There's a fan of glass cut into the top of the door, just above the 27-A. From here, the unit appears completely dark. Rolly snaps off his seat belt. "I'm going in."

Jay goes for the door handle on his side.

Rolly shakes his head. "I need you to watch my back out here. You don't hear from me or something looks funky, hit my pager just once." He reaches across the front seat for the glove box. He taps it twice, and the door pops open. From inside, he pulls out a crinkled bandanna, rolled as tight as a joint. Across the dash, he spreads out the fabric, revealing a set of lock picks, the metal dull from use. He chooses two, leaving the rest sitting on the dashboard.

Jay watches as Rolly slides the picks into his back pocket, just a few inches from the .45 that's resting in the waistband of his jeans. In under a minute he's across the alley, under the faux-Tudor awning over the entryway to Hollis's apartment, and inside the front door. Jay watches it all from the cab of the pickup truck. The radio plays softly in the background, the dial set to KCOH, Rolly being a longtime fan of its blues-and-news format. Tonight, the station is picking up a live feed from the Channel 13 mayoral debate, and one of the moderators, a political affairs editor at the *Houston Chronicle*, is just now introducing the candidates. KCOH, however, knows which side its bread is buttered on. They open up the phone lines early, cutting away from the debate before it even starts, betting on the fact that its audience would rather listen to one another than to either of the candidates. Tonight's topic: "What question would *you* ask the next mayor of Houston?" The first caller is a middle-aged woman from Third Ward—Terri, "with an *i*"—who launches into a tirade about the dirty seats on city buses. She's been looking for a job for three weeks and can't get nowhere clean half the time, looking like a street person every time she walks into an important interview. The call-in crowd is with her until the moment she starts complaining about the stinky food "them Mexicans be bringing on the bus." The next caller in line—Tammy, "with a *y*"—tells her she needs to mind her own damn business. "You doing them just like white folks used to do us." An argument countered by a first-time caller named Roy, who says, "But it *is* getting to a point where they're taking everything, coming over here, getting all the good jobs." To which the radio host says, "*Been* here, bro'man, long before you. You *are* calling from Texas. *Tejas*, baby." Jay snaps off the radio. He looks at his watch, wondering how much time he ought to give it.

A light blue Chevy Caprice pulls into the parking spot next to him. The driver shoots Jay a funny look as he's getting out of his car, and Jay, too late, realizes the lock picks are still laid out across the dash, a thief's tools in plain sight. "I help you with something?" the man says. His driver's-side door is only a few inches from Rolly's truck, and this close Jay can tell he's carrying something in his hands, but can't make out the shape or weight beneath the frame of the El Camino's passenger window. Wouldn't worry him none if it weren't for the good look Jay gets at his face, sweat and grease lit up by a yellow security light in a corner of the carport. He's a white guy, early thirties, with sandy, almost tea-colored hair, clipped at the sides, and long enough to touch his shirt collar in the back—a description that matches, almost to the letter, the one Lonnie gave for Alonzo Hollis. On instinct, Jay reaches for a piece, coming up empty, of course. He panics when he suddenly remembers where he left his gun. "I said, can I help you with something?" the guy says. He's watching Jay closely, but also darting his eyes up and down the parking lot every few seconds, as if he's checking to make sure there are no witnesses to whatever it is he has in mind. Jay has his cell phone open, dialing Rolly's pager number.

"Step out of the car," the guy says.

"Not looking for trouble, man."

"I said, step out of the car."

Rolly keeps a rusted tire iron beneath the front seat, or at least he used to. Jay reaches for it. He's about to hop out of the truck when Rolly comes out of 27-A, walking briskly across the alleyway. Seeing Rolly and the .45 in his right hand, the driver of the Caprice backs up slowly. In his arms, Jay sees he's carrying not a weapon but a paper grocery bag, a loaf of white bread sticking out of the top. He starts off, giving Rolly a sideways glance as they come within inches of each other in the parking lot. Rolly gives him a nod, as polite and casual as if they were strolling along the seawall in Galveston. The driver of the Caprice heads in the opposite direction from unit 27-A. Rolly opens the door to the El Camino.

"No girl?"

"No girl, no nothing," Rolly says. "The place is completely empty. No bed, no couch, no furniture, nothing, just some trash on the floor, a few ghost marks in the carpet. There's no way anyone's living in that apartment." He slides behind the wheel, throwing the truck into drive and pulling out of the carport. He makes a quick turn toward the entrance to Beechwood Estates and the 45 Freeway. Jay looks at the envelope with Hollis's address scribbled on the front.

"So either he lied to his ex about where he was living—"

"Or he moved out of 27-A in a hurry," Rolly says.

Jay lifts the cell phone from his lap as they ride, dialing home. Evelyn answers on the fourth ring. "Where are you?" she barks, forgetting that she's the one who's been out of touch for hours. It's Saturday night, and she has plans to see a show at the Magnolia Ballroom, she reminds him. At this point, there's barely enough time left for her to wash and dry her hair.

"I'll be home soon," he says. "But do me a favor, will you? Keep the kids out of my bedroom, okay? It's important, Ev. Don't let them go in there."

"Why? It's something dirty in there?"

Jay doesn't bother to correct her because, frankly, he'd rather have her think he sleeps with a stack of *Penthouse* magazines under his pillow than a handgun, the very thing he told his wife he'd never bring into the house again. But Tuesday night, after the break-in at his office, he walked right inside the house and slid it beneath his bedroom pillow, like old times.

"You hear me, Evelyn?"

"Fine. But don't you have none of that shit in this house the next time I come, you hear? You already got me over here babysitting somebody else's kid."

"What are you talking about?"

"Ellie's friend, what's her name?"

He knows instantly. "Lori?"

"They're holed up in Ellie's room now."

"She's grounded."

"Guess she found a loophole."

"Well, tell her it's getting late. Tell her it's time for Lori to go home."

"Don't look like the girl is planning to go home no time soon. She walked in carrying a big-ass duffel bag, both of them heading straight to Ellie's room."

Jay sighs. "Okay, I'll be there soon," he says.

As they pull out onto the feeder road, Rolly reaches across Jay's lap for the glove box. He returns the set of picks to its hiding place. "Come on, Counselor, let's get you home," he says, doing a piss-poor job of hiding his disappointment over the gaping hole he can't close. Tomorrow makes six days, and they are no closer to finding Alonzo Hollis.

CHAPTER 10

Ellie is on him the second he walks through the door. "It's just for tonight, I swear," she says. "She had a fight with her mom, and she just wants to get away from home, just for tonight." She's at his heels as he walks through the house. Evelyn bid a quick good-bye in the driveway, offering no more than a small wave before driving off. But she left a pot of oxtails on the stove, peas, and a chopped salad, for which he doesn't think he could be any more grateful. He hasn't eaten anything since a boiled egg at breakfast. He nods at his son, who's lying on the floor on a pile of couch cushions, watching *Star Trek*. "Hey, Dad," Ben says, barely looking away from the TV. Jay takes off his suit jacket, heading past the kitchen to the front of the house and the main hall that leads to the three bedrooms. Ellie, behind

him, continues to plead her friend's case. Lori, he guesses, is
hiding out somewhere, waiting to hear her fate.

"She tell her parents yet?"

"This isn't even about that," Ellie says. "She got into a fight
with her mom about leaving wet clothes on the bathroom floor.
Her mom's fine with her spending the night." Jay stops at the
door to his bedroom, not wanting her to cross the threshold.
"And the other thing, well, we're going to figure something
out."

"This isn't your problem, Ellie. Stay out of it."

"She's my friend, Dad," she says, in a way that makes it impossible for him to scold her or offer any better counsel than the
words that just came out of his daughter's mouth. She's compas-
sionate, not to mention loyal, two qualities he finds precious
and too fragile for his clumsy hands to touch, tonight at least.

"We'll talk about it in the morning," he says.

Ellie smiles.

She might have thrown her arms around her dad in gratitude if he weren't so stiffly guarding his bedroom door. "Did
you get something to eat?"

"Yes, sir."

"Okay," he says awkwardly. "Good night, then."

She gives him a strange look, suspicious even. It's not yet
seven o'clock.

"'Night," she says, before turning toward her bedroom.

Jay waits until he can hear the girls' voices, including Ellie's
laugh, on the other side of the door. Then he steps inside his
bedroom, closing the door behind him. The carpet is thick as
cream, and the room is softly quiet, too quiet, the mattress on
one side of the bed sagging lower than the other. He walks to
his pillow, lifting it, feeling the cool metal of the .38. In one
swift motion, he unlocks and unloads, feeling reassured by the

almost musical notes of the bullets brushing against each other in his hand. He looks around for a place to store them, settling on his sock drawer, where neither of his kids would ever think to check.

He tosses the gun in as well.

Later, he takes a plate into his room, eating his dinner in front of his bedroom TV. Untied dress shoes at his feet, he leans over a TV tray, sucking meat off a bone, as he catches the last ten minutes or so of the Hathorne-Wolcott debate on Channel 13. Wolcott looks good on camera, just as she looked during a series of television interviews following her sensational win against the famous defense attorney Charlie Luckman and his client's millions, a two-month trial that put Dr. Henry Martin, a surgeon accused of murdering his wife in the pool house of their River Oaks home, on death row. It was a trial no one thought she'd win, some even calling out her hubris for putting herself in the courtroom instead of turning the case over to one of her assistant district attorneys who had more trial experience. "I love when people underestimate me," she told Oprah Winfrey. On-screen now, she appears to be enjoying herself. But Axel looks like he's trying harder. The powder's worn off, and a faint sheen is showing across his chestnut skin, but it actually plays as a workingman's grace, a show of the sweat he's willing to break to win your vote. "Here's what I know," he says. "This city cannot grow without being a law-and-order city. We're losing business to Dallas, Oklahoma City, places like Charlotte, Atlanta, and Nashville, because of the current leadership. Bottom line, folks is getting robbed, left and right," Axel says, dropping into a plain speak that sounds straight out of Fifth Ward, and that manages to address the worries of the predominantly white west side of the city while using the cadence and rhythm of the inner city, straddling in a single breath a great cultural and economic divide. It's this asset, more than any other, that might ultimately get this man elected, and Reese Parker knows it. "Our ability to attract big business and grow out of our economy's dependence on oil and gas rests on a promise we can present to the world, a promise of Houston as a safe place to live and work and grow business," Axel says. "Or else this economic resurgence going on, this emergence of the 'new South,' it will leave Houston behind if we can't get crime in this city under control. When I ran the department, property crime was down nineteen percent from what it is today, violent crime down by eight percent."

The mention of the police department reminds Jay of his afternoon holed up in an interrogation room and the lingering questions surrounding Neal, specifically why his phone number was in Alicia Nowell's pager. It bothered Jay then, as it does now. Neal never answered his question. He never did say where he was Tuesday night between seven thirty and nine o'clock.

On TV Wolcott is saying, "You should ask Mr. Hathorne how he plans to pay for this 'revamp' of the police department, or any city services, when he's proposing a diversion of tax revenue into risky development ventures."

"Which was my next question, actually," the moderator says. "Mr. Hathorne, the *Houston Chronicle* has uncovered a political flyer circulating in neighborhoods to the northeast, a flyer that suggests your enthusiastic support for a development project along Buffalo Bayou, something one of your political allies, Cynthia Maddox, tried during her tenure in office. It didn't work then. What makes you think now is the right time to pick up the failed project, and what kind of commitment are you prepared to make in terms of spending the city's limited resources on private development?" Wolcott turns at the lectern, awaiting her opponent's answer. From the satisfied look on her face, Jay feels certain her camp leaked news of the flyer. Parker, he thinks. The shit stirrer.

"Let me be clear," Axel begins, leaning over the lectern and pointing his right index finger, the universal gesture of shady politicians everywhere. He should have spent a few more hours in rehearsals, Jay thinks. "The bayou development project is not now, nor has it ever been, a part of my platform."

"What then do you make of the appearance of these flyers?"

Axel looks down at the lectern, as if he might divine a right answer in the grain of its faux-wood veneer. He has his suspicions, but does he have the balls to make an accusation on live TV? "I think there may have been some confusion at a few candidate forums about my priorities," he says, stumbling over the words. On camera, it plays as evasion at best, outright fudging of the truth at worst. And then the candidates are instructed to move on to their closing statements. Axel goes first, then Wolcott gets the last word, reciting her belief in the need for "smart growth," lest a few poor decisions in city hall undermine the city's stability once again, something she believes Mr. Hathorne does not fully understand. It's smart of Wolcott to pick at this tiny pill of perceived difference between the two law-and-order candidates. On paper they are nearly identical, but saddling Axel with the cumbersome and expensive bayou project makes him appear unsophisticated about issues beyond crime.

Jay crosses the room to the armchair. He picks up his suit jacket from the day before, fishing through the pockets, inside and out. By the time he finds what he's looking for— the copy of the campaign's schedule for Tuesday, November fifth—the debate is over. The candidates are already shaking hands. Channel 13 cuts away from the debate to a promo for the nightly news broadcast, and the first image that pops up on-screen is Sandy Wolcott with her arm around Maxine Robicheaux, the lead story for the ten o'clock news: *Mayoral Candidate Reaches Out to Missing Girl's Family*. It's as if Reese Parker hand-scripted the day's narrative: the leaked question about the bayou project during the debate and then the footage of Wolcott providing succor to the weeping mother on the nightly news. No wonder Neal hates Parker. She's better at this than he is. Jay turns his attention to the campaign's Election Day schedule, searching through the messy grid for Neal's name or initials.

Some of it looks familiar.

Neal mentioned much of it in the car today.

Tuesday, he was scheduled at GOTV ("get out the vote") events in Westchase and Sharpstown; a media event in the parking lot of the Windsor Village megachurch; and visits to polling places, union halls, and community centers, among others, with time penciled in for several stops back at campaign headquarters. And of course there was the planned gathering at the home of a major donor, where the Hathorne family had plans to watch the returns with VIPs (not in Pleasantville as Sam had told their supporters). What is *not* here is any indication of Neal's whereabouts from his last GOTV stop, at a rally with volunteers at a satellite campaign office on the west side, to the time he was due at the viewing party, a window from about seven fifteen to nine thirty, which Jay finds highly odd. Neal simply drops from the schedule, right around the time Alicia was last seen. According to this, Axel's campaign manager could have been anywhere. Detective Moore probably had this information the whole time Jay and Neal were holed up in that interrogation room: Neal has no alibi.

Jay walks his TV tray and dirty dishes back to the kitchen, leaving the whole mess for tomorrow, Neal, all of it. He kisses his son good night, and puts himself to bed. He's undressed and knocked out cold by eight o'clock.

A few hours later, he hears a crash outside his bedroom window, a banging sound that so startles him he reaches for his wife's hand across the sheets—something he hasn't done in months. He sits up, feeling in the dark for his glasses, the ones he started wearing at night when he crossed forty. He's supposed to keep a pair in his car for night driving, but has only the one, which he never seems to remember he needs. They are resting on the nightstand. He slides them on and turns on the lamp beside the bed. The room is exactly as he remembers, lushly furnished, but spare of heart, the only sign of life his clothes left across the back of the armchair. The clock on top of the bureau puts the time past twelve. The house is completely still, save for the soft rumble of Ben's perpetually stuffed sinuses, which Jay can hear through their thin shared wall. The house is so still in fact that the fuzzy lamplight takes on a dreamlike quality, reminding Jay of those nights right after Bernie died, before she was in the ground even, when he would wake up not remembering any of it, when he wandered the rooms of his house, looking for his wife. He wonders if it was grief that woke him, tapping on his shoulder, demanding to be attended to.

But then he hears the sound again.

Trash cans, he realizes, the ones lined up along the side of the house.

Someone must have knocked them over.

The motion sensors in the backyard are going off, lighting up the garage and the back patio. Someone is creeping along the back of the house, setting them off, one by one. The black mastiff in his neighbor's yard is barking loudly.

Jay goes for the .38 in his sock drawer.

The bullets have scattered everywhere, some slipping to the bottom of the drawer. He feels around for them, feeling the time tick past, counting seconds by the beat of his own heart drumming in his ear. He slides two copper-tipped bullets, the only two he can find, into the cylinder, before slamming it back into place. Barefoot, he slips out of the bedroom and down the main hall and through the den to the sliding glass door leading to the patio and the backyard. There are two ADT consoles in the house, one by the back door and one in Jay's bedroom. He turns off the alarm so he won't wake his kids. Then, slowly, he unlocks the sliding door. It squeaks when opened all the way, has since they first moved in, and Jay is careful to give himself no more than a foot of space to squeeze through as he starts into the yard in cotton pajama pants and no shirt. The air outside is so damp it fogs his eyeglasses, momentarily blinding him, causing him to stab at the air with the nose of his pistol. When his lenses clear, he sees the side door to the garage is wide open. Someone picked the lock and let himself in. Jay starts toward it, and as soon as he crosses the threshold, he's hit by a burned singe in the air, the familiar smell of marijuana. He remembers the break-in at his office, just as he remembers the Nissan Z idling outside his house two nights ago. He imagines the kid with the red eyes and the taunting smile waiting for him inside the darkened garage.

He raises the .38 in his hand, flips the light switch, and takes aim.

The door to Bernie's car is standing open on the driver's side. Someone popped the trunk too. Jay stands staring at it, the bones of his rib cage rising and falling as he struggles to steady his breathing, the gun shaking at the end of his outstretched hand. He has a brief out-of-body feeling, a moment outside time itself, as if the dream he's been in for the past twelve months has come to an abrupt, heart-shaking stop, and his wife has finally come home, about to step out of the car at any moment, to ask for a hand with the groceries, could Jay bring in the soda and the charcoal. He actually whispers her name. But he's alone in here. There's no thief, no intruder, and Jay worries that he's finally cracked, that he imagined the whole thing. But then he sees the cardboard boxes strewn across the floor of the garage, each opened and overturned, picked over and picked through: boxes of stationery from his old office; some of Bernie's work papers; a video camera; and duplicates of some videocassettes that Jay recorded for his biggest cases, including the first images he took of the crude oil bubbling up in Erman Ainsley's backyard, the first interviews with Ainsley and his neighbors, as he prepared for the civil case against Cole Oil. Someone went through it all.

The girl, Lori, is standing in the kitchen when Jay stumbles in, confused by the sight of a child not his own. In a loose T-shirt and plaid boxer shorts, she is studying the contents of his refrigerator. She turns at the sound of his bare feet slapping on the stone tiles and drops the open bottle of apple juice in her hand. It bounces, but doesn't break, spilling juice in tiny waves across the floor. She is staring at the gun in his hand. "I was just getting something to drink," she says, eyes darting between Jay, Ellie's mild-mannered dad, and the .38, unable to put the two together. Lori is half Filipina and half white; her parents were high school sweethearts. She has black hair, stick straight, save for an unexpected and girlish curl at the edges. She backs into the refrigerator's open door, bumping against a ketchup bottle and a jar of Del-Dixie pickles. Jay sets the pistol on a nearby countertop, raising his hands a little to show he's harmless. "I thought I heard something outside," he says, trying to explain. "It's nothing. You should go back to

bed." He walks to the laundry room, pulling out a string mop
and a bucket. Lori leaps on her toes across the spilled juice,
skittering out of the kitchen as fast as she can . . . until Jay calls
her back. "Lori," he whispers.

When she turns, he's holding a fresh bottle of Mott's apple
juice for her. Bernie, he remembers, used to get up in the night,
both times she was pregnant with the kids. "You get hungry,"
he says, "take anything you want."

She grabs the juice and then hustles back to Ellie's room.

At the sink, Jay fills the plastic bucket with warm water.

He actually works up a sweat, mopping every inch of the
kitchen, even past the place where the juice spilled, because
it's Saturday, and he's sure no one's touched it in at least a week.
Later, the bucket put away and the mop drying in the laundry
room, he walks down the hall to his bedroom, trying to think
what to do next, what calling the police would do at this hour
besides frighten his children. To say nothing of the fact that
this recent incident, like the one at his office on Tuesday, feels
outside the bounds of what HPD is actually good at—solving
crimes with the bluntest, basest of motives, lust and greed,
hunger and hatred, cases put together as simply as stacking a
child's set of building blocks.

This was no theft, Jay thinks.

Not in any conventional sense, at least.

Someone sent that kid here, he's sure of it, just as he's sure that
the kid didn't stumble into his office by accident or opportunity. He was looking for something, something to do with Jay's
old cases. Jay remembers finding the business card of Jon K.
Lee in his office, a day after the break-in, and the car bearing
Lee's license plate idling at the curb in front of his house. He remembers Lee's connection to Cole Oil and curses that family's
name. It just barely crosses the threshold of coincidence, none
of it proven. But it's late and his wife is still dead and so this

is where it gets tucked in for the night, his unanchored rage. Somewhere, Thomas Cole is laughing at him. Plotting against him, as he did years ago, the first time he put a dangerous man on Jay's tail. *No*, Jay thinks. No cops. He called the police Tuesday night, and what good had it done him? He slides the loaded .38 across his wrinkled sheets, tucking it beneath his pillow. He throws himself across the bed, exhausted. It's after one in the morning by now. He stares at the ceiling, asking sleep to have mercy on him, trying to push out thoughts of yet another pregnancy under his roof, and all it stirs up for him.

Bernie thought she was expecting, that's how it started. The fatigue, the nausea, and the familiar, peculiar sensation below her navel, like lightning, she said, a sure sign of something growing inside her. They'd been down this road before, but Bernie was strangely ambivalent this time, thinking about her work at the school district, what a baby at thirty-eight would do to her newfound career, never mind her body. She waited a week or so for her period, lining her panties with Kotex, before finally giving in to the idea, going so far as to check the boxes in the garage for new-life inventory. They'd need a new crib and car seat, but they were covered for clothes, boy or girl. She took three drugstore tests before she finally made an appointment to see her doctor, who did an ultrasound right there in her office and then referred her to a specialist. Bernie tacked the doctor's business card on the memo board in the kitchen, the word ONCOLOGY printed clearly in black ink, the writing literally on the wall, a message Jay had missed on his many weekend jaunts home from Arkansas and the Chemlyne trial, whole hours swallowed up spending time with his kids, driving Ellie to the mall, and taking Ben to the movies, or catching up on his other cases. He hadn't noticed anything was wrong, hadn't noticed when the boxes of baby clothes went back into the garage, and Bernie never said a word. She went alone to Dr. Klotsky, on a day when Jay was at the courthouse in Little Rock and the kids were in school. Days later, it was Evelyn who drove her to and from the biopsy, sworn to secrecy. "Mama and Daddy will just worry," Bernie had said, never mentioning her husband, and Evelyn, she told Jay months later, had assumed that he knew, had even cursed him for not walking off the trial and coming home.

"Why didn't you tell me?" he says now, rolling over in bed to look at his wife. She tells him plainly, "It wouldn't have made more time." The woman next to him, it's Bernie as he first met her, at twenty-three, her hair in twin French braids. She looks tired, though, and uncomfortable, lifting her head every few seconds to find a cool spot on her pillow. Her forehead is damp, and her lips are chapped, as if she's been laboring at some task that has no end, not yet. He keeps thinking he should get up and get her a glass of water. But will she be here when he gets back? Will she wait for him? "It wouldn't have changed a thing, except throw away a case you worked years for, men and women bound to end up like me if they couldn't get to the right doctors. They needed you."

"You needed me."

"Oh, Jay," she says, sighing, reaching to touch his face.

He tries to put his hand over hers, but feels only his own stubble, the feverish skin beneath it. "Bernie," he says softly. "I'm worried about Cole."

"You did the right thing," she says. She closes her eyes, wincing slightly. She licks her dry, cracked lips. He worries she's in pain, a wave of it hitting her.

"Bernie?"

"I'm okay. It's *you* I don't know about."

"I'm going to be fine. I got a plan," he says, hot tears stinging his eyes, sliding down the sides of his face, pooling in the hollow of his neck. "I can just lie here and wait. I can wait it out, B, long as it takes. I can wait till I get to you. It's *this* I can't do."

"But you got to."

He hears the clang of a bell, a shriek and a command at once, like the ones that used to ring through the hallways of his junior high school, calling an end to the day. He turns when he realizes the sound is coming from his bedside phone. It's nearly shaking with the vibration of whatever is coming through the line. He goes to answer it, but Bernie grabs his arm. This he feels through to his bones.

"The girl, Jay," she says.

It takes him a minute to understand what she's saying. "Alicia?"

"The news, it's not good."

When he opens his eyes, Ellie is standing in the doorway to his bedroom, holding the cordless phone from her room, shivering in a nightgown. Through his window, pale blue light pours across the thick carpet, the first breath of dawn blowing in. Jay looks at the tangled sheets on his bed, touching the cold, empty place beside him. He doesn't remember falling asleep. "Dad," Ellie says, her voice quivering, on the verge of tears. Unable to say more, she simply holds out the phone. It's Lonnie on the line. Jay sinks back onto the bed at the sound of her voice at this hour. *The news, it's not good.* "They found her," Lon says.

Part Two

CHAPTER 11

Jay is dressed by seven o'clock, in a suit and tie. He wakes Ben and tells him and his sister to do the same. "Church clothes, please." But not Lori, he says. Lori is going home. The doorbell rings at quarter to eight. Ellie doesn't seem to believe he actually called Lori's mother until Mrs. King is standing in their foyer, literally wringing her hands. "Let's go," she says sternly, as Lori shuffles in her direction. Her mother grabs her oversize bag and kisses the top of her daughter's head. As the two leave, Mrs. King mumbles a thank-you to Jay. He closes and locks the front door, turning then to see Ellie standing across the room, pointedly still in her nightgown, her arms crossed in righteous anger. Behind her, Ben is in a navy sports coat and tan slacks, his big-boy uniform. He's nibbling the edge of a Pop-Tart.

"What's going on?" he says, looking between his sister and his dad. Jay doesn't answer, instead asking Ellie if she wants toast and eggs. "I can't believe you just did that," she says.

"Get dressed."

"You promised you wouldn't say anything."

"No, I didn't."

She glares at her father. "I will never trust you again."

"You told me *because* you trust me, because you wanted me to know, because, deep down, you wanted my help. Lori can hate me all she wants."

"You had no right to do that to her!"

"She's fifteen years old, Ellie! She needs her mother, not me." Which was the wrong thing to say to his daughter. He wants to take it back immediately, to say it with more grace, all of it, every word that's come out of his mouth since her mother died. He takes a step toward her, but she backs away, tears pooling. If there's an emotional place past devastation, he's looking at it right now. More than hurt, she looks stunned. "Don't touch me," she says, fleeing. He follows, calling her name as he hears her bedroom door slam. He puts a hand on the door, but can't bring himself to barge in on her. It's a line he feels he can't cross.

"Get dressed, we're leaving in ten minutes."

"I'm not going anywhere with you."

"Then don't do it for me, okay?" he says. "Don't do it for me."

Twenty minutes later, she emerges wearing a dark olive green dress.

She asks Ben, and not her dad, to help with the buttons, which tiptoe up the back of the silk bodice. It's the dress she wore to her mother's funeral, the only nice one she has. In silence, the three of them line up and go out the back door, Jay careful to set the alarm before they go. Outside, Ellie climbs

into the backseat of the Land Cruiser, leaving Ben up front
with his dad. This early, it's still cool in the car, and Jay can
see his breath all the way until they get to the 610 Freeway. He
takes it north, heading toward the neighborhood of Pleasantville.

Lonnie is waiting outside the church.

Along with reporters from every TV station in the city, including Univision and the UHF channels, standing under
umbrellas to block the rising sun, running through their lines
ahead of the cameras starting to roll.

"Cool," Ben says, seeing the media hubbub.

"Shut up, Ben."

"What?"

Ellie kicks the back of his seat. "Someone *died*."

"Oh," he says, because he will never again hear those words
and not know what they mean, the thorny path some family's
about to start down. He looks at his dad, next to him in the
driver's seat. "Is this the funeral?" he asks, sudden nerves showing. He'd had a terrible time at his mother's service.

"No," Jay says. "Just folks looking to gather. It's Sunday, son."

He pulls into the grass-and-gravel parking lot across the
street from the Pleasantville Methodist Church, Pastor Morehead's house of worship. Along the cracked concrete at the
curb, there are campaign signs, bent and softened by yesterday's rain, a cockeyed line of red-white-and-blue, waving like
parade drunks at passersby. HATHORNE FOR HOUSTON! A WOL-
COTT WIN IS A WIN FOR YOU! LEWIS ACTON MEANS ACTION FOR
HOUSTON! Jay squeezes the Land Cruiser between a Ford and
a white Pontiac, cutting the engine. The second he steps out of
his car, buttoning his suit jacket, he hears the music, pouring
through the open doors of the white clapboard church. The
hymn is a knee buckler, "What a Friend We Have in Jesus,"
daring God to say something about the organist's secular,

twelve-bar take on it. But blues is the only color for this solemn morning. Jay nods to the sisters in the parking lot. Decked out in feathered hats, decorated with plumes of purple and gold, bands of rose and coral, they walk quickly, making sure to get a seat for the ten o'clock service, their only chance to hear Pastor Morehead's sermon. Young and unmarried, he does not have children of his own, but he had coached the other two girls who'd been killed, in intramural girls' basketball and track, had held the hands of their grieving parents. Jay crosses Tilgham, meeting Lonnie at the edge of the church's lawn. She sucks down the last of a Parliament, then grinds the spent cigarette against the heel of her shoe. She's wearing a black pantsuit, too big through the shoulders. "Hey," she says, following Jay and the kids up the church's walk, whispering, "The boyfriend, he's got no alibi, by the way."

Jay sends Ellie and her brother ahead.

"Sit wherever you can," he says.

"There's no accounting for him Tuesday night," Lonnie tells him, the two of them standing in the doorway to the church. "He skipped dinner in the dorm and his roommate didn't see him until the following afternoon. And get this, the boyfriend, name of Kenny Ester, he had an eight A.M. statistics class Wednesday morning, but he never showed."

"You talked to the school?"

"The roommate. I bought him dinner."

"It would be something to look at those pager records again. Any sense from the roommate whether Kenny was in contact with Alicia on Tuesday?"

Lonnie shakes her head. "He'd never heard of her. Apparently, Kenny never mentioned word one about a girlfriend, let alone one that was missing the better part of a week." She raises an eyebrow as they enter the packed church.

The air inside Pleasantville Methodist is thick and warm,

tinted amber by the rows of stained glass windows on both
sides of the church, the sun pouring in from the east, spinning
a mélange of colors into gold. Folks are waving hand fans, Johnson's Funeral Home advertising on one side, a grim promotion
on this morning in particular. Jay and Lonnie take the two remaining seats in the back-left pew, sliding in beside Ben and
Ellie, who are squished against the congregants on the other
side. It smells of hair lotion in here, Love's Baby Soft, and aftershave, all of it together making Jay wish he had one of those
hand fans himself. He feels his armpits grow damp. He has to
reach over and touch Ben's leg to keep his son from fidgeting.
After the opening prayer, Morehead, in his deep blue robe, the
edges trimmed in gold braid, looks out across his congrega-
tion. "I think by now some of you have heard the news about
Alicia Nowell." There are a few gasps in the sanctuary, cries
of *Oh, no.* "The young woman, her body was found early this
morning along the railroad tracks behind Demaree Lane, just
a block from here." Here, his voice breaks, a wave of something
unexpected washing over him, choking his words. He pauses,
trying to gather himself. A few of the women in the church
hold up their hands in support. *That's okay,* they say. *Take
your time.* Morehead nods his gratitude for the encouragement
of his church family. "I'd like to call up one of our own now, a
man raised in Pleasantville, a good, god-fearing man, who tele-
phoned me first thing this morning asking if he could say a few
words to his people. For you *are* his people," he says, nodding
at the chorus of *amen* that follows. "Let's welcome Brother Axel
Hathorne to Pleasantville Methodist." He steps aside, ceding
the pulpit to Axel, who rises from the front-right pew, Jay's view
of which is obscured by the hats of the women in the congre-
gation. Axel, four inches taller than Morehead, towers over the
plain white pulpit. He is a gentle giant, utter humility written in
his hunkered stance. "I spoke with Maxine and Mitchell Robi-

cheaux earlier this morning," he starts, his voice dry and slow. "Beyond the pain this brings to their family, I also know this stirs up old wounds for the people of Pleasantville, in particular the families of Deanne Duchon and Tina Wells." He nods toward the girls' families in the front row. Jay can't quite see them from here, but he does see the four Hathorne sisters, Ola, Delia, Camille, and Gwen, well-kept women in their fifties, all as striking as their mother, Vivian, seated beside them. Jay is surprised Sam isn't here. Or Neal. Axel, in the same suit he wore to last night's debate, lowers his head solemnly, looking at the families. "I want to make the same promise to you that I made to Alicia Nowell's parents this morning. Whether I'm in city hall or not, whether I have to camp out in Chief Tobin's office, I will find who did this to your daughters," he says before stepping down.

After Councilwoman Johnetta Paul has a turn at the pulpit, dabbing her eyes throughout a tone-deaf declaration of commitment to the people of her district, shamelessly working in a few key phrases from her stump speech, Jay slips out of the church for a quiet moment on his own. He wants to see it for himself, the place where Alicia Nowell was found. He walks west on Tilgham, crossing Demaree to walk through a patch of tall grass and weeds, the thick strip of untended land between the neighborhood proper and the railroad tracks. There are four stakes in the ground, strung with yellow police tape meant to secure the scene from pedestrian traffic. Standing in waist-high weeds, Jay wonders why she was left *here* and not in the field where the other two girls were discovered. He can hear the church music playing. He can see the back of Pleasantville Methodist, the staff parking lot with a row of Fords and the Sunday school van. The hymn washes over the whole scene. Jay finds it easier to talk to god out here than inside any church. Away from the heavy robes and stiff pews, it's just him and blue sky. He strings together a few words for Alicia Nowell, a prayer whispered to the wind.

At the close of service, Jay meets Lonnie and the kids in front of the church, where a crowd has gathered under a cloud of hickory smoke. An enterprising neighbor has set up a barrel pit in the bed of his pickup truck and is selling hot links and brisket. There's a line forming, men loosening their ties and women dabbing their foreheads with eyelet handkerchiefs. It must have jumped fifteen degrees since the day started, a warm one for November, even in Houston. Ben asks his dad for a few dollars. Jay pulls a ten from his wallet, telling Ben to get something for his sister too. "I'm not hungry," Ellie says. Pastor Morehead, composed now, comes down the church steps to greet his parishioners. He goes out of his way to say hello to Jay, who introduces him to Lonnie and Ellie. "You a ballplayer?" he says to Ellie, asking about school, her grades, then asking Lonnie where she worships. Jay waits until he's moved on to say to Lonnie, "You should see what else you can pull on the original suspect."

"Hollis?"

Jay nods. "He's not at Sterling anymore, and he's moved around in the last few months. I just wonder if there's some clue in your old files as to where he might be. Relatives, previous employers, something. Maybe if you get a chance tomorrow, you could comb through your notes, see if anything jumps out."

"Maybe," she says, sounding stiff, distant. Jay turns to her. "I've got a job interview tomorrow." She shrugs, rolling her eyes to take the sting off it.

"At a paper?"

"At a restaurant."

And then, because she can't bear the look on his face, the concern inching toward pity, she says, "I figure I can sling drinks at night, still try to write some during the day. I'm not giving up or anything, I'll have you know. I'm not."

Jay nods absently, but is distracted by a distressing sight: his dissatisfied client, Jelly Lopez, with his wife and four-year-old daughter, Maya, walking through the crowd with a man Jay doesn't recognize. He's Mexican, like Jelly, with a Pat Riley slick-back and a very nice M Penner suit. They're with a few of Pleasantville's newest residents: Bill Rodriguez, Arturo Vega, and Patricia Rios, all clients of Jay's too. He watches as they make their way through the Sunday crowd, using the moment of community solidarity to press an agenda, crossing religious lines to make their pitch. They're shaking hands with their neighbors, making introductions, "Pat Riley" smiling covetously at everyone he meets. *Ricardo Aguilar.* Jay would put money on it.

He's about to confront the man when Johnetta Paul, likewise making the rounds, stops him. "Jay Porter," she says, dabbing at her hairline with a pink handkerchief, an act, he thinks. He has never ever seen her sweat. "I don't believe I've seen you at any of my fund-raising events this season."

"You don't need my money, Johnetta."

"Ha," she says, laughing at the very thought.

"Besides, I don't live in your district, remember?"

"Neither does he," she says, nodding across the church lawn toward Ricardo Aguilar. "But he understands the value of spreading a little goodwill around."

"Buying his way into your heart, I'm sure."

"Buying his way *in*," she says, as if this were obvious. "He knows how to play the game, unlike you, Jay. Whatever happens going forward, I want you to know I've always had the utmost respect for you. But I can't afford to ignore the concerns or interests of Mr. Lopez, Mr. Rodriguez, and their faction, not with the numbers the way they're going. Pleasantville isn't always going to look like this," she says, gesturing to the hot links and hair grease, Bobby "Blue" Bland playing on some-body's car radio, black folks as far as the eye can see. "You'd do well to take that into consideration," she says, before moving on through the crowd, shaking hands, maneuvering her way to the front of the barbecue line.

Lonnie rolls her eyes. "Is she for real?"

"Dad."

It's Ellie, tapping him on the shoulder.

She's pointing toward Tilgham Street, where the Hathornes' black Cadillac is parked. Vivian and her eldest daughter, Ola, slide into the rear as Axel climbs into the front. Frankie, the Hathornes' driver, is coming up the church walk toward Jay. He pulls off his hat, wipes a film of sweat from his freckled brow, and speaks, so softly that Jay has to ask him to repeat himself. "Sam wants you to take a ride with us to the house. Says it's urgent." Frankie's eyes dart left and right, looking at the crowd, the pastor nearby. "He said to come get you right away."

"What's this about?"

"I'm just saying what he told me to say, sir."

"I've got my kids here."

"I can take them," Lonnie says, as Ben arrives holding a hot link wrapped in a slice of white bread in each of his small hands. "I mean, if you need it."

Jay looks at Ben, then Ellie. "You guys okay?"

Ellie nods, and Lonnie puts an arm around Ben.

Jay turns to Frankie. "I'll follow you."

The ride is just a few short blocks.

He parks his Land Cruiser behind the Cadillac, right in front of Sam Hathorne's house. Axel's out of the car first. As he makes his way up the front walk, he doesn't look at Jay. Vivian and Ola decline to exit the car, and Frankie remains behind the wheel, letting the Cadillac's engine idle softly.

Jay lingers in his car, hesitating for a few seconds, a bad feeling in his gut. Finally, he climbs out, heading for the house. Inside, he finds Sam and Axel in the living room, Sam with his back to the door, standing by the bar, pouring himself a drink. "Absolutely not," he's saying to his son. "You stay as far the hell away from this as possible, for as long as possible. Wolcott gave us a head start with the press. She swears she had nothing to do with it, has promised to recuse herself from any supervision of the case." He's still wearing his hat and his overcoat.

"What's going on?" Jay says.

Sam throws back the scotch. "Neal's been arrested."

"I still think I should go down there," Axel says.

"Arrested for what?"

"Obstruction."

"The Nowell girl?"

"They think he knows more than he's saying."

"He's in custody?"

"Downtown."

"They picked him up at his house, six o'clock this morning, not even an hour after the girl was found," Axel says. "No way this isn't Wolcott's doing."

"I wouldn't have thought she'd go this low," Sam says.

"Then it's Parker."

"Either way, he's in trouble."

"They're holding him?" Jay asks, slightly incredulous.

Sam pours another drink.

"Slow down, Dad."

"He'll bail out today," Sam says. "They'll arraign him tomorrow."

He throws back the drink, setting the tumbler on the bar top. With his back still partially turned, he pauses in silence, taking a moment that only he knows the meaning of, staring at family photographs along the wall, his grown kids. Jay has never seen him so retiring, so waylaid by an emotion Jay can name only as dread. Sam turns to look at him, lifting his gray fedora to perfect its position on the slim pompadour on his head. "I appreciate what you did for Neal the other day. But he needs a lawyer *now* more than ever."

Jay looks between the two men, both of whom are staring back at him, waiting for him to do the simple arithmetic of why he's been summoned here.

They can't be serious, he thinks.

"He needs a criminal defense lawyer," he says.

"What he needs is someone to get him through the next thirty-six hours," Sam says. "Wolcott swore she gave us a head start, no leaks to the press, but—"

"We have no reason to trust her."

"And, one way or another, by tomorrow, the paper will have the story."

"If not sooner," Axel says. "I can't see any reason why she and Parker would fabricate a charge and then not call the goddamned newspaper themselves."

"We don't know they did that, Axe."

"The woman has a whole prosecutor's office at her disposal. And twenty-six days before the runoff, my campaign manager and nephew gets arrested for withholding evidence in the investigation into what is now a *murder* in the very neighborhood where her opponent was raised. It's front-page news."

Axel is pacing, fuming.

"We don't think the charges are of any substance," Sam says calmly. "We just want to get out ahead of the story, protect Neal, and also protect the campaign, of course. But the clock is already running on this thing."

"Where's Marcie, your press aide?"

"You're the only one we've told," Axel says.

"Me?"

"We need you to do us this favor."

"People *like* you, Jay," Sam says. "They trust you, think you're a man who's always on the right side of things. Neal walks into a courtroom tomorrow, you at his side, and it sends a message to the city that a man, a good man, a man Pleasantville has chosen to honor and to protect their interests, is standing by Neal. It sends a message that a whole community is standing by the Hathornes, a message to Wolcott in particular, making her question her tactics, how far she wants to push things, what with a voting bloc at play."

"You want to use me as a prop?"

"I want you to do me a favor."

"It's thirty-six hours," Axel says. "They're never going to take this to trial. They might even drop the charges before this goes to court, after squeezing a few front-page stories out of it. I'm fairly certain this will all blow over tomorrow."

"We just need to help my grandson, who, smart as he is, does not know as well as you and I what can go wrong inside a police station, let alone a courtroom, how quickly things can get out of control. We just need to get Neal out of that police station, and out of this whole mess safely," Sam says. "You have a son, don't you, Jay?"

"Stop," Jay says. He doesn't need that kind of pitch.

"I'm begging here, Jay, and I *don't* beg. And I never forget a favor."

"You must have at least fifteen lawyers you could call, all with more criminal experience than me, all more than willing to take your money."

"And don't think the press doesn't know it too," Axel says.

"It's a bad play." Sam is shaking his head. "I don't want anyone thinking I'm buying Neal's way out of something, or that we're hiding behind money, or that he has anything to hide at all. If we bring a gun to a knife fight, people will make more of it than it is, start asking questions about Neal."

"Questions like what?"

Jay looks at Sam, and at Axel.

They're too quiet, he thinks.

"You know where he was Tuesday night?"

"He says he was working," Sam says.

"Work that he didn't bother to put on the campaign schedule?"

"I have no reason not to believe him."

"They found his number in her pager, you know. Did it ever occur to you that the cops might be right, that Neal knows more than he's saying?"

"It's a stunt, Jay."

"I hate to back you into this," Axel says. "I hate to trade on our past."

"But there's no one else for this," Sam says. "You as Neal's lawyer in the courtroom, you'll put an indignant spin on the arrest, messing with Neal on a bullshit obstruction charge while there's a killer still out there. It's a thing of gold you got, really. A reputation like yours can be worth a lot of money."

"I don't want your money."

"That's the beauty of it," Sam says, smirking a bit and slurring his words, looking, despite the circumstances, almost pleased with himself. "You're clean, son. Not a soul in Harris County thinks Jay Porter does anything for money." He reaches into his coat pocket for a pack of cigarettes, wobbling a bit on his bad leg, ignoring his son's advice to slow down on the scotch. "But you and I know better, don't we, Jay?" he says, lighting a cigarette. He exhales, blowing a hot breath of nicotine and liquor in Jay's direction. "For what it's worth, I think Jelly Lopez is a fool for turning his back on you, and I am alarmed by the number of plaintiffs who've been swayed by Ricardo Aguilar's promise of a pipe dream, more signing that petition every day I'm told. I'd certainly be willing to do everything in my power to stem the tide, reverse it even." He comes closer, moving his short bowlegs like fragile twigs, using the edge of a nearby chair to steady himself. "How much have you laid out on Pleasantville so far? It must be in the hundreds of thousands by now. Tell me, Jay, has it hit a million yet?"

Jay puts out a hand, anything to make him stop talking.

"Thirty-six hours," he says.

He'll take the deal on the table, his name and likeness in exchange for Pleasantville, his retirement plan, his ticket out. *I can wait*, he thinks. *I can wait it out, B, long as it takes.* He nods toward the open bottle of scotch. "Pour me one of those too."

"**Everything okay?**" Lonnie asks, when he comes for the kids.

"I'll let you know tomorrow."

He's known Lonnie a good fifteen years and Neal Hathorne a matter of days, but Neal is his client now, and, for better or worse, there are things he's not at liberty to discuss, not now at least. He thanks her for the afternoon, walking his kids outside to the curb. Over the roof of her crumbling, redbrick duplex, he can hear the hum of the Cowboys and 49ers game playing on the outdoor speakers at the Ice House on West Alabama, the bar's patio abutting the rear border of Lonnie's weed-choked backyard. The howl of beer-soaked cheer floats over the wooden fence. They're smoking links and brisket on a grill behind the bar's kitchen. Starving, Jay takes the kids to James Coney Island for chili dogs on the way home. Walking into the house later, he tells them he needs them up and at 'em early tomorrow, something big going on for him downtown. "I don't have school, remember?" Ellie says, clearing away the leftover breakfast dishes without being asked, either out of genuine contrition for her outburst this morning or to soften this reminder that she was suspended from school. Jay had completely forgotten. He sighs, trying to figure just how this is going to work. He doesn't want her home alone, not with the mysterious man in the Z on the loose. "I guess this means you're coming with me," he says. "Dress for court."

"What does that mean?"

"No jeans."

CHAPTER 12

The formal charges of obstructing a government operation into the investigation of the death of Alicia Ann Nowell are to be read at one thirty this afternoon, sandwiched into a docket filled with DWIs and domestic-assault charges, and any other leftovers from the weekend arrests. Jay has arranged to meet Neal an hour before that, when most court watchers are out to lunch. He's to come alone, no campaign staff, as too many of them together at one time might as well be a campaign event; Neal on his own will draw far less attention.

Jay will be waiting.

Until then, he's holed up at his office on Brazos.

Eddie Mae has made a proper fuss over Ellie, bringing her glasses of lemon tea and letting her use the desktop computer.

Ellie's been asking Jay for an e-mail account for a few months now. "Maybe," he tells Eddie Mae, "it's something you can set up for her," as Jay doesn't know the first thing about how one would go about sending a message from one computer to another. He stows himself away upstairs, in the conference room, picking through the old Cole Oil files, still trying to see if anything's been stolen. A little after ten, he hears Eddie Mae coming up the stairs, the ancient wood steps creaking beneath her weight and the thick soles of her Clarks. About halfway, she stops and demands he meet her there, holding out a box full of invoices when he starts down the stairs. "It's everything. Every receipt for which we were billed on *Ainsley v. Cole Oil Industries*, from trial prep through litigation, years' worth."

"Thanks."

"And Jelly Lopez called," she says with a sigh, leaning her weight against the carved stair railing. "He'll put it all in writing, but he's officially informing you that he's releasing you of your duties as his attorney. His words, not mine. He wants his name off the suit, and he wants copies of any of the official case filings with his name on them, as well as a copy of his initial interview, his client forms, and his deposition. You got six more calls just like it. Rodriguez, Vega, Patricia Rios, plus Fred Poynter, Ned Werner, and Jim Wainwright."

That last one hurts. "Jim? Are you sure?"

"Don't shoot the messenger."

He tells her not to copy a thing. "Don't promise anybody anything."

"Yes, sir."

He takes the box of invoices back into the conference room.

He spreads them out across an open corner of the table. Hotel receipts, rental car slips, office supply delivery notices, plus a whole accordion file folder's worth of billing from experts and extralegal help. Most of it is organized by date. It

was late April 1982 when he went to meet a Nathan Petty in
Arizona. Petty's name was on a list of former residents of the
neighborhood across from the old Crystal-Smith Salt Company and the salt mines where Cole Oil had been illegally
storing crude oil for years. Like dozens of others, Petty and his
wife, Hannah, were bought out by a development company
that for months had been courting local residents, pressing
them to sell the homes they'd lived in for decades. The company originally said it was planning to build a shopping mall
on the site, then a beauty college. Erman Ainsley, stubborn
as shoe leather, was the only one who refused to sell. It was
their chance meeting, his and Jay's, that led to the lawsuit—
Ainsley's tales of a pretty young real estate agent sashaying
through the streets of his neighborhood, batting eyelashes
through sales pitch after sales pitch, that allowed Jay to lay
the final piece in a puzzle he'd been worrying over for days.
Crucial to proving the conspiracy was the testimony of Ainsley and the other men and women living across from the salt
mines, detailing the deception of one Elise Linsey, represen-
tative and sole employee, it turned out, of Stardale Development Company. The development company was nothing but
a front for Cole Oil, a scheme to cover what it had been doing
when crude oil started coming up in Ainsley's neighbors'
backyards; Elise Linsey was a plaything of Thomas Cole's, a
lover and disciple. It just had to be proved that the shell company was pushing for the home sales, faking countless property inspections, never mentioning the toxic ground just a
few feet below the surface, where black oil was seeping from
the unstable salt mines.

Which is why Nathan Petty presented a problem for Jay,
when he finally located Petty living in a suburb of Phoenix.
Mr. Petty seemed to remember a different sequence of events
from every single one of his former neighbors—or rather he

couldn't with any consistency remember the sequence of any events at all. Had Stardale pressured him to sell, or had *he*, in fact, been the one to reach out to Stardale? An improbability that left open the possibility that Stardale was not a vulture swooping down on unsuspecting homeowners at the behest of Cole Industries, but a legitimate business. "The thing is, I just can't remember how I got that gal's card," Petty had said to Jay. A good defense lawyer could make a meal out of this single crumb, if he or she was crafty enough. Petty's shitty memory was enough to win the case for Cole. Jay had been all set to take the man's deposition when he suddenly hesitated, stepping outside to call his wife for guidance. Two minutes later he was standing on the man's front porch telling the hired court reporter, who'd arrived late, that he wouldn't need her services after all. She shrugged and lugged her machine back to her Toyota Celica. The Phoenix-based agency billed Jay for the day anyway, because he'd canceled at the last minute. He is right now staring at the invoice, the only proof that he ever called a court reporter, with the implied intention to depose a witness, to the address of Nathan Petty—a man who, as far as opposing counsel was concerned, had never been found. "Do it for them," Bernie whispered to him that night, when he made it back to Houston. *Do it for your clients.* She told him he shouldn't tank his whole case because of the faulty memory of a senile old man (who died before a verdict was ever read, before anyone but Jay knew he had been residing in Phoenix for years). She came close to suggesting he had a *moral* obligation to omit this one fact in service to a higher truth, more substantive and meaningful than what usually manages to squeeze its way through the cracks in the rules of law. But Jay Porter was the one with the bar card, the one who took an oath to uphold those very rules, including but not limited to the rules of discovery. He was the one who knew better.

He folds the yellowing invoice, lining up the edges with precision, and tucks it into the inside pocket of his suit jacket. The agency itself surely has its own copy. Someone would just have to know to look for it. The question is whether or not Thomas Cole hired someone to break into Jay's office and snoop around for proof, whether he already knows about Nathan Petty.

Neal is late, of course.

Jay glances at his watch, then at his daughter, who is leaning against the tiled wall of the seventeenth floor of the courthouse, hands in the pockets of her denim skirt, perhaps thinking she should have listened when he told her to bring a book. "I'm bored," she says, staring down the tiled hallway at the lawyers lugging scuffed briefcases, and at the spectators and jurors loitering near the washrooms. He smiles at her, trying not to show his nerves, embarrassed by them in some way, a fish afraid to swim. He hasn't been in a courtroom since Bernie died, hasn't been in this very courthouse since before Ellie was born. It's warmer than he remembers; the lights are brighter too. But the smell is the same: coffee and industrial-grade disinfectant, and the musk of fear. It brings back a thousand memories, petty theft and solicitation, misdemeanor assault and the like, criminal cases that were the bottom rung of his practice for years. "Hey, you know about computers, right?" he says to Ellie, remembering her hunched over Eddie Mae's desk. "You want to do your dad a favor?" Ellie comes off the wall with a shrug. Jay reaches for a slip of paper from his jacket pocket. On it, he scribbles the name Ricardo Aguilar.

According to the state bar directory, a copy of which Jay keeps on a shelf behind his desk, Mr. Aguilar has been licensed to practice law for only three years and lists as his primary field "criminal law," which Jay finds odd to say the least. He has no idea if Aguilar has ever tried a *civil* case, let alone a class action suit as big as Pleasantville's. But at least here, in the *criminal* courthouse, he can access Aguilar's entire history as a defense lawyer. He sends Ellie down to the third floor. "Log on to one of the terminals and type in this name," he says. "Tell one of the clerks to print out everything that comes up."

Ellie nods, a tiny smile cracking through the facade of teenage weariness. She seems surprised, excited even, to be asked. "I can do that," she says.

"I know."

Jay watches her go, and he waits.

He's already been into and out of the 209th District Court twice, once looking for Neal when he first arrived, and then again fifteen minutes later so he could introduce himself to the judge's clerk, because he remembered that's how it's done. From her, he received a copy of the official complaint against his client, filed by the D.A. handling the matter, plus what little discovery exists at this stage. All of it–the arrest report, Detective Hank Moore's statement on the issue of probable cause, and notes from his interviews with Neal Hathorne and Tonya Hardaway, field director for the Hathorne campaign–is barely five pages long, but not without its share of surprises.

"You fired her?" he says when Neal finally arrives in wrinkled slacks and shirtsleeves, looking as though he's just come from the campaign office. He stares at the papers in Jay's hand and then makes a grab for them.

"Where did you get this?"

"Come with me," Jay says, pulling him down the hall.

Inside the seventeenth-floor men's room, he checks stalls one through five, all empty, then puts his back against the washroom door, turning to face Neal.

"You fired your field director a day after she talked to Detective Moore."

"I would have fired her for talking to my grandmother without running it by me first. You can't do that kind of shit in the middle of a campaign."

"It looks bad, Neal," Jay says. "It looks like obstruction."

"This is all Reese Parker, you understand that, don't you? The arrest, using Wolcott's office to file charges on *me*. This will go down in history as one of the boldest moves that's ever been pulled, having the opposing candidate's campaign manager arrested," he says. "My kids will be talking about this."

"Tonya gave them a copy of the schedule, Neal. Tuesday night, all key campaign staff can be tracked by the minute, everyone except you, from about seven to nine thirty that night. So again, where were you, Neal?"

Neal rolls his eyes at Jay's earnestness, his honest belief that there's anything to this little judicial charade. "Let's just get this over with," he says, pushing past Jay, through the washroom door and into the hall.

They are not even speaking to each other when they enter the courtroom, which is packed after lunch. Gregg Bartolomo is here, having received a tip in time to hear the judge call the first item on the afternoon's calendar. But the sight of Maxine and Mitchell Robicheaux in the second row of the gallery is Jay's first clue that something is wrong. Why, he thinks, are they here for an arraignment on an obstruction charge? Maxine, in a white T-shirt like the one she wore the morning of the search, is staring at Jay. The judge, nearing seventy, his pale, freckled pate shining under fluorescent bulbs, enters and takes a seat at the bench, calling the Hathorne matter first. "Do we have counsel present?" he says. He looks over the black rims of his reading glasses.

"Yes, Your Honor," Jay says.

"Is the defendant present?"

"Yes."

"Okay, approach, please."

There's a small wooden gate between the gallery and the well. Jay holds it open for Neal, nudging him to the defense table on the left. On the other side of a lectern, the assistant district attorney handling the matter has his head in a stack of paperwork at the state's table. "All right," the judge says. "I've got here *State of Texas v. Neal Patrick Hathorne.*" He looks up. "Appearances?"

"Jay Porter for the defense."

"Matt Nichols for the state, Your Honor."

The judge looks at Jay. "Is your client ready to be arraigned, Counselor?"

Neal speaks before Jay has a chance to. "No, Your Honor."

Jay turns to his client. "What are you doing?"

"Mr. Porter?"

"Your Honor, can you give us a minute?"

"A very short minute."

Neal, the former law student, lowers his voice. "I want to defer my arraignment," he whispers to Jay. "The runoff is in twenty-five days. If they still want to charge me, they can charge me after Axel's elected mayor."

Fine, Jay thinks.

That's way past his thirty-six hours.

"Judge, on the matter of the obstruction charge," he says, "we'd ask for a deferred arraignment on this. My client has already posted bond to the court."

"I'm sorry," the judge says, looking down at his papers. "I'm looking here at a charge of capital murder." He looks up, ripping off his reading glasses, staring down at Jay and his client. "What are you two talking about?"

The assistant D.A., Mr. Nichols, a sandy-haired lawyer in his thirties, raises a hand. "That's my fault, Your Honor, Mr. Porter doesn't have a copy of the amended complaint. This came down from the grand jury this morning."

"What's going on?" Neal whispers in disbelief.

Jay feels his stomach sink. "They think you did it."

"What?" He looks at his lawyer, then the judge. "Are they serious?"

"They have an indictment."

"This is absurd."

"Don't say another word," Jay tells him.

"*Stop* this," he hisses at Jay.

"I can't."

From her desk beside the judge's bench, the clerk holds a freshly stapled stack of papers. Jay, stunned, doesn't move right away. It's Nichols who crosses the courtroom to the clerk's desk, retrieving the amended complaint and delivering it to opposing counsel himself. Jay stares at the first page, the words laid out in black and white: they're charging Neal with first-degree homicide.

"Are we ready to proceed, Mr. Porter?" the judge asks.

"Uh," Jay says, stammering. "Just a minute, sir."

He turns to his client, who, for the first time since they met, is speechless. He appears to be in shock. Behind them, Gregg Bartolomo is scribbling away in a notebook. Jay can see him out of the corner of his eye. Ellie too. He hadn't noticed her before now. She's back from the clerk's office with a quarter-inch pile of white papers in her lap, and she's staring at her father. His breath jagged and quick, he seems fragile in a way she's never seen. "Dad?"

"I'm fine," he says, swallowing the sour taste in his mouth.

He looks at Neal and then the judge.

"Yes, Your Honor," he says finally. "We're ready to proceed."

"No," Neal says, shaking his head. "No, I want to postpone."

Nichols, the A.D.A., objects on behalf of the state. "Consider-ing the gravity of the new charge, Your Honor, I don't see how that's prudent."

"I agree," the judge says.

Jay listens as the judge reads the official charge into the record:

"*State of Texas versus Neal Patrick Hathorne. Case number HC-986723.*

"*It shall be noted for the record that the defendant is hereby charged with one count of criminal homicide, in violation of Texas Penal Code 19.02, a felony to wit the defendant did knowingly and intentionally cause the death of one Alicia Ann Nowell.*"

Neal, panicked, looks from the bench to Jay. "What the hell is going on?"

"They think you did it," he says again.

"Based on *what*?"

Jay hasn't a clue. For whatever questions Neal has yet to answer about Tuesday night, Jay can't see how they rise to the level of a capital murder charge. It makes it hard *not* to see the situation the way Neal does, as a political stunt.

"How does your client plead, Mr. Porter?"

"Not guilty," Neal says indignantly, practically shouting it.

"Not guilty, Your Honor."

"You have an argument as to bail, Mr. Porter?"

Neal grabs Jay's arm. "I am *not* going to jail."

In front of the bench, Jay stammers, trying to line up a simple argument. He hasn't done this in over a decade, and never in a capital case. "The defense would, uh, request that Mr. Hathorne be released on his own recognizance."

"The state can't allow that, Your Honor."

"Mr. Hathorne poses no flight risk, Judge. He's got roots in this community, is at this very moment, in fact, deeply involved in a citywide election, the details of which may be of some interest to Your Honor, since the candidate running against my client's employer runs the very department that brought these charges," Jay says, his words picking up speed, remembering the power of calling someone out in open court, the truth trotted out onstage. "Absent compelling evidence against Mr. Hathorne, it certainly gives the appearance that someone is gaming the system to gain an advantage that doesn't have the least bit to do with administering justice for Alicia Nowell," he says.

"Are we doing opening arguments now?" Nichols says.

"Save it for trial, Mr. Porter. Is the state ready to set a date?"

"Not at this time, Your Honor."

"Bail is set at five hundred thousand," the judge says. As he calls the next case on the calendar, a bailiff approaches Neal to handcuff and print him for processing. He is absolutely terrified, shaking all over. "Call my grandfather," he says to Jay, who, having walked in here to go through the motions of a misdemeanor arraignment, has just laid out, in open court, an explosive defense argument, one that Gregg Bartolomo is still busy getting down on paper. As Jay starts out of the courtroom with Ellie, he comes, for one tense moment, face-to-face with Maxine Robicheaux. Red-eyed, her voice low and quivering, she whispers, "Shame on you," before turning and walking out of the courtroom.

CHAPTER 13

Gregg Bartolomo catches them on the courthouse steps, along with a handful of television reporters, some court watcher having tipped off the local stations while Neal was in lockup waiting for a wire transfer of fifty thousand dollars from his grandfather's bank to a bail bondsman. Court staffers move aside, making way for the multiheaded beast moving down the stairs, the swarm of press and rubberneckers, Jay at the very center of it, his client on one side and his daughter on the other. Gregg, the seasoned newspaperman, doesn't let more than a few inches get between him and his subjects, making notes on the scene, letting the girls in heels and the men in shiny suits do the dirty work, shouting vulgar questions over their microphones and one another: *Did you have anything to do with* *the death of Alicia Nowell? Was she working for your uncle's campaign? Did Axel try to stall the investigation?* Gregg notes every twitch of Neal's eyebrow, every upward curl of his lip, but is smart enough to simply observe at this point, leaning in at just the right moment to whisper in Jay's ear, "You let me know when you want to tell your side."

Jay reaches for Ellie's hand, squeezing it tight, keeping her close as they push through the crowd. He turns to Neal. "Where's your car?"

"On Congress."

"Then you're coming with me," he says, as they start for Jay's car parked in the lot directly across the street.

He gets Neal as far away from the courthouse as fast as possible, taking whole blocks at forty miles an hour, Ellie riding shotgun. She keeps turning around every few minutes to sneak a peek at their passenger, the man in khakis accused of murder. Jay's cell phone rings the second they pull into the driveway outside his office. It's Lonnie. "You do realize you're going to be on the front page of tomorrow's paper. What in the world have you gotten yourself into?"

"I have to call you back."

Inside, he tells Neal to have a seat in the parlor. The phones have been ringing nonstop, Eddie Mae reports. Gregg Bartolomo. Channels 2 and 13, 26 and KCOH. The entire news community is already on to the story, must be if within half an hour it's already trickled down to Lonnie, who's now at a Birraporeti's on Gray, interviewing for a job at its bar. It's a quarter to three, and Ben will be of out of school soon, a circumstance Jay hadn't accounted for. He hadn't expected the day to take the turn it has, from misdemeanor arraignment to a looming murder case. Sam Hathorne is on his way to Jay's office at this very moment. Jay leans over his desk, dialing Mrs. King's number into his office phone. Her house is ten minutes from Poe Elementary School. Ellie stands on the other side of the desk, watching her dad. She's been asking a version of the same question since they left the courthouse. "Who was that woman?" she says, meaning Alicia's mother. "Why did she say that to you?"

When Alice King answers the line, Jay asks for a favor, running through a routine they've traded back and forth for months. Would she mind picking Ben up from school, and maybe swinging by to get Ellie too? She could take them back to her place. Jay promises to bring dinner later, if she wants.

There's an unexpected stretch of silence on the other end.

"Actually, I don't think Lori is going to be spending so much time with Elena anymore. I just don't think the girls are the best influence on each other."

"Oh," Jay says.

He's caught off guard at first, and then furious.

"Right, 'cause my daughter got yours pregnant."

"Excuse me?"

"Dad!"

"Never mind," he says. "Forget it."

He hangs up on Mrs. King.

"Eddie Mae!"

He calls her into his office and begs her to take Ellie to pick up Ben from school, to try to kill an hour or so. "You all right here on your own?" she asks.

"Yes, ma'am."

"Dad, what's going on?"

"Just go, El."

He locks the front door when they're gone and turns to Neal, sitting on the antique sofa, newly humbled from his brush with lockup, his clothes damp and wrinkled with sweat, circles of it spreading under his arms. He leans forward, head in his hands. "I can't believe this is happening."

"Do not listen to a word Sam says. You need a lawyer, and you need a lawyer *now*. Forget the campaign, your uncle. You need to protect yourself."

"I don't understand how this is happening."

"I'll tell you how: your phone number in her pager, the fact that yours was one of the last calls before she went missing, and the gap in the schedule, not to mention your failure to disclose any of this to Detective Moore. It's circumstantial, and it's thin, but it's there. They don't have any physical evidence. But the autopsy isn't set until tomorrow. That could change, I guess."

Neal shakes his head at what Jay is suggesting.

"I never touched that girl."

There's a loud knock on the front door.

Here they come, Jay thinks. He unlocks the door and lets in Sam and Axel, but blocks Marcie, the communications director, and Stan, the campaign's finance director, from entering the building. "They can wait outside," he says, closing the door on them and relocking it. He turns to Sam and Axel. "Your time is up," he says. "Neal needs a criminal lawyer, and a damn good one."

Sam's face is damp with perspiration.

Axel too looks as if he might have run all the way here.

"Can we just sit somewhere and talk?" he says, looking out the window, where Marcie and Stan have a view of this confidential meeting from the front porch. Jay shows them down the hall to his private office. Neal is the only one who sits, picking a chair directly across from Jay's desk. The others choose to stand. Because the heating system is funny in this place, Jay's office is always a good ten degrees warmer than the rest of the house. Sam, sweating, removes his overcoat, tossing it onto the back of a chair. He pulls out a pack of cigarettes.

"I'd rather you didn't," Jay says.

"Tell me you have something to drink at least."

"You're not staying."

Pacing the office, Axel seems utterly mystified, shaking his head over and over again. "You can't take someone to trial on what they have."

"You can if you don't care if you win," Jay says. "This isn't about a trial."

"The D.A.'s office hasn't even set a date," Neal says.

"They're going to let this sit out there," Sam says, "on the front page of the newspaper, until the runoff. It's a goddamned death sentence for the campaign."

"But why me?" Neal says.

"They saw an opportunity, and they took it," Sam says.

Jay asks Neal again. "Where were you Tuesday night?"

"Wait a minute," Sam says, stepping forward. "Before we get into potentially privileged information, we need to know that you're on board."

"With what?"

"We want you to represent Neal."

"I'm not a criminal lawyer."

"You *were*."

"Stickups and joyrides, sure, kids caught with a quarter ounce of weed. But I can't try a capital *murder* case." He nearly laughs at the idea, looking around the room, waiting for the others to join in, to hear how absurd it sounds. "Look, if you want to call their bluff, call their bluff. Hell, get an injunction to stop the election, invoke your right to a speedy trial, and hold them to it. Make Wolcott and Parker put up or shut up. But you don't need me for that."

You can almost hear a pin drop.

Neal looks at his grandfather. "Can we do that? Stop the election?"

"This is America," Jay says. "You can sue anybody over anything."

"Jesus, that's good," Axel says. "It's brilliant."

"It's dangerous, son," Sam says, looking uncharacteristically tentative and unsure. "We could lose the small lead we have. We could *lose*."

"We lost our lead the second they indicted Neal. But Jay is right. This is exactly the way this needs to be approached, a crusade against an injustice, to Neal personally, and to the city politically," Axe says, taking control of his campaign, maybe for the first time. "That's why it's got to be you, Jay. Former civil rights activist, from rabble-rouser to lawyer with a conscience, working the courts in the people's best interests. You'd almost be as big a story as the crime itself."

Jay winces at the thought, the crassness of the offer.

"I'm not interested."

"Otherwise, it's some Johnnie Cochran–type dream team."

Sam shakes his head. "We can't play this slick."

"I couldn't agree more," Axel says.

Jay shakes his head, adamant. "I can't go to trial, okay?"

"Yes," Sam says, his voice taking on an edge. "I think there are a number of your civil clients who are afraid of that very fact. Look, we need you, Jay, so let me make plain that my offer yesterday, to help squash the defecting faction in Pleasantville, the ones that want resolution quick and are willing to trade you in to get it? Well, it goes both ways, Jay. I'm just as happy to use my influence to give my blessing to Ricardo Aguilar."

Jay, in no uncertain terms, tells Sam to get the fuck out of his office.

Sam nods, unfazed. He doesn't move, though, not right away. "Let me ask you something, Jay. Do you really think my grandson killed Alicia Nowell?"

"I never touched that girl," Neal says again.

Sam holds out a hand to quiet him.

"Do you think for a second that with Neal up on these charges HPD is going to continue to look into the matter, to find out what really happened to Alicia Nowell, let alone what it has to do with Tina Wells and Deanne Duchon?"

"They're not even putting the cases together," Axel says.

Jay knows that too. He has a sudden flash of Maxine Robicheaux in the courtroom, the way she looked at him, as a man with no grief in his heart apparently, no clue what she was going through. *Shame on you*, she said.

"We can make this easy on you, Jay, get you all the help you need behind the scenes, the best defense lawyers and consultants in the state."

"No," Jay says. "I'm not the one you want."

Sam is grossly disappointed in him, almost to the point of disdain.

"I hope, for your sake, you don't come to regret this."

"That's enough, Dad," Axel says. He grabs Sam's coat. "I don't hold it against you, Jay, any of it. This is a mess, that's all. This is an absolute mess." He and Sam turn to go. Neal lingers, waiting, it seems, until his family is down the long hallway, almost to the front door, before he works up the courage to look at Jay one last time. Whatever he wants to say, it gets distilled, in speech, to the two plainest words: "Thank you."

Lonnie calls the house after dark. "What the hell happened?"

"Waded in too deep, that's what," he says, pushing pork chops, swimming in grease and onions, in a pan on the stove, the phone cradled to his ear. "Sam is holding Pleasantville like a golden carrot above my highly overextended head."

"How much have you shelled out so far?"

"Enough," he says, calling over his shoulder for his kids to come to the table. "Maybe it's for the best," he says to Lonnie, "this whole thing coming to a head. Maybe Pleasantville deserves a better lawyer than me. I hadn't been in a courtroom in over a year before today, and I was an absolute mess."

"That's not what I heard," she says. "Gregg Bartolomo said you fought back in there. That's right. Guess who wants to play ball now? But only if I get him on the phone with you. He wants to do a Sunday feature on you, the case."

"Tell him 'No comment.'"

"The killer's still out there, Jay," she reminds him, and he resents her for saying it. What does she expect him to do about it? "I'm not a trial lawyer anymore."

"Then what are you?"

"Hungry." He nods to Ben and Ellie, entering the kitchen, whispering to Ben to get forks on the table, Ellie to set out the cups. "I got the kids here, Lon."

"Okay, okay," she says. "I only called to follow up on Hollis."

"Right," he says, plating up the pork chops and black-eyed peas, potatoes roasted with carrots and tomatoes. He holds up a finger to the kids, to give him just one minute. Ellie has been remarkably uninterested in the telephone since she's called Lori's house at least ten times today and received not a single return call.

"You asked me about contacts?" Lon says. "Family?"

"Yeah."

"Well, most of them, from what I remember, are all down in Needville, but when I went back through my notes, I did find a brother in Houston. Well, Aldine, actually. He lives in an apartment complex off the 45 Freeway."

"Beechwood Estates."

"That's it."

"Tell me, what's the address, the apartment number?"

"It's here, hold on." Jay can hear her blowing smoke on the other end, can picture this whole scene playing out over beer and cigarettes. "It's 27-B."

So they had the wrong apartment.

Rolly had let himself into 27-A.

"Hmmph," Jay says.

He tells the kids to go ahead and get started. Then, walking the cordless into the living room, he asks Lonnie to run Hollis's description by him again. White male, she says, between thirty and thirty-five years of age. Sandy, almost reddish hair, clipped in the front and kind of long and shaggy in the back.

The white guy in the blue Caprice; he can't believe it.

He'd been standing right in front of him.

"That his name hasn't floated around any of this is unbelievable," she says. "It's shitty police work. But it's even shittier journalism. His name is all over the original police files on the first two girls. Mike Resner and his partner *talked* to Hollis, for god's sake, talked to his employer and his ex-wife. I don't know why the *Chronicle* is chasing this Neal thing down a rabbit hole," she says. "Unless you know something I don't."

"I don't."

Jay lowers his voice. "But it wasn't Hollis's semen, you said."

"Still, it's a door that's open."

"Neal Hathorne knew the other girls," Jay says, because he thinks he might actually sleep tonight if he can make it all fit in a box, put it high up on a shelf somewhere. Maybe there are a lot of questions Neal needs to answer in a court of law. Lonnie disagrees. "Please. He practically grew up out there. Anyone who ever spent more than a few days in Pleasantville knew those girls."

"You think it's a hit? On the family?"

"I think Reese Parker is a snake," she says. "But even she can't pull off something like this all on her own. There's some shit tied into this that we don't know the half of." Through the phone, Jay can hear the honky-tonk music from the Ice House floating over her back fence. "I got the job, by the way," she says.

Neal's arrest leads the ten o'clock news.

Jay checks Channels 2, 11, and 13 on his bedroom TV, all while skimming through those court records for Ricardo Aguilar. His legal history is shockingly thin and seems to mostly revolve around a single client by the name of T. J. Cobb, who's been in and out of lockup for years. On TV, each station is running the same written statement by Axel Hathorne, former police chief, about the arrest of his nephew and campaign manager: "It's important to remember an indictment is not a conviction. The mistake that's been made here, this rush to judgment in the middle of a heated campaign season, will be apparent in due time. My thoughts and prayers are with the family of Alicia Nowell, and I will redouble my efforts to find her killer." The ABC affiliate, Channel 13, has an exclusive interview with the girl's parents, standing in front of their wood-and-stucco apartment complex in Sunnyside, complete with the requisite neighborhood fools in the background, craning necks to get their nappy heads on television. Wolcott makes her second appearance at the parents' side, along with Pastor Morehead. She reiterates her determination to recuse herself from any decisions regarding the Neal Hathorne case, stressing that the charges caught her off guard as well. When asked how she thinks this will affect the tenor of the campaign going forward, Wolcott says she doesn't care a whit about the election right now. "My prayers are for justice for Alicia Nowell, and peace for her family." Jay stares into Maxine Robicheaux's red, watery eyes. The scene is painfully familiar. It takes him back to that last hospital room, Bernie staring at the television screen, day in and day out, waiting on a miracle that never came, feeling for the first time the limits of her maternal reach, the dark corners she couldn't make safe. It's for her, really, that he gets himself out of bed. It's for Bernie that he grabs his pants, hanging off the end of the bed, sliding them on first and then his shoes. He leans into the hallway and tells the kids to put on some clothes, something warm. He glances back at the television—Channel 13 is now playing a thirty-second Wolcott campaign ad—and turns it off.

Neal Hathorne lives in a clapboard cottage on a narrow lot in West U., not that far from Jay's house, actually. It's a cozier choice than he would have thought for a bachelor, and it makes Jay wonder if there isn't a woman in Neal's life, a romantic past other than rumored dates with dead girls. Jay parks the Land Cruiser by the curb. From the backseat, Ben asks, "What are we doing here?"

"I need to talk to someone."

"But why are *we* here?"

It's after ten on a school night. It's not ideal, he knows. But it was too late to call someone out to the house. "I could stay with Ben," Ellie had said.

"Not anymore."

He hasn't told either of his kids about the break-ins, the one at his office, or the one much closer to home, in their garage. But part of keeping them safe is making them feel so in their own minds.

"It won't take long, I promise," he says, cutting the engine.

Neal is home alone, having been, for the time being, banished from the campaign. He answers the door in blue jeans and a T-shirt. He looks at Jay, then the two kids, Ben in long johns and a Cowboys T-shirt, shivering in the night air. Bernie bought the jersey as a joke a couple of years ago, just to get a rise out of Jay, not realizing, of course, that she would up and die one day, and her son would never take it off. He sleeps in it most nights.

"Can we come in?"

Neal holds open the door. Inside, the house looks more appropriately like that of a man who, until tonight, was rarely home. The few pieces of furniture are covered in stacks and stacks of papers and campaign paraphernalia: mailers and T-shirts and oversize posters with Axel's face, plus county records and polling data. And there's a sour smell coming from the kitchen, like milk left out on the countertop. "Is there somewhere we can talk?" Jay says. "Alone?" Neal shrugs and starts out of the room. Jay tells Ellie and Ben to hang tight. Then he follows Neal down a narrow hall into a small study, clogged with more papers. Jay shuts the door behind him. Neal leans against the edge of a cheap chipboard desk, the kind that comes in a dozen different pieces in a box. There's no history in this place, this cheerless house miles from Pleasantville.

"What are you doing here, Jay?"

"Where were you Tuesday night?"

"Not your problem, remember?"

"I can't help you if you won't tell me."

"Hiring you was my grandfather's idea, not mine."

"Where were you?"

"I didn't touch that girl."

"Where *were* you, Neal?"

Neal looks down at his feet, in white sneaker socks.

He chuckles darkly to himself. "This is so fucked up," he says, his voice watery and weak. "If they go through with this, we're going to lose everything."

"*You're* going to lose everything."

Neal looks up, his dark, tea-colored eyes gone soft with emotion.

Man to man, it looks for all the world like he's on the verge
of tears.

"If you're my lawyer, it's confidential, right?"

"You graduated law school like me, you know as well as I do."

"Anything I tell you stays in this room?"

"If you want it to."

Neal looks down at the socks on his feet. When he looks up
again, he gives Jay a wan, almost pleading smile. He holds out
his right hand. Jay looks at it, then reaches out with his own.
The two men shake on their agreement, hammered out in the
simplest way. Neal leans back against the desk again, accidentally knocking papers onto the floor. "I went to see my father,"
he says.

CHAPTER 14

Lori doesn't show up at school Tuesday morning, at least she's not in their usual meeting place at the bottom of the school's front steps, just to the right a little, which is ordinarily Ellie's signal to get out of the car, to know that it's safe to cross the gauntlet that is the front walk of any American high school. This morning, she senses in an instant that yet another thing in her young life has changed, that another loss is looming. She lingers, reluctant to get out of the car.

Jay is running late.

He hates to push.

"I'll be here, okay?" he says, reminding her that he has to get into the office early today. "I'm the one who's picking you up today. I'll be here, El."

She turns to her dad and nods. A hand on the door's handle, she says, "She never called me back. I don't understand why she won't call me back."

"We'll talk about it tonight, I promise."

She nods again and exits the car with her backpack, her black Starter jacket puffed up around her ears. From the dry cleaner's parking lot, Jay watches her cross Westheimer at the light, watches her pass through the crowd of teenagers, walking through the doors of Lamar High School on her own.

When he arrives at his office a half hour later, there's a car parked in front.

Not the black Cadillac he might have expected, but a plain Town Car, midnight blue, with a thin silver stripe along the sides. It's not one of Rolly's either. Jay parks his Land Cruiser in the drive alongside the house, grabbing a briefcase off the passenger seat as he exits. He tucks it under his arm, a bruised and battered caramel-colored satchel he bought on a trip with Bernie to Veracruz right after the Cole verdict, their only real vacation in twenty years. He'd had to dig through his hall closet to find it. It's empty, except for a few Bic pens and a half dozen legal pads. He'll have to get used to the weight as it grows, swelling with briefs and file folders, witness interviews and the like, the raw materials for the building of any court case, like *State of Texas v. Neal Patrick Hathorne*, which, as of eleven o'clock last night, is Jay's to win or lose. As he approaches his office's front gate, the rear passenger-side window of the blue Lincoln slides down slowly, revealing Cynthia Maddox.

"Jay," she says.

He stops cold.

God help him, he still feels a jolt at the sight of her.

Her hair is different, the first thing he notices. It falls in a soft shag around her face, the color less artificially blond than he remembers. And here, in middle age, the handful of extra pounds the society pages loved to gossip about when she was mayor have come to serve her well. Her face is dewy, plump, and wholly unlined, a few brushstrokes from the girl he met thirty years ago.

His first impulse is to run.

Instead he says her name, because it's all he can think to do and because silence itself would be a lie. Whatever the fallout, their history has a sound, a ringing in his ear, the hum of a song's final note. He still remembers the night they went to see Lightnin' Hopkins at the Pin-Up Club in Third Ward, the night she first kissed him in the cab of her pickup truck. He remembers the grassy smell of her hair. He remembers everything, in fact, including the months she let him sit in a jail cell, never once explaining herself, or even coming to say hi.

"They're not here," he says, guessing she didn't come all this way for him.

Hoping, actually.

He is careful not to look directly into her eyes.

"I'm not looking for Sam. I'd actually rather he not know I was here." He hears the click of the door lock releasing. "Come on, take a ride with me."

What is it, he thinks, with people trying to put him in cars?

"I'm busy," he says, opening the front gate.

As he starts up the walk, she steps out of the car, calling after him, embarrassed, it seems, to be on her feet, asking him to turn around, to give her even the smallest unit of his time. "God damn it, Jay, don't make me chase you."

He'd like to see that, actually.

He'd walk in circles just to make her dizzy.

"There somewhere we can talk for a minute?" she says.

She's wearing a pale gray pantsuit that nearly matches her

eyes and, on her right wrist, a line of thin gold bangles, which she fingers nervously. Jay has never seen her so anxious, so undone by whatever emotion is stirring behind those blue-gray eyes. If he had to put a name to it, regret would come closest. She looks toward the door of the Victorian, but hesitates, as if she can't bear to cross the threshold into his private space, an intimacy they both know she forfeited long ago. The house, the porch swing—they're too much for her. She tells her driver to wait for her a block over on Travis. The driver, a white man in his fifties tanned the color of Jay's briefcase, eyeballs Jay from behind the wheel.

"You sure?"

"I'm fine," Cynthia tells him, watching and waiting as he puts the car in drive, pulling away from the curb. To Jay, she shrugs at the pomp and circumstance, how far she's come from the girl in peasant skirts, the one forever carrying a stack of leaf-lets, trying to rap her way into SNCC, SDS, and Jay's fledgling political groups, a journey he rode shotgun. She nods toward the Town Car, traveling up Brazos Street. "He used to be my bodyguard, in Washington. I ran into a lot of trouble after that Anita Hill thing, death threats," she says, rolling her eyes, but looking away, kind of, so that he can see she doesn't take it as lightly as she's pretending to. "I hate it, frankly, hate the whole idea of being watched, fussed over. But the White House in-sisted. Don't let anybody tell you folks on the left aren't hard-core. They can pull some scary shit."

"But you already knew that."

Cynthia smiles. "Let's walk," she says.

"I have a meeting at nine."

"That's why we need to talk."

Jay sighs, opening the front gate. He gestures down Brazos, pretending to let her take the lead, all the while ensuring that he never turns his back to her. They get all the way to the door of the Diamond Lounge before she stops, ducking inside the club's tiny entryway, stepping over cigarette butts and a broken pocket comb. The brick alcove, painted black and red, throws a dark shadow over this whole conversation. She keeps looking over her shoulder, again and again, as if she expects someone to be watching, as if someone somewhere is *always* watching. Jay glances in the same direction and sees a Chevy Caprice, blue, parked not far from his office. He tries to get a look at the driver, but can't.

"You can't take this case," Cynthia says.

"Why?"

"Because you'll lose."

"Thank you."

"No, I mean you will *lose*, Jay."

"Or maybe I'll find out who killed Alicia Nowell."

"You've already lost if you think this has anything to do with finding that girl's killer. Listen to me, you do not want to let Sam suck you into this."

"This is between me and Neal."

"Don't be stupid."

"Neal didn't kill that girl."

"I'm not worried about Neal, Jay. I'm worried about you."

"I don't understand. Axel's your candidate. If Neal goes down, so does he." He stares at her, trying to read something in those changeable eyes, gray, then blue, then gray again. "Unless, of course, you're playing both sides."

"You don't know what you're talking about."

"Is that why you don't want Sam to know you're here?"

"I *appointed* Axel police chief, remember? I fought like hell for him when the good ol' boys wanted one of their own," she says, laying out her racial bona fides, still bitter about the beating she took in her second term over the perception that she was not a friend to black folks, which had deeply hurt her brand as someone who had herself overcome prejudice to become the first woman to lead a major American city. So that's what this is, Jay thinks, the real reason she's publicly standing behind Axel. Cynthia Maddox is protecting her legacy.

Jay has followed her political rise over the years.

How could he not?

She was in the local papers, of course, when she was mayor, and her ouster was dissected for months, the blame resting with her about-face on issues of social equality and race or her inability to protect the city from the oil bust—depending on the side of town where you lived. A lot of folks held her personally responsible for the economic collapse of the mid-80s, as if the mayor were an inconsiderate party guest who'd failed to warn them that the keg was running dry. She let no grass grow beneath her feet, though, quickly working her historic election into a job at the EEOC in Washington, advocating for equal rights for women in the workplace during the Reagan administration, which was not as much as it sounded, she once quipped in a profile that ran in the *Post*. It was Reagan's successor, George H. W. Bush, who plucked Cynthia from bureaucratic obscurity to hand her a subcabinet post in the Department of Labor, a reward for her testimony during the Anita Hill hearings: that Clarence Thomas had never touched *her*, had never told a funny joke, let alone one that was the least bit risqué. It was a career boost that sputtered the second Bill and Hillary moved in. Jay knows Cynthia well enough to make an educated guess about her designs for her future: some local or statewide office that will shoot her back to D.C., a congressional seat maybe, or the U.S. Senate—a feat for which she'd need to, on paper at least, clean up her image among her more colorful prospective constituents. "This is all about you, isn't it?" he says, putting it together. "It's always about you."

"Oh, Jay." She sighs, exasperated, but also angry as hell. "Are we still going to be doing this twenty years from now?"

"God, I hope not."

"You have no idea how much I wish I could go back and do things differently."

"Like selling me out to the feds?"

"Tell me you don't still believe that."

"Tell me it isn't true."

She lowers her head, fingering those gold bangles again and making a grand show of how much it hurts, this lingering wound between them.

"I loved you, Jay."

"And what am I supposed to do with that?"

"I was a kid, a coward," she says. "But I have never intentionally set out to hurt you, Jay. And I am telling you now, *don't* do this."

"Who better than you would have known that saddling any candidate with the Buffalo Bayou Development Project, true or not, would burn political capital faster than a pile of hay? Did you slip them the idea about the bayou?"

"Listen to yourself, Jay."

"You talk to Reese Parker?"

"I don't even know Parker."

He has no proof she's lying, but neither can he shake the suspicion that she's up to something, that Cynthia Maddox is still, all these years later, double-dealing. Years ago, during the run-up to the longshoremen's strike, Cole Oil's stake in which Jay was in the perilous process of uncovering, he could never shake the idea that Cynthia was talking out of both sides of her mouth, working Jay with one hand while stroking Thomas Cole's dick with the other, delivering whatever Cole asked for in exchange for a spot on his gravy train. They had been close back then, Cole and Cynthia. "You want to do something for me, Cynthia?"

"I want you to *listen* to me."

"Get me a face-to-face with Thomas Cole, that's what I want," he says, playing on her incessant need to make things right between them. "No middlemen, no lawyers, just me and him in a room. Can you do that?"

"Why?"

"Just tell me when you have him, when and where."

"Jay," she says, as he pushes past her.

He won't stop for her.

He can't afford to.

By the time Jay makes it back to his office, Sam's black Cadillac is parked out front. Sam and Neal are already inside. They've been served coffee with sugar and cream, and offered what little resides in a kitchen that hasn't served a client in a year: rye crackers and some of Eddie Mae's leftover beans. She meets Jay at the front door. "There something you want to tell me?"

"Come on," he says. "Let me introduce you to our new client."

"Good lord." She reaches to touch up her hair.

Once formal introductions are made, she stays up front while Jay walks Neal and Sam back to his office. "I understand we have a deal," Sam says, not bothering to take off his overcoat. Jay tells him to have a seat, but Sam ignores him. Neal stands too. "Axel's meeting with the League of Women Voters this morning, else he'd be here too. The timing is brutal, but it'd look a lot worse if he canceled. But as you know, he's behind this, one hundred percent."

"*Neal* and I made a deal," Jay says, making clear the boundary that exists around a lawyer and his client.

Sam nods, reaching into his coat pocket for his cigarettes, getting one all the way between his thin lips before he remembers Jay's rule about smoking.

"What about the injunction?" he says.

"Let's consider that the nuclear option. I think there are a couple of steps between here and there," Jay says, glancing at Neal, who is still wearing the jeans from last night and has his hands in his pockets. Jay hasn't mentioned a word about Neal's father. That was also a part of the deal. "I've got a plan in place."

"Okay," Sam says, looking at his grandson, reaching for the young man's shoulder, almost turning to hug the boy, he's so relieved. "I'm going to put the best team behind you," he tells Jay. "Andrew Hastings out of Dallas is interested in second chair. I'll get you the best investigators, the best experts I can find."

Jay shakes his head.

He already put his team together, he says, late last night. After Ellie showed him how to make a three-way call, he put Lonnie on the line and then his old friend Rolly. Lon, the former *Post* reporter, agreed to work her police contacts and plumb the depths of her notes and knowledge of the Duchon and Wells cases, and Jay asked if she could get her hands on an early copy of the autopsy report for Alicia Nowell from the coroner. "Medical examiner," Lonnie had to tell him. "In Harris County, it's the medical examiner." And Jay nodded and said, *Right,* his inexperience already showing. Rolly, the former private investigator, would do pretty much anything Jay asked, whatever the case needs, starting with pinning down the whereabouts of the onetime suspect, Alonzo Hollis, last Tuesday. "If I'm doing this," Jay tells Sam, "I'm doing it my way."

"With *my* money?"

"You want me, you take them," Jay says, adding that Lonnie Phillips and Rolly Snow have something he's not likely to find anywhere else on short notice. "My trust."

"I don't know about this."

"I think Neal has made his choice."

"I want Jay, Pop."

"It's not just about you, Neal. Your uncle's campaign, everything this family's worked for, it could all go up in smoke if this thing is handled wrong."

"This was your idea, Pop."

Sam rounds his shoulders, trying to loosen them, testing the feel of a situation that's out of his control. He reaches for his cigarettes and then again remembers: Jay's house, Jay's rules. "So what now?"

"You let me do my job," Jay says. He lays out a few guidelines. "Publicly, I'd put no distance between Axe and Neal, don't send the message there's anything wrong, anything to hide, anything you should be ashamed of. And no cops, no press, don't talk to anyone, no matter how tempted you are, Axel too. Understand?"

Sam nods, sliding his gray fedora on his head.

"I'll messenger a check for the retainer," he says.

He looks once more at his grandson, who crosses the room and throws his arms around Sam. The two hold each other tightly, their foreheads pressed together, Sam whispering words that Jay pretends not to hear, as Neal starts to cry softly. "It's okay, son, it's okay," Sam says. "We'll make it right." He kisses his grandson's forehead before stepping back, forcing distance between them. Glancing at Jay one last time, Sam offers a curt nod and walks out.

"Why didn't you tell him?" Jay says.

"I thought that was between me and you."

"For now." He leans his head into the hall, checking to see that Eddie Mae has seen Sam out of the building. "But if you were with your father on Tuesday night, then he's your alibi, the man who's going to save your ass."

"I wouldn't count on it."

"I don't know that you have much of a choice." Jay leans against the front edge of his desk. "Why don't you want Sam to know?" He dips his head, trying to meet his client's eyes. "Whatever you're hiding, it's going to come out, and in court if this thing goes to trial."

"He hates him," Neal says finally. "No, worse than that actually."

"What do you mean?"

"To Sam, I don't have a father. He doesn't exist."

"Why'd they fall out?"

Neal shrugs. "I was born too late to know."

"Sam never mentions it?"

"He never mentions *him*. Sam Hathorne has only one son."

"Does Axel know what happened?"

"I never asked him. It's off-limits in the family, the whole subject."

"And I don't suppose you told Axe about the meeting?" Jay says, getting a picture now of how deep the secrets in this family go. Neal shakes his head, and Jay sighs, frowning. "So only three people know where you were Tuesday night, between seven o'clock and the viewing party in River Oaks? Me, you, and your father." He crosses his arms, thinking, trying to picture what could have happened to so tear the family apart. "What did you guys talk about?"

"Does it matter?" Neal says, looking up. "I was with him, okay?"

"Will he vouch for you?"

"If you can find him."

"How did you?"

Neal, uncomfortable with this whole line of talk, shifts his weight several times in the hard-backed chair. He rubs his hands along the front of his jeans and then stands suddenly, walking to the window across from Jay's desk. "I knew who Allan was. My grandmother, she said I had a right, damn anything Sam had to say about it. I guess over the years, despite the problems, they've had some contact. I told her I needed to see him, and she gave me an address."

"Why did you *need* to see him?"

Neal turns from the window but doesn't answer.

"I meet him, I'm just gon' ask him the same."

"Anything he tells you is a lie."

"Okay, let's start with this then. *Where* did you meet him?"

"Third Ward," Neal says. "A little gin joint hole in the wall. He must have had a gig or something."

"Your father, he's a musician?"

"You're joking, right?"

Neal pinches his brows together, a bemused expression on his face, surprised Jay hasn't already figured it out for himself. He steps away from the window. "A.G.," he says, playing the name slowly. "Allan George Hathorne . . ."

Jay stands for a long time, leaning up against his desk. He doesn't get it, not at first, not until his eyes land on the book-shelf a few feet from where Neal is standing, Jay's record collection sitting right there, his mint copy of *Belle Blue* facing out. "Wait a minute . . . are you telling me A. G. Hats is A. G. Hathorne?"

"One and the same."

"Your father?"

"Yes."

"Sam's son?"

Neal corrects him. "I told you, Sam has only one son."

"I have to find him."

"Good luck."

"*We* have to find him," Jay says, trying to make sense of Neal's silence, his stubbornness. "Have you forgotten you're looking at a capital murder charge?"

"I didn't do it."

"Oh, good, make sure you say that really loudly on the stand."

"I thought you said this wouldn't go to trial."

"I never promised that."

Jay turns and grabs a sheet of paper from his desktop. The seal of Harris County can be seen from all the way across the room. "What is that?" Neal says.

"A search warrant. The D.A.'s office is asking for a blood sample, they want you down at Central by noon. I can try to stop it, demand a hearing."

"Won't that make me look guilty?"

"So will your DNA on a dead girl."

"I thought you believed me."

"Don't want any surprises, that's all," Jay says, staring at Neal, at his bloodshot eyes. "You sure you never met her? All it takes, man, is a single hair, a single cell anywhere near that girl for you to be looking at a conviction."

"I never said more than a few words to her," Neal says in frustration over having to state this fact for the hundredth time. Jay makes the point that he had to have gotten her number somehow, that Alicia must have, in fact, called Neal herself, leaving her pager number. "Any idea why she would have done that?"

"I'm telling you I never touched her."

"And Deanne Duchon? Tina Wells?"

"What?"

"You heard me."

"No, I don't think I did," Neal says. "'Cause if I heard you asking me if I *murdered* Deanne Duchon and Tina Wells, then we're done here. I'll call Pop right now and tell him I made a mistake." He backs away from Jay, heading for the office door. Jay reaches for his arm to stop him. Neal slows, turns around.

"I believe you," Jay says. "I do."

That afternoon, Neal returns to work at campaign headquarters with a Band-Aid on his left arm from a phlebotomist's prick, and Jay sets out to find Allan George Hathorne, Sam Hathorne's second-born son, going on the only clue he has: the Playboy Club. It was here, a Third Ward shotgun house made over for a tiny dance hall, that Neal laid eyes on his father for the first time. Last Tuesday night, at a quarter after eight, the place was as empty as it is now, when Jay walks in at one o'clock in the afternoon. He's surprised to find the place unlocked and unoccupied, the only inhabitants being last night's empties: glass pint bottles and beer cans and crushed plastic cups. The interior, during daylight hours, almost resembles an abandoned church, with white clapboard walls and dark wood floors. The air in the room smells like stale corn chips and burned cigarettes, dried sweat and beer. There's a narrow stage in one of the front corners of the room, across from the front door. Onstage is an upright piano, black, the covers missing from several of the wooden keys. Somewhere Jay hears water running. He moves toward the sound, finding his way to a kitchenette at the back of the club. In a small porcelain sink, a metal bucket sits under the running faucet, filling with water. A rag mop rests against the wall nearby. The kitchenette's screened back door opens, and an older black man in a ball cap and stained carpenter's pants enters from the tiny scratch of a backyard. He's carrying a second metal bucket, this one filled with blue rags. "Ain't supposed to be back here," he says. "Place is closed."

"Looking for somebody that's all."

"That right?" the man says, setting the bucket on the countertop next to the sink. He turns off the water, running his other hand through the soapy bucket, stirring suds. Then he lifts both buckets by the handles and pushes past Jay and out of the kitchen, sloshing water on the tips of Jay's dress shoes. Inside the main hall, he sets the buckets on a tabletop and starts walking the room, turning chairs upright. "You know a man by the name of A. G. Hats?" Jay asks.

"Who don't?" the man says, wiping down the chair bottoms.

"He play here sometimes?"

"He don't play nowhere that I know of, not anymore."

"But he comes around sometimes?" The older man shrugs, cleaning a sticky table with one of the blue rags. "You know where I can find him?"

"Who's asking?"

"His son's lawyer," Jay says, thinking that this might move things along.

Jay had recognized him the second he saw him; the silhouette in the screen door was a near-perfect match for the one on the cover of his one and only album, a shot of the piano player backlit in blue. It's the ragged expression, the rough, unshaven skin, nearly as gray as the tufts of hair sticking out of the back of his ancient Oilers cap, the deep lines around his eyes that Jay doesn't recognize, time and circumstance having left a gulf of distance between his face and his older brother's. He looks a good ten years older than Axel. But it's A.G. all right, Jay is sure of it, if only because the man is trying so hard to hide it.

"Allan George Hathorne," Jay says.

A.G. turns slightly, looking up from the janitorial work.

"I owe you money or something?"

"I told you, I'm Neal's lawyer."

"And that's got what exactly to do with me?"

"You read the paper, sir? Your son's in a lot of trouble."

"Ain't seen the boy in twenty years, then all of a sudden you're the second person in a week to remind me I have a son." He turns back to his rags.

"That's right, Neal was here last Tuesday night."

"So he was."

"What'd you guys talk about?"

"The weather."

"What was it, the reason you fell out with Sam? Was it money?"

A.G. points to his bucket of rags, this low-rent gig. "You think I give a shit about money?"

"Must be something, man, to make you disappear like this."

"Sam's the one disappeared."

The words kind of catch Jay funny, filling him with a son's longing.

"What do you mean?"

He gives a cool shrug. "Nineteen forty-nine was a long time ago."

Yes, it was, Jay thinks.

Jerome Porter would have been twenty-one years old, if he had lived. Newly married and a young father, he might have made his way to Houston, the big city, hunting one job or another, might have rolled on the tiny hamlet of Pleasantville, a dream on stilts, wood-frame houses going up as fast as savings could be laid down. For a moment, Jay gives in to the fantasy, the boyish wish to rewrite history. He pictures his father scrounging up enough money to put down 10 percent on a future for his wife and child, a glittering city life far from the rural racism that killed him, that left him bleeding on a red-dirt country road.

A.G. dabs at his damp forehead with the back of his hand. "Some part of Sam just never left, those early days, I mean," he says. "The old way of doing things, with him at the head and everyone else walking two steps behind."

"Was anyone else here, Tuesday? Anyone else see you and Neal talking?"

"Place don't open till nine," A.G. says. "Owner lady, she come to work the bar around ten, sometimes she brings her son. I don't know no one else to come around. I only been working here a week, won't be here a week after this."

"Neal said you had a gig?"

"You're looking at it."

Jay watches the man dipping rags in the soapy water, wiping down the tables. "You really don't play anymore?" he says, finding it hard to believe.

"What you want with me, man?"

"Name's Jay Porter."

"Oh, I know who you are. Pleasantville's savior," he says mockingly. He stands over the bucket, wringing a stream of gray, steamy water from the rag in his hand. "You ain't ever gon' see that money, you know. The chemical company? You ain't figured it out yet, Mr. Porter, but the game is rigged."

"This isn't about me. I'm here for Neal."

"Murder," he nods. "I read it."

"You're his alibi," Jay says. "He needs you to vouch for the fact that he was with you last Tuesday night, from sometime after eight until almost nine o'clock, the longer you stretch it the better. I don't know what you talked about and don't need to know right now. I just need to know that if asked, you'll say he was here with you, and that if he was, there was no way he killed that girl."

"Is Sam paying you?"

"I'm *Neal's* lawyer, Mr. Hathorne."

Taking that for a yes, A.G. says, "Then I don't want nothing to do with it."

"This is about your son, not Sam."

"No, it's not," the older man says. "If Sam's got his hand anywhere in it, then it's all about him. I can promise you that. Man don't do nothing if it don't come back around to helping him. You're a fool if you think otherwise, a fool to trust a thing out of Sunny's mouth. I got out, and I'm not looking to go back."

He dips the rag in the suds again, starts in on another table.

Jay watches the older man, trying to make sense of one of the greatest blues piano players Texas ever created sopping tables, not even fifteen feet from a decent upright. "You know I saw you once, little place down past Edna, right off Highway 59. You played some Wilson 'Thunder' Smith, played it hard."

"Did I now?" A.G. says, showing little interest.

"*Belle Blue*, that's one of my all-time favorites."

"Bring it in, I'll sign it. Cost you twenty bucks, though."

"Look, if you don't want to testify in court, I can get an affidavit at least, get you to sign something saying essentially the same thing about that night."

A.G. looks up, sighing. "Look, I'm sorry for the boy, I am."

"Just a time and a place. That's it. That's all we need."

"Huh-uh," A.G. says, shaking his head.

"We'll subpoena you either way."

"Giving me a head start, that's all."

Jay shoves his hands into his pants pockets, his fists pressing against the seams, trying to understand what could have possibly passed between Sam and A.G. to taint A.G.'s relationship with his one and only son. Jay, who didn't have a father, didn't have a choice in the matter, says, "You're making a mistake."

A.G. slides the ball cap off his head.

He lifts the bottom of his T-shirt to wipe sweat from his forehead. "I never did much for my son. Some of that's on me, but a lot of it ain't," he says, glancing around the one-room juke joint. "Best I could give him now is a little bit of advice. You want to know what we talked about, Mr. Porter? I'll tell you the same thing I told him. 'Get the hell away from Sam while you still can.'"

CHAPTER 15

Lonnie meets him at the house after dark. Jay leaves a plate of baked chicken, peas, and cabbage for her on the table. The kids ate early, with him, and went to their own rooms, Ben to his comic books and his PlayStation and Ellie to whatever her breakup with Lori King has freed her to do. Homework, he hopes. Maybe Lori's indiscretion might actually land Ellie on the honor roll this semester. *Belle Blue* is playing on the hi-fi when Lonnie walks in, lugging the same beat-up cardboard box full of her old notes, this time with a six-pack of Shiner Bock resting on top. "A. G. Hats," she says when she hears the music, the black-and-blue keystrokes. She sets the box on one of the kitchen chairs.

"You a fan?"

Lonnie shakes her head. "Amy is."

The thought of it, any little thing about the woman she's both in love and enraged with, makes her smile, despite herself. "She plays it once a week, I bet."

"You know anything about him, why he quit playing?"

"He's dead, isn't he?"

"No," Jay says, leaving it at that.

Lon takes off her jacket, a red quilted vest with cotton sleeves, draping it on the back of a kitchen chair. She thanks him for the food, inquires if there's any pepper sauce or chow-chow for the cabbage, tearing into half the plate while standing up. Jay cracks open one of the beers and hands it to her.

"You get it?" he asks.

"I got it."

Then, swallowing, she tells him he's not to quote a word of it. "You never saw this, okay? If even a period or comma is different from whatever you get from the state in discovery, I don't want to hear it. You never saw a thing from me, understand? Resner did it as a favor. He's pissed as hell about all of it, being pushed off the case, the way they're playing this whole thing, not bothering to link this girl to the others." She reaches beneath the flaps of the cardboard box. Sitting right on top is a thin manila envelope. She picks it up and hands it across the table with a piece of advice. "Take a deep breath first."

Jay opens the envelope. Inside, he finds a copy of the autopsy report following the death of Alicia Nowell, age eighteen. The first thing he sees is a color picture of her pulpy, bruised face, swollen around the eyes. The flesh at one corner of her mouth has been torn, the flap of skin pulled back like a bloody curtain to show her chipped right incisor, covered with dirt and tiny bits of dried grass. Her eyes are open, staring out at him, the mud-coated skin above her eyebrows knitted into a tiny, woeful *w*. Jay stumbles back at the sight, dropping the handful of papers onto the floor. "Jesus Christ," he mutters.

"I know," Lonnie says.

"The other girls, they weren't beaten, were they?"

Lonnie shakes her head, picking up the pages.

"What is all this?"

Jay turns at the sound of his daughter's voice.

She's standing in the doorway between the hall and the kitchen, still in her school clothes. "You can't be in here right now," he says. "Go back to your room." She stands on her tiptoes, glancing over his shoulder at the pictures.

"Is that her?"

"Go," Jay says, gruffer than he meant to be. She backs out of the room, Lonnie watching her leave. Jay puts two hands on the back of the nearest chair to steady himself. He feels the chicken, cabbage, and peas turn to raw sewage in his insides. *Jesus Christ.* What in the world did he do, bringing this shit into his life, this monstrous, bruising death into a house that has already seen its fair share? What was he thinking? "Hey," Lonnie says. "You okay?"

He nods. But it's a lie.

Lonnie lays her drawings from the first two cases faceup next to this recent autopsy report. She moves the pieces around so that the photographs of Alicia Nowell and the images of the first two girls are all side by side.

"Check the time of death," she says.

Alicia Nowell, according to this report, was far enough along in the stages of decomposition to prevent the medical examiner from making more than an educated guess as to how long her body was hidden in the weeds: five days.

"She was already gone," Jay says.

"The whole time they were searching."

"She was already dead."

He looks at the images, the three girls lined up in a row.

"Why is this one different?" he wonders.

Lon doesn't know. "For whatever reason, Alicia was the only one who was beaten. She was killed almost right away and found in a different place."

"The railroad tracks behind Demaree Lane."

Jay pulls out a sheet of paper from her cardboard box, flipping it over to draw a quick, crude map of Pleasantville. The railroad tracks are an L-shaped ten-block stretch from the open field where the other girls were found.

"Who called it in? Sunday morning?"

"It was a transient who found her, guy pushing a shopping cart," Lon says. "When he saw the girl, he ran to the Methodist church nearby and knocked on the back door. It was one of the pastors who called the cops."

"Where are we with the boyfriend?"

"I put in another call to the roommate. I may have implied that I'm writing a story for a newspaper, and I may have been intentionally vague about which one. We'll see how much he likes to see his name in print. If I get him talking, he may be more loose lipped with me than a cop. We'll see."

Jay stares down at the medical examiner's work.

Lonnie says, "She fought like hell." She points to the M.E.'s notes about defensive wounds, the fact that there may be DNA under her fingernails.

"What about semen? He left that behind with the first two."

"Yeah, but it rained Saturday, remember." She taps her copy of the autopsy report. "No semen, no nothing."

"So by the time they found her, early Sunday morning, most of the physical evidence would have been destroyed, no way to trace any of it."

"Which makes this a hell of a lot easier to pin on Neal."

"And also explains why they're keeping the cases separate,"

Jay says. "If they put the girls together, they have to test his blood against everything. If it's not his semen in the first two cases, it makes it harder to prosecute for the third."

Jay feels his cell phone buzz once in his pocket . . . his signal.

"That's Rolly," he says. It's a little after six. He's got less than thirty minutes to get across town. He pulls out his car keys. "You okay staying here?" he asks Lonnie, not wanting to assume, or to treat her like a babysitter.

"I can make some calls from here," she says. "I'm just happy to have a gig again." Then, just so they're clear, she asks, "We are getting paid for this, right?"

"Yes," he says, forgoing any mention of the fact that, for now, at least, any and all money on this case is coming out of his own dwindling bank account. Sam messengered the retainer to the office this afternoon, just as he said he would. Twenty thousand dollars in black ink, paid from an account at Sam's bank. Jay, A.G.'s bitter words still in his head, put the check in his top desk drawer.

The campaign to elect Sandy Wolcott the next mayor of Houston, Texas, is in full swing, buoyed by the recent reports of the arrest of Hathorne's nephew, the architect of his campaign. Gregg Bartolomo's front-page article in this morning's *Chronicle* was, in Jay's opinion, irresponsibly vague about Alicia's employment history, calling her a "volunteer campaign worker," giving the reader the impression that she was working for Neal, who is now charged with her murder. There is likely to be champagne popping in some dark corner at tonight's fund-raising event. Reese Parker ought to put Bartolomo on the payroll.

They rented La Colombe d'Or for the night. The valet is set up at the end of a long brick walkway. There's already a line of cars in front of the hotel and restaurant, including a row of

black Town Cars, all registered to Rolly's Rolling Elegance,
Inc., a trick he pulled once before on a job. "Wasn't nothing
to it," he said to Jay when he reported in late this morning.
He got his girl to call—a woman's voice raising fewer red flags
than a man's—and offer free car service from an ardent supporter; and Wolcott's people, violating a handful of state
campaign finance laws, said yes. They might not get more
than an hour or two out of it before somebody realizes it's
a Trojan horse, but that's all Rolly and Jay need. One by one
and across the city tonight, they climbed into Rolly's fleet of
cars. Wolcott staffers, guests, and VIP donors, they're all getting custom service. Rolly, in a dapper black suit with pin-
stripes as fine as baby powder, made sure his pickup for the
night included the candidate herself, rightly assuming that
she wouldn't take two steps without Reese Parker by her side.
He pulled away from their headquarters on Richmond with
the two women in the backseat and adjusted his rearview
mirror so he could read on their lips whatever he couldn't
hear at a distance, asking as he did if the A/C was okay. Neither acknowledged him as he pulled into the street. Fine by
me, Rolly thought.

Jay managed to arrive a few minutes before Rolly, parking a
block over in the lot of a Walgreen's and approaching the front
of the famed hotel on foot. This was not the official plan, but
Jay can't help taking a look, wanting to see Parker's organization up close, what he's up against. Despite its Frenchie name,
La Colombe d'Or was the early-twentieth-century home of an
oil tycoon, Houston's architectural legacy having been built
with the bricks of new money. It looks to Jay's eyes like an old
schoolhouse, only one lit from inside by antique sconces and
chandeliers. Beyond the two French doors, that's where the
magic is: a rush of chilled air, perfumed with roses and tall
stands of white and pink lilies, and a plush Persian rug run-

ning from one wall of the foyer to the other. Wolcott's many
donors and supporters are lined up, checking in at a table clad
in white linen. This is no coffee-and-doughnuts neighborhood
social. This night is for high rollers only. Businessmen and developers, corporate lawyers on the payroll of the big petroleum
companies, and contractors wanting a piece of city business,
men and women who want to put their money on the right
horse before the window closes. Jay wonders what one of those
little nametags costs. Five grand? *Ten?* The phone in his pocket
vibrates again, and Jay turns and goes back through the arriving crowd. As planned, he walks to the third sedan idling in
the valet line, a black Town Car, and taps the back right-side
window. When he hears the doors unlock, he opens the back
door and slides in beside Reese Parker, just as Rolly pulls out of
the line and away from the curb, starting south on Montrose.
"What the hell?" Parker says.

"Just give me five minutes," Jay says.

Sandy Wolcott, sitting on the other side of Parker, leans
forward, her hand on the back of Rolly's seat. "What are you
doing?" she shrieks. "Stop this car."

Rolly turns up the radio, pretending not to hear.

Parker reaches into her leather tote bag for a cell phone.

Jay puts a hand on hers to stop her. "He has an alibi, you
know."

Parker shakes him off and starts dialing.

Into the phone, she says, "Tell Tom we're running a few minutes late." She hangs up the phone, dropping it into her bag.
Then to Jay she barks, "Talk."

"You ought to drop this whole thing before you make a fool
of yourself and lose the election anyway," Jay says. "Neal Hathorne wasn't in Pleasantville Tuesday night. He had absolutely
nothing to do with killing Alicia Nowell."

"You so sure?"

"He has an *alibi*."

"Tell it to Matt Nichols, the A.D.A.," Wolcott says. "I told Sam, I told the paper, I'll tell you . . . I've recused myself from this case, don't have a thing to do with it. I shouldn't even be hearing this right now. Stop this car."

"She's right," Parker says, tapping the back of the driver's seat.

Rolly, glancing at Jay in the rearview mirror, slows the car.

Parker reaches across the seat to manually unlock the back passenger door. "Get out," she says to Wolcott. "Let her go," she tells Jay, "and we'll talk."

Jay nods to Rolly, who pulls the car over, about a block from the University of St. Thomas, where Wolcott gets out on the left side, almost walking into street traffic. "Fix this," she says to Parker before slamming the door.

"So this is all your doing?" Jay says to Parker when she's gone.

"Much as I would like to take credit for this unfortunate set of circumstances for the Hathorne family and campaign, I'm afraid getting the captain of the other team arrested for murder is above my pay grade," Parker says, reaching down to the car's carpeted floor to lift her leather tote to her lap. From inside, she pulls a pack of cherry Trident, unwrapping a single piece and popping it into her wide mouth, before retrieving a compact from her purse so she can check her acid-blond hair. She's in a bulky red pantsuit, the fabric bunching at her shoulders. "I'm afraid Neal Hathorne made this mess on his own."

"I know she was working for you."

Parker smiles, maybe the teeniest bit impressed. "Even if she was," she says, snapping the compact closed, "what does that have to do with murder?"

"You set him up."

"I didn't put his number in that girl's pager."

"But interesting that you know about it."

Evidence, he thinks, that despite Wolcott's profession of having had no hand in the case, someone is sharing inside information with her campaign.

Parker waves that off. "That was in the paper."

"You and I both know there isn't enough evidence to take this to trial, not without someone pushing it from the inside. You don't think everyone's going to see that before this is all said and done? He has an alibi," Jay says again.

"One that he conveniently forgot to tell the cops about."

"It's all going to come out, including the failure of the D.A.'s office to prosecute the only suspect in the murders of Deanne Duchon and Tina Wells. Putting Neal on trial for the third girl, it looks like Wolcott's covering her butt."

"Those cases aren't connected."

"Says who?"

"The *Chronicle*, in black and white," she says with a knowing smile.

"This comes dangerously close to rigging an election."

"Don't insult me," Parker says, wrenching around in her seat to face him head-on. "You have any idea what I get paid, the kinds of people I work with? I don't need to rig some Podunk mayor's race in south Texas."

"You can't win without Pleasantville."

"If I want Pleasantville, I'll reach right out and take it."

"It's Sam's, and you know it."

"Sam's day is done."

"You think it's so easy to get around him? They love him out there."

"And he's done a lot for that community, he has," Parker says. "He built that precinct with his bare hands. But even Pleasantville, as anyone knew it, has an expiration date. And why shouldn't it? The circumstances that created it no longer exist. Wasn't that what you, of all people, were fighting for, 'back in the day,' as the kids say? The rules of the game have changed. The voting maps have changed. The whole math of how people win elections has changed. From here on out, *every* vote counts. And I, for one, am not willing to concede an entire precinct on Sam's say-so. People can make up their own minds. It's their vote, not Sam Hathorne's. All that paternalistic crap, it's a thing of the past."

"They know Axel out there, they trust him," Jay says. "At least they did before you and Wolcott started putting those flyers all across the neighborhood."

"Axel, God bless him, isn't a politician. He'd do his legacy a favor to stay in the role of beloved former cop, city's first black chief. You can tell him I said that. He's not cut out for the mayor's office. He's trading on a last name."

"Interesting coming from the woman who helped put Bush junior in the governor's office."

"You're wrong to underestimate him," she says.

Then, tapping the back of Rolly's seat, she announces, "I'm not walking all the way the fuck back." Rolly doesn't move, not without Jay's explicit instruction. Jay, running out of time, reaches into the pocket of his jacket, pulling out a sheaf of papers. "Last chance to end this," he says. "Tell Wolcott to drop this case."

"I believe she told you she doesn't have a thing to do with it."

"Bullshit."

But Parker doesn't budge.

Jay pulls the last card he has: he threatens Parker with the news of Wolcott's affair with a cop, a man who just happened to be a witness in one of her cases. "You sure you want that coming out ahead of December?"

"Please," Parker says. "If they wanted to use that, they would have by now. And I'll bet money they never will. We have opp guys too, you know."

"He's going to be acquitted."

"Congratulations," she says. "But by the time this goes to trial, Mr. Porter, Sandy Wolcott will already be a few months in office, and I'll be back in Austin."

"Not if there's no election."

"What are you talking about?"

He hands her a photocopy of his motion to enjoin the city's runoff election, scheduled for December tenth, and his request for a hearing on the matter in county court at the earliest possible date. Jay tells her it's her copy.

"You can't do this."

"I already did," he says.

Parker looks up just as Rolly, out of the driver's seat now, opens the back door for her, a signal that her ride is through. Parker, in a huff, shoves the motion into her bag and grabs her mobile phone. She ungracefully scoots her behind out of the Town Car. Rolly tips his hat to her as she goes.

Back in the Walgreen's parking lot, Rolly lights a smoke. Jay asks if he picked up anything on the ride over, stuff that Parker and Wolcott talked about.

"A lot that didn't mean much to me one way or the other."

"They mention Neal? Or the court case?"

"Not a word, just a bit of chatter about media interviews, general stuff," Rolly says, exhaling smoke. "And talk about the big donors in their pocket."

"Any names?"

"They got Cole."

"Hmmph," Jay mutters. Thomas Cole, Cynthia's old pal.

Looks like everybody is lining up behind Wolcott.

They part ways soon after this, Rolly to finish what they

started at Beechwood Estates, trying to get close enough to Alonzo Hollis to figure out his game, and Jay to make sure Neal's alibi, his one true hope of getting the case tossed, hasn't fled the county. From Montrose, Jay heads south, to Third Ward.

Come drinking hours, the streets around the Playboy Club are lit up like Christmas. Young men hang on street corners, sipping beer out of paper bags, waiting on the club's doors to open. Older women trade gossip between sips of spiked tea, sitting on the porch steps of shotgun houses, rows of them lined up like tiny churches right off Scott Street, not even a quarter mile from the rough-and-tumble headquarters of Jay's first fledgling SNCC offshoot–a group he started with Bumpy Williams, Lloyd Mackalvy, and Marcus Dupri–and where he first laid eyes on Cynthia Maddox. He thinks again about this morning, the fact that, for whatever reason, she went out of her way to warn him. But against what, she wouldn't say, not really, offering only a vague sense that all with this election is not what it seems, which he was already beginning to see with his own eyes.

Jay parks under a dim streetlight just a few feet from the door of the Playboy Club, not realizing he's been followed. But as soon as he steps out of the Land Cruiser, he sees his pursuer. The driver of the Z, the one who was in his office and outside his home–the one he assumes is after his legal records for the Cole case–is standing right in front of him. The unkempt hair, the same cutting smile, the familiar funk of marijuana smoke laid tonight on top of a sweet, sweet cologne. He's so close Jay could reach out and touch him, which he tries to do to block the first blow, an uppercut that lands under his chin, knocking his teeth together until he tastes blood. Jay, if he had a weapon, couldn't reach it anyway, not as fast as the kid comes on him again, this time socking him under his rib cage. The .38 is a mirage, a dream he once had. Irony of ironies, he left it with Lonnie tonight, worried someone might try something at the house. He would laugh out loud if he could catch his breath. Doubled over, Jay tries to speak. He spits blood on the kid's sneakers, white Air Jordans, earning himself another hit, a punch as near to the kidneys as he can take without passing out. And then he hears the unlikeliest string of words in the English language.

"Motherfuck that injunction."

Jay sees the grip of a 9 millimeter in the waistband of the kid's underwear, peeking out above his baggy jeans. He's lifted his shirt to make the threat clear, like something out of a Tupac video Jay once asked his daughter to turn off. Laid out in the street, he thinks he can hear the song's thumping bass in his head until he realizes it's his own blood beating against the walls of his skull. "You understand?" the kid says, kicking Jay in the gut. "Shut it down, Heathcliff."

CHAPTER 16

The headline: "Hathorne Camp Seeks to Halt December Runoff."

The photo caption: "Attorney Jay Porter Accuses Wolcott of Misconduct in Murder Charge."

The article, written by Gregg Bartolomo, gives the unfortunate impression that Jay is working for the Hathorne campaign, rather than doing everything he can for his client *and* for the parents of Alicia Nowell, who deserve more from the top prosecutor than having their daughter's murder used as a political pawn. The sloppy reporting is infuriating but not wholly unexpected. Lonnie last night had warned Jay of as much, guessing the *Chronicle*'s editorial slant, and they both suspected Reese Parker of leaking all kinds of information to the press. (Lead sentence, paragraph two: "Sources inside the district attorney's office say there is enough evidence for a conviction. . . .") Lon practically wrote the story off the top of her head while she helped dress his wounds. He'd staggered into the house a little after eight, blood staining the front of his white shirt—after first calling Lonnie from the driveway to make sure he could get from the back door to his bedroom without his kids seeing. At breakfast this morning, he tells them he took a fall, delivering the news offhandedly while passing a plate of eggs. Ellie stares at him across the table, and Ben stops eating, complaining of a sudden stomachache. "Come on," Jay says. "We're late for school." He shoves the newspaper into the trash on their way out.

They ride with the radio off.

Twice in the car, Ben asks if Jay, his last remaining parent, is sick, mistaking the bumps and bruises for a different kind of pain. "I'm fine, son," Jay says, reaching across the front seat for Ben's hand. He's actually better than fine. He woke up this morning feeling strangely, yet powerfully, numb, not so much unable to process the pain across his cheek and jaw as indifferent to it. Standing over his bathroom sink at dawn, staring at the blood-crusted aftermath, he found the darkest center of the blackest bruise and stuck his middle finger straight into it, feeling nothing that a year without his wife hadn't overprepared him for. What, after all, was a scratch on the surface of a body that had already been hollowed out? He looked at his hands, at his shirtless torso, in the bathroom mirror. He saw his whole body anew, imagining grief, of all things, as a kind of superpower. This, he thought, looking at the abrasions across his brow, the swelling of his lips and cheek, this is the least that I can endure. It was like powder in a bullet, this knowledge. He felt inexplicably, undeservedly free. And he owed it to somebody to do something with this, didn't he? *Do it for them.* He heard his wife's voice and understood, more than ever, what she meant.

"I'm going to be fine," he says to his son.

When Jay arrives at the civil courthouse at eight thirty sharp, Gregg Bartolomo is waiting outside. "You set me up," he says acidly, the second Jay starts up the walk and into the building. Jay is not surprised in the least to see him here. Bartolomo is at his heels the whole way, hovering behind Jay in the line for the metal detectors, the two men removing their watches, the change in their pockets. "You should check your facts next time before you rush to print whatever Reese Parker feeds you," Jay says as he passes through the parallel walls of the metal detector, reaching for his belongings in the dingy plastic cup on the other side. "You ought to be spending your time talking to Alonzo Hollis."

"I already did."

Jay pauses, a few feet from the bank of elevators, watching as Bartolomo puts on his watch and the belt the deputies made him remove. "I'm not a bad reporter," he says to Jay. "But I *am* a gratefully employed one. My editor told me to drop it, so I dropped it. Nothing about Hollis ever made the final cut of any of my stories. But it doesn't mean I didn't do my job. Honestly? They're going to play this story the way they want it played," he says. "Unless . . ."

"Unless what?"

"I can get an exclusive interview with you or your client."

"No comment." Jay turns and walks toward the elevators, sliding into one and watching, with pleasure, as the doors close on Gregg Bartolomo's face.

He presses floor six for the clerk's office.

Eddie Mae is in rare form when Jay arrives later that morning. She's dressed for the occasion, for her new status as secretary— "no, legal assistant," she says—to a man on the front page of the

city's only newspaper, with a murder trial no less, her very own
Johnnie Cochran. "Don't call me that," he says. She's wearing
a slim skirt, tight across the waist but otherwise demure, and
a cream-colored blouse, and her hair actually appears to be
her own. It's a soft, silvery gray, with a shallow spray of curls
in the front and an egg-size bun pinned at the back. "Cynthia
Maddox called," she tells him. "Twice."

"Cole's willing to talk," Cynthia says when he gets her on the
phone.

"I'll bet he is."

"But it has to be now."

"Where?"

"Houston Club."

"I'll be there."

"And, Jay, listen—"

He hangs up.

The Houston Club is the oldest private social club in the city,
and no one gets up to the tenth floor without an express in-
vitation. Jay's is waiting for him, a handwritten card resting
on a silver tray held immovably in place by a black man in a
penguin suit and white gloves standing in the lobby. Jay is instructed to walk the card to the elevator and up to the tenth
floor, where he is to hand it to the hostess outside the main
dining room. When Jay says, "Thank you," the black man nods
without ever making eye contact. Inside the elevator, Jay ticks
off the floors on the slow rise, passing, according to the buttons on the inside panel, the club's gym, indoor tennis court,
and pool; its private ballroom; and its barroom lounge. On
the tenth floor, the hostess is waiting for him as he steps off
the elevator. "Right this way, Mr. Porter," she says, motioning
for him to fall in line behind her as she leads the way through

the anteroom, past the hat check and the rows of Stetsons resting on individual racks. The room smells of tobacco and Colombian coffee and woodsy aftershave, and the champagne-colored carpet is so thick that Jay's knees nearly buckle as the soles of his shoes sink into it. The hostess fairly skates across it, carrying her weight in her youthful hips, swinging them left and right as she walks between the linen-topped tables in the dining hall, smiling her way toward her Christmas tips, nodding at each male club member she passes. And it *is* all men, in boots and suits, seated two and three to a table. Odd, Jay thinks, for an hour that rightly belongs to tennis wives and retirees, that dull stretch of time between Bloody Marys and the day's first chardonnay. But these are men whose money is being made whether they're in their offices or not, and there's a leisurely and fraternal air about the room . . . at least, there was.

The conversation comes to an abrupt halt.

Everyone has turned to stare.

The black and purple cuts and bruises across the left side of his face, the eye that's slightly swollen—these are not enough to disguise the fact that Jay and the man on the front page of the day's newspaper are one and the same. "Mr. Cole is waiting," the hostess says, pointing to a corner table in the back of the room with a view of the city's skyline. The man himself is seated in a chair against the wall, so he can't actually see the view he's paying for. He's older than Jay by a decade, and it shows in the silver hair and the feathered lines cut into his tanned skin, but he is otherwise still at a fighting weight, ropy and lean. He's wearing a button-down oxford beneath a hunter green collared cardigan, a pair of reading glasses tucked at the neckline; and a Camel cigarette is sitting in a crystal ashtray a few inches from the gold nugget on his right hand. He looks up from the newspaper in his hand, smiling amusedly at the sight of Jay, as if he were a gnat Cole had swatted at and missed, a winged thing that had bested him and lived to tell. "Jay Edgar Porter," he says, calling out Jay's full name—which appears in a single place, on his original birth certificate filed in the Trinity County courthouse on May 5, 1950—letting Jay know, in five syllables, that there is no part of his life that Cole hasn't dug for and found. "I wish I could say it was a pleasure."

"Likewise," Jay says, pulling out the nearest chair.

Despite their legal showdowns, Jay has not laid eyes on the man in the flesh in fifteen years. In fact, the last time the men drew breath within a few feet of each other was inside a men's room in the criminal court building downtown, when Cole had uttered these words: "Don't make me regret I didn't kill you when I had the chance." He had delivered this particular prick of poison as if he were doing Jay some big favor, one he might cash in at any time.

"Let's start with you calling off your muscle," Jay says.

"Excuse me?"

Jay unbuttons his suit jacket and takes a seat.

He leans across the table, lowering his voice. "I'll give you Nathan Petty, okay? He's yours," he says boldly. "But you can't have people following me."

Over a center vase of milk-colored narcissus, Cole stares at Jay. His eyes narrow slightly as he lifts the cigarette from the ashtray.

"I have children," Jay says.

"Two."

Jay feels his blood rush. "Yes," he says, watching Cole roll the tip of the cigarette between his thumb and forefinger before taking a slow drag. "So you can see why I can't have anything happening to me. I need you to call him off."

Cole lets out a slow exhale, still studying Jay.

He gently taps his cigarette against the side of the ashtray. "I'm afraid I don't have the slightest idea what you're talking about."

"The kid in the Z," Jay says. "Get him off my back."

"Let me get this straight," Cole says, glancing at his watch. Approving of the hour, he holds up a finger to signal a waiter. He orders a bourbon, offering nothing to his guest, and shoos away the server before he can ask. "A 'kid' named Nathan Petty is following you, and, what, you think I had something to do with it?" He smiles, offering this retelling of the bits and pieces of Jay's story with an air of incredulity, as if he thinks Jay is bullshitting him and he's personally insulted by the lack of sophistication. "Surely," he says, taking another drag on his cigarette, "this isn't the reason you asked to meet with me."

Now it's Jay who's feeling tricked.

He leans back in his chair, studying the blank look on Thomas Cole's face.

Either Cole's flunky hasn't yet found the link to Petty in Jay's records or Cole doesn't know the man existed, and doesn't, in fact, know what Jay is talking about at all, which Jay finds hard to believe. "You're not tailing me?"

Cole takes another drag on his cigarette. "Should I be?"

He exhales, a puzzled look on his face, just as his glass of bourbon lands sloppily on the edge of the table, a tiny wave of honey-colored liquid splashing over the side and soaking through the tablecloth. The hand that delivered it is white, a racial anomaly in his peripheral vision that causes Thomas Cole to turn and look up, directly into the face of Charlie Luckman, Esquire. "This one's on me, hoss," he says, pulling out the chair to Cole's left and squeezing himself right into the middle of the men's private meeting. Jay knows both of them, under wildly different circumstances, of course. Time was, Charlie Luckman, former prosecutor turned highly paid defense attorney, held a permanent position in Thomas Cole's Rolodex, as he did in the private directories of other moneyed men in Cole's set, Charlie having gained a well-earned reputation as a fixer of sorts, a lawyer willing to work cases high and low, as long as the price was right. Jay had gone up against him in one of the absolute lowest of the low, the case of a hooker who suffered an on-the-job injury in the front seat of a port commissioner's car. The commissioner had paid Charlie to make the whole thing go away. Charlie, Jay remembers, was a friend of Cole's back then, and had even represented Elise Linsey, the tartlet on Cole's payroll who was the face of Stardale, the shell development company. Charlie had inadvertently confirmed the breadth of Thomas Cole's involvement in the hoarding and hiding of barrels and barrels of crude oil—which had planted the seeds of Jay's civil case against the oil giant. Jay has never known how, or even if, the men's friendship recovered. This morning Charlie seems tickled as pink as the broken capillaries across the tip of his nose to see Jay and Cole together in the middle of the Houston Club. He sets his own tumbler of bourbon on the table and throws a hammy hand across Jay's shoulder. "So you're the one messing with little Georgie's election," he says.

"What?" Jay says, shucking off his oily grip.

"You're drunk, Charlie," Cole says.

"I prefer to think of it as a slow marinade," Charlie says, signaling one of the servers for another round. He is quite openly on the downslope of a once unstoppable career, having benched himself after his very public loss to Sandy Wolcott, a woman twenty years his junior, in the murder trial of the Houston-area surgeon. "She got me," he said, as if he'd been the one to take the knife and not Dr. Martin's wife. Jay'd heard that since his public loss, he's settled down—on paper, at least—marrying, in his sixties, the daughter of a Mexican textile magnate and raising two boys, nine-month-old twins. Here, even in the soft white light of the dining room, he looks tired, the collar of his shirt cutting into the flesh of his neck like a yoke, the seams of his size-38 oyster gray suit surrendering under stress. It's a costume he need not torture himself with, Jay thinks. Charlie hasn't set foot inside a courtroom in a year.

"Walk away from the table, Charlie," Cole says, irritated.

"Well, aren't you full of grace?"

He stands, lifting his late-morning cocktail with one hand and attempting to button his jacket with the other. Suit tails flapping, his shirt slightly untucked, he crosses the dining room, stopping at a few other tables to pull the same routine, dropping in unannounced and uninvited. Thomas Cole stubs out his cigarette. He lifts the glass of bourbon and takes a hearty sip, tapping a finger on the newspaper's front-page story as he swallows.

"You got a lot of people worked up over this. Sam put you up to it?"

"Sam wasn't too keen on it, matter of fact."

Cole nods approvingly. "Confrontation isn't much his style. More flies with honey, and all that," he says, belching softly. "He's a decent man, if a little foolish, trading an extraordinary amount of power for the mess of politics played in the light of day. Axel's strong, but naive, and Sam is too hot to see a Hathorne in city hall to appreciate what he's giving up as a 'behind-the-scenes' player."

"Every man's dream," Jay says, rolling his eyes.

"Maybe you don't know Sam as well as you think you do. I'm holding out hope some of his spirit of reciprocity has rubbed off on you," Cole says. "You don't want this court case, Porter, this injunction. Trust me when I tell you you're wading in water over your head. You don't want this for your career."

To which Jay only grins. "I don't have a career," he says, leaning back, his hands clasped behind his head, feeling punch-drunk still, hours after the beating. "You're looking at a retired man, Cole," he says, glancing at the plush dining room, the fine china and crystal. "What does this setup cost—ten, twenty grand a year? It'll be a stretch, but I guess I can manage. What do you say, Cole? You and me, members of the same club? They got a basketball court in here?"

"You're making a fool of yourself."

"We'll let a judge decide that."

"It'll never work," Cole says. "There's not a single goddamned judge in Harris County who's going to halt an election over what you're talking about."

"A candidate using her position as district attorney to discredit a member of her opponent's family and campaign team? To influence a city election?"

"Bullshit," Cole says, raising his voice for the first time. He glances furtively around the room, meeting the curious eyes of the men at neighboring tables. He lowers his voice, pushing the vase of flowers to the side. He leans forward, half his torso reaching across the table in Jay's direction. "You're wrong to hold this up as a crusade. There's serious evidence against that kid."

"Now, see, how would you know that?" Jay says. "Last I checked, grand jury testimony is sealed. Hell, *I* won't even see it till discovery. So unless you're prepared to admit to having an inside track to the district attorney's office, the head of which you just so happen to be backing in the mayor's race, I don't see how you could know the details of what went on in that grand jury room." Jay points to the newspaper, to his picture on the front page. "You know what else I find interesting? How quickly this story made it into print. The *Chronicle* goes to bed at what, eight, nine o'clock at the latest?" he says. "The district court is dark by five thirty. There would have been no way for Bartolomo to fact-check any of what he got straight from Reese Parker's mouth the second she and I finished talking. And yet here it is, for the whole city to read."

"So?"

"So I didn't file those papers until this morning."

Jay leans across the table too, getting within a few inches of Cole's tanned face. "You know what I think? I think you're all playing a game with this whole process—you, Wolcott, Parker, with help from Houston's journalistic finest."

"It's not too late to withdraw the motion," Cole says. Jay ignores him, pushing back from the table as he buttons his suit jacket. "Perhaps there's something we can still work out, Mr. Porter. I'm certainly willing to concede that our civil matter has dragged on longer than it should have. If we were able to speed up a final resolution for your clients, maybe I could get you to reconsider."

"I don't think so," Jay says. He stands to leave. "Call off your boy."

"Mr. Porter, if I wanted to"—Cole searches for the right word—"*neutralize* you, I can promise you'd look a hell of a lot worse than you do now. You're standing up right now on my say-so, and don't forget it." He reaches for a gold-plated lighter in his front pocket. He sets the blue flame against the end of a fresh cigarette, burning through half the tobacco with the first drag. "They have enough for a conviction, you know," he says, as if he's tossing Jay a lifeline.

"You talking about the phone number in the girl's pager? He admits to dialing it unknowingly. Doesn't mean anything," Jay says, turning away.

"I'm talking about the eyewitness."

Jay stops at this, that thick, rich carpet like quicksand. He feels himself sinking. Slowly, he turns toward Cole, trying to inch forward, if only to shorten the distance, to keep the man's voice from drifting too far past this one table. "There was an eyewitness on the stand," Cole says, admitting for the moment his insider knowledge of the grand jury testimony. "A local out there saw him struggling with the girl on the corner where she was last seen."

"Saw *Neal*?"

"It's all under seal," Cole says. "But not for long."

Jay cocks his head to the side, disbelief being his first anchor against the wild tide of panic rising in his chest. "God damn it," he mutters as he walks out.

When Jay walks into campaign headquarters twenty minutes later, the candidate has his long legs tucked under a vinyl-topped card table. He is working the phones, his poll numbers having taken enough of a hit on the news of his nephew's arrest that direct contact with individual voters is about the only thing that might swing things back in his favor. Texans are, for the most part, a friendly bunch, and Jay guesses as many as half of the names on that call sheet will at least hear Axel out. There are men and women milling about, block walkers waiting on the day's assignment, hovering near a grease-stained box of cold doughnuts. One woman, her blue Hathorne T-shirt knotted fashionably on her right hip, has a packet of nondairy creamer in her hand, opened sideways like a bag of Fun Dip. She licks the white powder off her index finger. The man standing next to her hasn't yet committed to the campaign T-shirt. His is tucked into the back pocket of his jeans, the tail hanging out like a flag, an accessory he hasn't yet pledged any allegiance to, not until someone shows up with a roll of twenties to distribute. Marcie, on the phone at her desk against the back wall, is rolling a wad of Kleenex over the ripples of fat on the back of her neck, mopping sweat. The room is poorly ventilated. Even with the front door propped open, it's warm and smells of damp carpet. Axel has rolled up the sleeves of his dress shirt, a constellation of sweat drops under each arm seeping through the fabric. "Yes, ma'am," he says into the phone. He nods, listening to her side. "Well, that's been my priority since I entered this race. We're going to make neighborhoods like yours safe again. If I make it to city hall, with your help we can prioritize city resources in such a way that—" Cut off, he leans back in his chair, listening, the tops of his knees knocking the underside of the table. "My team has done nothing to interfere with the investigation, ma'am." He rubs his face in exasperation. "I want to find the girl's killer as much as anyone."

Jay walks past the phone bank, past the copy machine and Marcie's cluttered desk, all the way to an unlocked metal door, behind which appears to be the only private space in campaign headquarters and the place where Jay guesses he'll find his client. He enters a small room lined with bolts of upholstery fabric. He passes two long folding tables, both sagging in the center of the weight of boxes and boxes of campaign paraphernalia, buttons and T-shirts, plus reams of copier paper. Besides the dusty fabric, there's a hospital-size scale in here, a blue Coleman cooler, a broken vacuum cleaner, and a stack of two-by-fours. Jay doesn't know what this place was before the campaign rented it, or what it will return to after the polls finally close on this twisted little election. Neal is laid out across a three-foot-long red pleather couch, his legs hanging off the arm of one side and his right forearm covering his eyes.

"Sit up," Jay says.

He grabs a chair from one of the folding tables and turns it to face the couch. He sits down, kicking his foot against the base of the couch to wake up his client. "You do understand that I'm about to walk into state court to try to stop an election?" he says. "And so far, man, I've taken you at your word."

Neal swings his feet to the floor, rising suddenly.

The door behind Jay opens, and Axel walks in.

Jay never takes his eyes off his client. "Leave us alone."

"It's okay," Neal says. "He can stay."

"There's an eyewitness," Jay says.

"That's impossible."

"What's going on?" Axel says, hands on his hips.

"Somebody got on the stand in front of the grand jury and testified that they saw you and the girl *struggling*, right at the corner of Guinevere and Ledwicke."

"They're lying . . . or just plain confused."

"Who is it?" Axe says.

"Something you want to tell me?" Jay asks Neal.

"I wasn't there," Neal says, raising his voice. "Didn't you talk to A.G.?"

Surprised, Axel turns from Jay to his nephew. "What?"

"Yes," Jay says, glancing at Axel then back at Neal, who's now on his feet. "And guess what? He doesn't seem the least bit interested in reclaiming his rightful spot in the Hathorne line, especially if it means testifying in open court."

"I wasn't there!"

"You talked to A.G.?" Axel says.

Neal looks at his uncle but doesn't say anything.

Jay can't exactly read the look between them, but Axel, whose skin is usually a warm maple color, looks downright ashen. "A.G.'s here, in Houston?"

"Tell me this," Jay says to Neal. "Why Tuesday night?"

"What do you mean?"

"Why were you so hot to see him last Tuesday? You said yourself you were in the middle of a massive get-out-the-vote effort that day. So with the polls still open, why did you take a detour to the Playboy Club in Third Ward? Why that night to talk to your father for the first time?"

Neal looks at the ground.

He's still reluctant to go any further.

"You got to give me something here."

Neal sighs. "We got a call from Rob Urrea."

"Who is that?"

"Our opp guy," Axel says.

"He had a report on A.G."

"Jesus," Axel mumbles, reaching for the nearest chair to sit down.

"What kind of report?"

"I don't know," Neal says. "I didn't order it."

"Sam did," Axel says, guessing.

Neal nods. "And Rob swore he wasn't at liberty to share it."

"Opposition research," Jay says. "There something there?" Was there some bit on his younger son that Sam Hathorne wanted safely contained, typed up, and presented to him personally? "I need to see that report," he says.

CHAPTER 17

The Harris County District Civil Court has long set, by its own bylaws, an ancillary judge, a name assigned and rotated every two weeks, to handle emergency motions, and Judge Irwin Little, through no choice of his own, got this one. A "doozy," he calls it from the bench. He leans his pudgy torso all the way back in his leather chair, resting his hands on the mound of belly beneath his black robe, waiting to be entertained. He took an oath to uphold the United States Constitution and administer fair justice to all, but it doesn't mean he's not entitled to a show every now and then. And that's what this is, of course, a farce, a joke in poor taste, at least according to the morning's front-page headline: "Amid Trailing Poll Numbers Hathorne Bid to Halt Election Seen as 'Hail Mary' Pass." After a docket of garden-variety requests for temporary restraining orders, this one ought to be interesting.

The 152nd Civil Court is packed this Thursday morning, just one day after Jay filed the motion to request an oral hearing on the matter. From his perch at the bench, Judge Little has a clear view of the gathered spectators: Dick Urton, the sitting mayor, plus multiple representatives from the campaigns of the candidates looking to replace him, including Reese Parker in the front row of the gallery, sitting on the opposite side of the courtroom from Jay, who is seated alone at a table just ahead of the bar. The only faces from the Hathorne campaign are those of Marcie, the communications director, and Stan, the money-man. Axel thought his presence would be cheap. And Sam, well, Jay has no idea where Sam is. He's slipped through Jay's fingers of late, slow to return his calls. Jay did not demand that Neal be present for this. "In fact, it's probably better that you're not," he told his client. "You're not the one on trial here." To which Neal plaintively replied, "Not yet." In addition to press from the Houston paper as well as the *Morning News* in Dallas and a reporter from the New Orleans bureau of the *New York Times*, there's on-air talent in the room too, a rarity. Melanie Lawson from Channel 13 is here. So is Dan O'Rourke from Channel 2, the NBC station. Jay recognized two people from the CBS affiliate coming off the elevator when he arrived this morning. Besides the high-profile lookiloos, there's also a gathering of prominent local attorneys, men and women who approach this as they might a wacky sporting event, or a high-flying circus act: part of the pleasure of watching is the possibility of total disaster, a very public fall. Johnetta Paul is here too, having filed a last-minute companion brief demanding to be heard on the matter, as did two other city council members who are up for reelection and prepared to argue orally all the ways postponing a city election just three weeks away would adversely affect their chances at the polls. Technically, only Jay and the county's elections clerk have been selected to address the bench, although Matt Nichols, the D.A. prosecuting the Nowell case, is sitting openly at the same table with the county clerk.

Jay is up first.

He's nervous, sure he is.

He's got a full house at his back.

Last he turned and stole a glance, he could see that Maxine and Mitchell Robicheaux had squeezed themselves onto a slim sliver of wood at the edge of the bench nearest the back of the courtroom, as if they weren't sure how much space they were allowed to take, how much this particular hearing has to do with them, or justice for their daughter. Maxine looks to have come straight from work. She's wearing slightly stained, pale pink scrubs from the previous night's shift. She cranes her neck slightly, trying to see over the crowd. Her husband is wearing a heavily starched plaid shirt. Mitchell put himself together for this, shaved and ran a pair of clippers along his hairline. He sits staring straight ahead. In all the television interviews, all the pleas for help and justice for their daughter, Jay has never heard the man speak. On the opposite side of Maxine, Pastor Keith Morehead is holding tightly to the woman's hand. He has, over the last few days, become the family's unofficial spokesperson, claiming, as a man of the cloth, to be unaligned politically and therefore able to offer, without earthly distraction, spiritual counsel to Alicia's parents in their hour of need. Jay does not try to make eye contact with Maxine, not sure she would understand that he has pledged himself to her as much as he has to his client, not sure Maxine Robicheaux would cross the street to spit on his shoes. Still, as he looks down at his notes to start, he hears the words, a whisper at his back. *Do it for them.*

"Morning, Your Honor," he says, his speech tightened by the pain still throbbing in his jaw. He had to chew a handful of aspirin just to get through this. Citing paragraphs one through three of his motion, a copy of which rests on the judge's desk, Jay lays out his argument, enumerating the ways the court is in danger of allowing a mayoral candidate to use her office as district attorney to infect and influence a city election, an act of malfeasance with wide-ranging implications for millions of individuals. Letting the election go forward under the current circumstances, "threatens irreparable harm to the entire electoral process in which the citizens of Houston are putting their faith, not to mention harm to my client and the family of Alicia Nowell, who are victims here as well. They're being used, sir," he says from his place behind the counsel table. "Thank you," he says, before returning to his seat.

The courtroom is remarkably still.

Not a cough, not a twitch, from the gallery.

For a brief moment, Jay can hear nothing but the soft sigh of air coming from the vents overhead. Even the judge's clerk has momentarily stopped her typing. It may be the first time that most of the people in this courtroom are hearing the actual details behind the filing for this injunction, particularly the fact that the dead girl was working for Sandy Wolcott, a fact that Wolcott never disclosed to the police and that the *Chronicle* never reported. Irwin Little has been doing this long enough to give no premature signal from the bench, but it's clear that he too has had his eyes opened. He leans forward, rolling his leather chair a few inches closer to his desk. He takes a second look at the motion in front of him, or maybe his *first* look, Jay thinks. The judge reads for a few moments, silently to himself, the desk's slim microphone picking up the sound of his slow breathing.

Finally, he peels off his reading glasses.

"Mr. Duffie?"

Wayne Duffie, the county clerk in charge of the elections division, among other things, stands so quickly that he wobbles a bit on his feet. In his fifties, he is as short as he is round, and has paired his brown slacks with a green sports coat, double-breasted, with gold-tone buttons, the uniform of a man content with the least amount of political power available to him, elected to count the votes that put other people into offices over his head. On his right ring finger, he wears a class ring, the metal cutting into the meat all around it. Jay can smell his cologne from here. "I'm afraid I'm at a bit of a loss here, Your Honor," Duffie says. "This is unprecedented. I, uh, if I could, Your Honor, would like to elect Mr. Nichols to speak for the county, as it's his office with which the complainant seems to have the problem." He gestures toward Matt Nichols, who stands.

"If I may, Your Honor."

"Go on."

"Judge, this is just a stunt, of the highest order, and a waste of the court's time. Mr. Porter's client is charged with a homicide, indicted by a grand jury in this county. There is no evidence of some big conspiracy against Mr. Hathorne, or frankly that his legal troubles have anything to do with the election. Where Mr. Porter would like to suggest that our office is somehow using a murder charge to influence an election, from where I stand he appears to be using the timing of an election to get his client out of a capital murder charge."

"That could not more greatly misstate my purpose here," Jay says.

"Your Honor, his 'purpose here' is to create a diversion for his client. It's a cheap stunt and a supreme show of disrespect to the people of this city."

"Not when we're talking about no less than the sanctity of the entire electoral process," Jay says, standing, taking a gamble that Judge Little is not so close to retirement that he's impervious to a good, old-fashioned argument about the power of a courtroom, the plain facts of why they're all here, why, two hundred years on, men and women like Jay, Judge Little, Matt Nichols, and Maxine and Mitchell Robicheaux even bother showing up. "My god, Judge, do you really think I would try something like this unless I thought that this is *it*, all I have? The court, Your Honor, this has always been the church of last resort, the place where we at least take a stab at doing the right thing, where we believe it's even possible," he says, pouring it on a little thick, sure, but only because he believes it. "All I'm asking is that my client get a fair trial, and Houston get a fair election." Judge Little is quiet a moment, twirling his spectacles by one of the stems; tiny rectangles of glass, they are prisms playing tricks in the light, reflecting green one moment, a hard red the next. Behind him, Jay can hear the scratch of graphite on paper, reporters and a few of the spectators taking notes.

Finally, Judge Little speaks. "Do you have anything more than the girl working for Wolcott?"

"Do I need more?"

"Do you have *proof*, Counselor?" The judge lifts the stapled pages on his desk. "I've got the affidavits here from Pleasant-ville residents, the ones who saw the victim handing out these anti-Hathorne flyers, but where is the hard line between the flyers and Wolcott's campaign? In theory, anybody could have printed up these deals," he says, holding up one of the Buffalo Bayou development flyers, "anybody wanting to tip the scales in Wolcott's favor."

"My office is working on that right now," Jay says.

He has both Rolly and Lon out in the streets, working every print shop from Galveston to Humble, north of the airport, trying to locate the one commissioned to design and print hundreds of flyers linking Hathorne to a bayou development project. "One of the problems with moving forward with an election on the current timetable is the possibility of *never* having the 'hard' answers. What happens if this trial is held in six months, or a year from now, and not only is my client acquitted, but it's been proved that there was outright conspiracy on the part of the D.A., and she's already sitting up in city hall?"

Judge Little sighs, looking from Jay to Nichols.

"He does have a point," he says.

Jay wedges himself into this slim opening.

"Absent some action on the court's part," he says, "this murder case will hang over the whole election. It will taint the whole process."

"It does stink," the judge says. "A sitting D.A. running for office while prosecuting a member of the other candidate's family, his campaign manager, no less? I can't even imagine why she would, in the middle of the runoff campaign, leave herself open to something this messy *unless* she stood to gain."

"We have an eyewitness, Your Honor," Nichols says, very nearly losing his cool. He's a state prosecutor used to criminal court judges bending over backward to see his every argument as just good old common sense. That they are even still talking about this appears to have stumped the young lawyer.

"You have an eyewitness who saw my client," Jay says, "or an eyewitness who saw someone 'matching his description'?" Which is the catchall phrase of lazy prosecutors everywhere.

Nichols makes a play for the judge's equanimity, his levelheadedness in the face of the absurd. "What exactly is Mr. Porter asking the court to do, postpone a citywide election *indefinitely*?" he says.

"No, just until my client gets a trial."

"Which is the same thing as putting it off indefinitely."

Jay taps the counsel table with his fingertips. "My client is prepared to invoke his right to a speedy trial. We're ready to go at any time, Your Honor."

The judge raises an eyebrow, throwing this over to Nichols. He's waiting to see if Nichols is at least willing to play.

"What if we were able to move the runoff back a month, maybe two? Is that even feasible on your end?" the judge says, turning to Wayne Duffie. The county clerk stands, catching a side-winding stream of sweat off his brow with the palm of his hand and clearing his throat several times. After a long, partially rehearsed statement about the date of the runoff having been set for more than a calendar year, tradition holding that thirty days out from a general election, the county settles each and every draw with another go at the polls, he concedes that the final ballots are not actually due to be printed until next week, and, no, he can't think of a single reason why the runoff election couldn't be postponed.

"Mr. Nichols?"

"Your Honor, I don't need to remind the court of the intricacies of trying a murder case. It's not something the prosecutor's office takes lightly, nor something that we can just throw together. I cannot try a capital case between now and December tenth, sir, nor do I think it's fair to hold up a city election."

"He can always drop the charges and refile after the election is over," Jay says, which is what he really wanted all along: for Wolcott to drop this.

"And let a murderer—"

"Alleged, Your Honor."

"—walk out the door? I'm sorry, Your Honor, but Alicia Nowell's family, the ones that Mr. Porter claims to be so concerned about, they deserve justice, first and foremost. And justice, sir, justice does not *wait*."

"I couldn't agree more. My client and I are ready to go when you are."

For the first time, Judge Little smiles.

The balls on this one, his expression says.

"I'm not gon' rule today," he says finally. "I'd ask for case law on the matter, but I suppose if you had it, you'd have already laid it out." He looks back down at his copy of Jay's motion, almost marveling at it, like a three-legged horse or a blind dog nosing its way through a maze, an honest-to-god wonder of nature. "I will say for the record, Mr. Porter, that I don't for one second take the halting of a city election lightly. I can't think of anything more grave than messing around with our democracy." He looks down again at the papers and sighs, his pleasure in the morning's enterprise slowly deflating, like a slow, whistling leak in a circus balloon. The show is over, and the cleanup doesn't look like nearly as much fun. He reminds all parties to hang near a phone for the next day or two, so his clerk can reach them. When it's all over, Matt Nichols looks pleased—that is, until he turns and sees Jay Porter looking equally optimistic. It *was* a stunt, a shot a mile long. And Jay just argued his way into another day, another twenty-four hours. He packs the satchel briefcase, fingering the brass buckles to secure it. As he turns to leave, he sees Keith Morehead escorting the Robicheauxs out of the courtroom, a hand at the elbow of Maxine's pink nursing uniform. She turns and glances back at Jay, a look as piercing as the last time their eyes met. Only it's not vitriol he sees, but a kind of stumbling confusion, a haunting terror at the thought of losing her daughter all over again, not to men in dark cars, on the dark street corners of her worst nightmares, but to men in dark robes, men in suits, men who, inside the walls of this hallowed courthouse, will wrest from her daughter's life what they can use and leave the rest, men who are no better to Maxine than the killer who snatched Alicia on the street.

CHAPTER 18

He pulls Lonnie off the road first.

Rolly agrees to put in another hour or so tracking down
print shops, and then he'll pick up Hollis's tail when Alonzo
clocks out of the tire shop in Aldine, where he's been on shift
since eight o'clock this morning. Rolly's only news to report,
after three days' surveillance, is thin: "He wasn't working last
Tuesday, election night," he says. "At least two of his coworkers
willing to talk said he wasn't on the schedule, but, hell, even if
he was, place closes at seven, giving him plenty of time to get
out to Pleasantville to snatch the girl." A scenario, Jay knows,
that does not match the grand jury testimony about the night
in question, the eyewitness who fingered Neal. Rolly is embarrassed to admit that after three days he has no idea where

Hollis was that night or any more details about the man's night-time activities. "Not much I can do staring at the man's front windows."

For the second time, he pushes for a different, more direct approach.

Jay still thinks it's a bad idea.

"If this goes like I think it will, we may have a shot at interviewing him, even getting him on the stand," he says. "You roll on him now and he might get cagey or, worse, he might run. I can't afford to lose him, not yet."

"You insult me, Counselor."

"What are you going to do, give him a ride home in a Town Car? Buy him a drink at his favorite bar?"

"I got more tricks than that."

"Save 'em."

Rolly feigns uninterest. "It's your money, Counselor."

You don't know the half, Jay thinks.

They agree to check in in an hour or so, before Jay flips his Motorola closed. He's sitting in the front seat of his Land Cruiser, which is idling in the parking lot of the West Alabama Ice House, just over the fence from Lonnie's duplex apartment. The saloon is little more than a red-and-white shack, a wood hut built sometime in the 1920s. The bar's interior is a dark, low-ceilinged hall that's lit by neon beer signs and the glow of five television sets. Most of the action happens outside, where faded red picnic tables practically spill out of the small front yard and into the rolling traffic on West Alabama. Around back is a wide dirt yard with more sticky tables and a big, black drum of a barbecue pit. It's a place where the smoking of meat is holy, and cleanliness is next to whatever comes way after beer and football, a place where men and dogs are welcome. Lonnie is petting a dog when Jay finds her at a table in back, a black-and-brown boxer tied to the leg of a neighboring table.

She's wearing camel-colored square-toe boots, black jeans, and an ice blue T-shirt, her headlights poking out in the cooling November night. It's a quarter after six, the sun rust red in the sky over the roof of the Ice House. Despite, or maybe because of, whatever in the world is going on with her and Amy, Lonnie is flirting openly with the dog's owner, a dark-haired woman in a University of St. Thomas T-shirt, a denim skirt, and boots almost identical to Lonnie's, only in a dark shade of gray. Lonnie makes a joke about swapping, winking. She's in a good mood, stealing glances at the dark-haired woman, who Jay believes is way too young for Lonnie.

"Hey," he says, sitting across the bench from her.

Lonnie turns, all business suddenly.

"The boyfriend's out."

"What?"

"Kenny, Alicia's high school beau. He's got an ironclad alibi. Turns out he *was* in Houston last Tuesday, with plans to meet up with Alicia at his parents' place for a birthday dinner for his sister, but she never showed. He had a house full of folks who saw him all night, who know he was waiting on the girl."

"How'd you find out?"

"Resner cleared him on his own, behind Detective Moore's back."

"He has doubts about the indictment?"

"Publicly, no. Privately, 'doesn't feel right,' he said."

"Why in the hell doesn't he say something?"

"He did," Lonnie says, "to me."

She reaches into the back pocket of her jeans for a pack of smokes. "This is just the kind of thing he used to slip my way," she says. "You don't like how the top brass is running your case, you drop a line or two to the newspaper."

"But Bartolomo's not biting."

She shakes her head, lighting up a Parliament. "The paper

has its angle, and they're sticking to it." She throws her head back, exhaling. "Resner, it's not his case. In-house, his hands are tied. He's just doing me a favor, that's all. When I mentioned we might subpoena the boyfriend, he said, 'Don't bother.'" Which leaves Alonzo Hollis as the only alternative suspect to present to a jury.

"What about the print shops?"

"I didn't find shit," she says, pulling from the same back pocket a sheet of notebook paper folded lengthwise. She opens it, laying it on the table, rings of leftover beer sweat soaking through. It's her notes from the field. "I had Kingwood to downtown, then west to Meyer Park. Every Kwik Kopy and mom-and-pop, and I didn't find anyone who knows a thing about the BBDP flyers."

"Rolly didn't either," Jay says. "We'll keep looking."

Lonnie looks up, pointing over Jay's shoulder. "There he is."

Rob Urrea, the Hathorne campaign's opp guy, was a onetime lifer at the *Houston Post*, where he and Lonnie Phillips met. She had graduated up to features by the time the owners sold the paper, and Rob was working the city politics beat he loved. He was one of the lucky ones who landed a job at the *Chronicle* when the *Post* died. "Lucky" being relative, Lonnie told Jay; those jobs were just for show, evidence of the publisher's benevolence and civic integrity—which he touted in the pages of his own newspaper, mostly so he wouldn't look like a vulture picking at the bones of his now dead rival. It was all bullshit, of course. Most of those folks were let go within six months. Rob is in his late fifties. His salt-and-pepper hair is heavy on the Brylcreem, and he seems emotionally worn out just by the walk to their table. He might have made a play for retirement if there had been anything to retire on. He got two weeks' severance just like everybody else. He's got, what, a month left on the Hathorne job, more if Jay is able to drag the election out, but other than that he's already on to the next hustle. Lonnie lured him to the Ice House on the promise of sharing her leads in the journalism corner of the World Wide Web. "Aw, hell, Lon," he says when he sees Jay at her picnic table. He lingers about three feet from the table, debating taking another step. The boxer is licking Lonnie's fingers.

"Come on, Rob. She won't bite."

"Thought you was gonna buy me a couple of beers, catch up a little." Deflated, he slaps his black messenger bag on top of the table before taking an open seat at the bench. "Guess everybody's got an angle these days."

"You know, for a guy doing opp research, you sure are earnest as fuck."

"We just want to talk," Jay says.

"What happened to your face?"

"Occupational hazard."

"For a lawyer?" Then he reconsiders Jay's injuries in light of the morning's events. "One trying to stop an election, I guess." He shakes his head, not sure he wants to stick around for this. "Am I getting the leads or what?"

"Hold your horses."

She signals one of the waitresses, a blond girl barely out of high school carrying a tin tray at her hip. "What can I get y'all?" she says.

Jay orders water.

"Dos Equis," says Lon.

She orders two, thinking this is still on Sam's dime.

Rob orders carne asada *and* ribs, and a stack of home-cut fries. "Beer too."

He watches the girl's backside as she walks away, then opens the front flap of his bag, pulling out a handkerchief. He wipes his nose, digging in deep.

"You wanted to talk," he says. "Talk."

"A. G. Hathorne," Jay says.

Rob thinks on this a moment and then shrugs. He slides the handkerchief into his pocket. "I don't have anything to tell."

"Oh, I think you do."

"We know Sam asked for a report on his own son," Lonnie says.

Rob shakes his head, "Huh-uh," he says.

Jay leans across the picnic table. "Look, I know you may have thought you had to protect Neal in some way. Nobody wants to hear shit about their dad, no matter how bad the stuff you've been imagining about the man for thirty years, but this is a potentially life-or-death situation for Neal. You want me to sugarcoat anything for him, I can. But I need to know what was in that report, what made him drop everything to go talk to his father that night."

"You don't understand," Rob says. "There *was* no report, or rather there was nothing in it, certainly nothing that Sam didn't already know."

"Like what?"

"Drugs," Rob says, matter-of-factly, as if he's stunned that Jay hadn't come to that conclusion on his own. "Guy's a musician, after all," he says, as if it were a medical condition, a curdling in the blood that can't be helped.

"What are you talking about? Weed? Pills?"

"Cocaine. Used to smoke the stuff before anyone else knew you could do that. Ruined his voice, his hands. You watch 'em close now, you can still see them shake, fifteen years or so after he got clean for the last time. Shame, really."

"And you're saying Sam knew all this?"

"Yes," Rob says. "There isn't much that gets past the old man. I get the idea he's kept an eye on his son all these years, even from afar." He smiles at the pretty waitress when she returns with their drinks, fumbling awkwardly with his wallet, all just to press two sorry singles into her palm. Jay notices Rob isn't wearing a wedding ring, no tan lines on the ring finger either. He tries to imagine what fifty must feel like, marginally employed and without a wife, before realizing if he just waits a few years he can find out for himself.

"So why use you?" Lonnie asks Rob. "I mean, if Sam already knew about his son, why the ask? I know you were doing other work for the campaign—"

"Like Wolcott's affair with the cop," Jay says.

Rob smiles, pleased with himself for that particular unearthing. "That's right," he says.

"Which Sam doesn't want to use."

"No, he's strangely squeamish about the whole thing."

"Maybe because of his own Johnetta Paul problem."

"Maybe," Rob says. "But does anyone really care who Sam Hathorne is fucking?" He downs half his beer, running grateful fingers along the sides.

"Or maybe Wolcott has something better on Sam?"

"Makes more sense," Lonnie says.

"Something maybe," Jay adds, "to do with his younger son."

Rob considers this a moment, sipping his beer. "Like what?" he says. "There's the estrangement, sure, for whatever Wolcott could wring out of that. But she'd sure look like a petty bitch for calling out his drug addict son, a man who has, for all intents and purposes, turned his life around. And anyway, it's Axel running, not Sam. I got the sense that Sam just wanted to cross every *t* and dot every *i* where A.G. is concerned, wanting to go over anything about his son that the other side could use. I think mostly he was worried that if A.G. was using again, he might be vulnerable, that he might say anything for a five-spot or a promise of something more. But I'm telling you, there was nothing there. A.G.'s recovery, it's real this time, at least that's my two cents on it."

"So that's it?" Lon says.

"That's it. I read most of what I had to Sam over the phone, asked him if he wanted me to type something up. He said no, and that was the end of it."

"When was this?" Jay says, reaching into his pocket for a pen. On the back of an alehouse napkin, he writes down the facts as they come.

One: Rob spoke to Sam at length last week, sometime after his initial call to the campaign on election night, the call that Neal intercepted.

Two: Sam, in the end, didn't want any of it in writing.

Three: It appears the two haven't spoken in almost twenty years. The last anyone remembers A.G. around the neighborhood, or around his father for that matter, was back in the late seventies, when the old-timers out there really started to see the neighborhood change. "First, it was the freeway that cut through, and then the chemical companies that moved in," he says, nodding his head at Jay, the man currently wrapped in a fight with ProFerma.

When the waitress arrives with the food, Rob tears into the ribs first. Chewing, he reaches for a stack of white napkins on the table. "Well, really it was integration, I suppose, that started it." He nods at Jay again, this too being a subject he knows a thing or two about. "When there wasn't any other place to go, Pleasantville, Fifth Ward, they were a haven for black folks, but Pleasantville especially. Teachers, doctors, a few principals, Pullman porters, and business owners. Nice houses, nice cars, a little place that was all their own. Did you know Louis Armstrong used to stay in Pleasantville when he came to Houston? Dinah Washington? Joe Louis used to stay with a lady right over on Ledwicke? Back in the day, when black celebrities came to segregated Houston, there wasn't that many places they could go. You could stay in a cramped boardinghouse somewhere, or Houston's finest Negroes would open their doors for you out in Pleasantville. All-night whist games, good scotch, bathtub gin if that was your thing, blues on the hi-fi. It was a party, what I understand. Between the money and the names, the strong sense of community, every politician from here to Austin on their personal Rolodexes, Pleasantville was untouchable. But now, with the old guard dying off—excuse me for saying so, but it's true—and young black folks with a little change in their pockets picking neighborhoods that would have been closed to them a couple of decades ago, MacGregor and Meyerland, Bellaire, and such . . . Pleasantville is *gone*, at least the way it was."

"Sad," Lonnie says.

"Why?" Rob says, wiping his mouth. "'Cause people who look like me are moving in?" he says, gesturing toward his vaguely Chicano features, his wide, bright brown eyes. He pushes the ribs aside for the carne asada.

"That's not what I meant."

"You really looking to return to an America that birthed a place like Pleasantville?" he says. "Jim Crow is what made that neighborhood possible."

"Still sad," Lon says, picking at the label on her beer. "It's still a loss."

"For some. Opportunity for others."

He fingers a charred green onion lying limp along the inside of his corn tortilla, angling it to ensure it plays a central role in his next bite. "The 'mighty 259' is going to look *mighty* different ten, fifteen years from now," he says, digging into the asada, leaning over the table so the meaty juices and chunky bits of salsa slop onto the paper lining of the red plastic basket instead of into his lap.

"If there even is a precinct 259 in ten, fifteen years," Lonnie says.

"My people vote," he says, swallowing.

"Just ask Johnetta Paul," Jay says wryly.

"Surprised she hasn't started conducting campaign stops in Spanish."

Lonnie shakes her head. "I'm talking about a threat from the outside."

She's talking, actually, about the flyers, the implied threat to Pleasantville from a development along Buffalo Bayou. Rob rolls his eyes. "There is no threat. That development has never gotten off the ground, and it never will. The flyers, that was just Wolcott scaring the old folks out there, who, when it comes to land use and the slow encroach of development, have been burned before." Then, remembering to whom he's talking, he cringes at his choice of language. "Sorry," he says to the plaintiffs' lawyer, before adding, "And either way, Axel is not a pro-development candidate. He really means all that 'a safe city is a prosperous city' stuff. It really is his top priority, dealing with crime."

"Which is the *Chronicle*'s worst nightmare," Lon says, smiling faintly, very nearly enjoying the publisher's perceived misfortune. "Three hundred and sixty-five days of running crime stats on the front page. 'How's the Mayor Doing?' 'Can Former Police Chief Meet His Goals?' That shit does *not* sell newspapers."

"Or attract business," Rob says before taking another bite, talking with his mouth full. "It only becomes a daily reminder to investors to spend their dollars elsewhere, on a city with fewer problems."

"No wonder the paper is pushing for Wolcott from the inside," Jay says.

"Even though they publicly endorsed Axel."

"There are two elections going on. The fiction in the *Chronicle* and the real story on the ground," Rob says, sucking down the foamy swirl in the bottom of his beer bottle. "Looks like I'm the only one who picked the wrong horse."

"They're setting Axel up for a fall," Lonnie says.

"You talked to folks in Pleasantville about A.G.?" Jay says, circling back.

Rob shakes his head, washing down the taco with his beer. "I was under strict orders not to. Most of what I got was from Sam himself, Vivian a little bit."

"What about Axel?"

Rob shakes his head again. "I was under orders." He burps softly, then reaches for the opening of his black messenger bag, unhooking the brass buckle with one hand. "There were, surprisingly, a lot of records to pull at the Hathorne Community Center. The women out there, they've saved everything. Newsletters, team rosters, and elaborate directories, listing residents street by street, their kids' names, birthdays. Plus hundreds and hundreds of photographs from community meetings, parties, voter registration drives, even photos of the fight to stop the 610 Freeway from cutting through the neighborhood. The archives are open to the public." He pulls out a few photocopied pieces of paper. "The story of A. G. Hats is as thin as they come, more myth than anything, a story that begins and ends with *Belle Blue*, his lone solo album. I was trying to put together what happened *after* he stopped playing."

"Which is?"

"Well, he came home sometime around '75," Rob says. "Viv nursed him off the drugs. He quit the nightlife, quit playing, and tried to settle down, back home in Pleasantville. Sam had moved out of the neighborhood by then, and A.G. moved into the family house on Norvic. He got a job at the high school, cleaning up. He even started coaching intramural basketball and football teams with the neighborhood kids, the same program that Keith Morehead runs now."

He shoves the red plastic baskets of food off to the side.

Across the table, he unfolds the photocopied pages.

There, on top, is a black-and-white image of A.G. at the head of a line of marchers, holding up one half of a printed banner that reads: DON'T POLLUTE PLEASANTVILLE! Behind him, Jay notices a young Arlee Delyvan, in her early forties, her black hair wrapped in a paisley scarf. Jim and Ruby Wainwright stand just to the other side. Given the multitude of belled pants legs, the wide, lank collars, it must be 1976, Jay thinks, the same year ProFerma Labs had to file a public notice of its plans to build along Market Street, and six years after Jay had walked away from his own activism for good, or so he thought. "He got heavily involved in the campaign to keep the area around Pleasantville residential, keeping industry out," Rob says. "But this is it," he says, pointing to a photograph from this same march, A.G. again, surrounded by a swarm of kids as young as five and six following him in the street, their mouths open in midchant. "This is the last shot of A.G. I could find anywhere. The *Post*, the *Chronicle*, the archives in the Pleasantville community center, he just disappeared. I drank my way through every juke joint and blues hall in south Texas trying to track down any trace of the man. It was a fluke to find him pushing a broom, right in Third Ward, an absolute shot in the dark."

The cell phone in Jay's pocket trills, buzzing against the side of his hip. He slides it from his pocket, reading the number on the screen—Rolly, calling from his cell phone.

"Rolly," he says when he answers.

"We got a problem, boss."

"What's going on?"

"Hollis is on the move."

"I thought he had another hour on the clock," Jay says, checking the time on his watch. "Plus, I thought you were still chasing print shops."

"I might have moved up the schedule."

"You mean you didn't follow my instructions."

"I'm thinking right about now you'll be glad I didn't."

"How's that?"

"He clocked out early," Rolly says. "I'm on him now since he left the tire shop, heading not to his apartment, the grocery store, laundromat, nowhere near home, but instead keeping south on 45. Then he hopped on 610. He just exited Braeswood, and now he's turning onto Rice."

"That's right by my place."

"Same thing I thought," Rolly says.

Hollis coming after me? Jay wonders.

He can't think fast enough to guess why.

He can't think of anything but his kids.

"That's a right turn on Glenmeadow, man. He's on your street."

"Get ahead of him," Jay says, standing quickly. "Get to the house and have Ellie let you in. Evelyn should be there, but don't say a word about it if you don't have to." He throws two twenties onto the picnic table. "I'm on my way."

When he arrives at the house on Glenmeadow, almost thirty minutes later, Rolly's El Camino is parked in the driveway, behind Evelyn's Pontiac Grand Am. And just down the street, between two lampposts, a blue Chevy Caprice is parked, the same make and model as the one that was parked next to Rolly's truck the night they staked out Beechwood Estates. "He's just watching the house," Rolly said, when he called from Jay's street a few minutes ago. Jay lost him after that, his cell phone dropping out during a tricky patch of poor reception on Richmond, and when he tried back, his calls went straight to Rolly's voice mail, and no one was answering the house line. Stepping out of his car, Jay has just enough time to register the lights on inside the house before Hollis is on him. "Hey," the man says, marching toward Jay, stepping from the darkness into the light of the streetlamp overhead, two white-knuckled fists already clenched at his sides. Jay looks back toward the house, aching to know what is going on in there, what would keep Rolly or Evelyn from picking up the home phone. "What in the fuck all do you think you're doing?" Hollis says.

He's drunk. Jay can smell it from here. He can practically count the number of empties lining the floor of the Chevy. "Take it easy," he says.

Hollis is shorter than Jay, but meatier in the places that give men permission to start shit on dark street corners, thick about the neck and upper arms. The ribbed seams of his black-and-gold GOLDWELL TIRES T-shirt are stretched by the width of his biceps. It's him, all right. The greasy-haired white guy who confronted Jay in the parking lot of the apartment complex: sandy, almost reddish hair, clipped at the front, and brown eyes, a perfect match for the description given to the cops after the deaths of Deanne Duchon and Tina Wells.

"You following me?" he says.

"Might I point out you're standing in front of my house right now."

Jay slides his hands inside his pants pockets, thinking he might dupe Hollis into believing he's got something in there other than pennies and his car keys. This is the last time, he thinks, that he's leaving the house without the .38.

"And wasn't that you out in front of *my* house? Coming around my old job, stirring up some ancient shit?" Hollis says, creeping closer. He's sweating despite the cooling night air, and his skin is sallow. His five o'clock shadow is rough enough to be a weapon. "I ought to have you arrested for trespassing, stalking or something," he says, fists tightening at his sides.

"You really want to invite police scrutiny right now?"

"I ain't done nothing wrong!"

It's here he makes his first move, a quick step on the ball of his right foot while raising his left hand. Jay is quicker, hooking him right up under his chin, a clean blow that catches Hollis by surprise. He stumbles back a few paces before doubling over, resting his hands on the front of his dirty jeans. "I'll kill you," he says, spitting blood, standing suddenly and charging Jay again. He wraps his arms around Jay's waist and thrusts him to the ground. Jay can hear the pop of his head against the concrete before he feels it, before the bass note of agony echoes in the tight confines of his skull. He rolls over to his side, his stomach lurching with nausea. Hollis gets in another blow to his head before Jay manages to push him off, knocking him to the ground. Hollis, drunk, trips on the toes of his cowboy boots as he tries to stand, falling back to the street. Jay has a straight shot to the man's head if he wants to take it, a single kick that would shut him up for good. But Hollis is already spent, hunched on his hands and knees, struggling to catch his breath. "I swear to God, I'll kill you."

"Like you killed Alicia Nowell?"

"You not putting no shit on me just to save your boy's ass."

Hollis stands slowly, cautiously reaching his arms out behind him to catch a potential fall, as if he expects the street to rise up and snatch him back.

He's even drunker than Jay thought.

"There was an eyewitness who saw you."

Hollis nearly laughs. "Saw me *kill* a girl? Bullshit."

"There was an eyewitness, several of 'em, actually," Jay says, "who saw you and your van loitering in the neighborhood. There was somebody who saw you outside the truck stop on Market Street, struggling with a teenage girl."

"Wasn't that the same thing the newspaper said about your boy?"

He's right, of course. The D.A.'s office *had* said the same thing about Neal.

Hollis stands to his full height. "Anybody can say they saw anything, don't make it true. I never touched no young girls, at least not out there, and I certainly never killed anybody. Worst I ever did in Pleasantville was catch a smoke on the boss man's clock, park my van, and nap awhile. You the only one still can't get that straight. That story about me and some girl outside the truck stop, it never happened. The date it supposedly went down, I wasn't even in the state. I had a special run up to Tulsa for Sterling. They vouched for me, not to mention the shipping company in Oklahoma who received a big shitload of pipe fitters from yours truly. The district attorney's office, the cops, they knew all this years ago, that's why I was never arrested in the first place."

Jay falls silent, momentarily stumped.

In the dim light, he searches Hollis's bloodshot eyes.

Why hasn't he heard this before?

And how did this never come up in Lon's talks with Detective Resner?

"It's not me," Hollis says, cracking his knuckles, as if this late show of menace might still put Jay on notice. "I see you around me again, I hear you throwing my name around a murder case, and it's gonna come down a lot worse than this," he says, before pivoting on his boots and walking back to the Chevy.

It's warm in the house, too warm. Jay can smell Evelyn's cooking on the stove, spaghetti for the kids, hot links and sweet onions for her. He peels off his suit jacket, the cotton shirt underneath sticking to the hairs on his forearms. He stretches out the muscles in his right hand, where a bruise is developing across his knuckles. The back of his skull throbs. He wipes his damp forehead as he starts for the kitchen, looking for Rolly and the kids, Evelyn too, feeling a strange stillness in every corner of the house. From the great room, the den past the kitchen, Jay hears the low murmur of a male voice, young and slightly gruff, can actually smell the man's cologne, sweetly overdone, covering god knows what. The pain in his head swells, as panic vibrates through his body. He immediately thinks of the guy in the Nissan Z. He doesn't think anybody could get past Rolly, but how else to explain why his buddy didn't answer his phone? He's about to start for his bedroom, for the .38 revolver, when he finally recognizes the voice in the living room. He turns toward it, inching past the kitchen and into the den, where Pastor Keith Morehead is seated on Jay's L-shaped sectional.

Evelyn has brought him a glass of iced tea. She's sitting with her legs crossed, batting her big brown eyes at the pretty pastor, regaling him with stories of her dad's tenure at First Love Antioch Baptist Church in Fifth Ward, as if his religiosity were her own, when Jay happens to know for a fact that Evelyn quit her regular churchgoing as far back as the eleventh grade, preacher daddy or no preacher daddy. She swears like a longshoreman and drinks like one too. He'd be surprised if she didn't have a little squeeze of gin or rum in that glass of iced tea she's so demurely sipping. Rolly, who once tried to date Bernie's older sister only to be shot down halfway through a first meal at a Ninfa's cantina off the Gulf Freeway, is eyeing Morehead with thinly veiled disdain. An ex-con with a perennial line of dirt under his nails, Rolly can't stomach a fussy man, let alone an overly religious one. The cologne, the pressed jeans, the white, white teeth–Morehead is a type that Rolly doesn't understand, and certainly doesn't trust. "You have a visitor," he says coldly, before turning to look at Jay and seeing the damage done to his face. He curses under his breath.

Keith Morehead turns and stands.

"Mr. Porter. Sorry to drop in on you like this."

Evelyn stands too, smoothing down her coffee-colored hair, the few strands of gray professionally colored over with red and bits of gold. "Can I get you something else, Mr. Morehead?" Her skirt is hiked a few inches above her knees from sitting. She makes no effort to lower the shade on his view.

"No, ma'am, I've got to get on." To Jay, he says, "Is there somewhere we can talk?"

Jay walks him to the living room. Once they're alone, Morehead tells him, "She's to be buried this weekend. Maxine, Mr. Robicheaux, they've asked me to consider speaking at the service. I'm to meet the pastor at Sunnyside Baptist to talk over the details of the home-going." Jay nods, reaching to rub the sore spot at the back of his head.

"What can I do for you?"

"This is delicate," the pastor says, clasping his hands together. "And let me first say I appreciate the degree to which you must be feeling split, between your commitment to the community and your fidelity to the Hathorne family."

"I have no commitment to anyone other than Neal, my client."

"You have other clients too," Morehead reminds him, in an overly avuncular manner that irritates Jay coming from a man at least ten years his junior and with no skin in the game, as far as Jay can see. Keith Morehead lives, not in Pleasantville proper, but in neighboring Clinton Park. "And the men and women in Pleasantville are suffering over this recent blow, what feels like a growing rift in their own family, a Hathorne accused of preying on their children. The very fact of the indictment raises questions about the other girls and Neal's involvement. Not everyone is willing to accept it," he says, speaking as if Neal's guilt were a foregone conclusion. "My only interest is looking ahead, to where we go as a community after this tragedy. I agree with Arlee Delyvan, that deep down you're doing what you think is right, and it's something I will personally remind folks of in the days ahead. I'd hate to see the good people of Pleasantville lose what little momentum they had in the civil lawsuit."

"Why didn't Arlee call me herself?"

"I think there are some concerns about where your loyalties lie."

"Neal didn't kill that girl," Jay says, raising his voice a little, as if trying to call forth his earlier convictions, which have drifted just out of his reach.

"See, it's that kind of pushy statement of absolutes, when so many others are feeling unsure, that has been off-putting to some, especially coming from a hired attorney. *Their* attorney, they thought." He sighs, looking down at his clasped hands and closing his eyes. For all Jay knows, he may be praying. "I'm not on anyone's side, I hope you do know that," he says. "I want only the best for the Robicheauxs and the men and women who put their faith in my hands." He puts a hand on Jay's shoulder. "Now or later, I hope that you'll likewise be prepared to do what needs to be done to make this right."

"For whom?"

"Pray on it, Mr. Porter." Turning toward the door, he asks Jay to please give a warm hello to his kids, Ben and Ellie, whom he met at the church. His last words are a sage reminder of faith in god in all things. "We will get through this."

"Guy's a phony," Rolly says, loping into the living room once he hears the front door close behind Morehead. "No better than Johnetta Paul getting herself on TV, making this all about him." He gets another look at the injuries on Jay's face. "Sorry, Counselor, I got distracted with the preacher, got my hackles up, him coming in the house like that, unannounced." He glances out

the front windows, making sure the street's clear in both direc-
tions. "What'd Hollis want?"

Jay turns; first things first. "The kids okay?"

Rolly nods. "They're in their rooms."

"Get Lonnie on the phone," he says, as he turns toward the
main hallway that leads to the bedrooms, checking on Ben
first and then Ellie, who is on the telephone. She looks up when
her dad pushes open the door softly. She's beaming. She puts a
hand over the mouthpiece and whispers, "Lori called." Despite
himself, Jay smiles, feeling a hiccup of joy that, where his kids
are concerned, can pop up in the most unexpected places. His
daughter's fifteen-year-old pregnant friend called, and Jay is
unquestionably happy, for both of them, actually. And happy
as well to have solved the mystery of why no one had answered
the home line when he phoned from the road. Ellie had simply
ignored the call waiting. "It's a school night," he reminds her,
before quietly closing her door.

Lonnie arrives about twenty minutes after Evelyn leaves.

The three of them gather at the kitchen table, Jay and the sole
members of his legal team, making sure to keep their voices
down so his kids can sleep.

"It's not him," he says.

"Hollis?" Lon asks, looking from Jay to Rolly.

"Any chance Resner's setting you up?" Jay says.

Lonnie is quiet for a moment, staring at the two men.

Her mind is ticking through the last few days, every off-the-
record chat.

The only words out of her mouth are a muttered, "Oh, shit."

"He knows you're talking to me?" Jay asks.

"Yes."

Rolly is rolling an unlit cigarette across the lacquered cherrywood tabletop, flicking it back and forth with his middle finger. He reaches for the bottle of scotch in the center of the table, the only anchor in this rocky night of twists and turns. He pours a finger for the former reporter. She bites through it in one gulp. "Wolcott, the A.D.A. Nichols," Jay says, "they knew I would reach for Hollis—walking reasonable doubt—and they knew all along it couldn't have been him." He feels sick to think how badly he may have been played, Wolcott holding game pieces behind her back, purposefully misleading him, or how wrongly he may have played himself, rushing into a trial he can't win.

"Are you sure?" Lon asks.

"That little story about Hollis trying to shove a girl into the cab of his truck at that truck stop on Market—the bit in this that sold you against a lack of physical evidence, the fact that the semen wasn't his—that story is bullshit. Hollis was out of state the date that supposedly went down."

"Which is information that cop Resner could have given you," Rolly says.

"But didn't." Lon reaches for the bottle herself, pouring double the last round. She winces as she remembers. "He also knocked out the boyfriend."

"Hollis was always the best lead we had," Rolly says.

"And I'm telling you, it's not him."

Under the kitchen light, Jay turns his face to the right, showing up the blossoming bruise coming in on the right side of his face, to match the ones healing on the other side. "The guy came at me with his left hand." From Lonnie's box of notes, he pulls out the autopsy report on Alicia Nowell. Across the tabletop, he lays out the photocopied pictures. The places where her face has been distorted, the skin a black-and-purple bed of ripe bruising, are all on the left side, meaning it had to have been someone punching her with his *right* hand. "It's not his semen, it's not his left hook," Jay says. "It's not him."

CHAPTER 19

The call comes the following Monday, a week before Thanksgiving.

Jay Porter and all interested parties in the matter of *State of Texas v. Neal Patrick Hathorne* are to be in Judge Irwin Little's courtroom at one that afternoon, the big man himself cutting lunch short to issue his ruling. The small room is packed with people—some of the same faces Jay saw before and some new ones. Sam is here. Neal too. They flank Axel Hathorne, who sits tall in a navy suit and slim red tie. Vivian and all four of her daughters are seated in the row behind them, the family turning the judge's ruling into a test of their genetic fortitude and grace under fire, a test they intend to win, as if the injunction is victory itself, a triumphant end instead of the beginning of a battle they are not assured of surviving. Neal anxiously crosses the bar to join his attorney, a man who is having a hard time looking him in the eye. Jay already knows how this will go. He was in Judge Little's chambers just two days ago for an off-the-record meeting with the judge, Matt Nichols from the D.A.'s office, and Wayne Duffie, the county clerk—not in the presence of a court reporter or even Little's longtime clerk. Little asked just two questions—would Jay's client waive his right to any pre-trial hearings if the state pledged not to play games with discovery, and did any of them have any holiday plans that might take them out of the city for a considerable stretch of time—after which Jay knew how he would rule.

From the bench, Judge Little says much the same as he said in chambers, that if thirty days are all it takes to have a clean election without the mess of a murder trial and the grave accusations of wrongdoing on the part of Ms. Wolcott tainting everything, then he's inclined to grant it. If her office truly has the goods on Neal Hathorne, it will have to prove its case in court; and likewise, if Mr. Hathorne is found guilty by a jury of his peers, then he will have had his day in court, and the voters can decide what, if anything, they choose to extrapolate from the Hathorne name on the ballot. Either way, the judge agrees with the argument put forth by Mr. Porter: that Mr. Hathorne's interests, as well as those of the city at large, are best served by holding this trial as quickly as possible. Given the highly unusual set of circumstances, he has already been in contact with the clerk's office at the criminal court building to be certain a courtroom will be available on such short notice, and a trial date—December ninth—has been set. Judge Little himself has reset the date for the runoff election: Tuesday, January seventh. Across the courtroom, Matt Nichols looks downright queasy.

"It's a hell of a tight timetable, but you asked for a trial and now you got it," the judge tells him. Again, he offers the simple way out: the D.A.'s office can drop the charges, to avoid any hint of impropriety, and refile after the election.

Nichols opens his mouth to speak.

But it's Sandy Wolcott, who Jay had not realized is also in the courtroom, seated on the left side of the gallery, who answers the judge's query.

Her integrity publicly called into question, she rises slowly.

In an aubergine pantsuit, her dark hair pulled into a severe bun, she looks almost martial, armed and ready. With permission to approach, she crosses the bar and stands before the judge. "No, Your Honor," she says. "We're more than prepared to go forward." Judge Little nods, because what the hell else was she going to say? Admit in a room full of city officials and reporters that she pushed for a shitty indictment just to gain leverage in an election? Thanks to Jay Porter, her name has been tarnished almost as much as Neal's. She has more invested in this trial than ever before.

The whole thing takes twenty minutes.

Jay is out in enough time to pick up both of his kids from school. This will be his last time for a while. He'll have to arrange with Evelyn or Eddie Mae to get them home from school every day for the next month, while he's knee-deep in this trial. He asks Neal for this one thing, this one afternoon, before he promises to pledge his life to his client, every morning, noon, and night.

Ben gets out of Poe Elementary before his sister.

Jay's is the first car in line waiting for the bell.

They get ice cream at a market on Bissonnet, chocolate and strawberry for Ben, praline for Jay, and a scoop of peppermint in a cup for Ellie; Ben holds the cup in his lap all the way to Lamar High School.

"You won," Ellie says when she arrives at the car.

"Dad got ice cream," Ben says, teeth clicking from the cold. He climbs around to the back, ceding the front seat to his older sister without being asked.

"Your court thing," Ellie says again. "You won."

"Where'd you hear that?"

"Mr. Jensen heard it on the radio," she says, swiping the paper cup of melting ice cream from her brother. "He announced it in government. He said it's kind of a big deal." She dumps her backpack on the floor as she climbs in.

"I didn't *win* anything, not yet."

He takes the ride home to explain what he's doing and why, laying out the timetable, what it will mean for their lives, Thanksgiving upended, and probably Christmas too. He mentions, awkwardly, their mother's name, and their family's own firsthand experience with loss, how desperate it makes one for answers, even sharing with them Bernie's feelings about the other girls who'd been killed, wrapping it all up in a stumbling speech about cynicism and electoral politics. For an opening statement, it stinks. In the backseat, Ben is digging the last of his chocolate-strawberry swirl out of the soggy waffle cone with the tip of his pale pink tongue. Jay is not sure he's heard a word of it, save for his mother's name. Without the least preamble, Ben asks, "Can we get a tree this year?" In the front seat, Ellie turns to look at Jay. Ben, in the back, catches his father's reflection in the rearview mirror. They're waiting on him, Jay knows that. They are waiting on their father, their unelected leader, to show the way.

Last year, their first without Bernie, he had dreaded this very question, and nearly shook with relief when it never came. Christmas, any thought of it, went unspoken. They simply got into this car and drove as far away from it as they could get in a day. His kids, they had saved him by not making any extraordinary demands on life after death, and now he feels selfishly, shamefully angry at being so emotionally tethered to them, at having to grieve in lockstep with his children. He's already gotten himself into a murder trial this month. He doesn't think he can handle a Christmas tree too. He would, if he could, kick his own ass for thinking he was strong enough for any of this, for involving himself this deep. "We'll talk about it," he says, without explaining why the time to talk about it isn't right now, the three of them alone in the car, idling at a red light.

The first roundtable takes place in Jay's office Wednesday morning. In the conference room upstairs, they start at eight sharp. Jay, Lonnie, Rolly, Eddie Mae taking notes, and Neal pacing around the hard edges of the long table; they're all gathered. With a black Sharpie, Jay makes the first stain on a large white pad, starting with a list of the facts that are not on their side. They're three weeks from voir dire, and this is what they're up against.

1. Neal called the victim, Jay writes, an hour before she was last seen.

"It was seven thirty-two, to be exact," Lon says, reading from her notes of the phone records from Alicia Nowell's pager. Matt Nichols, to his credit, had been true to his word. They'd met in his office yesterday morning, combing through every inch of the state's file, making detailed notes, and working through lunch. "Alicia was last seen at the corner of Guinevere and Ledwicke."

"Waiting, the old lady said," Rolly adds, for in a day he too had memorized the state's file, and after seeing the evidence against Neal—all of it admittedly circumstantial—had asked a second time if Jay was sure about this dude. Here in the conference room, Rolly watches the client pace.

"Elma Johnson saw her at about eight forty-five," Lonnie

says. "And, yes, she said it looked to her like she was waiting for someone."

"Which suggests a rendezvous or a planned meeting," Jay says.

"Or some prior contact," Rolly adds.

"Plus there's the boyfriend's story," Lon says, "about the meeting at Jones High School in the spring, at that meet-the-candidates forum or whatever it was called. Kenny told the cops that Neal was extra chatty, flirting." Neal, halfway through his fifth lap around the conference table, rolls his eyes impatiently. He has not said a single word since they began, except to answer a phone call from his grandfather, to assure Sam that he was fine. Jay has held Sam to his directive that he would run this thing his way, without any interference from the elder Hathorne, and Sam, unable to control a situation he in fact engineered, has already called the office three times this morning. He must have figured out by now that Jay never cashed his check for the retainer. It is still sitting in Jay's top desk drawer, tucked away, as useless to him now as the deal he cut with Sam. He doesn't want to lose the Pleasantville civil case as his retirement plan, but neither is he willing to gamble with Neal's life over money.

"And he gave Alicia his card," Lon adds, flipping through her notes.

Jay nods. He marks down this fact along with the others.

2. Neal was evasive with the campaign staff about his whereabouts.

"The obstruction charge was dropped when the murder indictment came down," Jay says. "But they'll line up staffers on the stand to tell the same story."

"It's Tonya Hardaway that matters," Lon says. "She did the schedule."

"The one that he fired," Rolly says.

Jay adds this regrettable fact to the board too.

Eddie Mae steals a glance at Neal.

He makes her nervous, a man who won't eat.

She laid out a plate of Shipley's doughnuts first thing this morning.

Again, she asks Neal if he won't sit down, nibble a little something.

Neal, his back to them, is at the window, the one Jay had to replace.

He never answers.

3. Neal lied to police detectives about knowing the dead girl.

"What difference does any of this make?" he says finally, erupting to the exact degree that he'd been keeping his mouth shut, turning from the window and laying into Jay, as if *he* and not the state were the accuser, as if Neal blames Jay for the situation he's in. "You'll put A.G. on the stand and he'll say I was with him, and that's the end of it. The rest of this is bullshit."

"We're getting to that," Jay says, otherwise ignoring him.

He's had clients blow up at him before. Carl Pritchett's sister, screaming that she was in debt up to her eyeballs, once threw a coffee cup at his head, at a Days Inn in Little Rock—where Jay had rented a conference room to explain to his 157 clients the traps in the settlement they were being offered. The eruptions, the raw emotion, the exhaustion and mounting fear, not a breath of it matters, nothing beyond the facts he's putting on this board.

4. Neal was seen by an eyewitness, struggling with the girl on the street.

The room goes quiet for a moment, with only the squeak of Jay's marker against the white paper on the board. *This* is the one that could send Neal to prison. "Can I have one of those?" Jay turns to see him pointing to Rolly's cigarettes, one of which Rolly keeps near him at all times, lit or unlit, fingering the seam along the filter, worrying it like a rabbit's foot. Rolly gestures to the one that's on the table in front of him, as if to say to Neal, *It's yours, man.* His tattooed fingers then fish for a lighter in the front pocket of his jeans. "Not in here," Jay says. But Neal lights the cigarette anyway, exhaling slowly. In his pressed khakis and pale peach cotton oxford, he stands alone at the window, thin gray swirls of smoke curling around his head.

"I didn't want him to run," he says, with a bemused shrug of his shoulders. "I don't even know that Axel deep down really wanted it, at least not at first. Not that I don't think he'd make a good mayor. I do," he says, glancing over his shoulder at them, but never making eye contact with anyone. "I wouldn't have gone this far if I didn't believe that. It's just that this was always Pop's deal, you know, what Sam wanted for the family, and not just for Axel, but me too, I guess. Looking ahead, he thought I might get on a state race. Most everyone I know thinks Bush is going to make a run for the White House in 2000. I could work my way into a campaign for the governor's office, and down the line, who knows, maybe a national race, a place in Washington. He wanted that for me."

He shrugs again. Sam's dream for both Axel and Neal is about as within reach at this point as the pitted surface of the moon. Jay, undeterred, draws a black line along the outer edge of the list of "facts," creating a T shape on the page, leaving room on the right side to refute every point of the D.A.'s case.

A. Neal can explain the mistaken call to Alicia's pager, but it's weak.

B. Same with his explanation to the police that he didn't *lie* about knowing Alicia Nowell; he simply didn't remember her, for whatever that means to a jury.

C. He can likewise explain his reluctance to share with the staff that he was planning a meeting with his father, because of both the personal nature of the visit and the fact that it was a potential point of controversy for the campaign.

"It can work," Jay says, "especially if we can get him to tes-tify."

Neal turns from the window. "*If*," he says. "He *has* to testify."

Jay turns to Rolly. "How are we doing on that?"

"He hasn't run yet," Rolly says. "I got a guy on him I trust, a cat I contract out to sometimes. Mr. Hats don't get around much, Playboy Club and home."

"Which is where?"

"Garage apartment he's paying by the week, off Dowling."

"All this time?" Neal says.

"He's been in and out of places around Third Ward."

Neal shakes his head at the absurdity of it, his father right under his nose this whole time.

Jay writes their biggest problem in bold strokes on the board.

D. The eyewitness.

"Do we know who it is?" Eddie Mae asks.

"Nichols is stalling on his witness list," Jay says. "But ac-cording to what we could pull from some early police reports, Magnus Carr, a neighbor of Elma Johnson's, told the first beat cops who were called out that he not only glimpsed the girl through the window of his study, which faces Ledwicke, but also saw what he took to be a black man with her, 'struggling' was his word. He told the cops it was dark, a little past the streetlamp, and he couldn't be totally sure what he saw."

"He's one of your clients," Eddie Mae says, surprised.

"Who somehow went from thinking he *might* have seen a black male with Alicia to fingering Neal, in particular, in front of a grand jury," Lonnie says.

"You sure it was him?" Neal asks.

"Who else?"

"He was the only one in the D.A.'s file who intimated that he'd seen something more than what Elma Johnson reported," Jay says. "But until Nichols turns over a witness list, with some indication of who he's planning to put on the stand, we're not entitled to anything they might have said in front of the grand jury, not without calling a hearing in front of the judge to force the matter."

"Which I waived my right to."

"Exactly."

Neal shakes his head, adamant. "I wasn't there."

"He has to be mistaken," Eddie Mae says.

"The problem is we don't have any other viable alternatives as to who could have done it," Lonnie says. "Hollis is out, so is Alicia's boyfriend."

"Eddie Mae," Jay says. "See if you can find in here the client records for Magnus Carr, his neighbors too, on both sides. He's across the street from Elma, if I remember. There may have been someone else out there who saw something different. Plus, if I can get a look at his client file, I can get a better feel for the guy, what makes him tick, what might have made him susceptible to the D.A.'s suggestion that it was Neal out there, and not someone else." Eddie Mae nods, pushing back from the table and smoothing her tight skirt as she stands; she's the only one besides Jay who can make sense of their crude filing system, the boxes they never adequately unpacked in the move to this office. Jay's client files are essentially mini dossiers on the individual plaintiffs, based on their answers to an extensive questionnaire that Jay designed himself. The files can grow to twenty, thirty, sometimes forty pages long, containing every detail of his clients' lives, from birth dates to the names of spouses; those of their children and their ages; their parents; city and county of birth; their schooling, income, religious affiliation, political inclination; social clubs they belong to; how long they've owned their homes; previous addresses and places of employment; criminal history and/or any pertinent facts in regard to any previous involvement with the legal system—not to mention copious information about their medical history, including surgeries; and hospitalizations; and pregnancies, miscarriages, or forced terminations—all of it going back to birth. Clients are not obligated to answer every question, but most do. In civil suits, they're not the ones with anything to hide. The forms help Jay get a more complete picture of the people he's serving, who they were before and after the inciting injury, in this case, the establishment of the ProFerma chemical plant in Pleasantville's backyard. "Carr's a quiet one, what I remember, reluctant to get involved in the civil suit."

With Rolly's help, Eddie Mae lifts a banker's box to the other end of the conference table from where she was sitting. With her plum-colored fingernails, she flips through the plastic tabs on the hanging file folders within.

Lon glances around the table. She has on black jeans, and her kneecaps are pressed against the side of the table. She tugs at her button-down shirt, pulling it closed over a lacy camisole underneath. It's cool in here. One week before Thanksgiving, Houston has gone and got itself a cold, with thick phlegmy clouds overhead, gray and swollen, coughing a light mist of rain, and the glass replacement for the window is thin and cheap. "Don't shoot me for saying it," she says. "But anybody else got a hinky feeling about the girl's stepfather?"

Jay, in particular, doesn't want to touch this.

It brings back a host of bad memories of his own stepfather, nights he crept past Jay's bedroom door, heading for Jay's baby sister.

He draws another line down the paper on the board, writing in a third column the name Mitchell Robicheaux, followed by a question mark.

"Based on what?" Neal says.

"I may be reaching, but haven't we wondered from the beginning why this one was different from the others?" Lon says.

She reminds them of how badly Alicia was beaten, which Jay couldn't forget if he wanted to, and the fact that she was found in a different location. "Maybe this one is different because it *is* different," she says.

"Different killer?" Rolly speculates. He, as much as anyone else, had staked a resolution on the idea that one man had done all three girls, otherwise what in hell had he been chasing Alonzo Hollis for? He looks at Jay, to gauge his response. Jay is staring at the board, at the name Mitchell Robicheaux.

"Instead of a pattern, maybe it begins and ends with her," Lon says, pointing to a photo of Alicia, the high school graduation photo from the *Chronicle*, which Eddie Mae had carefully cut from its pages, tacking the image to a corkboard to the right of Jay's notepad. They all stare at her face.

"Which brings us back to what she was doing out there," Rolly says.

"Where are we with the flyers?" asks Jay.

Rolly shakes his head. "We combed the north and to the east, south down to Pearland. We'll push to the west next, but so far we haven't found anything."

Lon scrunches up the freckled flesh along the bridge of her nose, pondering something. "They found one in her purse, didn't they?" she says, tapping a Bic pen against her right knee-cap. "One flyer she'd folded up and saved. If she was out there to distribute Wolcott's flyers—"

"Then why'd she keep one for herself?"

Jay is ashamed he didn't see it sooner. "She called you that night," he says to Neal. "You returned the call, leaving your number on her pager, not knowing whose call you were returning, but the point is she reached out to you."

"You think she knew?" Neal says. "What Wolcott's team was up to?"

"She had to," Jay says. "They put her in a blue T-shirt, looking like one of Hathorne's people, like a local, an insider who was concerned about Axel's motives. She knew what they were using her to do. And she called Neal."

"You think she was trying to tell me?"

"I think it's possible."

"We should subpoena the phone records, the campaign's, your cell phone," Lonnie says, pointing to Neal, who is shaking his head. Jay seems to agree. "It could backfire," he says. "Any evidence of prior contact only bolsters the state's claim that the two knew each other, that they were planning to meet."

"But we had no plan. We never *spoke*. So who was she waiting for?"

Jay turns, looking at the corkboard. Below Alicia's picture is a map of the Pleasantville neighborhood and nearby Clinton Park, torn out of an old Key Map of Houston in Jay's office. Jay stares at it, zooming in on a detail he hadn't noticed before, a tiny blue M at the corner of Guinevere and Ledwicke.

"That's a bus stop!"

"It's probably unmarked," Neal says. "Metro hasn't been out to replace the signs in Pleasantville in years. It came up in one of our town halls."

"That's the problem with eyewitness testimony. What Mrs. Johnson thought she saw set the tone for the investigation, the assumption that she was waiting for someone when she might have been waiting for a bus ride home."

Turning back to the easel, he flips to the next clean white page on the oversize pad of paper. He starts a list of witnesses they'll need to interview ahead of trial. Magnus Carr. He adds the name Elma Johnson and leaves a blank space for any other neighbors they might find; Maxine and Mitchell Robicheaux; and the architect of Wolcott's campaign, Reese Parker, who probably designed the flyers herself. They'll start at the top, heading out to Pleasantville this afternoon. Neal stares at the board, frowning. He stabs the cigarette into the base of a cream-colored teacup. From the other end of the conference room, Eddie Mae looks up from the box of files in front of her. "For the devil of me, Jay, I can't seem to find Mr. Carr's file," she says. "Some of the C's aren't even in here." She waves Rolly toward another stack of boxes at the back of the conference room, directing him to lift and carry them down to her end of the table. She ferrets through the boxes, going through the hanging files, one by one. "These files are all mixed up, Jay. They're not in any kind of order."

"You're not seriously talking about putting Reese Parker on the witness stand?" Neal nods toward Jay's list, his hands balled into fists in his pockets. "If we go in there making this about politics, we could end up turning the jury off."

"*Wolcott* made it political," Lon says. "We're just pointing it out."

"It's important to get it in," Jay says. "The flyers, the lying, it sets up in the jurors' minds their inclination toward playing in the dirt, that they're willing to engineer a murder trial to gain advantage. It's a seed we have to plant, that these guys are fucking around, wasting the court's time with weak evidence."

"Not to mention letting a real killer walk free," Rolly mutters. In his low-slung Levi's and a BIG EASY BLUES FEST T-shirt, he's lifting boxes for Eddie Mae. Flustered and perspiring lightly across her forehead, Eddie Mae is pulling out folders, trying to make sense of what happened to her filing system.

Lon sits up, dropping two legs of her chair to the floor. "They're messing with a city election. I thought that was the whole point of what we're doing."

"The whole point is to keep me out of jail," Neal says acidly.

He's the client, he reminds them.

It's his life on the line. And he wants a clean defense strategy, low risk.

"We'll put A.G. on the stand," he says. "He'll tell them I was with him."

"And if he doesn't?" Jay says. "I mean, if he doesn't show."

"He will," Neal says. Adding softly, desperately, "He's got to."

He appears, over the past few weeks, to have changed his mind about his father's trustworthiness, to be so uncomfortable about, or downright afraid of, going after Reese Parker that he's placed his chances at victory in the hands of Allan George Hathorne; it's a boyish faith, a longing for a father that Jay understands, but is no less wary of. This plan of putting Parker, Wolcott's whole campaign, on trial, "Sam thinks it's a bad idea," Neal says, sounding to Jay less confident than he's straining to appear. There is another looming presence in the room, tugging at Neal's sleeve. He may as well have pulled up a chair for Sam at the table.

"This isn't Sam's case," Jay reminds him.

"No, it's mine," Neal says, his voice hardened. He tells of his utmost respect for his grandfather's wisdom, his faith in a man who has done so much for folks in this city, who has sacrificed so much for Neal in particular, and how profoundly grateful he is for his grandfather's love. "And I agree with Sam."

CHAPTER 20

Magnus Carr is a seventy-six-year-old retired postal worker whose eldest daughter, Jackie, a dentist who married and moved to Chicago right out of college, bought her father the four-bedroom, two-bath, one-story faux-colonial with union blue shutters on Ledwicke so that her kids would have a place to stay when they visited their paw-paw. His wife, Shirley Carr, never got to see the house, one of the last built on the street; she died when their kids, Jackie and her kid brother, Darryl, were still in their teens. Mr. Carr had raised them on his own, in a one-bedroom apartment not far from Hobby Airport. He lives alone now, on a comfortable pension. "Come on," he says to Jay. "It's back this way." Lonnie follows the two men, staring at the photos on the dusk-colored walls, straining to make

out faces behind the glass. The light is dim in the hallway, in
the whole house in fact; a gold-plated floor lamp in the living
room is the only spot of cheer in all seven rooms. The curtains,
thick rolls of wheat-colored linen, are pulled shut, and the air
is still. It smells of sweet onion and pickled chowchow. Mr.
Carr was reheating a plate of chicken for his lunch when Jay
and Lonnie arrived at his front door. Elma Johnson's view from
her kitchen window was at an angle of about forty-five degrees
from the south side of Ledwicke, but the window in Mr. Carr's
study faces the street directly. He had the radio on that night,
following the election returns. He had made a last-minute
switch inside the white cubicle at Pleasantville Elementary
where he'd voted that morning, impulsively pulling the lever
for Ross Perot, and forty-five minutes after the polls closed in
Texas, he was regretting it terribly. He'd never in his life voted
for a Republican, so Dole was out, but there had to be a better
man than Clinton to sit in the White House, a good Christian
and a decent husband. "I was fixin' to put in for the night, had
a little hot tea and then I went to close the curtains, in the back
bedroom and this room," he says, as they walk into his study,
a pristinely kept room without a desk or a book, just the radio
on a pedestal table next to a putty-colored recliner, and a neat
stack of magazines on the floor. "And I did just like this," he
says, pulling on the cord for the curtains. "And there she was,
right there." He points to the south side of Ledwicke, where the
corner is empty except for a gathering of flowers and notes left
on torn pieces of poster board and a small white cross, all of it
damp from the rain.

"You saw a man?"

"I saw a man," Mr. Carr says, nodding. "He was pulling at her,
like this."

He turns and for the purposes of reenactment uses Lonnie in
his demonstration, pulling on her wrist and twisting the arm a

little as he goes. "She wasn't hollering or nothing, but it looked to me like they were in a struggle of some sort. At the time I didn't think much of it, a lovers' quarrel or something like that, something that wasn't my business no way. Not until the cops came."

"And you told the detectives it was Neal Hathorne you saw?"

"No, I said just what I told you now, and I gave a description. It was a black man, looked like it to me. Maybe your height," he says, nodding to Jay, eyeing him, "maybe a little taller. He was bigger than the girl, that's for sure."

"How'd you get from that to Neal?"

"It was later, when they said they were going to have me to testify for the grand jury. It was a man from the D.A.'s office come around–"

"Matt Nichols?"

"No, it was an investigator with his office. He showed some pictures and, well, excuse my language, but hell if it didn't look like Neal."

"And you're sure it was him?"

"I'm sure it *looked* like him, that's all I said to the grand jury, all I'm willing to say if they put me on the stand again." He sighs. "I hate to speak anything against Sunny," he says, referring to Sam by his old nickname. "He's a good man, but I don't really know the young 'un, Neal, and you can't judge a man by his last name. I got kin of mine I don't hardly recognize, not down in their souls." He looks out at the corner, the makeshift memorial. "I never heard of nothing like this in my day," he says, the words rolling over the gravel in his voice. "But things is changing, even in Pleasantville." He shakes his head. Outside, damp flower petals litter the sidewalk, ink runs on the poster board. In a pale yellow windbreaker, Arlee Delyvan comes walking down Ledwicke, cradling a small box of pink camellias clipped from her garden, headed with great purpose for the makeshift memorial. She kneels at the gathering, taking time to pick away dead leaves, to set upright a pink teddy bear with a red ribbon, its fur spiked into thorns from the rain. Magnus clears his throat. "I hate to do this, Mr. Porter, god knows it's bad timing. But I need to tell you I'm moving on."

He appears vaguely ashamed, to quit on a man. But resolved, nonetheless.

He starts with a familiar refrain. "I like you, son."

"For a guy who's so well-liked, I sure am losing business left and right."

"It's just we've waited and waited, and time you decide to step back into a courtroom, it's over this here," he says, gesturing with his ashy brown knuckle toward the windowpane, the memorial for the missing girl on the other side. "I don't know if Neal did this thing they're saying, and I guess he's as entitled to a lawyer as anybody, but I don't know why it had to be *ours*. I'm seventy-six, I'm tired of waiting for ProFerma to pay for what they did. I don't need the moon and the stars, just something fair. They're saying this other fella can deliver."

"Aguilar."

"I was hesitant at first, figuring Jelly Lopez is getting too big for his britches, thinking he's running everything now. But now I just want it done."

"You're right," Jay says. "It is bad timing."

At the curb outside Mr. Carr's one-story house, Lon offers to talk to the rest of the neighbors, starting with the house to the right of Mr. Carr's. Jay is looking to the south, where Arlee is tending the memorial site. Overhead, the clouds have parted, white sunlight peeking through their cottony strands. Arlee has shed her yellow windbreaker, laying it beside her on the concrete. She looks up and sees Jay, but doesn't say anything, not right away, her hands keeping busy, and he has a stinging, disconsolate worry that she too is angry with him. He didn't realize until this moment how deeply he thinks of Mrs. Delyvan as more than just a *client*, or rather the depths of care and concern that word can hold, something, in fact, close to love. Perhaps it's this little-known facet of practicing law that truly threatens his legal career. When it comes to love, on the other side of his wife's death Jay is a foundling, a newborn, thin skinned and pink, sure of nothing save the sting of loss, the B side of every breath he takes. And for a man like Jay, whose cynicism is only skin deep, little more than a pose, a cover, it occurs to him that he will eventually be made to reconcile love with loss, one way or another. As he looks closer at the parade of crepe myrtles down Ledwicke, the carefully tended lawns and proud homes, lived in and loved by settlers, pioneers who, a generation before Jay, had paved the way for everything he has in his life, starting with the power of protest, the example they gracefully laid, brick by brick—and as he thinks of Arlee on her knees, caring for the memorial of a girl she didn't know—it dawns on him that he may have kept Pleasantville on his desk not for the money, his supposed way out, but for a back way *in*, a way back to himself. He wants Pleasantville to survive the hits it's taken in recent years. He wants Pleasantville to *survive*, whatever change is waiting around the corner. "Go on," he tells Lonnie, speaking softly. "I'll catch up."

As Lonnie starts for the house next door to Mr. Carr's, Arlee stands slowly, pushing herself up and waving off Jay's offer of help. "Well, aren't you having one hell of a month, Mr. Porter?"

"Yes, ma'am."

"Well, you're doing the right thing, whether you know it or not."

She pulls a small handkerchief, white with a pattern of faded blue hyacinths tracing the edges, from her pants pocket and

wipes a few pebbles of dirt sticking to her hands. Her pink camellias now hold a humble place at the foot of the memorial.
Above them, the clouds close in again, but the smell of rain is
gone, leaving behind the damp, milky, sweet scent of wet grass.
Jay shoves his hands into his pockets, wishing in the cool gray
air that he had on a real coat.

"Can't help feeling I've let you all down."

"Why? 'Cause Magnus Carr lost faith?"

"He's not the only one."

"Folks is scared, that's all, don't even know half of what
they're scared of, it's just a feeling out here that the ground is
unsteady, that Pleasantville, as most of us have known it, is in
trouble. First, there was the whooping and hollering over the
bayou development, if it's even real, and what it might mean
for us. And now this thing with Neal, the idea of a Hathorne
mixed up in this," she says, gesturing toward the marked spot
where Alicia Nowell was last seen, the corners of the paper
notes lifting in the breeze. "And when folks get scared, they act
out, make bad choices. We've made that mistake before, in our
first fight with ProFerma. We'd been so stunned by the freeway
coming through, our first big loss as a community, that when
it looked like we couldn't keep ProFerma out, we just kind of
gave in. Sam went in and negotiated a good number of jobs for
the community, the best we thought we could do. But you see
how that turned out in the end. Now folks is henny-pennying
that the sky is falling, moving too fast out of fear. You still got
plenty of clients," she says assuredly, reaching out to pat his
forearm to show her support. "You'll do what you need to do
with this trial, and then we'll finish up what we started on the
other thing."

"Nobody out here really thinks Neal did it, do they?"

"They don't know what to think."

"Let me ask you something," he says, swinging wide of the

question of whether *she* believes Neal did it, and asking, instead, "You know A.G.?"

"What in the world are you asking about him for?"

Jay shrugs, playing at nonchalance, mild curiosity. "There's a story there."

"More than one, in fact."

"Start with Sam then, what you know about it. Why'd the two fall out?"

"Oh, honey," Arlee says, drawing out the last vowel like the opening note of a torch song. "I can't remember a time the two of them ever got along. They're just different, always have been. Sunny's a moneyman, a buttoned-up banker type, likes to rub elbows with potentates. A.G., all he ever wanted was to bang a piano. It started when he wasn't nothing but a pup, used to play in the Methodist church, funerals and weddings, and that was fine, respectable. But when he come home from Prairie View, barely one semester under his belt, saying he was through, he was going to play for a living, well, you could hear the fights all the way over to Market Street. Sam cut him off, kicked him out. It was cold, sure it was, but that's how black folks used to do sometimes, if they thought you were walking off a cliff. They'd kick your ass before anybody else got a chance to—excuse my language, baby. There was a sense that people hadn't worked this hard and struggled for a better way of life just so you could run off and do what you *wanted* to do. No, you owed something for what you got, something you had to give back. Me, I can't understand what we struggled for if it wasn't to let our kids cut loose a little, be free," she says. She shakes the dirt from her handkerchief before returning it, folded, to her pocket.

"Sam was a taskmaster, that's for sure. But you got to understand how hard he worked for his kids, how much all of this," she says, gesturing at the suburban vista, the streets of Pleasantville, "was for them. Axel was in the academy at that time, Ola in graduate school at TSU, and Delia was just starting medical school. And A.G.'s out in the streets, playing in juke joints every night. It just goaded Sam something awful. And Vivian, the more she stood up for A.G., the madder it made him. There's not a soul out here who'll tell you this, but I will. Sam and Viv, they almost broke up over A.G., *twice*," she says.

"Who is Neal's mother?"

"Oh, some little sorry gal he met along the way, on the road. Nine months later, she found him playing a gig halfway up to Austin and dropped that baby at the foot of the stage, least that's the way the story made it back here."

Jay, surprised at the news, especially considering how close Neal and his grandfather are, asks Arlee, "And Sam just accepted him? Just like that?"

"Of course he did. Just like he had accepted A.G."

"Excuse me?"

Arlee gives him a knowing look, politely waiting for him to catch up.

Finally she says, "Sam didn't invent stepping out."

"Not his, huh?"

"The general consensus, especially after dark, what folks have whispered about for years, is *no*. Allan is not a Hathorne. And Sam knew from day one."

"Hmmph," Jay mutters.

He closes his eyes, taking this in, attempting, with this new information in hand, like a freshly unfolded map to a new territory, to trace the demise of their relationship in reverse, back to its original wound, whether Sam's or A.G.'s.

"But they patched it up, for a little while, didn't they?"

"He got off the drugs, came home for a while, that's right. And god bless him, I think he really tried to *come home*. He threw himself into coaching, getting involved with the kids.

This was around the time we were fighting ProFerma's plans to set up the chemical plant. And he got involved in that too."

Here, she sighs, reaching up to pat a few flyaway curls, wiry gray strands at her temples. The air has lifted a bit, picking up fallen leaves, rolling them across the sidewalk like marbles. Arlee shivers, crossing her arms across her chest. "But I don't know. I guess it didn't take," she says. "But there were a lot of things around that time that didn't turn out the way any of us wanted."

CHAPTER 21

The first big surprise of the afternoon turns out not to be
the lingering rumors about the paternity of Allan George Hathorne, not by a mile. It comes before Jay even breaches the
boundaries of Pleasantville. Lonnie phoned to say she had no
new information about the night Alicia disappeared, Elma
Johnson and Magnus Carr being the only two neighbors who
saw anything on the night in question. Plans were made to
meet back at Jay's car, which was parked a few doors down from
Mr. Carr's, on Ledwicke. After walking Ms. Delyvan back to
her home on Tilgham, crossing, in the process, some ten blocks
through the heart of the neighborhood, Jay doubles back, walking alone to the Land Cruiser to meet Lonnie. And that's when
he sees them. They're in red T-shirts, every last one, even Tonya

Hardaway, whose braids he recognizes at a distance of thirty yards. She's wearing a Wolcott T-shirt, like the others, a team of block walkers she's directing from an impromptu command center at the corner of Josie and Gellhorn. Jay halts in his tracks, pausing initially because it's a sucker punch—the naked campaigning during an electoral injunction, which, though not expressly forbidden, seems for sure in bad taste, especially given the knowledge that it was Wolcott's campaign that sent the dead girl into the streets of Pleasantville in the first place. It's tacky, at best, and sinister, at worst, another bit of chicanery, the outcome of which Jay can't divine from here. Would neighborhood residents really take to this kind of bald-faced proselytizing, in Axel Hathorne's political backyard, no less? Curious, he watches the procession for a while, the zigzag pattern of volunteers on Josie Street, not going door-to-door, as he would have thought, but rather skip-hopping houses by some internal logic he can't follow. Jay has never run a field campaign in his life, but what he's witnessing here is different from any way he would ever have imagined going about it, what common sense would dictate: that you hit every door, every house, making contact with each and every voter, every potential step toward victory. Tonya can't see him, not with her back to Ledwicke. And Jay is careful to hang back and observe what he can. Down Josie Street they go, knocking on doors, checking off street numbers and names on the small clipboards they're carrying, returning periodically to their field director and sage, who distributes more slips of paper, directing the block walkers to specific houses and advising them to completely skip others. Jay recognizes, from his client list, some of the houses they're canvassing.

2002 Josie Street is Mary Melendez's place.

2037 is Robert Quinones and his wife, Darla.

2052 is Linda and Betty Dobson, sisters who've lived together for years.

2055 is Rutherford Tompkins, widower and retired fire-fighter who was home alone when the explosion happened last spring. One of the first on the scene, he established a safety zone, past which he wouldn't allow any of his neighbors to cross, and joined firefighters from three counties battling the blaze.

"What in the hell?" Lonnie says when she catches up to Jay, following his gaze across Ledwicke. He doesn't know if she's cursing the fact that Wolcott's team, on the eve of the trial, is still campaigning, or the bizarre manner in which the block walkers appear to be going about it. Either way his answer is, "I don't know."

"You want to talk to her?" she says, meaning Tonya.

"Not here."

"Well, at least now we know where to find her."

"At Wolcott's campaign office," Jay says, still watching.

The second surprise of the day is an unexpected visitor. He's parked across the street from Jay's office, waiting, when Jay swings by in the late afternoon. Lonnie is back on flyergate with Rolly, who, through his subcontractor, is likewise keeping tabs on A.G. at the Playboy Club and his apartment on Dowling. Eddie Mae has been working all morning to set up witness interviews, drawing a giant grid on poster board in the upstairs conference room, representing nearly every hour they have left until jury selection. Jay is returning to check in with her when he sees the late-model navy blue Mercedes sedan, a two-seater with the dealer plates still on, parked on the opposite side of Brazos from the office's front door. The driver, early thirties and Asian, is wearing aviator sunglasses and a thickly knotted striped tie. "Can I help you with something?" Jay says, rapping on the roof of the man's new car with his knuckles. These days, the sight of a strange car idling outside his place of business sets his teeth on edge, the muscles in his jaw twitching, on high alert. The man in the Mercedes peels off his sunglasses.

Looking at Jay, he expresses surprise. "I know you."

"I don't think so, man."

"No, I mean I've seen you, in the newspaper." Then, regarding him further, he asks, just to be sure, "*You're* Jay Porter?"

"Now that we've got that out of the way." He crosses the car's threshold, leaning into the open window, his face coming within inches of the driver's, his eyes darting around the whole of the leather interior. But the car is empty, not a weapon or an alarming item in sight, nothing except a black leather briefcase on the Mercedes's passenger seat. "You want to kindly offer me some reason why you're sitting here, watching my front door?" he says.

"You called *me*, remember?"

"I've never seen you before in my life."

"You called about my car. It was stolen last month."

Jay steps back from the car door, staring at the driver.

"The Z?"

"The Nissan, that's right."

Well, well, Jay thinks.

"Please," he says. "Come inside."

Jon K. Lee was born and raised in Clear Lake, where his dad, a Korean immigrant, worked for NASA and his mom, a Texas native of Japanese and European descent, gave piano lessons in the living room of their Spanish-style suburban home. He is an only child, and the sports car was a gift for graduating from law school at UT in the top 5 percent of his class. "That's the only reason I'm even bothering," Lee says, standing just inside the foyer of Jay's office. He seems exasperated by this errand, self-imposed though it may be. A man in his late twenties, he's snappily dressed in a deep olive green suit. He has thick black hair, long strands of which he runs his fingers through in frustration. "I feel like I'm somehow letting them down if I can't get it back, if I don't even try, you know, even though I told them I would never see that car again. The cops basically said as much. They said even if they did find it, it would likely be stripped for parts." Upstairs, they can hear Eddie Mae singing to herself in the conference room. In the kitchen, there's another pot of beans on the stove. "And then *you* called," Lee says, looking around the old house, with its creaky floors and antique furniture and the smell of soul food wafting through.

"I found your business card in my office," Jay says. He points to the spot on the floor, just inside the shadow of Eddie Mae's desk, where it was discovered after the break-in. "You work for Cole."

"And you're suing them."

"*Sued.* And won, actually."

"Yes." Lee sighs as the story grows more complex. "I looked you up, after you called, and you can imagine my surprise when I realized your connection to the company I work for. Frankly, I thought this was some kind of trick."

"That makes two of us."

"I'm just looking for some information about my car."

"Well, let's start with the fact that my office was broken into shortly after your car was stolen, and whoever it was, it appears he dropped your card."

"I certainly didn't have anything to do with that."

"Thomas Cole didn't involve you in this, breaking into my office?"

"Mr. Porter, I have never laid eyes on Thomas Cole in my nearly two years on the job. I handle contracts, writing leasing agreements with oil fields, that sort of thing. I work in legal, but I don't have a thing to do with your case."

Jay rocks back on his heels, eyeing Lee.

The thing is, Jay actually believes him.

"This whole thing has wasted way more of my time than that car was worth, I swear. I told the police officers when I filed the initial report that I was fairly certain I knew who'd taken it. I gave them a name and everything."

"You know who did it?"

"I have a pretty good idea."

"How can you be so sure?"

"Because I fucked up," Lee says, the word sounding tart and foreign in his mouth, something he's more than happy to spit out. "I hired the guy," he says, sighing. "This young man, he was walking my neighborhood, and he comes up and says he's making money for college, mowing lawns, and could I use a little help. He offered to do the front and back for twenty-five. And I don't know, I had a funny feeling about the guy, just something a little too happy-go-lucky about him, something about his smile didn't look like he'd ever worked hard a day in his life. But I caught myself, thinking like that. I mean, I joined the Black Student Bar Association at UT, mainly because there wasn't one for Asians, but still, all that 'give a brother a job, give him a chance' stuff, I got it," he says, raising up a hand as if he thinks Jay might, on the spot, pick up the preaching where the black law students had left off. "So I said, yeah, sure. And he got right to work, did a decent job on the front and back, earned his twenty-five dollars, so that it only dawned on me after he left that I never actually saw him knocking on any other doors. It was just mine, like he had specifically picked me. Two days later, I wake up and the Nissan is gone." Lee shakes his head. "He had been asking about the car, how it drives, what it costs, you know, but at the time, I just shrugged it off. What young man isn't interested in sports cars?"

"And you had a name?"

"Only the one he gave me, T.J. something or other," Lee says, shrugging at his own stupidity, as if the initials themselves had spelled calamity. Thieving Juvenile. Troublemaking Jackass. But the initials mean something else entirely to Jay. They had imprinted themselves on his brain after their repeated appearance on the pages and pages of photocopied court documents Ellie had brought him the day of Neal's arraignment, the day Jay was looking into Ricardo Aguilar's history with the courts—the first time he heard the name T. J. Cobb. He was Aguilar's client. Jay thinks Jon K. Lee *was* specifically picked because of his tenuous connection to Jay's ongoing legal drama with the oil giant. The license plate on the stolen car and the carelessly dropped business card, with Lee's name and employer on it, were meant to leave a trail back to Cole Oil. *Aguilar is one slick motherfucker*, he thinks. All the while Jay had Eddie Mae looking for potentially stolen papers from the Cole case, Aguilar had come in and helped himself to Pleasantville.

"How many are gone?"

"Lord, Jay, it may be worse than I thought," Eddie Mae says. "Dozens of client files . . . they're just gone."

"I need a list of all the names that are missing," Jay says.

He's calling from two blocks away, already en route to the office of Ricardo Aguilar Esq., listed in the bar directory as Suite 101 of a commercial building on Dunlavy. He hasn't called ahead, wouldn't dream of giving Aguilar a head start. At the corner of Marshall and Dunlavy sits a squat concrete-and-glass building two stories high, one of those late-sixties space-age-style constructions done on the cheap. Thirty years on, there are cracks running on the south side of the building, and the aging film of window tinting has bubbled from decades of Texas sun. The dentist who shares the first floor with Ricardo Aguilar must write the building's biggest rent check each month, for he has earned the right to erect an oversize tube of toothpaste over the front door, a dirt-caked line of it snaking a few inches over Jay's head. There is no front buzzer, no doorman or directory. Jay, on his own, finds his way to Suite 101, through a modestly adorned door on his right. The accompanying brass plaque reads simply: LAW OFFICE. Inside, he's struck at once by how similar it looks to *his* first office, complete with the mirrored glass reception window, probably left over from a previous tenant, a doctor or some other medical practitioner, and a bonus for a young lawyer with a criminal clientele and limited staff. It allows a secretary to see out even if visitors can't see in. Jay walks through the anteroom, carpeted in blue, past the banquet chairs and the coffee table littered with ancient, feathered issues of *Texas Monthly* and *People*, before brazenly opening the door to the inner office. Turning to the right, he sees the face behind the glass. Aguilar's secretary is a bottle blonde who perhaps missed her true calling as the makeup director for an esteemed clown college, so painted is she in shades of red and purple and pink across her eyes and lips and cheeks, an orange line of foundation running just under her milky white jawline indicating the point at which she appears to have stopped caring about her looks. The woman is very nearly three hundred pounds. Jay ignores her calls to stop, to give his name, and to state just what in hell he thinks he's doing. He walks right past the L-shaped desk that houses her workstation, knowing that in the time it will take her to negotiate a release from the grip of her desk chair, he will have already found his foe. He starts for the first door he sees, down a short, harshly lit hallway, the walls decorated with photographs of the attorney with an array of Texas talent, from Houston Rockets center Hakeem Olajuwon to Congressman Bonilla of San An-

tonio to a young George W. Bush, then a partial owner of the
Texas Rangers; Aguilar is leaning in at the edge of the frame in
each and every shot, as if he'd had someone snap it before the
subject of the photo even realized he was there. Behind door
number 1 sits Aguilar himself in another razzle-dazzle suit,
this one a pin-striped number with slim lapels. He's got his feet
up on his desk when Jay walks in. The soles of his shoes look as
though they've never been worn. When he sees Jay, the phone
in his hand slides to the floor. "Oh," he says, more a moan than
an actual word. Eyes wide, he quickly contemplates his options.
His polished shoes drop to the carpet, very near the phone's
receiver, through which Jay can hear a high-pitched voice still
talking on the other end.

What follows next is as absurd a thing as Jay has ever seen.

Aguilar, in his nine-hundred-dollar suit, wheels back from
the edge of his desk and swivels to face the office's back wall
and the rectangular casement window cut into the drywall.
Jay, who promised himself he wouldn't hit the man first thing,
stands dumbstruck as Aguilar jumps out the window, thinking
to himself, *Did this motherfucker really just go out the window?*
He swears Aguilar must be the luckiest son of a bitch ever, a
lawyer with an escape hatch right behind his desk. "What
the hell?" Jay mutters, momentarily considering making the
leap too. It's a short drop, less than six feet. Aguilar did a tuck
and roll, barely creasing his suit on the patch of brown grass
that borders the back alley behind the building. Through the
window, Jay sees him scrambling to his feet, taking off toward
Kipling Street. Jay himself turns and runs back through the
office, the woman hollering behind him, through the anteroom
and the building's grim lobby and out the front door. Running
north up Dunlavy toward Kipling, he feels a burn at the base
of his sternum, the effort to gain on Aguilar boring a hole in
his lungs. He gulps whole mouthfuls of exhaust-filled air, can't

get it in him fast enough, the oxygen blazing to nothing by the time each breath lands in his chest. He has a fleeting thought that he could drop dead right here, right in the middle of the street. And for what exactly? Aguilar is long gone.

By the time Jay limps his way the four blocks back to the Land Cruiser, there's a squad car parked next to it. Aguilar's secretary called the police.

Well, this is rich, he thinks.

He ends up wasting the rest of the afternoon explaining to two uniform cops the illegality of poaching another lawyer's clients, and then traveling to the nearest HPD substation to amend his initial burglary report from the night of the election to include his suspicions about Ricardo Aguilar of 8791 Tidewater Drive, his home address, printed right in the white pages, behind Renaldo Aguilar and ahead of Roland Aguilar. Ricardo never returns to his office that day, nor do the lights come on at his home address that night. Jay knows because he parks himself right in front of the one-story bungalow, watching for hours, his penance for being totally checked out for the past year and letting a scoundrel walk right into his life. Never again, he tells himself.

Part Three

CHAPTER 22

Trials tell a story, of course, at least two sides of one, the witness list playing like chapter headings, signposts along the way, directing your attention this way or that. By the Sunday night before voir dire, Jay has interviewed everyone on the state's list of potential witnesses, all except for Maxine and Mitchell Robicheaux, who have refused the three overtures Jay has made, twice reaching out to the family directly and once going through Keith Morehead, who is still acting as their media and legal liaison. Jay's team lost a little steam this week when another seven days passed with them no closer to tracking down the printer that manufactured hundreds and hundreds of flyers; their hoped-for evidence linking the flyers, Alicia Nowell, and the Wolcott campaign through an invoice or eyewitness testimony is, at present, still outside their reach. With little time left on the clock, they are literally defense-less at this point, hanging their hat on the weakness of the state's physical case, which is no guarantee of anything; they have zero presentable evidence of another perpetrator, nothing to buttress the standard I didn't do it.

Meanwhile, Axel dropped another four points in the latest poll.

It was Sam's suggestion that they halt the campaign until after the trial.

"We're just bleeding money," he said in Jay's office yesterday.

It was meeting that had ostensibly been set in an effort to craft a visual strategy for the family during the trial. Since none of them was likely to be called as a witness, they were free to sit through its entirety, which was Jay's suggestion, as their absence would do more damage than any of them could imagine. But before long the gathering had devolved into naked debate about the political ramifications of Axel sitting in the courtroom day after day. His core advisers were now down to a party of three—Marcie, the communications director; Sam; and a highly distracted Neal—as Stan the moneyman and Russell Weingate had both quietly left the campaign the week after the injunction. Marcie and Sam disagreed about calling a halt to the campaign. "Unless you're just going to hand the whole thing over to Wolcott," she said. But they both believed that Axel should sit in the front row of the gallery, righteous and upright, for opening statements only, then make a show of his complete faith in the system and his nephew's lawyer to handle the rest. If he sits there for the length of the trial, which would certainly last a week, maybe two, voters will only be reminded that he's unemployed, that he hasn't held a leadership position in years. Sam wanted to reprise the idea of Axel getting his picture taken in the streets, out there looking for the real killer.

"I want him there," Neal said.

"Sure," Sam said, nodding at the obvious wisdom of it.

His hands, though, were shaking.

By then, he'd heard word that their potential savior was his ex-junkie of a son, A.G., illegitimate and angry as all get-out with his father.

"That does it," Axel said, with a thin smile in Neal's direction. "I'll be there."

Jay told them to arrive early and wear black.

He saw them to the door, where Sam lingered, sending his family ahead and waiting until they were all the way down the hall before asking to speak with Jay alone. The older man shut the door and asked, "Where's my money?" Jay walked to his desk and opened the top drawer, pulling out Sam's check.

"This one's on me."

Sam, frowning, took the check, folding it in half and tucking it into the inside pocket of his coat. "If you mess this up for my grandson—"

"Good-bye, Sam."

When he was alone again, Jay did his own form of prayer, playing side 2 of *Belle Blue*, dropping the needle on "My Back Is My Best Side," track number 5. "Come on, man," he whispered to the sound of A.G.'s voice, willing him to go against the spirit of the man in the song, one who's ever on the run. "Come on."

It's not that all hope is lost.

It's that Jay won't have faith in A.G. until he's in the witness chair.

And even then, it's a toss-up.

Rolly has assured Jay he has the situation under control, their peripatetic subject under his direct supervision. Last night he'd planted his girl, the amply endowed, doe-eyed mother of three and grandmother of five, at the bar at the Playboy Club in a V-neck T-shirt the color of grape bubble gum and a tight pair of jeans. She had teased her cinnamon-colored hair, even touched up the roots, and been given strict instructions to bat her eyelashes in one direction and one direction only, holding nothing back. She was probably A.G.'s age or older, and he fell for the whole picture: a gal, no, a *woman*, who knew blues, but not enough to recognize him—that Rolly figured would only make him skittish—and who was on her own for the night, willing to wait around until he got off shift. All she had to do was get him to walk her to her truck, parked on Rosalie Street, and Rolly would take care of the rest. Jay asks Rolly to stop the story there, not wanting to hear another word, lest he pick up his own kidnapping charge before Neal's trial. He does, however, anonymously send a plate of hot links from Lott's Barbecue to room 209 at the Holiday Inn on Broadway, where A.G. is holed up. Rolly's second hand, a driver of his by the name of Bitty who did time with him way back when, is currently stationed outside the hotel room door. Jay sends along a fifth of Hennessy as well, and a flight of tobacco: Kool menthol, Camels, and a carton of Newports, whichever his pleasure.

Meanwhile, Ricardo Aguilar has been dodging Jay, ignoring his calls, always "out" when Jay stops by his office, even staying clear of his own house, and with trial preparations kicking Jay's ass, his resources are stretched way too thin to pin Aguilar down. He's in the wind, and so is his heavy, T. J. Cobb.

The Sunday night before the trial, Jay takes his kids to get a tree.

Thanksgiving had been a spindly roasted chicken Lonnie brought over and a can of green beans, which was Rolly's contribution, along with a six-pack of cream soda and Crown Royal for the grown-ups. The kids watched TV while Jay and the others worked until Evelyn, fed up with waiting, finally came to get Ben and his sister so they could have a proper meal, or what was left of it, with their grandparents, Ellie begging at the last minute for her aunt to drop her at Lori King's house instead. Lori was almost twelve weeks along by then, and there was an actual picture of the thing, a little bean-shaped hope that will turn that girl's life inside out. It had been the Porters' first holiday apart, and Jay wants to make it up to them. The nearest tree lot is a small, dirt-packed field at the edge of the parking lot for Meyerland Plaza, which is already decked out with holly wreaths on its light fixtures, each with a red bow resting on the bottom, the ribbon turned up at the ends like a painted smile. Jay parks under one of these oversize holiday displays. He takes forty dollars, his absolute limit, out of his wallet and tosses the leather billfold into the glove compartment.

This was Bernie's deal, the tree and all that.

She did it with the kids every year.

They're excited at first, Ellie and Ben, even briefly reaching for each other's hands in a way that Jay hasn't seen in years as they take off toward the line of white tea lights ringing the field, the free apple cider, and the jingling carols playing on a boom box and the rows and rows of fragrant fir trees, skipping off like storybook children into an unknown forest. He loses sight of them within moments, dizzying himself in a maze of trees, six feet, seven feet, eight feet tall, his head light with pine and cinnamon. He leans over, hands on his knees. Over the treetops, he hears his son's voice.

"This one!"

"Let's let Dad decide."

Jay stands upright, turning the nearest corner to see both of his children the next aisle over, hands on different tree trunks, needles up to their jacketed elbows as they try to hold them upright. Ellie's is a noble fir, thin, prayerful branches pointing up, a Charlie Brown tree, as Bernie used to say. Ben has chosen a short, squat, sumo-looking tree that looks on the verge of toppling over. Unable, or unwilling, to choose between his children's two separate dreams for their first real Christmas without their mother, Jay makes the pick for the family, going with a thick Douglas fir. It's eight and a half feet tall and costs sixty-five dollars, and he has to run out to the car to get another twenty and a five.

They're quieter on the ride back, all three of them.

It's a heavy silence, breathless and strained, as if they were actually carrying the tree on their backs, so weighty is the expectation of holiday cheer, the dream of an easy, uncomplicated return to normalcy that they've strapped to the roof of the car. They seem, not a one of them, to have thought this through past the actual acquisition of the tree, failing to consider what more might be asked of them once the thing was in hand, that they would have to eventually bring it into the house, amid the ghosts of Christmases past, and decorate it, eight and a half feet of green to color with memories. Jay doesn't even know where in the house the box of ornaments and lights is hiding, or the dusky angel that his wife found in a clearance sale at Walgreen's. Bernie was the last one to put them away.

Ben sits next to Jay in the front seat. He's staring out the window, a tiny O fogged on the glass where his breath lands, the edges expanding and contracting every few seconds. He's looking at the decorated houses along the drive, lights in red and green, white and blue. From the backseat, Ellie breaks the silence. "Ms. Hilliard said I could come watch the trial, if I want to."

"Your principal?" he says, remembering suddenly the woman's wide-set eyes, her quietly solicitous manner. "I don't think so, El."

"No, really," she says, leaning forward to grip the back of the driver's seat, speaking over her father's shoulder, her face lit up in the rearview mirror by the passing streetlights. "She thinks it's an important thing to witness."

"I don't think they want a bunch of high school kids in the courtroom."

"She thinks it's an important thing for *me* to see," Ellie says, nudging her father's shoulder with the pads of her fingers. He can smell her lemony lotion, the sweet, plastic scent of her strawberry lip gloss. "She thinks it's important for me to see you . . . 'standing up,' or something," she says, trying to get the woman's words just right, but leaving the impression that Jay on his feet is in itself a major accomplishment. "I thought I could come by and watch some of it."

"There's a lot of stuff in this trial I don't want you hearing."

"I already know everything. I even know how they found her."

"El," he says. He nods toward her younger brother, reminding her of his presence.

"I'm just saying, I know enough," Ellie says, sinking back into the leather seat, throwing her head against the headrest. "I feel sorry for her," she says, so softly her father can barely make out the words. He tries to catch sight of her in the rearview mirror, but she's behind him, her face obscured by his own.

Ben finally turns from the window. "Are you going to win?"

"I don't know."

"Oh," Ben says, pinching his eyebrows together.

It appears he hadn't considered this as a real possibility. He sighs, as if preparing himself, or Jay, for defeat, as if the entire prospect has aged him in just the last few minutes. Then, with great care, he repeats to his father the very words he's been made to hear in the wake of every C grade he's ever received, every third strike at bat. "Well, you tried your hardest."

True, up to a point.

There is, in fact, one more thing Jay would like to try.

He asks the kids if they'll make a single stop with him, turning even before they answer toward the freeway, 610 East to 288 and Sunnyside, a working-class, historically black neighborhood in southeast Houston, with its own subheading in every crime report tracking citywide data and statistics. As they ride down the neighborhood's main artery, Ben and Ellie stare at the sights rolling outside the tinted windows of the Land Cruiser. Liquor store, liquor store, laundromat, liquor store, church, church. Tire shop, beauty shop, 7-Eleven, barbecue stand, dirt field, liquor store. Ellie doesn't remember their first apartment in Third Ward, and his kids have never seen their city quite like this. Jay doesn't know if that means he's sufficiently protected them, or done them a terrible disservice. This place is someone's home after all, as precious as the one they have. Maxine and Mitchell Robicheaux live in a two-story apartment complex off Cullen. Theirs is the door directly facing the street, next to a small carport.

Jay parks on the street in front of the complex, close enough so that he can see his kids from the front door of the Robicheauxs' two-bedroom apartment. He keeps an eye on them as he rings the doorbell, following the ring with a soft rap of his knuckles. It's Maxine who comes to the door. Jay doesn't know if Mitchell is home. The rooms behind her are cavernous and dark. Looking down, Jay can see the fraying yarn of the yellowing carpet, coming loose under the threshold.

Finally, he looks up to meet her eyes.

Maxine leans against the doorjamb, wondering, it seems, what this is all about. She's wearing a man's T-shirt, Mitchell's maybe, over a loose, faded pair of jeans. The peeling letters on the T-shirt read: BIG WIND TOOL & DIE. Her head cocked to one side against the wooden door frame, heavy with suspicion, or just plain exhaustion, she waits for him to speak first. He's not technically breaking any rules, or doing anything even half as unethical as kidnapping a witness ahead of trial, but this is not the way he would have wanted to go about this. Still, it's something he feels he has to say. "Ma'am," he says, nodding in gratitude for her time, for not slamming the door in his face. "However this all comes out in the end, I just wanted the chance to tell you that I'm sorry for your loss," he says, his voice slowing to a crawl, something salty and hot rising at the back of his throat, choking off each word. "I just needed a chance to say that."

Maxine stares at him a good long while.

Whatever is playing behind those dark, bark-colored eyes, it is not rage.

She nods toward his car at the curb, the two shadows in the windows.

"Those your kids?"

Jay glances over his shoulder, reminded of this one miracle.

"Yes, ma'am."

Maxine nods. "I only ever had the one," she says plainly.

She repeats the words, a whisper this time. "I only ever had the one."

CHAPTER 23

They're the same words she says on the stand three days later, when she's called as the state's first witness, the one who will start this story with that Tuesday, election night, when Alicia failed to return home from "work," which Maxine had assumed was a shift at her job on the grill at a Wendy's not far from their home. Maxine is wearing a dark gray dress with a wide patent leather belt. She sits with her shoulders hunched up a bit, as if she's cold, shivering actually. She leans forward, speaking softly into the microphone. Matt Nichols is at the lectern. At the state's table, a second lawyer and Detective Moore watch the proceedings. Jay, seated at the defense table on the left side of the courtroom, has no second chair, just Rolly riding shotgun in one of his work suits, looking, except for his single black braid, like a funeral director. He sits on the other side of Neal. Lonnie is still running leads in the streets, and behind Jay in the first row of the gallery, close enough that he can whisper in Jay's ear, sits Sam Hathorne, center in a row of Hathornes, Axel, Vivian, Ola, Gwen, Camille, and Delia. The courtroom is packed to the wood-paneled back wall. The media have doubled in size since the injunction, with reporters from across the state and a few national bureaus, the *Washington Post* and the *New York Times* again. Nichols, his back to them, walks Mrs. Robicheaux through the remainder of that night and her first call to law enforcement the following morning. Judge Carolyn Keppler watches from the bench. She is a white woman in her late sixties, with hair dyed the color of coffee. On her right hand she wears a large turquoise and coral ring, on her left wrist a line of silver bangles, chiming softly as she takes notes. As Maxine testifies, Jay glances at the jury: three white men; two Latinos; four white women; one man from Pakistan; and two black men, native Texans both, born and raised, and the only two brothers to survive the state's peremptory challenges during voir dire. Jay will play this whole trial to the back row, where they're seated. Surely at least one of them has been accused in his lifetime of something he didn't do.

"Mrs. Robicheaux," Nichols says, looking down at his notes.

"Yes," she says, anticipating the next question. She's been well coached; most of her answers to the D.A.'s questions have been a simple and easy yes.

"Finally, ma'am, as Detective Moore and his partner, Detective Oakley, asked you during your very first interview, and if I could have you reiterate it here, do you or your husband have any idea what happened to your daughter?"

"Objection, hearsay," Jay says. "She can't testify to what her husband knows." It was sloppy phrasing on the D.A.'s part, but for whatever it's worth, Jay got in the fact that Maxine and

Mitchell might have two wildly different stores of knowledge of what happened to Alicia Nowell. It was a tiny crack in the state's presentation, but he'll take it. "Sustained," Judge Keppler says, not looking up.

"Do *you* know what happened to your daughter between the time she left your home Tuesday, November fifth, and the day her body was discovered?"

"I don't know anything, no," she says softly.

"Do you have any idea what she was doing in Pleasantville?"

A sigh into the microphone, and then, "No."

The last question was Nichols doubling down on statements he'd made during his opening this morning, promising the jury that the state's was a straightforward, commonsense case: the defendant met the girl; the defendant flirted with the girl; the defendant gave the girl his phone number; the defendant pursued the girl; the defendant met the girl on a street corner in Pleasantville; the defendant was the last person seen with the girl; and, most important, he lied about all of the above. "Defense counsel is going to put on a show for you folks," he said. "Political espionage, corruption, and election tampering, and I ask you good people of Harris County what in the world that has to do with the price of tea in China?" Jay has yet to meet a young lawyer south of Kansas who doesn't put on his best Atticus Finch every time he stands in front of a jury, who doesn't speak in an overly folksy manner, as if he'd dropped years of sophisticated law schooling and legal prolixity like bread crumbs on his way to the courthouse, leaving a trail to find his way back once the audience is gone.

"It's all smoke, people, subterfuge," Nichols said. "A way to distract you from the fact that his client has no alibi for the time in question, that his client lied to law enforcement about knowing the victim. It's cheap and, make no mistake, it's a trick, and it speaks to the very cynicism that defense counsel will try to make you believe is the reason we're all here. Politics. Gamesmanship. When the truth is, a young woman is dead, and *that* is the reason we're all here. The defense will try very hard to present to you that Alicia Nowell was working for Sandra Lynn Wolcott, a candidate for mayor and the current district attorney for this county. But there is no evidence that supports this. I know that. He knows that. And soon you will know it too," he had ended, trying to get out ahead of anything Jay might present during trial. Jay, who frankly wasn't sure he would present *any* defense testimony at all—and was still unsure as to whether he could bank on A.G. being present in the courthouse at the needed time—had given the shortest opening statement of his career. "Well, as long as we're on the subject of *no* evidence," he said, "let's start with the fact that there isn't a single piece of *physical* evidence that ties Neal Hathorne to the murder of Alicia Nowell. In fact, we could pretty much start and stop there. There is no way any man could do what was done to her without leaving a trace of himself behind. But what you did *not* hear in Mr. Nichols's opening, and what you *won't* hear during this entire trial, is any physical evidence to show that my client did this horrible crime. No blood, no hair, no DNA of any kind." He spoke, total, for less than ten minutes.

"I have nothing further, Your Honor," Nichols says to Keppler.

"Mr. Porter," she says.

Jay stands, passing Nichols on his way to the lectern.

"Good afternoon, Mrs. Robicheaux."

She nods, but doesn't utter a greeting.

"Did you know your daughter was interested in politics, ma'am?"

"I don't believe she was, no."

"Are you aware that in the spring of this year, your daughter attended a candidate forum at Jones High School, where she was a senior?"

"I am now, yes. I believe it was a mandatory thing."

"It wasn't, actually," Jay says. "Alicia elected to attend that event, along with other students interested in volunteering; were you aware of that?"

Maxine shakes her head.

The judge has to remind her to speak up for the court reporter.

She clears her throat, leaning toward the microphone. "No."

"At this candidate forum, are you aware that all three major candidates for mayor in this election sent representatives to the high school?"

"Objection, beyond the scope of direct," Nichols says, standing.

He's late, Jay thinks, but right.

Keppler looks at the defense table. "Mr. Porter?"

"The state asked the witness if she knew why her daughter was in Pleasantville on election night—"

"And I believe she said no."

"I am, with the court's permission and in as few steps as possible, trying to broaden our understanding of her knowledge of her daughter's activities."

"The objection, as to *that* question, is sustained."

Jay looks down at his notepad on the lectern, stalling.

The pages in front of him are completely blank.

By habit, he usually maintains a separate legal pad for the questioning of each individual witness, but without the chance to interview the Robicheauxs prior to trial, he was at a loss as to how to prepare, or what Maxine might say.

He clears his throat. "Mrs. Robicheaux, your daughter's personal effects were discovered a day before her body was found, is that correct?"

Maxine sighs, closing her eyes briefly. "Yes."

"They found her purse, is that right?"

"Yes."

"And inside there was a wallet and a pager."

"*I* didn't buy her that," she says matter-of-factly.

"Yes, ma'am."

He glances at the jury.

In the front row, one of the white jurors, a woman, nods approvingly.

"There was also a campaign flyer in her purse, was there not?"

"It was some kind of flyer they said, yes."

"I'm sorry, Your Honor," Nichols says, the chair creaking as he comes to his feet. "I'm going to have to object to this whole line of questioning as hearsay. Where is she getting this information from, from what the police told her?"

"They showed it to me, her purse," Maxine says, looking up at the judge.

"Overruled."

"It was a flyer bad-mouthing one of the candidates, was it not?"

"Something like that."

"Bad-mouthing Axel Hathorne, right?"

"For all I know that's why he killed her," she says, looking at Neal.

Jay winces at the glass wall he just walked into. He's got nothing here and he knows it. He needs to retreat from the mess he's making as fast as he can. He looks at Judge Keppler, about to signal an end to his questioning, but then looks once more at Maxine in the witness chair and reaches for the only arrow left in his quiver, poisoned though it may be. "What year were you married, ma'am?"

"Excuse me?"

"What year did you and your husband marry?"

"In 1990."

"And Alicia was how old at the time?"

"She was twelve."

"They get along?"

Maxine leans back a little in her chair.

"Yes," she says, crossing her arms, guessing what he's getting at and hating him for it. She glances at the judge, as if she can't believe Keppler can't stop this, as if she can't believe someone is allowed to spread lies in open court. The D.A.'s chair is again creaking under the springy weight of a lawyer on the verge of getting on his feet again. Jay imagines he'll never get this line of questioning past the coming objections. It's pure innuendo, as thin as it is sly, and not worth it, not when Maxine's defensive posture is doing the job for him.

"Nothing further, Your Honor."

Next up: Elma Johnson.

She is led into the courtroom by the bailiff, a short white woman with a reddish buzz cut and a thick middle who takes extra care with the elderly witness, guiding her by the elbow to the edge of the witness stand, where she will be sworn in. Elma is wearing a floral blouse, black polyester pants, and thick-soled shoes. The newly pressed gray waves on her head are oiled and shining under the white lights, and she cradles a small black purse like a baby, the gold-link strap hanging over the side of her arm. She got all dressed up for a mere twelve minutes on the stand, the length of time it takes her to repeat a story that by now Jay has heard half a dozen times. Election night, at approximately eight forty-five, Mrs. Johnson looked out her kitchen window and saw Alicia Nowell standing at the corner of Guinevere and Ledwicke; she is sure it was her. "It looked like she was waiting for someone."

Jay stands for cross. "That's a bus stop, isn't it?"

"Pardon?"

"The corner of Guinevere and Ledwicke? That's a Metro bus stop."

"Objection, beyond the scope of direct."

"She said the victim was 'waiting for *someone.*' I think it's fair to probe her knowledge of the fact that there's a bus stop where Ms. Nowell was standing."

"But that's a misstatement of the witness's testimony, Your Honor."

"That's right, she said it *looked* like she was waiting for someone," Jay says, making sure that the distinction is on record again. "I'm trying to understand the basis on which she formed her opinion, the testimony she gave on direct."

"Overruled," Keppler says, turning to the witness. "You may answer."

"It's not marked," Elma says.

"But it's a bus stop, isn't that right?"

"Yes," she says softly.

"Why, then, did you tell police the victim was waiting for 'someone'?"

"She was looking north, up Ledwicke. The buses come from the south."

"But if someone, like Alicia Nowell, was fairly unfamiliar with the neighborhood, they wouldn't necessarily know that, would they?"

"Objection, speculation."

"Sustained."

But Jay had already got what he needed. "Nothing further, Your Honor."

Next up: Magnus Carr.

The retired postal worker is wearing a dark green, thickly knotted necktie and spectacles, round and gold plated, which he had not been wearing the day Jay visited him in his home. The shoulder pads of his camel-colored sports jacket are scrunched up around his ears and one side of his mouth is screwed up in a sort of half grimace, telegraphing his reluctance to be here. Every few seconds he keeps looking past Neal to Neal's grandfather. He has said, under oath, at least three times, "I hate to say anything against Sam," as if it were the elder Hathorne he's accused in open court and not Jay's client—whom Mr. Carr had no trouble pointing to and identifying as the man he told detectives he saw outside his study, struggling with a young girl, who he now knows was Alicia Nowell.

When it's Jay's turn at bat, he begins with the obvious. "Are those prescription eyeglasses, sir?" he says, liking the start of this, feeling comfortable enough to slide his hands into his pockets and lean his hip against the lectern.

"Yes, sir."

"You nearsighted or farsighted?"

"Barely sighted," Carr says, coughing out a laugh before realizing the implications of his joke. He swallows hard, looking at Nichols and then again at Jay. "Uh, nearsighted, sir," he says finally. "I have another pair for reading."

"And were you wearing your glasses on the night of November fifth?"

Again, Carr looks over at the D.A. "I believe so, yes."

"You're not sure?"

"I, uh, well, I had been reading some magazines earlier but I don't remember switching from one pair to the other. But I must have had these on," he says, tapping on the right stem of his current pair of glasses with his finger.

"Because otherwise you wouldn't have known what you were looking at."

"Objection, Judge. That's not a question."

"Sustained."

Jay moves on.

"And what you actually told Detective Moore is that the man you saw outside your window *looked* like Neal Hathorne, not that it *was* Neal Hathorne, isn't that right, Mr. Carr?"

"That's right."

"Earlier you testified you were closing up the house for the night, pulling curtains, that sort of thing; tell me, Mr. Carr, was the light in the study on or off at the time you saw the commotion outside the window?"

Mr. Carr squirms a little in his chair. "I can't say I rightly remember."

"You agree that it would make a difference, though, in terms of what you would have been able to see outside, on a dark night, don't you?"

"Well, yes, the light would have created a reflection on the window."

"And you wouldn't have been able to see clearly outside?"

"But I did see it, so, yes, the light was off."

Jay, not gaining much traction, tries a different tack. "How long would you say you stood at the window, Mr. Carr: a few seconds, less than a minute?"

"No, it was a little longer than that."

"But you weren't standing there recording 'evidence,' were you, sir? I mean, you didn't really know what it was you were looking at, did you, sir?"

"Objection, compound question."

"Sustained."

"You didn't call the police after you witnessed this 'struggle,' did you?"

Magnus Carr looks down, fiddling with the tail of his tie. "I should have."

"You glanced at something out the window, as you were closing your curtains for the night, glasses on or off, the lights on or off, but you can't be—"

"The light was *off*."

"In passing, sir, you can't for certain say what it is you saw, can you?"

"Wasn't in passing. Naw, I stood and looked," Carr says. "We've had some problems out there, you know, so I looked, I watched for a little bit. Some of the old-timers out there, we've kind of put it on ourselves to do what we can to keep the place safe, calling in things here and there. But we've been wrong before, not seeing what we thought we were seeing, so I guess I kind of hesitated." He pauses here, clearing his throat a little and straightening his spine, a corrective posture against the shame written all over his face. "As to not calling the police, well, I'm gon' have to live with that one. I think about that girl, I do," he says, and this time he looks out, searching the courtroom for the face of Maxine Robicheaux. Given that she and her husband are the closest kin to the victim, they have been afforded seats in the front of the gallery, just behind the state's table. Pastor Keith Morehead sits beside them in a black suit and paisley tie. Jay, because of what Mr. Carr has just said, turns to look in Keith Morehead's direction.

And that's when he sees T. J. Cobb in the courtroom.

In a black T-shirt and a faded denim jacket, a toothpick sticking out of the side of his mouth, he has been watching Jay's back for who knows how long, and now, given the chance to regard the man face-to-face, he gives him that same overbroad smile, the one that so disturbed Jay the first night he came across it. What in the world is this piece of shit doing in here? The courtroom has fallen silent, and the witness is fidgeting on the stand. "Mr. Porter," the judge says.

"A moment, Your Honor."

He turns to the defense table, but doesn't have to say a word. Rolly is already on his feet, buttoning his suit jacket. As the two men pass each other, Jay whispers two words in his ear. "Crush him." Rolly nods, jaw tight, as he starts out of the courtroom, just a few strides behind T. J. Cobb.

Jay finally returns to his witness.

"I should have called the cops," Carr says, shaking his head, reaching into the side pocket of his sports coat for a handkerchief, dabbing his forehead. "But I just didn't put it together, what was happening. I didn't see a van. When the other girls, Tina and Deanne, were taken, there was talk about a white van—"

Nichols is fast on his feet.

"Objection," he says. "May we approach?"

Jay follows Nichols to the bench. The D.A.'s cheeks are red. "Stuff about the other girls is inadmissible, and he knows it," the D.A. says to Keppler, who is twisting the turquoise and coral ring on her right ring finger, which is long and thin as a blade of grass. Up close, Jay can smell the stale coffee on her breath.

"That came out of Mr. Carr's mouth, not mine," he says, making clear that he is honoring the judge's single pretrial ruling, that the murders of Tina Wells and Deanne Duchon would not be a part of these proceedings. "The state should have coached its own witness not to touch on the other murders," he says.

Judge Keppler agrees.

Still, she is bound to instruct the court reporter that the last piece of Mr. Carr's testimony should be disregarded and will be stricken from the record. On his walk back from the bench, Jay steals a glance at the jury box. The jurors are as alert as he's seen them since Mr. Carr took the stand. One of the white men in the back has his arms folded tightly, his brow deeply wrinkled. The judge's direction to ignore the mention of the two other dead girls has only drawn more attention to it, a lucky break for Jay, and the last he will receive for the rest of this first day of testimony. On redirect, Nichols presents Mr. Carr with a copy of his affidavit, reminding him of his words at his second police interview, when he was shown a picture of Neal in a photo lineup. "I said, 'Well, hell if the man didn't look like Neal Hathorne.'" To Judge Keppler, he adds, "Excuse my language, ma'am."

They are, by then, nearing the hour of five o'clock.

Judge Keppler adjourns for the day, asking for the principal players to return at eight thirty the following morning. It takes a long time for Neal to stand as the courtroom starts to clear. And when he finally does, he takes one look at Jay and says matter-of-factly, as if he were getting used to the idea, "We're going to lose." He turns and joins the Hathorne family in the gallery. Sam puts a hand on his grandson's shoulder, guiding him out of the courtroom.

CHAPTER 24

Jay's phone rings before he's out of the courthouse.

"Rolly," he says.

But it's Lonnie, calling with news. "I got it," she says. "I got the flyer."

"You found the printer?"

"Tracked the invoice, everything," she says.

Passing through the front doors of the criminal court building, Jay is rather grateful for the useful prop of the cell phone, pressed to his ear. It has a strange, pacifying effect on the throng of TV and newspaper reporters, bringing their questions down to a reasonable pitch, as if they're hoping to pick up the other end of Jay's phone conversation. Gregg Bartolomo leans against the railing at the bottom step, waiting for him.

Jay ignores him as he did every day of jury selection. Walking faster, Jay thanks Lonnie for making something out of this shitty first day of trial. "But there's a problem," she says.

Of course there is, he thinks.

By the time Lonnie finds him at the office, about a half hour later, Eddie Mae is already gone for the day. Having a week ago completed an extensive inventory of all things Pleasantville—every environmental report from the civil case, every deposition and client file, the ones that were there and the 290 files that are still missing—she is, by Jay's own instructions, free to leave by five. She left some sliced ham and a pot of soup for them on the stove, and upstairs in the conference room an updated key and map to the filing system she set up for *State of Texas v. Neal Patrick Hathorne*, every piece of paper associated with the case accounted for. The only thing she hasn't touched is the cardboard box from Lonnie's days at the *Post*. The corners are starting to tear, and Jay is careful to lift the flaps gently. He is rooting around in the interior when Lonnie walks in. "You heard from Rolly?" he asks right off. "He's not answering my calls." It's not like him to disappear, not at all.

Lonnie shakes her head as she sets her leather hobo bag on the conference room table, followed by a plate of ham and a stack of dill pickles. She stopped by the kitchen on her way up. She nods toward the box. "What are you doing?"

"Looking for the person who delivered Alonzo Hollis to the cops."

"It was the van, remember? They had an ID number off the side."

"Right," Jay says, nodding. "And maybe he was parked out there once or twice, catching a smoke or a nap sometime in his van and someone made note of it. But Magnus Carr today . . . that's what reminded me. The community has been keeping their eyes out for years. So who was the one who told that bogus story about Hollis trying to get a girl in his van, over at the truck stop on Market Street, the one the cops refuted because Hollis wasn't in the state when it happened?" He slaps a stack of papers down, digging into another pile.

"Jesus, that's him," she says, realizing. "That's the guy."

"Why else would anybody make something like that up?"

"Unless they wanted the heat on somebody else," she says.

Jay nods, because he knows it too. "It's someone in Pleasant-ville."

Lon jumps in, nudging him aside. "Let me. I have a system."

She starts in on the years of handwritten notes of police reports and witness statements, digging her way to the bottom of the box. "You better hope I'm as good a reporter as I think I am. If I didn't write it down at the time, it's not here. Resner never gave me copies of any police reports, just a quick peek."

"What happened with the flyer?" he says, getting to the other big news.

"Yes," she says, moving away from the cardboard box to reach for her leather bag. Inside is a photocopy of a handwritten invoice. Jay takes it from her. Stapled to the back is a copy of the printer's original mock-up. It's the BBDP flyer all right, exclamation points and all. "It was a special order," Lonnie says. "The guy had to find a special typewriter to make it look that old."

"Where?"

"Print shop out Highway 6, edge of the county."

Jay flips back to the copy of the invoice, the line just below the date.

The invoice is made out to "America's Tomorrow."

"Wolcott's name is nowhere on this."

"And therein lies the problem."

"You're saying this *wasn't* Reese Parker's doing?"

"No," Lon says, bending at the waist to reach for a dill pickle.

"I'm saying I don't know who or what 'America's Tomorrow' is, and until I find out, we don't know anything." She crunches into the pickle on the side of her mouth, looking comically like the Vlasic stork. She reaches for a slice of ham.

"He have a description for who placed the order?"

"White male," she says, chewing. "They grow on trees out here." She shrugs. It's hardly useful.

Jay's mobile phone rings.

He slides it from his pants pockets, checks the number on the screen. He should have heard from Rolly by now. But it's Evelyn. "I have to go get my kids," he says, sighing. He starts scooping up Lonnie's handwritten notes.

"Leave it," she says. "I'll go through it."

"You sure?"

"Go get your kids. I'll stay and pick at this and find out what I can about what's happening with Tomorrow in America, or whatever the hell it's called."

"How are you going to do that from *here*?"

"That little box down there called a computer," she says. "I got all night."

"I don't know if I like the idea of you here by yourself."

Lonnie smiles, sheepish.

"Well, Amy might stop by," she says. "Her man's out of town."

"Right," Jay says. "The mysterious Amy."

Across the table, Lon stares at him, searching for something.

"Go on and say it. You think I'm being played for a fool."

"I think it's none of my business."

"I hate when you do that, you know," she says, hurt or disappointed, he can't tell. "You think you're making some kind of grand show of respect, giving people their space, but what you're really saying is that you don't give a shit."

"I care," he says. Then, as if there were a need to clarify, "About *you*."

"Well, this is my life we're talking about, Jay, and I'm inviting you to chime in for once. It's called a friendship, man, you should try it sometime."

"You sound like Bernie."

"Smart woman."

He sighs. He doesn't do this well, not at all.

But Lonnie, she *is* a friend, one he's willing to wade in the muck of human emotion for. "I think if you give her an inch, she's prepared to go ten miles, so, yes, you should make her choose. She has no kids, right? Then it's got to be you or him. And if you don't press her, then you *are* a fool." He winces, bracing himself for the blowback, as if he thinks it's entirely possible she might deck him.

But Lon only smiles.

"Go get your kids," she says.

Jay nods, heading for the door.

At the threshold, he stalls, turning back. "If you're looking for my approval or something, you got to have the balls to bring her around sometime."

Lonnie gives him a mock salute. "Yes, sir."

"And if you want to be my friend, you can't disappear on me like you did." It's the first emotional need he's expressed to another soul besides his wife.

"I know."

"This year has been hell."

"I know," she says. "But I'm here now, Jay." This case, it's more than just a paycheck, she says. She would never let him out on a limb like this on his own. Jay nods, tapping the door's wooden frame. "Don't stay too late, huh?"

She nods. "Yes, sir."

Rolly lost T. J. Cobb before he even got out of the courthouse, in a crowded swirl of bodies on the first floor near the elevators, and was too pissed at himself to call Jay; at least he couldn't call right away, not until he tracked Cobb down. He had a name after all. He'd done more with less, and the night was long. He left the courthouse alone, heading to his El Camino, parked in a lot off Franklin, peeling layers as he went—jacket, tie, dress shirt—so that by the time he made it to his truck, he had stripped down to his white undershirt and his slacks, getting the smell of justice off him, at least the kind that comes drenched in a D.A.'s cheap cologne. He was planning to swing by his garage, to make sure it was still standing, make sure his drivers and mechanics hadn't made off with his best tools, make sure they were still getting to their gigs on time. He'd been given the all-clear on the A.G. situation that afternoon: only one weak-ass escape attempt reported. The bluesman had claimed the toilet was backed up and when the motel's maintenance man knocked at room 209, A.G. opened the door and ran out, knocking the super on his ass. But seeing as he had made it through half a carton of Newports, he didn't get very far, out of breath and doubled over before reaching the motel's stairs. Since then, "I ain't had no trouble with him," Rolly's pal Bitty had said. Frankly, he was starting to suspect the old man was finding solace in his surrender, happy to put his feet up for a few days, his meals paid for, a little drink in hand. Through the stucco walls, he often heard the TV going. Reruns of *Good Times* and *One Day at a Time*. And westerns at night. It had to be better than cleaning toilets in a gin joint. Relieved, Rolly had planned a night with his girl. He owed her a steak-and-bake after her valiant service to the cause. He had a dime bag in the glove compartment of his truck and was going to pick up a couple of T-bones on the drive down to Hitchcock, some charcoal too, until the kid, strolling into the courtroom, had fucked things up, rearranging his whole night.

He was hardly through cursing his name when god himself seemed to have a change of heart about ol' Rolly Snow, rolling a gift right across his windshield, at the corner of Franklin and Crawford, while his truck was idling at the light. He leaned over the steering wheel, peering past his headlights. It was T. J. Cobb, all right, there in front of him on the street. Long and lean, with a mean, skulking walk. Among the gray army of office workers and bank tellers, women in shoulder pads and high heels, he stood out like a peacock in a flock of pigeons. He was wearing that same faded denim jacket and black T-shirt, his right index finger curled around a cigarette.

Rolly, feeling lucky, tailed him for a few blocks.

Not so easy when the man was on foot.

He was about to ditch the El Camino and put his own two feet on the ground when T. J. Cobb ducked into the vestibule of a bar. The Last Call sat behind a windowless brick wall painted black and unadorned, save by a small wooden sign over the door. Rolly rolled past the bar's front door just as Cobb slipped inside. He made the block before deciding to pull over and roll on him. The man had come to Jay's home, near his kids. And Rolly wasn't having that. He found a dirt lot and parked, not far from the old abandoned Union Station. This part of downtown, heading toward the menacing shadows of the 59 Freeway overpass, is grimly pastoral, the natural world taking back what the city no longer wants. There are weeds shooting up three feet from cracks in the sidewalk, and between the many vacant brick buildings, dirt lots dot the landscape. Rolly grabbed his piece from under the driver's seat, the Colt .45. But he never got to use it. He was made before he even got out of his truck. By the time he got to the Last Call, Cobb was hiding in the dark vestibule, waiting for his mark, the real one he'd been eyeing in the courtroom. He put the muzzle of a handgun to Rolly's chest, a .38 Rolly guessed, realizing too late that he'd been set up. It was his last coherent thought. He doesn't remember the shot itself, remembers only the sound of his tooth cracking when his face hit the sidewalk, and then footsteps, sneakers on pavements, slipping far, far away.

Jay got the call this morning, after failing to reach Rolly all night.

It was Marisol, Rolly's girlfriend, phoning from St. Joseph's Hospital.

Court was due to start in less than five minutes, and Jay's attempts to obtain a delay were rebuffed by Judge Keppler, who reminded him they'd put a city election on hold for this trial. To Nichols, she said, "Call your next witness."

Next up: Kelley Young, crime scene technician.

Jay glances at the empty chair on the other side of Neal. He has not told his client the reason for Rolly's absence, nor does Neal seem in the least bit curious about where the investigator is. He is staring straight ahead, watching as Ms. Young, a blonde in her thirties, takes the witness stand. Jay, on the other hand, is distracted to the point of near incompetence. He is sweating in the warm courtroom, his dress shirt a thin film against his damp back, and his throat is dry. He actually misses the D.A.'s first two questions for the witness, and makes a guess in his notes that they had to do with the correct spelling of her name and her years of service to the county. She is here to establish that a body had indeed been found in the early morning hours of Sunday, November tenth, and under what conditions. Matt Nichols needs to get in the fact of the rain that fell between the girl's disappearance and the discovery of her remains—an explanation as to why no DNA tying the defendant to the crime was ever found. Ms. Young also processed the items that were in the deceased's purse, which had been discovered one day before the body. One by one, she holds up the bloody items, individually sealed in clear evidence bags, for the jury to see. Jay glances at his client, thinking the same as Neal: we are going to lose.

Next up: Roy Singh, medical examiner.

It's testimony Jay has been dreading. No one should have to witness what was done to Alicia Nowell, least of all her parents. But there it is, up on a three-by-five-foot projection screen, just to the left of Judge Keppler's seat at the bench. The courtroom falls silent as the first image pops up. The only sound Jay hears is Maxine Robicheaux's footsteps as she walks out of the courtroom. A couple of the jurors, two older men, squirm in their seats. One of the black men in the second row has his hands clenched tightly in his lap.

Nichols walks the doctor through the gruesome facts, the beating and the suspected sexual assault, the bruising around her pelvic area and across the face and neck. The cause of death was strangulation, the manner of death homicide. On cross, Jay gets as far as he's likely to get in dismantling the state's case. There is, he reminds the jury, stealing a look at the black men in the second row, not a single piece of evidence on the victim's body that suggests his client ever came into contact with Alicia Nowell, let alone killed her. "Testing of the material underneath the victim's fingernails was inconclusive, yes," Dr. Singh says.

"And again, to be clear, Dr. Singh, that means none of it matched the DNA sample of my client, Neal Hathorne, isn't that right?"

"That is correct."

On redirect, Dr. Singh, with the D.A.'s prompting, reminds the jurors that the testing was "inconclusive," as he turns to give them an impromptu lecture on the adverse effects of moisture on DNA material. "It's terrible, in fact."

"So the fact that the DNA test results were inconclusive doesn't mean that it *wasn't* the defendant's DNA, does it?"

"Objection, leading."

"Sustained."

"Let me ask it this way, then," Nichols says. "Can Mr. Hathorne be ruled out as the contributor of the DNA found under the deceased's right fingernails?"

"You cannot draw any real conclusions from this test, no."

"Oh, I think we can," Jay says on recross. "Inconclusive, by definition, means you cannot conclude that it was the DNA of my client, isn't that right?"

Dr. Singh sighs. "Yes, that is correct."

Next up: Derek Menendez, Sprint technician.

He's here to pick up the story of the pager, found in the victim's purse, and to get into evidence the phone records attached to the ten-digit pager number that Alicia Nowell was using. At 7:32 P.M., November fifth, Ms. Nowell's pager did receive a call from 713-457-2221, digits that were stored in the small device. Jay, in a few questions, reminds the jury that there is no recording of any phone conversation between Neal and Alicia, nor proof that any such conversation ever took place. "I wouldn't know anything about that," Menendez says.

Next up: Tony Perlman, AT&T rep.

His only role is to establish that the above phone number

belonged to a cellular telephone account paid for monthly by Mr. Neal P. Hathorne.

Jay passes on a cross.

And Judge Keppler breaks for lunch.

Lonnie agrees to meet him at the hospital. As soon as he steps through the sliding glass doors of the emergency room at St. Joseph's, Jay starts to feel short of breath. It's the stark scent of industrial-grade bleach and the cold, cold recycled air that tighten his chest, making him feel light-headed. He hasn't been inside a hospital, or a doctor's office for that matter, in a year. "Rolly Snow," he tells the intake nurse, before being sent up to the third floor, to room 312, where the man himself is sleeping, seventeen hours out of surgery now. He's lying on top of the bedsheets, bare chested. Jay can see the thick bandages, just under his left clavicle but, thank god, above his heart. Marisol, in a rather demure pair of brown slacks and a flowery blouse, is standing to the side of the hospital bed, leaning over the brushed metal railing to sweep damp black hairs away from Rolly's face. "He's okay," she says, barely turning when Jay walks in. Maybe it's the clothes, or the hospital setting, but she actually looks like someone's grandmother today, cooing words into Rolly's ear in Spanish. "He's going to be okay," Jay hears again, this time from Lonnie, who is sitting by the room's one window, a slim rectangle just to the left of the door. For a moment, none of them says anything, just three sets of eyes on the patient and the soft whir of the compression pump attached to his legs to prevent blood clots. Bernie'd had to wear the same. The steady rhythm of it, like a ghost's breath in the room, used to keep her up, day and night. To Marisol, Jay says, "I'm sorry."

She won't look at him. "You're trouble, both of you."

"He's very lucky," Lon says, which leads Marisol to cut her eyes at the white girl. She suddenly grabs her purse off Rolly's rolling meal tray. "I'm getting coffee," she says, sliding the beaded strap onto her right shoulder. "He wakes up, you tell him just like that, tell him I said I'm getting coffee," she says rather cryptically. Jay watches her walk out, wondering if he or Rolly will ever see her again. He will never forgive himself if he cost Rolly his girl. He inches closer to the bedside, reaching for the tattooed knuckles of Rolly's good hand. The very warmth of it is such a comfort, Jay nearly cries. "He *is* lucky," Lonnie says.

A few moments later, they step outside to let him sleep, leaving the door ajar. They lean against the wall just across the hall from the nurses' station, Lonnie with an update on America's Tomorrow.

"It's a 527, a PAC."

"A political action committee?"

"It was registered with the FEC early this year." From her shoulder bag, she pulls a photocopy of a Federal Election Commission report. "This is a list of donors for the first quarterly reporting period, January to March of this year." She hands it to Jay, who scans it quickly. "Those are some big names, my friend."

"Yes, they are," he says, reading.

AT&T
Bush, Dorothy
Bush, Marvin
Carlton, Jeffrey

Chevron
Cole Oil Industries
Cole, Richard
Cole, Mrs. Richard
Cole, Thomas
Dorian, Paul
Enron
Fox, Sam
Hunt, Ray L.
Koch, David and Julia
Lay, Kenneth and Linda
Luckman, Charlie
Maddox, Cynthia
Merrill Lynch
Mosbacher, Robert
National Rifle Association
Nunez, Pedro and Rita
PhRMA
Pfizer
ProFerma Chemicals
Philip Morris
Rose, Mark and Leanne
Stoney, Lee
Wyly, Charles
Wyly, Sam

"What does any of this have to do with Wolcott? These people are all donating to her mayoral campaign?" he says, looking down at one name in particular. It would mean he was right all along. Cynthia was double-dealing.

"I don't know," Lon says.

Jay folds the paper lengthwise and slides it into the inside pocket of his suit jacket. "I've got to get back to court," he says, glancing through the crack in the doorway to Rolly's hospital room, watching for a few moments the rise and fall of his chest. "Can you stay for a little bit?" he asks. "In case he wakes up?"

"Sure thing," she says. "And I'll check in with Rob Urrea too. Maybe this list of names means something to him."

CHAPTER 25

The court has thinned for the day's second act, with half the seats in the gallery empty after intermission. The Hathornes are here, of course, and the Robicheauxs, both in the front row but on opposite sides of the courtroom. The *Chronicle* still has reporters present, including Bartolomo, but the usual court watchers and trial junkies got their fill from the autopsy photos before lunch.

Next up: Kenny Ester, the boyfriend.

"Mr. Ester, did you know a person by the name of Alicia Nowell?"

"Yes," he says, the tears starting. He cries through his entire testimony actually, led gingerly by Matt Nichols into the story of meeting Alicia Nowell in fifth-period trigonometry during their junior year. "She was smart," he says, "a lot smarter than people gave her credit for, smarter than she even knew, my opinion. I wanted her to go to college, tried to get her to apply to Lamar University, in Beaumont, with me. But she was worried about money, you know. She figured she'd work a little, save some cash, and maybe there'd be a scholarship or something. I think that's why she wanted to volunteer on a campaign. She thought some school might look at that and put her at the top of the pile."

"Well, let's get to that, Mr. Ester," Nichols says.

The jury hears the story for the first time (and all from Kenny Ester's point of view) of how Neal Hathorne participated in the candidate forum at the high school, representing his uncle's campaign, and how he had singled out Alicia and flirted openly with her, right in front of her boyfriend. "I didn't like the dude." Kenny's alibi on the night in question is unimpeachable, and Jay doesn't bother trying to dismantle it on cross. Instead, he attempts, suceeding rather easily, to make Kenny look like the jealous type who misread a situation that was as simple as the description of the event: campaigns looking for volunteers.

"But he *gave* her his card."

"How else was she supposed to reach him?"

Kenny leans back, crossing his arms.

He's in a boy's idea of dress attire, a pressed golf shirt and baggy black jeans. He got a new fade for court, S-curls shining on top.

"Your girlfriend, she took other business cards that day, didn't she?" Jay says, letting the boy testify, with his body language, to the fact that his grief is now hiding behind anger, an emotion that rarely ever works on a witness stand.

"I guess."

"In fact, Alicia reached out to the Wolcott campaign, didn't she?"

"That day, naw. It was her and him talking," he says, pointing to Neal.

"But she eventually reached out to their campaign, didn't she?"

"Objection, calls for hearsay."

"Sustained," Judge Keppler says, her first word on record since lunch.

"Your Honor, he may have personal knowledge of Alicia Nowell's activities in the days and weeks leading up to her death," Jay says, wishing almost as soon as the words are out of his mouth that he'd quit this cross three questions ago. Judge Keppler peers over the lenses of her purple eyeglasses at the witness stand. "Do you," she says, "have personal knowledge, not something Ms. Nowell told you, but that you yourself witnessed?"

"Naw," Kenny says, wiping his nose on his sleeve. "When me and her got together, we didn't talk about politics. I never heard of no Wolcott having to do with Alicia until *he* brought it up in the newspaper." He is pointing right at Jay.

Next up: Tonya Hardaway.

Jay turns as she's being led into the courtroom by the bailiff, only to see his daughter sitting in the second row of the gallery, behind Ola Hathorne. Just as Tonya Hardaway, in a black sheath dress and ballet flats, her braids pushed back with a yellow headband, is being sworn in, Jay stands.

"Can I have a minute, Your Honor?"

"Something wrong?" Judge Keppler says, blowing steam from the mug of tea her clerk just handed her. She glances above Jay's head at the courtroom's clock.

"Just one second, Judge."

He slips past the bar into the gallery, pulling his daughter with him into the hallway as half the courtroom watches. Outside the double doors, Ellie holds her backpack against her chest, almost as a buffer against her dad's rising anger. She's in the same jeans and roll-neck sweater she left the house in this morning.

"What are you doing here?"

"I want to watch."

"How did you even get here?"

"I took the bus."

Which, the way Metro runs, means she might have left school as long as two hours ago. "I thought we agreed, no more skipping class."

"I didn't," she says, reaching into the front pencil pouch of her backpack, retrieving a slip of yellow paper, folded in half. She hands it to Jay. It's a permission slip for an excused absence, signed by Principal Debra Hilliard.

"I told her you said it was okay."

"Jesus, Ellie."

The bailiff leans her head outside the courtroom. "Mr. Porter?"

"Yeah, I know," he says to the deputy, glancing at his watch.

To Ellie, he says, "Get inside, we'll talk about it later."

Nichols barely waits for Ellie to take her seat, for Jay to get to his place at the defense table, before he starts in on his direct examination of the former field director for Axel Hathorne. "And how long did you work for the campaign?"

"Eight months. I was the first hired when they put the official campaign together. I worked through the general election, just up until a few weeks ago."

"Well, we'll get to that," Nichols says, leaning against the lectern.

Neal, sitting beside Jay, closes his eyes. He knows what's coming.

"I want to discuss the night of the general election, November fifth. Were you working in the campaign office that day, Ms. Hardaway?"

"I was coordinating GOTV, get out the vote, from the main office, that's right. I was in contact with precinct captains throughout the day, but I was mostly in the office, yes," she says, glancing over at Neal, almost leading Nichols right into his next question. Was the defendant in the office that day?

"He was in and out," she says. "Election days are pretty hectic."

"Well, let's narrow our focus then, shall we? Was Mr. Hathorne in the office on the evening of November fifth, around eight forty-five?" Nichols says, verbally drawing a line under the time Alicia Nowell was last seen across town.

"No, he had left the office almost two hours earlier. He asked me to take him off the schedule for the rest of the day."

"Was that unusual?"

"Highly," Tonya says. "He said he would be on his cell phone. I didn't see him again until after the polls closed, when he met up with the family and top staff at a viewing party at one of the donors' homes."

"And did you try to reach the defendant during the time he was missing?"

"Objection, assumes facts not in evidence, that my client was 'missing,' rather than simply in a place that was none of this witness's business."

"Objection, Your Honor, to counsel's argumentative tone."

"Overruled," Judge Keppler says, making a face at the objection to the objection. To Jay, she says, "Defense counsel's objection is sustained, but he is admonished to refer to the witness in a more respectful tone."

"Yes, Your Honor."

Jay can only imagine Ellie behind him, thoroughly enjoying

herself, having found the one place on earth where her dad's mouth actually gets *him* into trouble. Nichols, in a charcoal suit today, steps forward a few inches past the lectern, turning his back to Jay, as if he could block him out that way. Tonya shifts in her seat, adjusting the stiff neckline of her dress. Nichols asks her, "Did you try to reach Mr. Hathorne on the evening of November fifth?"

"Several times."

"And?"

"He never answered his mobile phone or pager."

Nichols glances back at his notes on the lectern, letting her words linger for a bit. Then, looking up, he asks her when she stopped working for the Hathorne camp. "After the girl went missing," Tonya says, "Neal fired me."

It's a specious presentation of the facts, suggesting causality where none has been proved. But it isn't worth the spotlight a verbal objection would put on it.

Jay stays in his chair.

"Do you know why you were fired, Ms. Hardaway?"

"For talking to a cop about Neal."

Neal's knee finds and nudges Jay's beneath the table.

Jay nods without turning to look at his client.

He'll handle it.

"You had discussed Mr. Hathorne's sudden absence from contact with the campaign staff on Tuesday, November fifth, with Detective Moore?"

"Yes. He came into the office and asked about some of the staff, including Neal, and he asked questions about the schedule on the night of the fifth."

"And how long after that were you let go from the campaign?"

"It was that afternoon."

"I don't have anything further, Your Honor."

"Mr. Porter?"

"Ms. Hardaway," Jay says as he stands. He walks to the lectern, slapping down his legal pad. "The Hathorne campaign has a strict policy regarding the chain of command when it comes to communicating on behalf of the organization, isn't that right?" He looks up, staring at the witness.

"That's right."

"In fact, it's in writing and known to all staff members that no one in the office is allowed to speak on behalf of the campaign, or distribute an in-house memorandum, such as a campaign schedule, to *anyone*, without going through Marcie Hall, the communications director, or Mr. Hathorne, the campaign manager, or the candidate himself, isn't that correct, Ms. Hardaway?"

"Yes."

"So it is a misconception and a false impression to give this jury to suggest that it was talking to law enforcement about Mr. Hathorne's whereabouts that got you fired, when, really, you weren't following the rules."

Tonya shrugs. "I talked to a cop, I got fired."

"Which would make a nice title of a country song maybe, but not necessarily the way it happened, is it?"

"Objection, Your Honor, argumentative," Nichols says, standing again, hands on his trim, athletic hips. He actually turns and glances at Jay, a pointed look of gleeful anticipation on his face, a sibling awaiting the punishment of an eternal foe. "Sustained," Judge Keppler says sternly. "Be careful here, Mr. Porter."

"Yes, Your Honor."

Jay turns to address the witness again. He knows he's taking it out on her, the whole charade of this trial, his impatience with the slow drip of *Isn't it true?* and *Didn't you?* and with the yawning gulf between where they're standing and the truth.

"Where are you working now, ma'am?"

Nichols is on his feet again. "Objection, beyond the scope of direct."

"Her employment was the whole point of direct."

"Overruled."

Tonya looks at the judge, then the D.A., hesitating.

"That means you can answer," Jay tells her.

Tonya sits up a little straighter. "I am currently the field director for the campaign to elect Sandra Wolcott."

"Working for the opposition, huh?"

"It's a job."

"Might also suggest a lingering bitterness toward the Hathorne campaign, my client in particular," Jay says, gesturing toward Neal, who glares at Tonya.

"Like I said, it's a job."

"Okay," Jay says, turning to grab, from the corner of the defense table, a single sheet of paper labeled STATE'S EXHIBIT NO. 37. "Permission to approach, Your Honor." Nichols immediately calls for a sidebar at the bench.

At her desk, Judge Keppler peers down at the exhibit, a single sheet of paper.

Nichols, standing next to the court reporter at the bench, says, "This is a murder trial, not a dissection of election politics. This has no business here."

"This is part of the *state's* evidence. It was in the girl's purse."

"He's trying to prove something without laying any foundation for it."

"I want to ask a simple question as relates to her employment with Hathorne. I'm not going to ask her to authenticate the document, just if she's seen it before, in the course of her employment with the Hathorne campaign."

"I'll allow it," Judge Keppler says.

Jay lays the BBDP flyer in front of the witness. As he walks back to the lectern, he sees Sam Hathorne leaning over the bar to whisper something to his grandson. "Have you seen this before, Ms. Hardaway?" he asks. She nods, says yes, and sets it on the corner of the wooden banister in front of her.

"Can you tell the jury what this is?"

Tonya sighs, pressing her lips together for a moment.

It's clear this is an area she wasn't expecting to get into.

"It's a flyer, something that came to the campaign's attention."

"A flyer that was circulating around Pleasantville, yes?"

"That's right."

"And why was this of significance to the campaign?"

"We all thought it was a stunt by one of the other campaigns."

"Which campaign, Ms. Hardaway?"

Tonya looks down for a second, fiddling with the hem of her dress, where it rests just above her knee. "We all thought it was the Wolcott campaign."

"Including you?"

Following a small, sharp exhale, Tonya says, "Yes."

They break for the day earlier than usual, following a quick conference at the bench to discuss the pace of the schedule, Nichols wanting to know if Jay plans to call any witnesses, so he might prepare. Jay assures the judge no decision has been made as to whether he'll offer a defense, and Nichols, put on the spot by Judge Keppler, admits he has plans to call only one more witness before the state rests. Jay is momentarily stunned by the news. The state's case, laid out in open court, is even weaker than he thought, not so much a condemnation of Neal as a light scolding for not doing everyone the courtesy of at least *appearing* less guilty, making Nichols stand up and sit down, stand up and sit down for the past two days. Neal, leaving the courtroom with his uncle and family, shows the first hint of a smile in days. He looks at his lawyer and gives him a grin, lopsided and unsure, but hopeful nonetheless. Sam pats Jay on the back on their way out. Axel's sisters are not in court today, but Vivian, in a teal coatdress, the color deep and stormy, holds her grandson's hand as they exit the courtroom. Ellie, slinging her backpack onto her shoulder, follows her dad down the fifth-floor hallway to the side stairs, both of them avoiding the crowd at the elevator bank. Outside, the air is cold, Houston being famously late to the fall dance, waiting until the second week of December to wring the last of the summer's humidity from the air. It's dropped below fifty for the first time since last Christmas. There's a curling wind snaking through the high-rise buildings downtown, rolling sideways down the length of Franklin Street, lifting wayward leaves and gum wrappers along the curbs. As they approach the Land Cruiser, parked in a twelve-dollar-a-day lot on Caroline, Ellie, in her cotton sweater, shivers. Jay peels off his suit jacket and drapes it over her shoulders. Then he hands her the car keys. "Now?" she says. She seems nervous, not just because she's never driven downtown, but also because she senses another talk coming on. She's slow to put herself behind the wheel. By the time she's in place for this impromptu driving lesson, Jay already has his seat belt on in the passenger seat, the photocopied list of donors to America's Tomorrow sitting faceup on his lap.

Earlier Lonnie left a message on his cell phone, calling from Rolly's hospital room to say that Rob Urrea had never heard of the PAC but was spooked by the donor list. "I definitely picked the wrong horse," he said, before wondering openly if he could break his contract with Hathorne. If it were up to him, Jay would fire his ass. While Urrea was busy digging into Wolcott's sexual imbroglios, a group of high-profile political players had dipped a toe in the city's mayor's race, unseen. They included

ProFerma, Thomas Cole, and Cynthia Maddox. Three of the biggest headaches in Jay's life were tangled up in this somehow.

Ellie puts the key into the ignition. The engine turns, rumbling softly, and lighting up the radio console. KCOH is running a predinner debate on its boards: "Christmas or Kwanzaa, people?" The host, Big Mike, chuckles at his own personal act of provocation. He announces the phone lines are open, before playing a scratchy recording of Otis Redding's "White Christmas." The horns sting Jay, so painful are the memories riding on that sound. He had just gotten used to the idea of the tree—erect, but undecorated still, in a corner of their living room—and now there's music too, the breadth of his loss finding a new sense to explore. It kills him to think that there are notes of his life that will never be played again, save by rolling in circles in his mind, old recordings on a turntable.

Ellie pulls the car out of its parking space, narrowly missing the tail end of a Subaru as she turns the wheel. Jay tells her to make a right turn out of the lot, as Big Mike announces the first caller, Danielle, from Northside Village. "Now, I'm a Christian, y'all, but I do think we need to have our *own* celebrations."

The next caller, Don, from Fifth Ward, takes it a step further, starting with *"Assalamu 'laikum*, brother," before launching into a lecture about Christ being a tool to keep the black man down since slavery time. "Brother Farrakhan is our true prophet and the Nation of Islam our true religious home."

"You telling me you never gon' eat another Christmas ham?" Big Mike says, with no small amount of skepticism. "You had me up till that point."

"Naw, brother, I'm done with that hog."

"I'll eat his, shoot," the next caller, "Bullet, they call me," says. "I was raised in the church, I was raised in Christ, and I'm gon' eat what the lord provide, pork, beef, or chicken. We got to raise these kids out here with Jesus."

Jay reaches for the knob, turning down the volume.

"Don't ever do that again," he says. "Don't you ever walk out of school and get on a city bus without telling me where you are, you understand me?"

"Okay."

"'Cause I could show you autopsy photos of what happens to a girl walking around this city alone—"

"I said, 'Okay.'"

"I'm serious, El."

"*Okay.*"

"I don't know what you and your mother talked about, at the end, I don't know what she said to you, but I need you to understand—"

"Stop it!" she says. She slams on the brakes, fifteen feet short of the nearest stoplight, leaving the two of them stranded, a stone stuck in the sand against the tide of traffic pulling around them. "Stop talking about her! Just stop!" Jay stares at her across the front seat, not sure which one of them is going to break into tears first. "Why don't you want to talk about your mother, Ellie?"

"I can't," she says, shaking her head slowly. "I can't do this."

He takes off his seat belt. "You want me to drive?"

She grips the steering wheel, her eyes watering.

"I don't know if I can do this, Daddy."

Tears falling, she appears unsure, literally, of how to go forward. Jay reaches over and touches her right hand on the wheel. "Come on," he says, telling her to come off the brakes, to start moving slowly. "You can do this, Ellie. Just drive."

CHAPTER 26

"Here, turn here," Jay says, gesturing for Ellie to pull into a small parking lot off Bissonnet, worrying too late that the only open space, one of three slots, is too narrow for the Land Cruiser, at least in a novice's hands. But Ellie does fine, missing the other car in the lot and only barely scraping his front bumper on the concrete barrier between the parking lot and the wooden fence bordering it.

"What are we doing here?" she says, peering past her father.

They are parked in front of a shaded house on a stretch of Bissonnet, between Main Street and Greenbriar, once residential and now a tony spot for art galleries and florists, high-end psychiatrists and, yes, lawyers, cozy bungalows and Craftsman homes made over for the commercial needs of the upper class.

This one is a narrow white two-story with black shutters and a flat roof, a line of Japanese maples out front, their plum-colored leaves shivering in the twilight. Hanging from a post just a few feet from Jay's car is a swinging sign that reads: CHARLIE LUCK-MAN, ESQ. Of the dozens of names on the list of PAC donors, his is oddly the only one Jay trusts. Charlie Luckman may be a lot of things, but a liar is not necessarily one of them, at least not where Jay is concerned. A long time ago, Charlie went out on a limb when he didn't have to, when he and Jay were established adversaries in court, by giving him inside knowledge about Thomas Cole, information that solved a mystery and saved Jay's ass. Ellie asks to stay in the car, but Jay tells her to follow him. Inside, the carpet is thick, the walls as creamy as churned milk, and there is a smell of cigars and good coffee, a Mexican blend, strong and faintly sweet. The soft light in here is as gentle as a madam's reassuring touch, letting any virgin souls crossing the threshold know that they're safe here, that there's no safer place in the world, actually, than a defense attorney's office. There's a wall of Texas license plates going back to the 1930s behind the receptionist's desk, which itself is empty, with only a small Tiffany lamp on top illuminating open magazines, *Cosmopolitan* and *Glamour*. Across the front parlor, above the studded leather couches, there are framed prints, cowboys and ranch scenes, a steer in a stand of prairie grass. "Carla!" Jay can hear Charlie, calling from a back office. He tells Ellie to have a seat on one of the leather sofas.

Following Charlie's voice, he starts down the nearest hall-way.

"Carla, honey, is that you?"

Charlie's office is a long rectangle along the south side of the building, the desk halfway to the back wall. He's sitting with his feet up, the heels of his buttery calfskin boots pointing toward the office's one window; the view is a direct shot into the dance studio next door, a line of women in leotards visible from here. Charlie, seeing Jay, sits up. "Where the hell is Carla?"

"Your receptionist?"

"My wife," he says, standing and walking to the door, sticking his neck out into the hall, her absence more alarming to him, apparently, than the unexpected presence of Jay Porter in his office.

"Your wife is your receptionist?"

"You know a better way to keep track of her?"

Standing in the doorway a few inches from Jay, Charlie adjusts his necktie. Seeing Ellie on the couch in the reception area, he frowns. "God, is that a client?"

"That's my daughter."

Charlie, his black-and-red-striped tie wrenched between his hands, steps back, taking a good look at Jay for the first time, then looking, again, at Ellie. "Where the fuck is Carla?" he barks, walking back to his desk. He picks up the phone, pressing a few buttons. "There a silver Mercedes out there?"

"No."

"God damn it," he says, slamming down the phone. "I swear, I can't keep her ass out of Neiman Marcus to save my life." Throughout the office, there are photos of Charlie and the wife, a tall, thin brunette with caramel-colored skin, and a shot of the two of them and their twin boys. The office decor also includes dozens of glossy images of Luckman with his celebrity clients over the years: an Oilers quarterback, the anchor of a local morning TV show, and the bassist of a bluegrass band out of Austin. Charlie pours himself a drink from a tray on the leather-and-wood sideboard behind his desk, dropping a spoonful of Carnation milk into his scotch. He offers the same to Jay, who declines. "So, Mr. Smith goes to Washington," Charlie says, smirking. "How's politics treating you? I heard you're riding a sinking ship in Keppler's courtroom. I'd be down there to take a look for myself, but I don't really give a shit." He sips the milky scotch.

Jay lays the copy of the list of PAC donors on Charlie's desk. "Then why are you donating to Wolcott's campaign?"

"What the hell are you talking about?"

"America's Tomorrow," Jay says.

"What is this?" Charlie picks up the list, studying the printed names and then setting it back on his desktop without comment, except to say, "I would think it need not be said that I am no fan of Sandy Wolcott." He tops off his scotch and again offers Jay a piece. From down the hall, Jay can hear the phone ringing at the receptionist's desk. Charlie, his face florid and pink, his once sandy hair streaked with gray, like needles stacked in hay, looks as bitter as a man can, well aware that he inadvertently unleashed Sandy Wolcott on the world. Had she not beaten *the* Charlie Luckman in court, she would still be slogging through a caseload of rapes and burglaries and felony manslaughters and not at present be considered the front-runner to lead a city Jay would bet a hundred dollars she can hardly find her way around. She was Charlie's monster. Well, Charlie's and Oprah Winfrey's. Charlie was humiliated, but his client, a prominent heart surgeon who used his considerable skills to gut his cheating wife, is sitting on death row. "It spooked me, losing like that," Charlie says now, sipping his drink. He's had a few doping cases since then, an outfielder from the Astros and a track star who almost lost every medal she won in Atlanta this summer, and he can count on his clients' recreational drug use to keep him solvent for years, but murder, "I can't do that shit anymore," he says. He got married, became a father. "I'm in the goddamned PTA." He raises his glass to Jay. "You're a brave man. Or a fool." He tosses back his toast. "I will say this. You have scared the ever-living shit out of quite a number of men in this town. They think you're crazy. Or worse, reckless and undomesticated. You ever wanted to push your luck, ask for a cushy appointment, get on a board or two, now is the time to ask. Or, hell, *don't*. I won't say this other thing isn't fun to watch. You got folks running scared," he says, remarking on a quality he'd once had in hand and lost. Charlie has always had a grudging respect for Jay.

"What is America's Tomorrow?"

"That?" He nods toward the donor list. "Thomas pulled me in on that."

"Cole?"

Charlie nods. "He's been telling everyone to get in early. First checks written, first names remembered when the time comes." Charlie shrugs, glancing briefly at the phone lines flashing on his desk. "A Texan in Washington again, it could open up a lot of doors for folks down here, grease a lot of wheels. I figured I'd put in my down payment now, instead of playing catch-up in four years." He looks up, his gaze hovering on the view outside his window, the bodies clad in Lycra. "Maybe a judgeship down the line," he says, lost in his thoughts, some far-off dream for his future. "I might want something different one day," he says.

"But what does any of this have to do with Wolcott?"

Charlie nearly laughs.

"Wolcott?" he says. "Oh, hell, nobody gives a shit about Wolcott. That money is for Reese Parker, a grant, shall we say, for her little experiment. She says she can deliver, that was the sales pitch. She and Cole, they had a bunch of high rollers out to his place, cocktails and fifty-dollar steaks, and she laid it out, the way the game is changing. The way elections are run, it's all changing. It's not precinct by precinct anymore, not for the ones who want to win. Four years from now, it's going to come down to a handful of votes. 'Trust me,' she said. Folks were signing checks on the spot. We're talking money to win the *big* prize." He walks back to the bar behind his desk, hovering a little, as if he's debating whether or not he has to behave himself if his wife is nowhere on the premises. "The mayor's race," he says, "this is just a test case for Reese Parker."

Outside, Jay sits in his car, staring out the front window for a long time, so long in fact that Ellie starts to shift in her seat behind the wheel. "Dad?" She touches his arm, and he nods. *I'm fine.* But, still, he doesn't move, looking through the windshield, playing in his mind an image of his last time in Pleasantville, when he'd seen Wolcott's volunteers making an aggressive play for votes in what should have been enemy territory for a right-leaning political candidate; they were following a pattern of attack that Jay still doesn't completely understand. What he does know is what he tells Lon when he calls her that night from his bedroom phone. "They're trying to break Pleasantville." The mighty 259 no more, he says, but a voting bloc that can be destabilized. The misleading flyers, the targeted approach in the streets—if they were able to do something similar in urban precincts across the country, pull votes that shouldn't on paper belong to them, they could actually swing a national race. "This isn't about Wolcott, or even about Houston. This is about the White House in 2000."

"Holy shit, Jay."

"Didn't Parker work on Bush's governor's race last year?"

"She worked for Karl Rove's firm for a bit."

"We've had our eyes on the wrong game this whole time."

Detective Herman "Hank" Moore takes the stand on Monday morning, the sixteenth, a day after a center-foldout story on the trial appeared in the pages of the *Chronicle*, written by Gregg Bartolomo and detailing the strengths of the state's case against mayoral candidate Axel Hathorne's nephew and campaign manager—evidence that he apparently watched in a different courtroom from the one Jay was in all of last week, so puffed up and laid out in a way most favorable to the D.A.'s office are the facts. But such is the power of the press: to get it right, or dangerously wrong. Nichols, in a blue suit, is especially smug this morning, moving with the assured strut of every prosecutor with a cop in the witness chair—which is as good as writing the testimony himself. He leans against the lectern, hands in his pockets, barely glancing at his notes, so certain is he that the detective's testimony, with little help from the prosecutor, will roll out with ease to produce the desired effect. As Detective Moore takes an oath to tell the truth, Jay, at the defense table, glances behind him. Sam is not in the courtroom today, nor are his daughters; just Vivian and Axel are there. Ellie, with her dad's permission, and after he had a weekend chat with her principal—"It's good for her, Mr. Porter"—is sitting beside them. Lonnie is at the city's central library on McKinney, using one of their computers to search for any more information on America's Tomorrow.

Jay can feel the rat-a-tat-tat of Neal's left knee, up and down, up and down, bumping up against the underside of the table. At the lectern, Nichols walks Moore through the evidence, none of it new to Jay. One, the girl was reported missing by her mother. Two, Neal Hathorne came to law enforcement's attention because his phone number was in her pager, a call that came in shortly before she disappeared. Three, Mr. Hathorne lied about knowing the girl and about calling her. Last but not least, in a follow-up with neighbors of Elma Johnson's, Magnus Carr positively identified the defendant as the man he saw struggling with the victim on the corner of Guinevere and Ledwicke. The jurors are as stone-faced as Jay has seen them to date. Worse, a few of the women look directly at Neal, with something new: contempt. Even one of the black men in the second row, the older one by a decade, is eyeing Neal differently. He's frowning, his arms crossed, both hands tucked into his armpits. It's nothing they haven't heard before, but words out of a cop's mouth are like nuggets of iron pyrite: everyone wants to believe it's gold.

Jay is left with little room to maneuver on cross-examination, especially because in Neal's first interview with law enforcement Jay was the only other witness in the room, and Moore knows it. "Detective Moore, isn't it true that my client, Mr. Hathorne, said he didn't *remember* meeting the victim?" he asks first.

"That's what he said."

Moore, in another interesting ensemble of slacks with a checkered sports coat, has his hands clasped together, resting in the center of his lap. His afro is neatly clipped, gray hairs greased and glistening in the fluorescent lights.

"And you would agree that saying he didn't remember is different from *asserting* that he had never met the victim, Ms. Nowell, wouldn't you?"

"A misdirect is a misdirect," Moore says. "It wasn't the truth."

"Within moments of saying he hadn't called the victim's pager, my client made clear that he might have called the number *by mistake*, didn't he?"

"I don't remember it that way."

And there's no one here, besides Jay, to say otherwise.

Moore patiently waits for him to land a jab, seemingly enjoying the spectacle. He lifts his russet-colored tie, fiddling with a loose thread along the bottom before returning it to its place, and resting his hands again in his lap.

"Mr. Hathorne indicated to you that he was returning a call, didn't he?"

"That's what he said."

"Which suggests, does it not, that the victim, Ms. Nowell,

had previously reached out to Mr. Hathorne?" Out of the corner of his eye, Jay senses movement behind him, behind Nichols at the state's table. He turns and sees Maxine Robicheaux leaning forward a little in her seat, a curious look on her face, part surprise and part fret. Had they really not put that together for her? That for Neal to have called Alicia's pager, she had to have given him the number or left it for him at the campaign office, the number on his card.

"I don't know what their relationship was," Moore says.

"Did you check the phone records for the Hathorne campaign office?"

"We declined to get a warrant."

"Why?"

"I didn't think it was pertinent to our investigation."

"You didn't think it was pertinent to investigate why the victim called the defendant in the days leading up to her death?" He presents it as a given fact, which is what trips Moore up, his eyes going blank, as if they're scrolling through reams of information about the case in the back of his head. He shifts in his chair.

"I, uh, don't know that she did that."

"You found a number of items in the victim's purse, didn't you?"

More shifting. "Yes."

"The pager, of course."

The thing with his tie again. "Yes."

"Some cosmetics, a wallet, a little money?"

"Yes," Moore says, glancing past Jay to Nichols. Behind him, Jay can hear the faint squeak of Nichols sitting at the edge of his chair. Jay walks to the clerk's desk beside the bench, reaching into the evidence box for state's exhibit no. 37, the BBDP flyer. He walks it to the witness stand, laying it faceup on the banister.

"This was also among the victim's belongings, wasn't it?"

Moore pushes the sheet of paper an inch or two away from him. "Yes."

"If the victim had knowledge that these flyers, disparaging Axel Hathorne, were circulating around Pleasantville, wouldn't that be a reason she might have reached out to Mr. Hathorne's campaign manager, Neal, to let him know?"

"Objection, speculation."

"Overruled," Keppler says.

"I never said she called him," Moore says.

"Well, you wouldn't know because you didn't check."

After getting the detective to repeat, for the fifth or sixth time, that law enforcement found no physical evidence that tied Mr. Hathorne to Alicia Nowell and her murder, Jay sits down, telling the judge and the witness he has no further questions. Maxine Robicheaux, in the gallery, is staring at Jay, sudden doubt on her face. When Keith Morehead leads her and Mitchell out of the courtroom, she seems turned around, lost, even in the few steps it takes to get from her seat to the door. At the close of court, Nichols again asks for some heads-up as to whether Jay is planning to call any witnesses or mount a defense at all. Jay is cagey, knowing he doesn't owe the prosecution a look at his playbook, the thing he has planned for day one of defense testimony.

"I want to go after Parker."

"Absolutely not," Sam says.

It's after six o'clock, and they have all gathered in Jay's office on the eve of what they believe will be Nichols's announcement the following day that the state is resting its case. Sam even brought over a bottle of Macallan from his personal collection, so confident is he that they are that much closer to putting this whole awful thing behind them. Eddie Mae, who stayed long enough today to see Ellie off safely with Evelyn and Ben, passed out paper cups, and helped herself to a couple of swallows. Neal hasn't held back either, downing three shots in as many minutes. Only Jay and Axel have refrained from drinking this early in the day, or this early in the judicial process, for that matter. Vivian stayed outside on the front porch, smoking a cigarette. Through the windows of the front parlor where they're gathered, Jay can see her hugging herself against the night air. A few doors down, music is pouring out of the Diamond Lounge, a lick of blues guitar followed by a long harmonica note, a wounded man's howl.

"I'm willing to give in on A.G., and anything else he might say on the stand," Sam says. "I'm willing to forgive him *anything* if he comes through for Neal, but I think it's a grave mistake to turn this into a crusade, especially when we're so close to a win. When this is over, and Neal is acquitted, we can walk back into the mayor's race, heads held high, knowing we didn't sling mud."

"That's not your decision to make."

"Neal," Sam says, turning to his grandson.

Neal, warmed by the whiskey, is sweating. His skin looks dewy and flushed, as if he'd run a mile, as if he's warming up to get back into a fight. "I don't think we need it," he says, nodding at his grandfather in agreement.

The candidate is leaning against the armrest of one of the room's chairs, his long legs splayed out so far in front of him that the argyle design of his socks is visible. He has his arms crossed. "I feel that I, of all people, ought to abstain from a vote, given that it's my campaign Dad is trying to protect, and the fact that I pushed for this, the injunction and all of it, putting Neal on the line. But let me ask, isn't my brother's testimony enough?"

"All we need to do is dismantle the eyewitness's story," Neal says.

"And A.G. does that."

"Parker on the stand just confuses the issue," Sam says.

Axel stands. "Or worse, like we're making this all about politics."

"It *is* about politics," Jay says. "She sent that girl into Pleasantville with an agenda. And here's your chance to air it in open court, what they're doing."

"Reese Parker isn't the reason that girl was killed," Sam says.

"You do understand what I'm telling you?" Jay says. "They put a mark on Pleasantville, a test case for the rest of the nation. Some of the biggest names in this city, in this state, including Cynthia Maddox, your supporter, they are funneling money into Wolcott's campaign, not because they want her to win, but because they're willing to fund Parker's work to win the next election and the one after that. If you don't make this plain right now, you will lose, understand? Not just the mayor's race. But everything you fought for during the past forty-plus years. The power of your vote, the power of Pleasantville, you will lose it all."

The room falls silent.

Axel lowers his head, looking queasy. Neal turns to his grandfather, everything, for him, hinging on Sam's reaction. The man himself clenches his fists at his sides, his dark eyes narrowing behind his spectacles. "Which is why we need to get back out there and fight," he says, "just like we always have."

"Pop is right," Neal says, nodding vigorously, too vigorously, Jay thinks.

"I'll handle Cynthia," Sam says.

Neal crosses to Jay, putting a hand on his attorney's shoulder, standing so close that Jay can see the dots of sweat above his lip, can smell the whiskey on his breath. The fear is still there, in the quivering of his lower lip, the searching look in his desperate, bloodshot eyes. "Just get A.G. on the stand."

Jay spends the rest of his evening at St. Joseph's, where Rolly is up and eating well, thanks to Marisol, who, thank god, really was just going for a cup of coffee. Tonight she brought him ceviche and a T-bone from Tampico, a cantina around the corner from his house in the Heights. He's sitting up in bed, a robe over the bandages and a paper napkin tucked up under his chin. His black hair has been freshly washed and braided, also thanks to Marisol. She's watching *Jeopardy!* on television, her butt in the hospital room's only chair and her bare feet resting on the edge of the bed, near Rolly's waist. Her man awake and alert, she's dressed herself accordingly, in a tight sweater and black jeans. She said hello to Jay when he walked in and not much else. Rolly washes down his steak with a swig from a contraband bottle of Negra Modelo. He snatches the napkin from beneath his chin and wipes his mouth with it. "So what do you want to do?"

"You know what I want to do."

"Then what the hell are you doing here, man?"

"Well, you *were* shot," Jay says.

"My own damn fault." Rolly sits up, using his fists to adjust his position in the bed and wincing from the residual pain in his left shoulder. "But if that earns me a window of grace, let me say my piece now. You think you can handle it?" He looks at Jay, a cockeyed grin forming across his plump, almost ladylike lips. "We're friends, right? I mean, we can call each other that?"

"Yes, sir," Jay says, smiling faintly.

"I like you, man, I might even love your ass," Rolly says. "But anything I owed you for shit you've done for me, I paid back years ago. That ain't why I'm here. I don't need your money, I got a job, a good one. That ain't it either. Hell, I'd pay *you* just to see you this up and at it again, this, I don't know, *alive* again, man. This is you, Jay, this is where you belong, stirring shit the fuck up. And what I did *not* do all this for," he says, gesturing at the white walls of the hospital room, the monitors, and, yes, the bandages, "is for you to come all this way only to half-ass it. Parker, her crew, they're tromping on your legacy too, shit you and your boys marched for." He stares down the length of the hospital bed to Jay, who is standing with his head down slightly, his hands tucked into the pockets of his pants, still in the suit he wore to court today.

"It's just the way this works," he says to Rolly; "it's his game to play, his life. He's my *client*, man."

"Then counsel him, Counselor."

Hours later, just after midnight, the telephone on Jay's bedside table rings, echoing throughout the house. Having just dozed off after a late-night conference at Neal's house, Jay doesn't pick up until the sixth ring. "You son of a bitch," Reese Parker hisses in his ear, before hanging up, never bothering to identify herself, not that she needed to. He was expecting her call. Though Neal and Sam didn't know it, Rolly either, Jay had actually filed a subpoena two full days ago for her to appear in Judge Caroline Keppler's courtroom. He'd had his eye on this moment all along. He hangs up the phone and rolls back to sleep.

CHAPTER 27

Word of Reese Parker's expected presence in the courtroom
must have gotten out. The 181st District Court is more packed
than it was on the morning of opening statements, with a few
spectators waiting out in the hallway to see if they might get a
spot, if someone faints maybe in the unusually hot courtroom,
leaving an extra seat for the next person in line. Johnetta Paul
is here; the county clerk, Wayne Duffie; and a few other names
on next month's ballot. There are reporters, of course; lawyers
from neighboring courtrooms, come to watch; and the families on both sides. The entire Hathorne clan is in the front row
of the gallery, behind Jay's client. Maxine and Mitchell Robicheaux sit somberly, staring straight ahead, as Nichols stands
and announces, just as Jay had expected, "The state rests, Your

Honor." Keith Morehead, their spokesperson and ardent supporter, has been pushed to the other side of the courtroom
because of the overcrowding. He is sitting today beside Ellie,
who is behind her father, taking notes for her government class.
She and the principal and Mr. Jensen worked out a deal: for a
heaping dose of extra credit, Ellie will take notes and deliver
a report to the class when the trial is over. She's taken her role
seriously, borrowing some authentic-looking steno pads from
Lonnie. The pastor smiles at her, patting her on the leg for her
good work. Jay can hear their whispers behind him. He looks at
his client, seated beside him. It's his last chance to change his
mind. But Neal just nods. Behind him, Sam sits with his arms
folded. He was not present last night when Jay showed up on
Neal's doorstep, when he'd asked him, point-blank, why he was
interested in politics in the first place, what any of this meant
to him if it wasn't about protecting the work of men and women
of his grandfather's generation. "Any gratitude you owe Sam is
for that, not for taking you in," he said, alluding to the family
secrets. "You have to do what *you* think is right."

And when Neal had grown quiet, chewing on his bottom lip,
Jay said to him, stoking a buried rage, "You really think you
would have been charged if Sandy Wolcott weren't running for
mayor, if Parker weren't involved?"

"Mr. Porter?" the judge says.

After a perfunctory motion to dismiss the case for insuffi-
cient evidence, which Keppler denies, Jay is free to start. "The
defense calls Reese Parker."

Nichols is on his feet too. "Your Honor, may we approach?"

Keppler waves them both forward.

There's a low murmur rolling through the courtroom.
Lonnie is watching the commotion from the last row of the gallery. At the bench, the D.A. makes clear his objection to this
witness. "On what grounds, Mr. Nichols?"

"Relevance, for one."

"The victim was working for Ms. Parker when she was assaulted," Jay says. "I expect this witness to shed light on why she was in Pleasantville."

"Sounds relevant to me," the judge says.

Nichols looks stunned. "Based on what evidence?"

"Well, let's let the woman take the stand and find out."

"He's trying to bring in stuff that has nothing to do with this trial."

"If she knows anything about the girl's last hours, it does," Keppler says.

"He's been picking at this for weeks now," Nichols says. "Ms. Parker has repeatedly said she never hired Alicia Nowell, that the girl wasn't one of hers."

"You know, for someone who claims he didn't know this witness was going to be called, who claims he had little time to attempt to interview her, you sure do know a lot about the inner workings of your boss's campaign," Keppler says, eyeing him over the rims of her glasses. "Bring her in," she says, before nodding to her clerk to find someone to come check on the heating system.

Reese Parker dressed up for this.

She pressed a suit, tamed her blond, overprocessed, almost white hair into a chic sweep off her face. She put on panty hose and pinned a demure brooch to her lapel, a small star, glistening stones in red, white, and blue: rubies, diamonds, and tiny sapphires. She raises her right hand, smiling through her oath. All the way up until she's plopped her considerable heft into the swiveling witness chair, she never stops smiling. "Good morning, Mr. Porter," she says, addressing him before he's even looked up from his notes on the lectern.

"Spell your name please," he says.

"R-E-E-S-E P-A-R-K-E-R."

"And where are you employed, Ms. Parker?"

"I am currently doing some consulting work for the Wolcott for mayor campaign." She glances at the jury, another smile for the ladies in the first row, as if she imagines she might as well try to pick up a few votes while she's here.

"For how long?"

"The campaign hired me six months or so before the general election."

"And what are your duties with the campaign?"

"I consult."

"On?"

The smile again. "Well, I wouldn't want to give away any trade secrets."

"Objection, Your Honor," Jay says. "Witness is being unresponsive."

"Sustained," Keppler says coolly.

"You strategize, oversee media buys, raise funds, that sort of thing?"

"Sure."

"Go over policy?"

"Yes."

"Print campaign literature?"

Here, Parker hesitates. "Something like that."

Jay notices she keeps looking over his shoulder toward someone in the back of the courtroom. Dabbing at his forehead, he turns slightly to scan the faces behind him, his eyes landing on Cynthia Maddox. She's in a winter white pantsuit. Of everybody in the courtroom, she has the seat closest to the exit sign. She's made no show of her presence, pointedly sitting herself behind the back of most of the reporters in the courtroom, watching the proceedings silently. The heat across his forehead spikes. "Ms. Parker, have you heard of an organization called America's Tomorrow?"

Parker blanches, her skin going nearly as white as her hair.

Biting through another stiff smile, she says, "Yes, I've heard of it."

"Is it a political action committee?"

"I believe so."

"You do any consulting work for them?"

"Objection, relevance," Nichols says.

"Sustained."

Keppler shoots Jay a look from the bench.

He'll have to come at this a different way.

Jay walks across the well between the lectern and the clerk's desk, reaching into the box of evidentiary material for exhibit 37, the flyer. As he did with Detective Moore, he lays the flyer in front of the witness chair. It's on his walk back to the lectern that he again catches sight of Keith Morehead. In the front row of the gallery, positioned just to the left of Neal, their faces are almost side by side, though Morehead is a few inches behind the defendant. Jay can't believe he never noticed it before, the stark resemblance, the same nut brown skin and the hooded eyes. If he had to guess, he would put the difference in their heights at no more than an inch, and if either one of them was standing on a dark street corner, he might easily mistake one for the other.

The heat spreads down the sides of his neck, across his damp chest.

"Is there a question, Your Honor?" Nichols says.

Jay swings back around, stumbling slightly, flustered by a sudden, creeping suspicion. He leans against the lectern to steady himself, staring at his own handwritten words jumping across the legal pad in front of him.

"Have you seen that flyer before, Ms. Parker?"

Parker surprises him by answering, right off, "Yes."

"And that's because you wrote it, isn't that right?"

"Objection, leading."

"Sustained."

Jay, out of the corner of his eye, watches Morehead next to his daughter.

"Did you write that flyer, Ms. Parker?"

Here Parker chuckles softly, at Mr. Porter's innocent misunderstanding, her look to the jury says. "No, no," she says. "I just, you know, during a campaign, stuff gets around. I'd heard these were circulating. I'd seen it."

"Are you telling this court, under oath, that you are not the author of this flyer connecting Axel Hathorne to a bayou development project that would, according to that sheet of paper, negatively affect the residents of Pleasantville?"

Parker's eyes narrow ever so slightly. "No."

"No, that's not what you're telling the court, or no, you didn't write it?"

"I didn't write it."

"But you paid for it, right?"

"Me?" Parker says, carving her answer with a scalpel. "No."

"That's right. America's Tomorrow paid for it."

"Objection, Your Honor. Is he testifying now?"

"Sustained."

"Are you aware that the political action committee America's Tomorrow wrote a check in the amount of three hundred and eleven dollars to print up eight hundred of these flyers?" When she doesn't answer, he says, "Ms. Parker?"

"Objection, Your Honor, lack of foundation."

"I have the invoice right here. I'm happy to move it into evidence."

"That's usually how this works," Keppler says.

During the time it takes the clerk to stamp the back side of Jay's copy of the Prince of Prints invoice and write the evidence number and case file ID on it, Parker has started to breathe more heavily. She is sitting too close to the microphone, and her ragged breath is amplified across the courtroom. Finally, Jay shoves the invoice in front of her. "Were you aware that the PAC, America's Tomorrow, paid over three hundred dollars to have that flyer printed?"

She smiles tightly. "That amount, no."

In the jury box, one of the men in the front row frowns. He's not the only one who looks slightly confused. But to Jay, it's as good as a confession. He's ready to ask the question more directly. "Are you, at present, doing any consulting work for the political action committee America's Tomorrow?"

"Objection, relevance," Nichols says. "We went over this, Your Honor."

"Overruled," she says, peering over her glasses.

Jay looks at Parker. "Answer the question."

She takes so long to say the word that when it finally comes, it is just an echo of what the courtroom has by now already guessed. "Yes," she says flatly, pushing her chin out in defiance, shooting a cold look across the room at Jay.

"And did you oversee the creation of this flyer?"

"I didn't write it if that's what you mean."

"No, that's not what I mean."

The courtroom falls silent for a few seconds.

Overhead, Jay hears the clicking of the broken heating system.

"Did you, Ms. Parker, participate in the creation and distribution of this flyer disparaging the intentions of mayoral candidate Axel Hathorne, who is an opponent of the woman whose campaign you're working on right now?"

"Can you define 'participate'?"

"Why don't *you*?"

Finally, Parker sighs.

She's grown huffy and impatient.

This is stupid, she might as well be saying. "It was my idea," she says, perfectly happy to take credit for the maneuver. At the state's table, Nichols lowers his head. Neal turns and looks at his grandfather, behind him, as if he needs Sam to confirm that he actually just heard what he thinks he heard. Sam appears stunned. Parker is unrepentant. "I've done better, and I've done a hell of a lot worse. It's politics." She shrugs, as if this was the most elementary thing in the world and of absolutely no consequence. "I didn't kill anybody," she says, looking pointedly across the courtroom at the defendant.

"Are you aware that the victim had one of those very flyers in her purse when she was killed?"

Maxine Robicheaux has a hand on the bar in front of her, gripping the wood.

Parker considers this for a second. "At the time she was killed, no."

It's another equivocation, and everyone, from row one of the jury to Judge Keppler to Nichols himself, has grown tired of it. Jay actually turns to look behind him, to see if Bartolomo and the other reporters are taking good notes.

And that's when he sees the two empty seats in the front row.

Directly behind him, to the left of the Hathornes, there's a harrowingly hollow space where, just moments ago, two people were sitting: Keith Morehead and Elena Porter. He was about to ask Parker the next question, the answer to which had set this trial in motion: had Reese Parker hired Alicia Nowell to distribute those flyers in the neighborhood of Pleasantville? But he can't get the words out, feels his throat choking on the rising bile of fear clogging up his speech, scrambling his thoughts. He thinks of Morehead putting his hand on Ellie's knee, and feels ill. His back to the judge, the witness, he scans the courtroom from corner to corner looking for his daughter. When his eyes meet Lonnie's in the back row of the gallery, she sees something in his face that makes her stand and intercept him by the doors. Behind him, the judge calls his name. He ignores her, ignores everyone. "Ellie," he says to Lonnie. "Where's Elena?"

"She walked out."

"And Morehead?"

"He was a few steps behind her," she says. "What's wrong?"

But when the moment comes to put a name to his panic, he finds he can't.

He instantly starts to doubt himself, the madness of what he's thinking.

"Mr. Porter?" Judge Keppler says. "What's going on here?"

"I have to find her," he says to Lon, to anyone within earshot.

He glances at the judge. "I'm sorry," he says, before shuffling out of the courtroom. She is standing at the bench now. "Just what do you think you're doing, Mr. Porter? You'll need to return to this courtroom immediately—"

He hears nothing but the door swinging closed behind him.

He's already in the hallway, looking left, looking right.

It's quite empty, except for a few lawyers on the benches against the wall, and a young woman in white jeans and Keds talking on a pay phone.

"Ellie!" He screams her name, not sure which way to run.

He checks the ladies' room first, kicking in stalls.

By the time he's back in the hallway, his voice is almost hoarse from screaming. When the door to the men's room opens and Keith Morehead walks out, adjusting his belt, Jay flies at him, grabbing the man by his suit lapels and slamming him against the nearby wall. "Jay!" Lonnie is right behind him, running to what is fast becoming a scene. The bailiff from Keppler's courtroom is in the hall too, her right hand hovering over the grip of the pistol on her belt. Others start spilling out from the courtroom, Gregg Bartolomo, Sam, and Vivian. "What did you do with her?" Jay says, slamming him against the wall again.

"Hey!" the bailiff says, moving closer.

Lonnie puts a hand on Jay's back. "Calm down, Jay, just calm down."

"What did you do to them?" Hearing that word, that *them*, Lonnie steps back, staring at Morehead, her mind lighting on some meaning. "Where the hell is my daughter!" Jay screams. Morehead is so spooked by Jay, by the brewing commotion in the hall, that he can't quite speak. Stuttering his way toward a response, the beginning of a word that keeps tripping on his tongue, he keeps darting his eyes over Jay's shoulder and down the polished floor of the hallway.

Lonnie turns first, and then Jay, in time to see T. J. Cobb slipping through the door to the stairwell at the end of the hall, a flash of something red moving just ahead of him and then gone from sight. *Red*, Jay thinks, lights turning off one by one in each chamber of his brain as he races through it trying to remember what Ellie was wearing when they left the house this morning. Why, oh why can't he remember what was just in front of his eyes only a few minutes ago?

"Call the police," he tells Lonnie. "Get Axel, and call the police."

He takes off running for the stairs.

In the grayish light of the stairwell, he hears the footsteps below him, two sets, he's sure of that. He calls his daughter's name, over and over, and hears nothing but the tin echo of his own panic. They are just beyond his reach, it seems, just past the landing of every floor before he gets there, never in full sight.

When he gets to the bottom, he barrels through the door, nearly tripping over his own feet as he stumbles into the crowd in the first-floor lobby. Jurors, cops, lawyers, translators, social workers, teary relatives, and nervous defendants out on bail, all moving in a reluctant swirl through the metal detectors. Jay grabs the arm of the nearest deputy on duty, causing the man to cuff Jay's wrist with his own oversize hand, its force nearly crushing the bones. "A girl," Jay says quickly. "Did you see a teenage girl, fifteen, black? She might have been wearing red." It *was* red, he remembers now, a cardigan with a rosette above her heart. She'd dressed up for court. "There was a man with her, a black guy, really tall." He doesn't see either of them anywhere in the main lobby.

"Okay, calm down, buddy, calm down."

But as he says it, the deputy sees the bailiff from Keppler's courtroom coming out of the same stairwell from which Jay recently emerged. She's still got her hand in position, over the pistol, and she points directly at Jay.

"Wait a second, guy," the deputy says, tightening his grip.

Jay shakes him off and pushes his way through the incoming crowd and out onto the front steps of the criminal court building. He's screaming her name, scanning the faces on the street for any sign of his daughter or Cobb.

"Jay?"

It's Cynthia Maddox, in that white, white suit.

She must have come down for a cigarette at some point and is standing by the sand-filled cement ashtray at the top of the steps. She has a cellular telephone in her right hand. The look on his face absolutely terrifies her.

"My daughter," he says, breathless. "I can't find my daughter."

Behind him, Keppler's bailiff and the sheriff's deputy are coming through the glass doors. Jay is probably a few moments from being arrested. "Come on," Cynthia says, tossing her cigarette and pointing to her waiting car, her driver behind the wheel reading a newspaper folded into a square. Even with the officers on his tail, Jay hesitates, still afraid, after all these years, to trust her.

"Don't be stupid, Jay," she says. "Let me help."

She climbs into the backseat of the car first, leaving the door open for him. Jay, desperate, slides in behind her. "Where to, ma'am?" the driver says. Jay barks out an address, reaching into his pocket for his cell phone. He calls Lonnie, who hands the phone to Axel, to whom Jay gives a detailed description of his daughter and T. J. Cobb. "I started a file on him with HPD," he says. Axel tells him, "I'm on it, man." Jay slams the phone closed. He squeezes his eyes shut against the terror, the image of that empty seat in the courtroom, his daughter *gone*. But it's worse in the dark, and so he opens his eyes and stares out the window instead, hearing nothing but his breath, his heartbeat, and the rush of pavement beneath the car. After Parker's turn on the witness stand today, the things Jay must know by now, Cynthia wants her chance to explain.

"Listen, Jay—"

"Don't say a fucking word."

Ricardo Aguilar has apparently been conducting all of his business between the hours of nine and four thirty, when he expected Jay to be in court, and then, just to be safe, had actually moved his personal office into a small storage room just off the reception area, so certain was he that Jay, or Rolly, the long-haired dude in the El Camino, was coming after him. Should anyone ask, it gave his secretary a perfect cover to answer honestly, "No, Mr. Aguilar is *not* in his office." Jay storms in, barreling past her and her threats to call law enforcement. "They're already on their way," he informs her.

She never actually reveals Aguilar's hiding place, not verbally at least.

She merely bats her heavily made-up eyes in the direction of a wooden door, repeatedly nodding her head in that direction too. The door isn't locked, but someone is attempting to hold it closed from inside. Jay kicks it in with the heel of his shoe. When the door flies open, Aguilar falls back on his butt.

Jay grabs him off the ground. "Where is he? Where's Cobb?"

Aguilar holds up his hands in retreat. "Now, look, let's talk about this."

"He's got my daughter!"

"What?"

Aguilar nearly tumbles back to the ground, his eyes wide. He seems genuinely bewildered. He looks at his secretary, but she has her head down, avoiding all eye contact. "I swear, I don't know what you're talking about."

"Where is Cobb!"

"I don't know," Aguilar says, holding up his hands again as if he expects to be hit. He's wearing another one of his fancy suits, the cuffs of the pants legs dragging dust from the floor of the storage room. "I haven't seen him in weeks."

"That's not possible."

"It's true, I swear."

Jay stumbles back, the line of the doorjamb ramming into his spine. He remembers then the press of concrete into his back the night Cobb jumped him outside the Playboy Club in Third Ward. What had he said? Nothing about ProFerma, or the civil suit. No, it was a threat about Jay's push for the injunction to stop the city's election, a warning to back off. By the time the question forms on Jay's lips, he already knows the answer. "You didn't send him after me, did you?" Aguilar stands up straight, smoothing the black sheet of hair on his head, putting himself back together as if his coming confession were about to be televised on a stage filled with push brooms and bottles of Mr. Clean, and a makeshift desk with a single phone, whose cord snakes all the way out of the closet and down the hall to Aguilar's real office.

"Jelly Lopez and me, we go way back, Jester Hall, freshman year," he says, catching his breath. "He's got this case he tells me, the fires, the chemical company, they're stalling, he says, and, *you*, he thinks you're not much better, and he thinks it's all a game to you guys and meanwhile his kid's sick and part of his house he still can't live in. So we get to talking. And I'm thinking maybe I can help, maybe we can help each other, you know. I'm dying here, this low-rent criminal bullshit," he says, motioning to the whole of his small law practice.

"So you *did* steal the client files."

Aguilar hangs his head. "I had Cobb do it."

Behind them, Aguilar's secretary has been quietly and methodically packing up her desk: framed photos; pencils and the coffee mug they were stored in; a few notepads; and a small paperweight, a starfish suspended in resin, all of it goes into her purse, a cheap black satchel, plastic tubing showing at the seams. Without saying a word, she stands and walks out of the office, moving faster than Jay would have thought possible. Her departure seems to destroy whatever shred of dignity Aguilar had left. He looks at Jay pleadingly, wanting to be understood. "But, as god is my witness, I haven't seen that kid since he turned those files over to Sam. I haven't heard from either one of them, in fact. I'm starting to feel like he set me up. I think he was just using me all along."

"Sam?"

Aguilar makes a face, as if he thought this was obvious, as if he thought Jay was right behind him on this trail but now sees he'd lost him a few steps back. He sighs, starting the story from the beginning. "Jelly Lopez has a lot of friends in Pleasantville, but he can't sway over four hundred plaintiffs, not on his own. Sam was quietly pushing this thing the whole time. He and I had a deal. I get the files for him, and he would make sure I got the civil case. But I haven't heard a fucking thing from him since. He won't even return my calls."

"Sam," Jay says again. "He was trying to push me out?"

"He said you'd be so busy with the murder trial, it'd be easy to get the residents to go against you, to say you were distracted, not the right man."

A murder trial that he hired me for, Jay remembers.

"But I think he's trying to cut some deal with ProFerma on his own, coming up with some number everyone can live with and presenting it to the residents directly, not using any attorney, that's what I think he's really doing now. All those rumors about bayou development affecting Pleasantville, those flyers that were going around, that just made it that much easier to convince people to take what they can now. Jelly says he's hearing sixty-three thousand a family," Aguilar says, shaking his head at the bum deal. "And no lawyers' fees."

"And you haven't seen the files since?"

"I *never* saw them. I had Cobb deliver them directly to Sam, and then I lost control of him. I guess he's working for the old man now."

Jay walks to the chair at the receptionist's desk and sits down, trying to find his daughter somewhere in this maze of deception. If Cobb is working for Sam now, then it was the elder Hathorne who delivered the warning to back off the injunction, just as he had tried to move Neal away from any public confrontation with Reese Parker about the flyers—flyers that actually benefited Sam and his plan to work out a private settlement between ProFerma and Pleasantville. Even though it was all a lie. There is no bayou development deal. Meanwhile, Sandy Wolcott and her ace in the hole Reese Parker had gone on campaigning, picking up percentage points in the polls for every day the situation with Neal Hathorne wasn't

resolved. The march of the volunteers' feet crosses Jay's mind
again, that day he'd seen them out in Pleasantville, block-
walking, making a naked play for the precinct. And what's
more, he remembers Charlie's description of Parker's pitch to
donors: *It's not precinct by precinct anymore, not for the ones
who want to win. Four years from now, it's going to come down
to a handful of votes.* That day, on Josie Street, it looked for
all the world as if they were cherry-picking the voters they
could get the most out of, skipping some residents completely.
And now he finally understands how they had chosen which
houses to target: they were using the information in his files.
"My god," he mutters, as he turns the final corner in the maze.
He pictures the street addresses, the zigzag pattern of the volunteers, each of whom he now believes was armed with highly
sensitive information about the people living inside. He can,
by memory, name them all.

They're his clients, after all.

2002 Josie Street is Mary Melendez's place. She'd had a complete hysterectomy in her early thirties after a botched abor-
tion, a fact that was included in her medical records, and she
had therefore had only one child, a son, David, who was killed
in Vietnam. She was woeful about her "mistakes," and was
staunchly pro-life. She did not, in her seventies, drink or take
drugs.

At 2037 are Robert Quinones and his wife, Darla. Mr. Quinones had a preexisting injury to his shoulder when he'd
caught buckshot on a hunting trip with his son, who was thirteen at the time. He was an NRA member and a weekend did
not pass that he wasn't hunting some kind of mammal somewhere.

At 2052 are Linda and Betty Dobson, sisters who've lived together for years, who are not actually sisters at all, but "dear
friends," and who Jay has always believed are lovers, in a rela-

tionship for over thirty years. Because copies of their medical records and birth certificates were included in their client file, along with tax records and the names on the deed to the house, Jay is the only one who knows this, and he was sworn to secrecy by both of them. They were serious, three-nights-a-week-at-church Baptists who did not like "queers," they told him.

2055 is Rutherford Tompkins, widower and retired firefighter, who was home alone when the explosion happened last spring. Jay had seen his tax returns too, and received an earful about how much he was still paying to the government, chunks of money taken out of his Social Security checks. Jay had noted all of this in the file, along with the name of his deceased wife and dozens of other personal facts about the man's life, from birth to his sixty-seventh year.

My god, Jay thinks again, if Parker could swing any one of them *away* from Axel, if she could reach into traditionally black precincts throughout the country, for that matter, and pluck out the registered Democrats with the slightest tear in their liberal fabric, a weak thread that could be pulled until the stitches came apart, could she, four years from now, swing them for a Republican candidate? If you could take Pleasantville from a Hathorne, you could do anything. *They're trying to break Pleasantville.* And damn if they didn't have help.

The car is a surprise, still idling there.

He was sure she would have left him here, abandoning him at the worst time, as she had done nearly thirty years earlier. But Cynthia, of all people, is right here when he needs someone most. He has no car, no other way out of here, back to his real life, before Aguilar and T. J. Cobb, before the Hathornes and this mess of a trial, when his daughter was still safe. He opens the rear passenger door of the Town Car and collapses into the leather seat. The car is filled with gray smoke, swirling from the end of the cigarette in Cynthia's shaking hand. She looks pale, her blond hair lank in the warmth of the car, the smell of her sweat mixed with the woodsy scent of her perfume, looking at this angle like the girl he once knew, the one who leaned across the cab of her green Ford Econoline truck and kissed him at dawn. She's staring out the tinted window. "I told you not to fuck with Sam."

"Where's my daughter, Cynthia?"

"I don't know."

Turning from the window, she leans forward, tapping the back of the driver's seat. "Get him out of here now," she says before turning to Jay, who leans forward, elbows on his knees, his head in his sorry hands, and weeps.

CHAPTER 28

The Sam Hathorne that the people of Pleasantville rarely get to see resides in a five-bedroom colonial on three-quarters of an acre on North MacGregor Drive. The house sits on a bend in the winding road, with a view, through a parklike stand of trees in the front yard, of the landscaped path along Brays Bayou. MacGregor Drive, north and south, is lined with palatial homes owned almost exclusively by moneyed blacks who took over the neighborhood after segregation and its hand tool, deed restrictions, were outlawed. They were suddenly free to leave places like Pleasantville for something better, for there is always something better, and soon the first black families were moving to MacGregor—running out the Jews who'd built the homes, who had themselves been run out of WASPy

River Oaks—and leaving empty properties along Pleasantville Drive, Norvic, Ledwicke, and Guinevere, homes that were then bought up by the likes of Jelly Lopez and Bill Rodriguez, Patricia Rios, Arturo Vega and his family. It was a snake that bit its own tail, the way some things changed only to remain the same. Sam's driver, Frankie, answers the front door. Inside the foyer, the dark wood floors gleam under the twinkling light of a teardrop chandelier overhead. Jay hears Sam's voice coming from the great room. Down the hallway ahead, he can see the length of Vivian Hathorne's toned calf and the pointed heel of her left shoe dangling off the edge of a leather couch. They have gathered in the living room, the whole family, all except Axel, who is still at the central police station downtown, coordinating from there a citywide search for Jay's daughter. Cynthia pushes past Frankie into the house, down the hallway, and into the living room. When Jay enters behind her, he tells everyone—Vivian, Ola and Camille, Delia and Gwen—to get out. "Not you," he says to Neal. "And definitely not you," he says to Sam, who is in the same dove gray suit he was wearing before court was abruptly halted this morning. He takes off his wire-rimmed glasses, slowly wiping the lenses with a handkerchief embroidered with the initials SPH. He doesn't say a word. Vivian stands, a drink in hand. "What's going on here?" she says to Sam when she sees Jay and Cynthia eyeing him, when she senses the electricity running under everything.

"If you could give us a minute," Cynthia says.

Vivian turns to her husband and whispers, "What did you do?"

"You're drunk, Viv."

"Come on, Mom," Ola says, leading her mother from the living room, looking nervously over her shoulder as her three sisters follow her out. Frankie stands guard by the front door, as if he's expecting another intrusion any second now. In the living room, it's just Neal and Sam, Cynthia and Jay.

"Where's my daughter?"

Neal looks from Jay to his grandfather, then back again, confused. "Axel's still at the station. I'm sure we would have heard by now if he knew something."

"I'm asking *you*, Sam. Where is my child?"

Sam carefully folds his handkerchief, then slides his glasses back on, taking time to adjust the stems, to smooth the tightly coiled hairs along his temples. Jay crosses the room, closing the gap between them by pressing his face close to the old man's. "I will kill you, Sam, understand? I will kill you with my bare hands if you don't tell me right now where she is."

"I don't know where she is." Sam shrugs, the gesture as cold as the ice cubes he drops, one by one, into the bottom of a crystal glass resting on the bar behind him. "Cobb is a loose cannon." He starts to pour a finger of whiskey, but Jay knocks the glass, the whole bottle, out of his hand. It shatters on the parquet wood, the brown liquid creeping across the polished floor, seeping into the fringe of an Oriental rug in the center of the room. "He was supposed to scare you, that was all," Sam says.

"By going after my kid?"

"No," Sam says softly. "I told you, he's a loose cannon."

Cynthia falls into the nearest chair, her hands landing in a perfect prayer position. They are, even now, still shaking. "You have to fix this, Sam. Fix this."

"Did you know?" Jay asks her.

"Not about this."

Neal, taking in the scene, unsure of what exactly he's seeing, turns to stare directly, pleadingly, at his grandfather. "What are they talking about, Pop?"

"Ask him," Jay says. "Ask Samuel P. Hathorne, HNIC, Mr. Head Nigger in Charge, ask him how he sold out his own people, his own family even."

"What?"

"Why'd you do it, Sam? What did Parker promise you?"

"You don't know what you're talking about, don't know a thing about what I've done for Pleasantville, for my family, for every colored person in this city, including *you*. It's easy to stand on the outside, son, raising a fist, not so easy to get close enough to power to twist a wrist, to work this city from the inside out. Those folks out in Pleasantville have never wanted for anything on my watch. So don't talk to me about selling out. I know what I'm doing here."

"As long as you're the one sitting on top, the one holding all the cards, folks lining up to kiss your ring, to have you take their walk to the big house for them, coming back to deliver crumbs, streetlights, an elementary school—"

"Don't you dare! You haven't earned the right to speak to me like that. I was out there marching these streets when you were in short pants. You late ones think you invented struggle, invented the right to stand up to something."

"That's right, Sam, you and I were both out there once. We both marched for something better, for *change*, but you're not letting it happen. We're sitting here four years from a new century, man, and you're still trying to run it like we're standing still, putting up a black candidate, when behind the scenes you're planning to keep everything business as usual." He thinks of his old comrades, his running buddies during the Movement. Bumpy Williams, shot up by the feds in 1970. Marcus Dupri, lost to drugs and the Texas penal system a long time ago. And Lloyd, Kwame, whose heart gave out before he got to see a brother get within arm's reach of running the good ol' boy city of Houston, Texas. They didn't die for this shit, he tells Sam. "Did you even want Axel to win? Or if he loses, do you get to hold your place in line, stoking the flames of Axel's loss as proof that black folks can't win, that they can't have nothing without you? You at the head and everyone else walking two steps behind. Isn't that what A.G. said?"

"You leave him out of this."

"Where the hell is Cobb!"

"You've got to have a number," Cynthia says, "some way to reach him."

Sam looks at Jay. "Leave A.G. off the stand, and we'll talk about it."

Jay lunges at Sam, straight for his throat.

Neal has to pull the men apart.

"Drop A.G. and we'll talk."

"Pop!"

"You don't need him, Neal, you don't," Sam says, damp desperation on his face, sweat on his brow, spittle in the corners of his mouth. "You saw the state's case, how weak it is. You can close the trial without him. I'll protect you, no matter what happens, I promise, son. You're *mine*, Neal," he says, claiming the boy against everything, as if that could stem the fallout of his betrayal.

"What are you so afraid he's going to say?" Neal whispers.

Jay's cell phone rings.

He yanks it from his pocket, checking the screen. It's a number he doesn't recognize, one with the new area code 281. He looks at Sam, as if this is it, as if he's prepared to force Sam to negotiate a hostage release. He answers the phone, nearly collapsing at the sound of the first word: "Dad?" It's Ellie. She's crying.

"Are you okay?"

He can hardly hear her for the noise in the background: car horns and loud music, someone yelling in the distance. "Where are you?" he says.

"I don't know why he grabbed me like that," she says.

"Where *are* you?"

"I don't know," she says, crying harder. He listens to the street noise in the background. She's outside somewhere. "Are you on a pay phone?" he asks, turning to Neal to tell him to get Axel on the phone right now. "Start describing everything you see, Ellie, especially street signs. If you see a cop, flag him down. I'm going to put out a countywide bulletin right now. But I'm on my way, El. I'm coming to get you right now, do you understand? Ellie? Ellie?"

The line is dead.

Jay starts for the front door, Cynthia right behind him. Outside, they climb into the back of the waiting Town Car. She's on the phone with a contact at the FBI by the time her driver pulls away from the curb. She reaches for Jay's hand and he lets her take it. Ellie calls two more times, each call shorter than the last, but she's finally able to give him a street name, and how she got there. She ran from Cobb the second they were through the courthouse doors. She used the crush of downtown pedestrians as cover and then jumped on the first city bus she saw, too frightened to get off until she was miles and miles from downtown. "I'm scared he's coming back," she says. "I'm scared, Dad." It takes an hour for them to find her on a street corner halfway out to Missouri City, hovering in the vestibule of an abandoned medical supply company. He opens the door before the car stops, and she runs to the curb, throwing herself into his arms. They stand for a long time on that street corner, the blue Town Car idling nearby, just holding each other, the front of Jay's shirt soaking up her tears. "I got you," he says.

They spend two hours at the police station downtown—Axel standing close by while Ellie is interviewed by two detectives—before Jay is finally allowed to take her home. Cobb is apprehended that afternoon, at a pool hall around the corner from the address on his driver's license. He's arrested without incident while Jay is across town, getting his daughter settled in at the house. He is loath to ever leave her again. But Ellie, who is leaning into Lonnie on the couch in the den, with her aunt, Evelyn, on the other side of her, swears she'll be okay.

"I won't be long," he says.

He kisses his kids and walks out the door.

Neal agreed to meet him, but not at his house. He doesn't feel safe there. He doesn't feel safe anywhere anymore, he says. He's at the bar when Jay walks into the Marquis II on Bissonnet, a few blocks from Neal's house. He's drinking a Texas Tea, running the black straw through the soup of ice cubes and liquor. He's not talking much, but Jay came for the answer to only one question. "It's your deal," he tells Neal. "Your case and your life," he says, waving off the approaching bartender. This won't take more than a few minutes.

"I can't tell you what to do, not on this one," he says.

And Neal nods because he understands the logic of it. He went to law school after all. But it doesn't help him one bit. "He used you, Neal."

"I know," he says, looking down at his drink, losing interest fast.

He nods, to himself more than anyone else. "Do it," he says.

Next up: Allan George Hathorne.

On day five of the trial, and after a lengthy conference in Judge Keppler's chambers, the agenda of which was a single item—a long apology and explanation from Jay, complete with a police report regarding the attempted abduction of his daughter at the hands of a felon—they are back on the record in the matter of *State of Texas v. Neal Patrick Hathorne*. Reese Parker claimed a hardship—regarding her time, not her conscience—as the reason she could not appear again in court on such short notice, and Jay, who had only one last question for her, gladly accepted an affidavit signed by Ms. Parker, clarifying some confusion she'd had on the stand (and so as not to appear that she had perjured herself). Yes, in addition to her work for the Wolcott campaign, she *was* doing some freelance consulting work with the PAC America's Tomorrow. Yes, she *did* know about the bayou development flyer. And, *yes*, she hired Alicia Nowell and paid her two hundred dollars in cash over the course of a week to paper the flyers all over Pleasantville, which in and of itself was a violation of state campaign laws, since the work was not reported to any governing agency. It lacked the pomp and circumstance of the same being said into a microphone, echoing from the witness stand across the entire city. But it was evidence now. And Jay would take it. Lonnie was in the back of the courtroom, writing everything down. Ellie, thank god, was back in school, in second-period trigonometry.

A.G. walks into the courtroom, hunched over and squinting, kind of, as if he's just stepped out of an after-hours club into the harsh white of daylight, his pockets full of empties and regrets, his legs unsteady beneath him. He keeps looking around the courtroom, as if he's never been inside one before, as if he doesn't know where to look or where to find his son. Neal almost stands when he enters, forgetting himself, and where they are and why. He watches his father walk to the stand. Twice, A.G. asks the bailiff if he's going the right way. He's wearing a black blazer, something out of Rolly's closet that's too tight through the shoulders. The cuffs of his pants drag behind him on the floor. He takes an oath to tell it like it is. Straightening his spine, he adjusts himself in the chair.

His famous hands, they're shaking.

"Morning, Mr. Hathorne."

"Good morning, Mr. Porter."

"Mr. Hathorne, do you know the defendant, Neal Hathorne?"

"Yes, sir," he says, his gaze finally landing on Neal. "He's my son."

At the defense table, Neal lowers his head. Jay hears a soft exhale. Behind him in the gallery, his grandmother Vivian cries softly. Axel holds his mother's hand. They are the only two Hathornes in court this morning, though the presence of A. G. Hats on the stand has brought out quite a number of surprise guests. Fans, Jay guesses. Young white boys in homemade T-shirts with a bootleg mock-up of the Peacock Records logo on the front. Plus music reporters from the *Chronicle* and the *Times-Picayune* in New Orleans. And a good number of the "original 37," the families who founded Pleasantville. Arlee Delyvan is here. Jim and Ruby Wainwright. Elma Johnson and her husband. But also Jelly Lopez, who appears to have cut out from work to see this, a piece of his neighborhood's history on display. Jay, facing the witness stand, asks Mr. Hathorne if he's ever gone by a different name, and when he nods and says, "A. G. Hats," the white boys in the gallery, blues geeks every one of them, nearly break into applause. The stage name is a segue into his career, which is a segue into his current job as a janitor and all-around helper at the Playboy Club in Third Ward—an explanation, if one is needed, as to why a man of his background, from such a well-respected family, is so employed. "I like to be close to the music," he says on the stand. And Jay nods and walks him right up to the night of Tuesday, November fifth of this year, when Neal walked into his father's club. "He come in a few minutes after eight o'clock that night."

"And you're sure about the time?"

"Oh, yes," A.G. says. "We don't open the doors until nine most days, and I had just done all my rounds, checked the bathrooms, stocked the fridge, made sure the floors were clean, and I was sitting down at the keys. I like to play a little sometimes, if ain't nobody around. You can imagine how surprised I was."

"Why 'surprised'?"

"I hadn't seen him since he was"—and here he holds his right hand, palm down, kind of low around his knees—"just a little thing, since he was a boy."

"But you recognized him?"

A.G. smiles. "He's my son."

"But this wasn't the first time you'd seen his face since he was a boy?"

"No, sir," A.G. says, polishing his language for the court-room. "Mama sent me some pictures here and there. And I'd followed his career, seen his picture, his name in the paper." He looks at Neal, at the wonder he's become.

"Your mother, Vivian Hathorne?"

"Yes."

"And your father is Sam Hathorne?"

"He raised me, yes," A.G. says. "That's my daddy."

"Why is it that *you* didn't raise your son, Mr. Hathorne?"

A.G. nods toward his mother, in the front row. "They offered, and I took 'em up on it. Didn't see he'd do any better with me. I used to have a problem, drugs, you know. And I was right to give him up," he says, nodding toward his son, as if to say, *Look at him*, as if he expects Neal to stand up and thank him right here. "I could have done better by him, though, not stayed away so much."

"And why did you?"

"Objection, Your Honor, relevance," Nichols says. "It seems we're veering into a family drama that has little to do with Mr. Hathorne's purported purpose of providing an alleged alibi for his long-lost son," he says, building into the objection a poten-tial motive for A.G. to lie on the stand.

"If the court will allow it, I think the family dynamic and the history of estrangement make clear why the event was so memorable to Mr. Hathorne, and why there can be no mistake for him about when and where he saw Neal."

"I'll allow it," Keppler says. "Overruled."

"Mr. Hathorne," Jay starts in again. "Why didn't you reach out to Neal?"

"Me and Sam, we don't get along," A.G. says. "Actually, that's a hell of a nice way of saying it. My dad and I don't exist in the same world, we just don't see eye to eye on anything. He hovers above the earth, and I'm down in it with the rest of the regular folks." He dabs at his forehead. It's cooler in here than it was yesterday, the heating system purring softly, kindly. But A.G. is sweating.

"How long is this, since you've been estranged?"

"We fell out years ago, when he cut a deal with the chemical companies."

In the front row, Axel's whole posture deflates, and he sinks into the pewlike bench. He looks at his mother, who has her head down still. Axel looks at Arlee, at Ruby and Jim Wainwright. Did they know this too? Did everyone know this but him? But Arlee and the other Pleasantville residents look stunned.

"Which chemical companies?"

"It was ProFerma that started it, then every Tom, Dick, and Harry started moving factories in, brewing all kinds of nasty shit you can't hardly pronounce. Once one of 'em got in, they all started setting up shop in Pleasantville's backyard. We fought it at first, we did. It kind of meant something to me the way the community came together, and it was good for me too, to keep my head up and out of trouble, channel all this stuff I got inside of me," he says, gesturing vaguely to his gut, "to put it toward something outside of myself. Neal was a boy then, and I was getting my act together, and I thought, 'This is it for me.' I felt proud to be a Hathorne, like I was really one of them. Axel was busy with the police department around then, and this was something Sam and I could share, like I was finally living up to that name, what Daddy had done for people over the years." A.G. looks down, rubbing the palms of his hands along the front of his borrowed trousers. "And then one day, he took me aside and told me to stop. The marches, the flyers we was putting out, the plan to take the ProFerma fight to city hall. He told me to stop all of it."

"Do you know why?"

"He said people didn't really know what they wanted, let alone what they needed, that maybe there was something in this ProFerma deal after all. It was good jobs, he would tell people. He would go in and negotiate, be the hero who delivered a hundred, two hundred jobs to the community. And what he didn't tell anyone is that they were paying him to do it, cooked up some kind of 'neighborhood relations fee,' a consultancy of some sort, and gave him five hundred thousand dollars for it. I know 'cause he offered me fifty G's of it." He looks around the courtroom, at the jury especially, as if *he* were actually the one on trial, for failing to stand up to his father years ago. "It really hurt me that he offered the money to me and not Axel, not the girls, that he thought I, of all of them, was dirty, like I wasn't a Hathorne at all. After that, I walked out."

At the state's table, Nichols stands.

"Your Honor, I'm going to have to object. This is just straight narrative. Mr. Hathorne's relationship with his father is totally irrelevant to the matter."

Offended, A.G. says, "Hey, my father and I haven't spoken in twenty years over this." He looks right at Nichols, as if the D.A. had popped his head into A.G.'s confessional. "And it ruined everything between me and my son."

"And he's still talking, Your Honor."

"All right, the objection is overruled, Mr. Nichols. But the witness is instructed not to speak unless a question has been posed to him, and especially not if an objection is pending. Do you understand, Mr. Hathorne?"

"Yeah, yeah, I got it," he says, waving a hand in the air.

"Did Neal ask you about this on the night of November fifth?" Jay says.

"He didn't know what to ask. He didn't know any of it. He wanted to know why Sam was investigating me, what he was scared I might say during a campaign. And I danced around it. I know how it hurt me to find out the truth about Sam, so I was scared to get into it. We talked for about an hour or so, catching up about Neal, about my brother. I asked a lot about Mama."

"So that means he left the Playboy Club at what time?"

"It was about ten minutes to nine," A.G. says. "I know because I have to be off the piano when the boss lady come in, and I was checking the clock. Neal said he had to go to some party. And that was it. I looked at the Budweiser clock above the bar. It was ten minutes to nine." He taps his finger on the railing in front of him for emphasis. And when Jay asks him if there's any way he could be mistaken about what time Neal arrived at the club and what time he left, A.G. says no, he remembers everything, the whole thing is burned into his brain. "I'll never forget it, Mr. Porter," he says. "When my son walked in, it was a miracle."

The jury gets the case that afternoon, following a straightforward closing statement from Jay. Beyond the indisputable fact of Neal Hathorne's alibi, there was also just the plain weakness of the state's case, Jay said, the lack of any physical evidence tying Neal to the murder, and frankly the lack of a clear motive for Neal, on the night of his uncle's election, to go after a girl he'd met only one time, a girl standing on a street corner clear across town.

"You know who did have a motive?" he said.

Sandy Wolcott, and so did the woman running her campaign.

Wolcott and Reese Parker both had a motive to make Neal Hathorne look guilty of *something* in the middle of a neck-and-neck campaign. "But a district attorney elected in this county should not be allowed to bring up charges on the family members of her opponent and get away with it," he said, "else we'll see no end to this kind of trickery. And that's exactly what this is, a trick and a waste of your time and the voters' time and, most egregious, a waste of that family's time," he said, pointing to Maxine and Mitchell Robicheaux. "They deserve justice. As does the next family out there who don't even know it's coming, the phone call after midnight, or a police officer on their front door, a trip to the morgue . . . because make no mistake, he's still out there." He glanced at the empty seat next to Maxine, where Keith Morehead would have been sitting if he'd shown his face since Jay attacked him in the courthouse hallway. "And a *thing* like that, he will kill again, all the while Reese Parker is playing games with this election. The voters in this county, you deserve better," he said. "My client deserves better, and most of all, Alicia Nowell deserves better than what the prosecutor has presented in this case and tried to pass off to you as truth."

The state's rebuttal, he didn't listen to even half of it.

As far as Jay was concerned, it was over.

The jury walked out, and he left to wait it out at home.

Neal went with his uncle and his grandmother and his father, A.G. Jay patted Neal on the back and said he'd be the first to know whenever Jay heard word from the courthouse. Lonnie went to her place to write, trying to get it all down on paper: America's Tomorrow and the donors for George W. Bush, Reese

Parker's experiment in Pleasantville and the death of consolidated black voting power, which the Voting Rights Act and the tireless work of activists from Sam Hathorne to John Lewis to Dr. King to Diane Nash and James Bevel and countless others across the country had created, which people like Parker were now looking to poison from the inside. With help from Sam. He'd delivered Jay's client files to Parker in exchange for her help greasing a just-good-enough settlement from ProFerma, which just happens to also be a major donor to her PAC. Lonnie's already gotten calls from two different newspapers that are interested in the story. Sam, who had been careful to leave no paper trail, no phone records or letters or electronic mail of any kind, between himself and a Terrence Jerard Cobb, was, as Jay had heard through Lonnie, on his second interview with the Houston Police Department regarding the attempted kidnapping and the break-in at Jay's office, this time without his elder son, Axel, as an advocate. He was spending the night, on his own, in an interrogation room. Rolly was home by now, convalescing in his girl's arms. All this left Jay free to be with his kids. They had finally agreed it was time to tackle the tree.

It's Jay's job to find the box of decorations in the garage.

Ornaments, a tangle of lights, the angel from the clearance sale, it's all out here somewhere, along with his fishing gear, the three-piece dinette set from their old apartment, Ellie's first bicycle, and his son's train set, which Ben doesn't want anymore but had begged his mother not to throw away. There are some of Jay's old law school textbooks and a quilt Bernie started and never finished and on the top, top shelf just past the garage's side door, a white box with pages and pages of something Bernie was writing in her last year, which Jay is not ready to touch.

And there's Bernie's car, of course.

After he finds the Christmas stuff, in a cardboard box along the rear wall, he sets it all on the roof of his wife's Camry and climbs inside. The air is dry in here, but without the film of dust covering everything else in the garage. It's as it always was, the leather soft and clean, the radio still set to KTSU, the carpet on the driver's side with the same mud stain under the gas pedal from the last time Bernie drove the car, the last appointment she was able to drive herself to, last September, a few days before El-lie's birthday, when it had rained and rained and rained, Bernie stumbling into the house after dark, her whole body shaking. She knew then. He can still see the haunted look on her face and knows that she knew then what was coming. But she had sol-diered on. For them, he wants to believe, and it's true too, but he also knows she did it for herself. Just as he knows he's got to do this now, to beg her forgiveness. "I'm sorry, B," he says, sitting in the same spot he's been in so many times this past year, nights he thought this was his way out, engine idling, garage door sealed shut, his way back to her. "I can't wait," he says. "I can't sit out this life for you, Bernie." He takes a deep breath, pulling in what's left, the last he can smell of her, Dove soap and sandalwood. "I've got the kids, I've got Christmas, I've got the next day and the one after that." He's crying by now, the tears fat and warm, rolling down his chin as he lays his head on the steering wheel. He's got to stay. Bernie said it herself. But what's harder to admit is that he *wants* to. He asks her to forgive him for staying behind, speak-ing the words out loud inside his wife's car, knowing, even as he does, that he's only talking to himself.

When he leaves the garage, lugging the box of decorations, he spots a white van parked on the street in front of his house, its rear bumper blocking part of the driveway, the words PLEAS-ANTVILLE METHODIST CHURCH written beneath the back win-dows. He stares at the white van, his mind doing somersaults, as he turns for the house. Inside, it's quiet, a thick silence.

He hears nothing, not a single sound, even after he calls his daughter's name. "El?" he says, setting down the box on one of the couch cushions. The TV in the den is still on, a rerun of 227 playing, the canned sitcom laughter echoing through the empty room. Jay doesn't hear his son either. "Ben," he says, turning off the TV and walking through the kitchen, where their dinner is still sitting on the table, plates of chicken bones and buttered rice, even though Jay asked Ellie to clear the dishes before he went out to the garage. He knows almost instantly that something is wrong. He walks into the living room at the front of the house.

Ben and Ellie are on the couch, their knees touching, not far from the Christmas tree.

Pastor Keith Morehead is standing in the living room, hovering over them. He's in civilian clothes, black jeans and T-shirt, the front of which is stained with a dull grayish brown splotch. "That's a pretty little family you got."

Ellie tries to explain. "I answered the door, and he pushed his way in."

She is gripping her brother's wrist, keeping him as close to her as possible.

"What's going on, Dad?" Ben says, his lower lip trembling.

"Ben, Ellie, go into the den."

Morehead shakes his head, weaving a little on his feet as he reaches out to grab Ellie's wrist. He's drunk, Jay realizes. The stain on his shirt is red wine.

"Let them stay," Morehead says.

Jay steps between the man and his kids. "Ben, go with your sister."

"I said let her stay," Morehead slurs, making a move toward the kids.

Jay shoves him back, and it seems to loosen something in Morehead, giving him just the provocation he needs to unleash himself on Jay. He clocks Jay under his chin. Jay, stumbling back, hears his son shouting for Morehead to stop.

Morehead hits Jay again, this time in the gut.

Ellie runs for the kitchen phone, and that's when Morehead reaches for something in his waistband. "Stop!" Jay screams. "Don't move!" he tells his daughter. Morehead stands back, his hand still lingering under his shirt, fingering something Jay can't see. "I just want to talk."

"Leave my kids out of it."

Morehead stares at Ellie and at the boy.

He blinks his eyes a couple of times, as if he's seeing double.

Jay stands upright and tells his kids to wait for him in the den, but not before reaching out to squeeze his daughter's hand, secretly pressing the keys to her mother's Camry into it. She grips them as her dad looks over her shoulder, through the kitchen to the sliding glass door in the back. "Go," he whispers. "Just drive." Ellie, shaking, walks her little brother into the den.

Jay turns his attention to the drunk pastor.

Morehead sits on the edge of the embroidered sofa, pulling out the palm-size .22 automatic that was inside the waistband of his jeans. He rests it on his right thigh, eyes cast downward, to the carpet. "It was you, wasn't it?" Jay says.

"No," he whispers as he starts to cry.

"What I don't understand," Jay says, "why mess around with the girls' parents, why hold their hands, knowing all the while what you did?"

"I feel bad for them," he says, tears falling. "You don't think I feel bad?"

"I don't think you feel anything. Sidling up to the parents, that was all just a cover, just like calling in the story about Alonzo Hollis trying to kidnap a girl at the truck stop." *Local preacher*, those were the words in Lonnie's handwritten notes, words she copied, in quotes, from Resner's file. It was a call that had come into the Northeast station last year, a message left for the detective; a police report was filed, but nothing came of it. "It was you."

"I said *no!*" Morehead says, standing, pointing the .22.

Jay, on reflex, raises his hands in front of his chest, trying to think his way out of the room, knowing what a fight with this man will cost him. *This.* This is why the last one was different, he now understands. Alicia Nowell fought. The other girls, they knew the pastor. He was their coach. They trusted him. But Alicia fought like hell. Morehead, as if following the same thought, lowers his head. He weeps openly. "Deanne and Tina, it wasn't the way you think. It wasn't nasty the way you think. It was something between us, something special. But I should never have touched the Nowell girl. I should have known better. But once I saw her . . . it's like the devil got to whispering in my ear. It's like I couldn't stop. I got her in the van, got her all the way to the west side of the neighborhood when she ran. The lock in the back, it ain't ever worked exactly right and she got out of the van and ran, straight into the weeds along the railroad tracks. I had to stop her," he says, looking up, as if he expects understanding from Jay, compassion even, all while pointing the pistol at Jay's chest. "Whatever it took, I had to stop her, right there by the railroad tracks. By the time it was done, I heard music coming from the church, choir practice, and I was too scared to move her that night. Then the cops started coming around, and I just froze," he says, as if stunned by the entire sequence of events that led to tonight, the gun in his hand. "I just froze, and now I've got to fix this. I got to fix it."

"Taking me out isn't going to change things," Jay says. "Your DNA was under her fingernails. It's locked in an evidence box downtown right now. I bet there's traces of all three girls in the back of that van parked outside. If I put it together, you can bet someone else is going to be right behind me."

"You've ruined my life."

"I didn't kill those girls."

"I didn't mean to hurt them!"

Jay hears the garage door open, followed by the squeal of tires as Ellie backs out of the driveway at a fast clip, knocking over garbage cans and, by the sound of it, grazing the side of his Land Cruiser. Morehead looks panicked, not sure if it's a car leaving or one arriving, a squad car maybe. Just as the head-lights swing from the driveway and out onto Glenmeadow, Morehead turns, peering through the curtains, and that's when Jay runs. He knocks the tree down as he goes, clumsily blocking the exit from the living room. He races to his bedroom, leaving the light off and feeling his way to the bed, to the pillow under which he left the .38, loaded. He hears a shot in the dark, burn-ing the air, mere inches from his head. It shatters the window that faces into the backyard, setting off the sensor lights on the patio. When Jay swings around, Morehead is standing in the doorway to his bedroom, bathed in the sickly yellow light from outside. His right hand is shaking badly, the barrel of the gun jumpy and unpredictable. Something about seeing this killer, this coward, inside his bedroom, the room where his wife died, where so much was taken from him, sets Jay off. He raises the .38, pointing it at the preacher.

But Morehead only smiles.

It's the wide, grotesque grin of a clown, makeup melting at this late hour, under the glare of the lights. "Please," he says, begging. "Deliver me, Jay."

"Naw, man. There's no way you're getting off that easy."

Morehead's expression hardens. He levels his gun, aiming.

But Jay gets him first, a clean shot to the right side of his chest.

Morehead drops the .22, falling back against the doorjamb and sliding to the floor. Jay crosses to the man's feet, kicking the .22 out of his reach, his last move before he grabs the telephone to call the police. He sits on the side of the bed, watching trails of gun smoke curling in the air, as the phone rings and rings.

Election Day

TEXAS, 2000

Axel Hathorne starts the day a clean ten points ahead in the polls, on track to win his third and, by city law, last term as mayor of Houston, Texas. The polls have just opened, and the Bush-Gore race is anybody's guess, the two running neck and neck in every poll from the *Washington Post* to the *Los Angeles Times* to the *Chronicle* and the *Dallas Morning News* and *USA Today*, and several pundits on the cable news channels suggesting that it may be the closest presidential race in U.S. history. Jay still remembers Reese Parker's prophecy: *Four years from now, it's going to come down to a handful of votes.* She's still working her magic, he's heard, with her name popping up in a few feature articles in the *Chronicle*, about the inner workings of the Bush campaign–her involvement in "flyergate," the stunt that tanked Sandy Wolcott's career, reduced to a few sentences, nearly forgotten by now. But if Bush wins, she'll be a star. Cynthia too. After Axel distanced himself from Cynthia during the runoff campaign and the election that put him in office, she went to Austin, taking a position at a lobbying firm with close ties to the capitol and then chairing the Bush campaign's state operation this year. Jay hasn't seen her since that day at Sam's house. She sends him e-mails from time to time. He reads them, sometimes more than once, saving them in an untitled folder on his computer. But he never writes back.

He's at his desk this morning, typing notes for his opening statement, two index fingers attacking the keys. It's still warm for November, and he's opened his office window a few inches. He smells the garlic and chiles from the house next door, where a vegan restaurant opened last year. The Diamond Lounge is still around, thank god. He and Eddie Mae have their whole last day together planned out: a long lunch at Brennan's, anything she wants, champagne and oysters Rockefeller, a porterhouse and lobster tails, and then beer and a little blues at the Diamond Lounge tonight. He can hear her down the hall right now, training the new girl in her own special way. For all Jay knows, they're buying shoes online. He's holding out hope that this newest hire will work. Eddie Mae has been trying to retire for two years now, but Jay has, until now, refused to let her go, wondering how he would find someone who can type *and* cook. Who, in this house (hers as much as it is his), will ever know him the way she does? But she bought a little house in Galveston last year, spending more and more time on the water, and when she came in last month and said, "Jay, honey, I'm tired," he couldn't think of anything to do but kiss her cheek and tell her that he loved her.

This new one, Natalie somebody, he's hoping Eddie Mae can have her up to speed before the trial starts later this month.

She's one of Neal's students at South Texas, a young mom working her way through law school, taking classes at night. There may be something more to it, between Natalie and Neal, but it's none of Jay's business, and anyway he trusts Neal's judgment, has actually come to like his former client. It was a case that nearly killed him, nearly sent Neal Hathorne to prison for the rest of his life, but, four years on, it's just a story, one of many in his life—and one that just happened to end with the best cocktail party brag of all time, about the time he had Christmas dinner with A. G. Hats, played his record all night, and drank whiskey with the man. Neal, newly acquitted then, heard his father's music for the first time that night, really *heard* it. And Amy, Lonnie's girlfriend, her hands shook every time she had to pass A.G. the potatoes. Ben still teases her about it now. They're having a viewing party at their place tonight, Lonnie and Amy, to watch the returns. Rolly is planning to come too, with lots of beer. But Jay promised Eddie Mae a night out and this one is hers. At quarter to eleven, she comes in, tapping her watch, reminding him that their reservation is for twelve sharp. Then she drops a heap of mail on his desk.

"Ms. Ainsley called about her check."

"I'll call her."

Dot Ainsley's grandson, the dentist from Baytown, died two years ago, and she started having the biannual checks she receives from the Cole Oil settlement sent to Jay's office instead of to the tin mailbox in front of her one-story house in Texas City. Jay takes the time to call her monthly, and when her checks arrive, he puts them in one of his office envelopes, with his return address, and then sends them to the very same tin box. She feels safer having them come from him.

He settled with Cole Oil Industries about a month after the Hathorne trial, calling Thomas Cole at home and driving, alone, to the man's house. If they could wrap this up for $35 million, in a structured payout, could they put an end to this for everybody, no more trials, no more delays? He was betting on what Charlie Luckman had said, about folks being afraid of what Jay might do, what he was capable of, and Cole had readily agreed to the terms, believing he'd singlehandedly brought Jay Porter to his knees, not knowing that this was Jay's way of disposing of the case before Thomas Cole ever discovered Nathan Petty, the witness he had buried. It was twenty million less than Jay won in court. But if he forewent his fee, the money for his clients would be the same, even a little more. It was his self-imposed punishment for skirting the law. He could drag this thing out for another ten years, or he could finally get Cole to pay the people who needed the money more than Jay did.

There's a postcard from Ellie's school in the mail, an ad for an art exhibit in Lafferre Hall, open to students and parents. It reminds him that he has to write her a check. Two hundred a month, they agreed on, just to help out, something to put on top of her work-study job. She's in her first year at Lonnie's alma mater, studying journalism at the University of Missouri in Columbia. She called him this morning from her dorm room, excited to have voted in her first election. She'd voted for Gore, even volunteered at his local campaign office, answering phones and canvassing neighborhoods. Jay had bought and overnighted her a cell phone as soon he heard. He wrapped it in a sheet of his letterhead. *Love, Dad.*

There are bills and bank statements to go through. Yet another America Online CD. There are store catalogs, an issue of *Sports Illustrated*, and coupons.

And at the bottom of the pile is a pale pink envelope, the rose logo of the American Greetings card company embossed on the back. He knows who sent it before he opens it. She sends one every year on November fifth, the day of her daughter's death. This year the card is a garden scene: a toddler wearing a floppy purple hat stands in the center of the frame. In one plump brown hand she holds a metal watering can, in the other a clump of dandelions. *Thank you.* It's all Maxine has ever said. A note to him every year since Keith Morehead was arrested for the murders of Alicia Nowell, Tina Wells, and Deanne Duchon. There was a little blip about it in this morning's *Chronicle*, a timely reminiscence about Houston's oddest election in history, which involved a murder trial and the resolution of two other unsolved crimes—and the undoing of one of the city's oldest African-American leaders, a man once revered who has since retreated from public life and politics, along with his wife. The article's last line mentions his estrangement from his elder son, Mayor Axel Hathorne.

The article was written by Gregg Bartolomo.

Jay shoves all of the mail to the side of the desk, in the spot he considers his pre-inbox, a messy stack of unopened mail and lists of things he needs to add to other lists that are floating somewhere on his desk. He has to get back to work before lunch. He'd like to have a good grasp of his opening statement by the end of this week, thirteen days before *Pleasantville (Arlee Delyvan et al.) v. ProFerma Labs* is set to finally go before a jury, after years of fits and starts and stalling on the part of the chemical company. Four years ago, when he stood before his clients in the Samuel P. Hathorne Community Center to make a pitch to regain their trust, he'd prepared them for this kind of prolonged fight. But not before seeking out the one man he knew he had to win over first. It was about a week after Christmas that year. Jelly Lopez, the new leader of Pleasantville by default, had let Jay into his four-bedroom ranch-style house. His wife had poured him sweet tea spiked with lemon and ginger, and Jelly's four-year-old daughter played with Legos on top of the coffee table while the two men talked. "I didn't fight as hard as I could, I didn't," Jay said. "But I'm here now, and if you'll put your trust in me, I'd like to represent your family in a court of law." Jelly, Jules to his wife, looked at her, and together they asked for a minute to speak alone in the kitchen. Jay passed the time building a car for Maya, their daughter, flicking its wheels with his thumb and watching it ride across the polished coffee table. And when Jelly came out of his blue-and-yellow kitchen, Jay stood and said again, *I'm here now.*

ACKNOWLEDGMENTS

With each book I feel ever more grateful for the creative support I have in my life. Richard Abate, who is part agent, part counselor, part dreamer like me, championed this book from its very beginning and helped push the story to where it needed to go. How lucky I am to call you a friend. Claire Wachtel was patient and exacting in equal measure, and this book is better for it. Thank you for your faith in me, and your enthusiasm for this book. Rebecca Gray recognized the ambition of this project, and offered keen insights along the way. You are kind, funny, and wise—and know where to find good Mexican food in London! Hannah Wood, thank you for your hard work and support. And Dawn Davis, thank you for seeing the potential in this book from just a few lines of description, and for being one of my biggest cheerleaders, near and far.

I could not have written this book without reading Sasha Issenberg's *Victory Lab*. Big thanks to Jesse Dickerman for suggesting I read it, and for sitting down with me to talk about campaigning and Texas politics. Additional thanks to Rusty Hardin for answering some very important questions about Texas criminal law. Erik Eriksson answered my questions about the Ship Channel and the Port of Houston, and I dearly appreciate his generosity. And though it seems odd to thank my dad, Gene Locke, for `one of the most painful experiences of my life, I couldn't have written this book without bearing witness to a cantankerous and complicated mayoral race, one that shed light on some very dark corners of our democracy. Thanks also, Daddy, for answering a million trivia questions about Houston's political history and where to get the best barbecue.

To the real Eddie Mae Loston, who passed away as I wrote this book, you were a beautiful part of my childhood and will be remembered forever.

To the folks in Pleasantville who opened their homes to me and shared their personal stories—Talmadge and Geneva Sharp, Clinton Johns, Evelyn Mouton, James and Carolyn Campbell—I cannot thank you enough.

To my family, thanks, as always, for your big, beautiful love.

To Cheryl Arutt, thank you for Thursdays.

Tembi, thanks for the light, love, and laughter, and for reading this book while your own writing life has been so full. Karl, my dear husband, you are a writer's dream mate—patient, quick with a joke, willing to do dishes, and full of legal knowledge. I couldn't do any of this without you. My darling Clara, your love is my true muse. You and Zoela, my dear niece, keep me light. Finally, to my brother-in-law Saro, I started this book in your hospital room. And when I finished, you were the first person I told, a whisper in the wind. Thank you, Sa.

ABOUT THE AUTHOR

Attica Locke's first novel, *Black Water Rising*, was nominated for a 2010 Edgar Award, an NAACP Image Award, and a Los Angeles Times Book Prize, and was shortlisted for the prestigious Orange Prize (now the Baileys Women's Prize for Fiction) in the UK. Her second book, *The Cutting Season*, published by Dennis Lehane Books, is a national bestseller. It was named an Honor Book by the Black Caucus of the American Library Association, was long-listed for the Chautauqua Prize, and is the 2013 winner of the Ernest Gaines Award for Literary Excellence.

A graduate of Northwestern University, Locke was a fellow at the Sundance Institute's Feature Filmmakers Lab. She spent many years as a screenwriter for Paramount, Warner Bros., Disney, Twentieth Century Fox, Jerry Bruckheimer Films, HBO, and Dreamworks, and is a writer and coproducer on the Fox drama *Empire*.

For more information, visit www.atticalocke.com.